The Healing Rose of Savannah

Inspired by a true story

by Jenny Elaine

Copyright © 2020 by Jenny Elaine

This novel is a work of fiction. Though actual locations are mentioned, they are used in a fictitious manner and similarities of characters to any person, past, present, or future, are coincidental.

ISBN: 9780578649498

Dear Reader,

I have always been fascinated with history, soaking up any and every story told by friends and family members through the years. It's from those stories that I created "The Healing Rose of Savannah". I did, however, take creative liberties to enhance the storyline of the book. For example, the murders of Mrs. Gibson, her daughter Cathy, and Mrs. Willingham were based on a real-life crime committed right here in Savannah in 1909, but I changed the names and some of the facts to better fit my story. If you're interested in reading more about it, search the internet for "Axe murders in Savannah, Georgia". It's one of Savannah's most intriguing unsolved mysteries. Also, if you read to the very end of the book, you will find a detailed list that further explains what else is fact and what is fiction.

Now, onto "The Healing Rose of Savannah". I truly hope you enjoy!

Prologue

-1965-

Darkness could not begin to describe the heavy cloak that surrounded me. Loneliness, desperation, terror, and hopelessness all grasped at my heels as I ran through a dense, dark, and unfamiliar forest. My eyes searched through the trees for something or someone to help me, only to come up empty. I could hear it coming closer, the thing that chased me, and I glanced over my shoulder to see it drawing nearer every second.

Suddenly, the clouds broke open, and moonlight began to shine through the thick branches, revealing a black, hooded figure only a few feet away, with long, gnarly fingers reaching out for me. I couldn't let it catch me, I just couldn't. Heart pounding in my ears, I pushed myself to run faster, my legs burning and lungs screaming for air. Then, without warning, I caught my foot on a protruding root and began to fall, my arms flailing, mouth opened in a muted scream...

My eyes snapped open, revealing more darkness, only this time it wasn't so thick, so oppressing. I turned my head to find my husband lying beside me, his deep, even breaths calming my nerves. I quietly withdrew the covers and stood to my feet, my legs weak and body drained from the terrifying nightmare. I walked to my dressing table and sat down in the chair, staring at my dim reflection in the mirror. Big, black eyes gazed back, the laugh lines that cold cream couldn't erase seemingly more pronounced than usual. Thick, dark hair billowed out around my shoulders, and I suddenly wondered how long it would take before it started to fall out.

I could still see the heavy look in the doctor's eyes as he studied me earlier today. We'd known each other for so many years that I knew instantly something was wrong.

"You have breast cancer, Savannah," he told me.

Never in a million years had I expected such words to be spoken to me. I don't think anyone could ever be prepared to hear them, to accept their meaning. I'd never been more terrified in my life.

"We'll do surgery first," the doctor's words rang in my ears. "Then we'll follow up with treatments. The tumor is rather large, but I believe your chances are good."

I could only hope he was right, but as a nurse, I knew the odds. I'd seen them first-hand. I just never expected to face such a battle at only forty-five years old. I was still young, I had many more years left to live, more places to see. I wasn't ready to die.

"What's wrong, sweetheart?"

Strong, gentle hands rested on my shoulders, and through the darkness of our room I raised my eyes to see the look of concern on my husband's face.

"I had a bad dream," I said.

"Why didn't you wake me?"

I shrugged, feeling like a little girl when my eyes filled with tears for seemingly no reason.

"Ah, honey, don't cry," he said, turning my chair around as he knelt before me. "Everything is going to be alright. You believe that, don't you?" He asked, taking both my hands in his.

"Of course," I whispered in a small, non-convincing voice.

He reached up to wipe a tear off my cheek, his beautiful eyes full of concern. "I promise to do whatever it takes to make you better. I'll go to the ends of the Earth and give everything I've got to find you a cure."

"What if there is no cure for me?" I asked softly.

"Don't say that," he said, sitting on the floor so he could pull me into his lap. "You're going to be alright," he whispered into my ear, cradling me like a child. "We've weathered tough times before. We'll get through this together."

We sat there for what seemed like hours, our tears mingling together as our thoughts travelled in a thousand different directions. I wondered what I would do without him, without his strength, love, and support. We'd never been blessed with children, but instead of tearing us apart, it seemed to have only drawn us closer together.

It hadn't always been this way. I never expected to fall in love with this man, never intended on spending my life with him. It took so much for us to find our way to each other, for the stars to align and for my heart to be opened.

My eyes started to grow heavy as my mind travelled back to a different time, a different place. To a million years ago, to yesterday. To the beginning of our story. To the beginning of our lives.

Chapter One

-1940-

I stared out the train window, watching the scenery pass by, and wondered fleetingly if in reality the train sat still while the world spun madly by, instead of the other way around. Trees...grass...rivers...it all bled together into one shapeless blur, adding to the fog in my brain, the confusion in my spirit.

It was the summer of 1940. A war was being waged in Europe, causing unease in every American home. The United States had declared its neutrality, claiming they wouldn't become involved in the war, but Daddy, and many others, seemed to think they would.

As the scenery slowly began to change, I drew a breath of relief that we were finally drawing closer to the coast. I'd lived the first 10 years of my life in Savannah, Georgia, spent every summer there since, and would recognize the familiar landscape anywhere. The golden marshland, the muddy banks of a river at low tide, the smell of salt in the air. It was like going back home, only I hadn't planned on returning this summer. I was supposed to be getting married instead.

I closed my eyes, a sigh passing my lips, and wished I could stop thinking about him. If only it were possible to totally wipe a memory from one's brain, to remove all recollection and pain. I wondered, if it really were possible, how it would feel to have empty spaces from the past, holes that couldn't be filled, missing pieces that couldn't be explained. I wondered how different things would be for me right now if I'd never met him.

I could still remember the exact moment it happened…

It was almost three years ago at our church bazaar. I was in charge of selling cakes and pies when I realized I was out of dollar bills. I hurried over to the next booth to get some more and, not watching where I was going, bumped right into him, knocking the donated box of books right out if his arms and scattering them all over the ground.

"Whoa," he laughed, grabbing my elbow to steady me.

"I am so sorry," I gasped, my cheeks flaming red.

"It was totally my fault," he said, helping me gather the books. Once we were finished, he stuck out his hand and said, "I'm Doctor Jake Bradley."

"It's nice to meet you," I smiled, accepting his offered hand. "I'm Savannah Adair."

"Adair?" He tapped his chin. "Your father wouldn't happen to be Edward Adair, would it?"

"Yes," I nodded, swiping a tendril of dark hair behind my ear. "You know my father?"

"I've played golf with he and my father a couple of times, and he's also one of my father's...well," he chuckled sheepishly, "actually, I guess he's one of my patients. I just moved here and took over my father's practice three months ago."

"Congratulations." I glanced back at my table to find a couple of ladies looking through the selection of desserts and told him I was on a mission to find some change.

"I've got some," he said, pulling a billfold from his back pocket. We exchanged money, and I turned to go back to my table, stating once again that it was nice to meet him.

"And," I added, "welcome to Atlanta."

As I assisted the two ladies with their purchases, I noticed that his booth was only a few yards from mine, and I wondered how his father's patients would feel about such a young man taking over the practice. I didn't give him much more thought, and at the end of the night, I was surprised to find that he'd stayed around to clean up.

"This is my church and community now, and I plan on being involved as much as possible," he explained.

We bumped into each other quite often after that. At church, at local events, and even once at the park. We became friends, something I'd never experienced with a male before, and started seeing more of each other. I learned that he was nine years older than me, but our level of maturity was the same. I'd always been mature for my age, and we both soon discovered that we had a lot in common.

I didn't realize at first that Jake was interested in me romantically, as I didn't feel that way about him. He was a handsome man, with bright blue eyes and wavy, auburn hair, but I was studying to become a nurse, something I'd dreamed of my whole life, and I was focused and driven, with no intentions of courting anyone until I graduated, if even then. My mother died when I was a baby, and growing up with a distant, workaholic father and cold, harsh stepmother had left me apprehensive when it came to relationships. Jake sensed this and kept his feelings very well hidden. He never said anything to make me think he liked me, and never attempted to touch or kiss me. Instead, he slowly earned my trust. He was so different from the other men my age. He listened to me and seemed to really care about my thoughts and feelings. Little by little, he wormed his way into my heart, and when he finally told me how he felt, I told him I felt the same. We began officially courting and became engaged six months later.

I still remember the day I went to his office to surprise him. It was two weeks before the wedding, and he was working late. I slipped quietly inside, the basket on my arm filled with roasted chicken, biscuits, and apple pie. I hadn't seen him in three days and wanted to eat supper with him. When I opened the door to his office, the basket slid from my hands and I gasped.

There, by the window, stood Jake and his assistant, Pamela, in an embrace. They were kissing and hadn't heard me enter until I dropped the basket. I turned and ran from the room, Jake calling my name as he chased me. I was heartbroken and sick to my stomach, my faith and trust completely shattered. How could I not have seen this coming?

Jake caught me and tried to explain, but I never even heard his words. It was as if my brain shut down and closed off my hearing. I refused to talk to him or see him and cancelled the wedding. My stepmother, in her typical fashion, kept making comments about my staying with her and father when she'd planned to use my room for her sewing after I moved out, people kept asking questions, and I just couldn't take it anymore. I called my mother's older sister, Debra, and told her what happened.

"Why don't you come home, honey?" Aunt Deb said. "You can stay with us for as long as you like. Goodness, you could even finish up your last year of nursing school here with Maxine! You know how much she would love that."

It was as if she had read my mind. I readily agreed and, after packing my things and saying my goodbyes, got on the next train to Savannah.

Chapter Two

-1940-

"Next stop is Savannah!"

Sometimes, when you're deep in thought or reliving a memory, a voice from the present is like a splash of cold water to the face. With a start, I was jerked back to the time at hand. Pushing thoughts of Jake out of my head, I hurriedly slid my gloves on and began gathering my belongings. We pulled into the station, and I was one of the first to get off, the excitement of being back "home" finally starting to sink in and override the gloom.

"Vannie!" I heard a familiar voice call and searched through the crowd until I found her. There was only one person who called me by that nickname.

Dear, sweet Maxine. She was my cousin, yet how we were related I didn't really know. She'd lived with Aunt Deb and Uncle Ray since she was fifteen, and we became the best of friends the moment we met. I tried to ask once where she came from, only to receive a curt, evasive reply from my aunt. I never attempted to ask again.

"Oh, Vannie, it's so good to see you!" Maxine cried, throwing her arms around me. She drew back, cheeks blushing, to make certain no one noticed the spectacle she was making.

"It's wonderful to see you, too, Maxi," I smiled broadly, leaning down to kiss her cheek. At 5'7", I towered over her short 5'2" frame, a trait that, along with her shy disposition, always made me feel protective towards her.

"I'm so sorry about... about what happened," Maxi said, her big, blue eyes filling with tears of sympathy.

Before I could respond, Aunt Deb appeared, her green eyes blazing as she scolded Maxi for rudely pushing her way through the crowd.

"You should have waited for me," she said, reaching up to adjust the hat that tilted precariously atop Maxi's blonde curls.

"You're just sore she got to me first, Auntie," I teased.

"Of course, I am," Aunt Deb winked, pulling me into a hug.

I only had one picture of Mama, but every time I saw Aunt Deb, I was reminded of her. She was five years older than Mama, with strawberry blonde hair and sparkling green eyes. Standing at barely five feet tall, she made up for her small stature with a boisterous, opinionated personality. Daddy always used to say, "*Your aunt and mother may have looked alike, but never were two people more different. I don't think I've ever seen such a bossy woman as Debra Coleman.*"

Smiling at the memory of his words, I squeezed my aunt even tighter. Bossy or not, I loved her dearly. She and Uncle Ray helped raise me before we moved to Atlanta, and I loved them both as if they were my own parents.

"I'm so glad to have both my girls with me again," Aunt Deb said, blinking back tears as she grabbed both our hands. "Let's head home, shall we? We have a lot to catch up on."

As we drove through the old, familiar streets, I couldn't help but feel calmer, more at peace. I rolled down the window of Uncle Ray's bright blue, 1935 Lincoln K Sedan, and let the warm, humid breeze ruffle the black curls around my face. The azaleas had already bloomed and gone, but the roses, camellias, and hydrangeas were in full season, their brilliant colors in stark contrast to the gentle, silver moss that hung from the massive oak trees. I took a deep breath and let it out slowly. It felt good to be home.

Twenty minutes later, we pulled up in front of the house and parked on the curb. My aunt and cousin each grabbed a suitcase and headed up the tiny, dirt driveway while I stood by the car and gazed up at the old, familiar house with its red door and twin peaked roof, memories flooding my mind. The swing still hung on the front porch, drifting back and forth listlessly in the breeze with a gentle "creak", and the spindles and columns looked as if they'd recently been painted, for they gleamed bright white in the afternoon sun.

"Savannah banana, is that you?" A voice to my right exclaimed.

I turned, a smile already forming on my lips, and cried, "Leon!" I stretched out my arms, rushing forward to give him a hug.

Leon (pronounced Lee-uhn) Danes had been my aunt and uncle's neighbor his whole life. We were the same age, and so we'd gone to nursery school together, as well as elementary school until Daddy's job transferred him to Atlanta when I was ten. Leon always had a very outgoing, charming personality, with curly brown hair and a smile that could melt any girl's heart. One couldn't help but adore him.

Pulling me into an embrace, Leon lifted me off my feet and spun me about.

"Leon Danes, you put my niece down this instant!" Aunt Deb called from the upstairs window. "You are making a scene carrying on in the street like that."

Laughing, Leon sat me down and took a step back, whistling as he took a good look at me. "Savannah Rose Adair, you are more beautiful every time I see you. And," he added with a wink, "I heard the wonderful news that you're back on the market."

"Shame on you for saying such a thing," I gasped, wiggling a finger at him. "I don't know whether to laugh or cry."

"Well, you most certainly shouldn't cry," he said in a stern tone. "The fool isn't worth it."

I smiled, reaching out to loop my arm through his as we walked up the driveway. "How is your mother?" I asked, changing the subject.

"Just wonderful," he replied. "I've tried to convince her to quit her job at the bank and take it easy, but she won't hear of it. Says she'd go stir crazy sitting around not doing anything all day."

"Do you still live next door with her?"

"I do," he nodded. "Once I graduate next year I plan to move out, but until then I'm the man of the house. Or, at least, I am when Con isn't here."

I forced my face to remain neutral at the mention of Leon's older brother. I'd never liked him. Connor was four years our senior, bossy, and arrogant. He used to tease me mercilessly, and although I hadn't seen him in nearly six years, I still held a grudge.

"How is Connor?" I asked politely.

"He's a Lieutenant now," Leon gushed proudly. He continued to list all his brother's accomplishments, but I wasn't paying much attention. Connor joined the military when he was eighteen, and I hadn't seen him since, nor did I care to.

"Is your mother seeing anyone yet?" I asked when Leon stopped to take a breath.

"No," he shook his head, stuffing his hands in his pockets. "I've tried talking her into courting again, but she swears she'll stay a widow until she dies."

The spark in Leon's eyes dimmed a bit at the mention of his mother being a widow. His father had died in a car accident about eight or nine years earlier, and I knew he missed him terribly.

"Tell her I'll come over for a visit soon, alright?" I said. Emma Danes was like an aunt to me. She'd been one of my mother's closest friends, and I loved to hear the stories she'd tell me about her. She was one of the kindest, most generous souls I'd ever known. How she'd managed to finish raising two teenaged boys on her own I'd never know.

"I'll do that," he nodded, opening the front door for me. "See you later?"

"Of course," I stepped through the door, turning back to add, "Thank you for being my welcome home committee."

"I'm just glad you are home," he smiled warmly.

As I walked through the house, I smelled the warm, familiar scent of apple cider potpourri my aunt always used and heard the massive grandfather clock still ticking the minutes away in the foyer. Uncle Ray's prized grand piano held its proud position against one wall of the living room next to Aunt Deb's China cabinet, and as I slowly made my way up to the second floor, I remembered all the times I'd slid down the slick, shiny railing of the staircase I now brushed my hand across.

"I have most of your things unpacked for you, dear," Aunt Deb said when I entered my room. It didn't matter that I was already twenty-one years old, she still acted as if I were twelve. "Some of your dresses need ironing, but Lizzie can do that tomorrow."

"Thank you for everything, Aunt Deb," I said, pulling her into a tight hug.

Maxi joined us then, and we all sat down on the bed and had a long talk. Going through everything that had happened with Jake, crying it out and explaining how hurt I was, helped more than I could have imagined. They understood me better than anyone else ever had, and I remember feeling a deep sense of overwhelming gratitude for them, their love, and support.

Later that evening, after Uncle Ray got home and we'd all eaten supper together, I lay in bed, unable to sleep. It had been such an exhausting day, but it was a typical hot and humid summer night in the South, and all I could do was toss and turn. My window was open, and I watched as a soft breeze gently ruffled the curtains, causing the moonlight to bounce along the walls. I was thankful we had screens, or else there would be blood-sucking mosquitoes and gnats swarming about.

The door that adjoined mine and Maxi's rooms opened slowly, and I turned to find my cousin peering at me through the darkness.

"Vannie, are you asleep?" She whispered, her thin nightgown sticking to her sweaty body.

"Are you kidding?" I sighed, kicking off my sheet and pushing myself up to sit Indian style.

"I'm going down to the kitchen for some cold lemonade. Want to join me?"

I readily agreed, and we tiptoed down the stairs and into the kitchen where we pulled a large pitcher of lemonade from the ice box. We poured two glasses and sat down at the table to enjoy the cool drink, both of us fanning ourselves with a magazine.

"It's normally not this hot in June," Maxi frowned, taking a sip from her glass.

"I dread what August has in store for us," I sighed. As we sat in silence, both sipping our drinks, I studied my cousin in the dim light, and realized that as close as we were, I didn't truly know anything about her past. "Could I ask you a personal question?" I asked, breaking the silence.

"Of course," she replied, looking a bit surprised.

"How did you come to live here with Aunt and Uncle Coleman all those years ago?"

I immediately regretted my direct question when a look of discomfort...or was it pain?...passed over Maxi's face.

"You don't have to answer that, Maxi," I said gently.

Maxi shook her head, causing the curlers in her hair to bounce back and forth. "No, no, it's fine," she smiled reassuringly, her lips wobbling a bit. "I've often wondered why you never asked me before."

"I tried once, but Aunt Deb sort of cut me off," I shrugged sheepishly.

"That's not surprising," Maxi chuckled. After a moment of hesitation, she cleared her throat and said, "My father is Aunt Deb's second cousin. During the depression, things were very hard for us, especially with four mouths to feed, and Mama just couldn't keep up. So, she...well...sort of...divided us all up among whatever relatives she could find." A short, humorless laugh at the word "divided" passed Maxi's lips, which had been curled into a slight grimace.

"Four mouths?" I asked.

"Yes," Maxi nodded. "I have two younger sisters."

"Oh," I murmured, trying to take it all in. "What about your father?

15

Why couldn't he help?"

Maxi hesitated, as if unsure of what to answer, and I immediately thought that he must be dead. I opened my mouth to apologize when she said in a small voice, "I…never knew my father. He and mama were never married, and after I was born, he married someone else and they didn't want anything to do with me." She raised her eyes to meet mine, and I saw a look of shame in their depths as she added in a near whisper, "My sisters never knew their fathers, either. Mama wasn't the most…reputable woman in town."

I was shocked and didn't know what to say as I pondered this newly found insight into Maxi's life. A wave of compassion passed over me as I studied my cousin's tight, pained expression. What must it feel like to not be wanted by your own father? To be, as Maxi said, "divided" up among family members? How terrible it must have been for Maxi to leave her mother and sisters, to be forced to live with strangers. Thankfully Aunt Deb and Uncle Ray were kind and loving people, but how frightening it must have been to come here at so young an age and face such uncertainty.

"I'm sorry, Maxi," I said, reaching out to gently squeeze her hand. She raised tear filled eyes to meet mine, and my heart clenched. "I didn't mean to bring up painful memories for you but thank you for telling me. And," I added with a smile, "no matter what we've both gone through, I'm glad we're here and that we're together."

"Oh, Vannie," she sniffled, "I'm sorry I never told you. I was afraid you'd think badly of me."

"Don't be ridiculous," I huffed. "I could never think badly of an angel. It's a sin."

Maxi laughed, the sound bringing relief to my heart. "Thank you," she smiled at me. "And I'm glad we're here together, too."

We began gathering up our glasses to wash them when she asked if I planned to stay and go to college there. "Since we're both going for nursing, we'll share the same classes," she said, glancing hopefully over at me.

I washed my glass in silence as I considered her question. Why should I go back to Atlanta? Everyone who truly loved me and cared about my well-being was right here. I could finish school alongside Maxi and live here with my aunt and uncle for as long as I needed. I wouldn't have any trouble finding a job at one of the local hospitals, and I'd never have to see Jake's face again if I didn't want to.

"Yes," I said, turning to look at her with a smile on my face. In that moment I'd made a very important decision about my future, a decision I hadn't given much thought or consideration to, but somehow, I knew it was right. "Yes, I'm staying right here."

Chapter Three

-1965-

"I think it would be wise to have a double mastectomy," Doctor Roberts stated, looking me directly in the eye. I trusted his judgment, but I'd also seen the disfigurement a mastectomy left behind, and the thought made me sick. "You don't want to run the risk of developing a tumor in your other breast later. As you know, that happens quite often."

"No, we certainly don't," my husband said, giving my hand a squeeze. He turned to look at me, his eyes serious and direct. "I think you should do as the doctor says, but it's up to you."

Up to me. I didn't want it to be up to me. I wanted this whole thing to disappear, to be some sick, twisted dream I would wake up from at any moment.

Taking a deep breath, I turned to look at Doctor Roberts and said, "A double mastectomy it is."

"Good," Doctor Roberts nodded his head in approval. "I've got the surgery scheduled for one week from today."

As we walked out, I noticed a woman that looked to be in her mid-thirties sitting in the waiting room, a girl of about six or seven years old seated next to her. Doctor Roberts called to the woman, and she stood to walk bravely into his office, leaving the child behind. She looked at me as she walked by, and I couldn't help but notice the familiar look of fear in her eyes. I wanted to ask what was wrong, to offer words of encouragement, but I couldn't. I didn't have any. As we left the building, I glanced at the girl, who sat quietly in the corner coloring a picture, and I realized that maybe I was luckier than I'd first thought. At least I didn't have a child I'd be leaving behind.

The drive home was quiet. I flipped through a few radio stations until finally turning it off. There just wasn't anything I cared to listen to.

"When all of this is behind us," my husband said, breaking the silence, "I think we should take a vacation. How does Canada sound? Neither of us have been there, and I hear it's beautiful in the summer. We could even stop by Niagara Falls on the way."

"We probably won't have the money after paying all of the doctor's bills," I said, immediately regretting my words. He was trying to make me feel better, to give me something to look forward to, and all I could do was tear his efforts down. "But," I added, turning to smile at him, "if we can afford it, I think that sounds like a wonderful idea."

His face relaxed into a smile of relief, and he reached across the console to take my hand. "Have I told you lately that you're just as beautiful now as you ever were? Even when I wanted you so badly I thought I'd die, but you were being stubborn."

I couldn't help but laugh. "I wasn't stubborn, just…confused, I guess," I shook my head, grinning at him as I added, "But aren't you glad you were so relentless? I believe my making you work so hard to win my affections taught you a very valuable lesson."

"Oh?" He cocked a brow at me. "And what lesson was that?"

"Patience," I winked.

Rubbing his thumb across the back of my hand, he slowly nodded his head and said, "I think you're right, and yes, I'm very glad I was so relentless."

Chapter Four

-1940-

He walked among the crowd, sticking as close to the tall, willowy figure as he dared. It was a busy day in the city, with shoppers and workers bustling all around. He was glad, however, for the crowd, as it gave him a sense of obscurity. He wouldn't want her to realize she was being followed.

His jaw clenched tightly together, he stepped into a doorway, peering out around the edge to watch as she quickly turned the corner, glancing over her shoulder to make certain no one saw. Once she was gone, he hurried on with his mission, intent on finding out where she was going.

He rounded the corner, allowing a bit more distance to grow between them as they moved further and further from the busy market area. He made certain to move quietly and to keep his hat pulled low over his face. If she saw him, she would run, and he may never find her again.

They'd been in love once, or so he thought until they'd had an argument and he turned violent. He'd tried to explain, to apologize, but she wouldn't listen. Instead, she packed her bags and disappeared in the night, leaving absolutely no trace behind. It had taken him days to track her down, but still he didn't know where she was staying.

He followed her for blocks, crossing streets and even the railroad tracks, until she finally arrived at an old, rugged boarding house. He watched as she climbed the steps and went inside, closing the door behind her.

So, this was it. This was where she'd run off to. He circled around the house, noting its surroundings and all of the entrances. He wouldn't make his move now, not in broad daylight, but he would be back very soon. She would pay dearly for ever leaving him.

It was Saturday, and I'd been in Savannah for almost a week. Maxi wasn't feeling well, and Aunt Deb was playing bridge with her friends, so I decided to go for a walk. I wandered for miles, taking in the beautiful sights the city had to offer. I walked along the path that surrounded the city's beloved, thirty acre Forsyth Park, where several young couples sat picnicking on the green grass, and I stopped to watch a young boy playing with his dog, laughing when the dog knocked the boy onto the ground and licked his face repeatedly, smearing wet slobber all along his cheeks. I glanced over and noticed Candler Hospital just across the street, and the fleeting thought that I may be a nurse there some day crossed my mind, a thought that pleased me a great deal.

The path carried on, leading me to an opening on my left where a very wide, beautiful stone walkway stretched out before me. A recent rain had left puddles all along the pathway, the reflections in the water twinkling as tiny little birds drank their fill. On either side stood massive, live oak trees that draped gracefully across the path like an archway, while wooden benches and old, iron lamp posts rested quietly beneath their branches. What truly stood out, however, in such a breathtaking scene was the huge, two-tiered fountain that stood majestically at the end of the walkway, its water spouting gracefully in all directions. The fountain, I had once been told, is reminiscent of the Place de la Concorde in Paris. It was built in 1858, but was still sparkling, stark white, and I walked closer to study the lovely, classically robed female figure that stood at the very top, holding a rod from which bursts of water spilled into the bath below where several triton figures rested.

Tearing myself away from the magic of the park, I continued on, walking through a couple of the 22 public squares the city was so famous for. James Oglethorpe, the city's founder in 1733, was the master behind the planning of the picturesque squares, which are set within a unique grid of streets and lanes and offer benches upon which one can sit beneath the silken branches of majestic oaks. William Dean Howells wrote almost 100 years ago that "the noble sequence of wooded and gardened squares forms the glory of the city", and I couldn't have agreed more.

After a while, my stomach gave a loud rumble, and I realized it had been hours since I'd last eaten. Heading further downtown, I soon arrived at a familiar location and gazed up at the large building looming before me, its sign reading "Leopold's Ice Cream". I hurried inside, taking in the long counter with a row of stools perching just beneath, the tables and booths off to my left. Soda jerks hurried back and forth behind the counter, some taking orders while others prepared them, and the smell of grilled hamburger patties and chocolate malt filled my delighted nostrils. I took a step forward, only to stop in my tracks when I spotted a certain young man working behind the counter amongst the others. The place was crowded, and he hadn't seen me yet, so I tip-toed over and quietly perched on one of the barstools, leaning over on my elbows as I spoke.

"Well, well, well, I didn't know you were a soda jerk," I spoke to the bent head before me.

Surprised hazel eyes rose from the bucket of ice cream he was scooping from, and a slow grin spread across Leon Danes' face.

"There's a lot you don't know about me," he winked. Handing the glass cup filled with strawberry ice cream to a young girl with pigtails, Leon turned back to face me and made a show of straightening his white hat and uniform. "Now," he cleared his throat, trying for a professional tone of voice, "what can I get for you, miss?"

Laughing, I ordered a cheeseburger with extra pickles, and a chocolate malted shake for dessert. "With extra whipped cream," I added.

He joined me minutes later with an extra plate, announcing that his shift was over, and dove hungrily into his thick, juicy burger.

"How long have you worked here?" I asked, wiping a bit of mustard from my lip. I had to admit, the burger was the best I'd ever eaten.

"I started at the beginning of the summer," Leon replied. "Last year, as you know, I made deliveries for Joe at the market, but this job pays better. Once school starts back, I'll only work on Friday afternoons and Saturdays, but every little bit helps."

I hadn't realized until then how much the Danes' must struggle financially. It had been hard for everyone the last several years with the Depression, but losing Mr. Danes must have made things doubly hard for them. I now understood why Connor had joined the military.

"What are your plans once you graduate?" I questioned, pushing my half-finished burger away as I started in on the delicious malted shake.

"Mom's boss is going to give me a management position at the bank," he replied, taking a gulp of his cold Cola. "Are you going to finish the rest of that burger?"

I had barely shaken my head "no" when Leon snatched up my remaining burger and transferred it over to his own plate.

"Where is Connor stationed?" I asked, the thought of Connor joining the military still on my mind.

"He is at the Albrook Army Airfield in Panama for now, right by the

Panama Canal." As always, pride shone from his eyes when he spoke of his older, more accomplished brother. "We're hoping, though, that he will be transferred to the new base they're building here at the Hunter Airfield."

"Oh, yes, I heard that the army was building a base just outside of town," I said, recalling that bit of information in a letter from Aunt Deb a few months ago. "It's not completed yet, is it?"

"No, but they're saying it will be by next year." His plate now clean and his stomach full, Leon leaned back against the booth and, with a satisfied sigh, folded his hands behind his head and smiled, studying me. "So, how do you like living here again? Do you miss your family in Atlanta?"

Offering him the rest of my malted shake, which he heartily accepted, I sat quietly for a moment as I pondered his question. "I miss Daddy, of course, and some of my school friends, but that's about it," I finally answered. "Savannah has always had my heart and always will, I suppose, and I'm glad to be living here again."

"You don't miss your stepmother?" Leon smirked.

I cocked my brow and replied drolly, "What stepmother?"

Laughing, Leon shook his head and set aside the empty glass. "Well, I'm glad you're back. I've missed my friend." He smiled warmly at me, and my mind was suddenly filled with happy childhood memories of the two of us teasing each other, telling secrets, and playing hide-and-seek. Mrs. Emma, his mother, always said we'd end up getting married some day, and the thought brought a wry smile to my face.

"What's going through that pretty little head of yours?" Leon wanted to know.

Before I could answer, a shrill, high pitched voice interrupted, "Hi, Leon!"

We turned to see Lucy Michaels walking our way, a dazzling smile on her face as she beamed at my handsome dinner date, and my stomach immediately began to sink. The first time I met her was at a summer barbecue when I was eighteen, and I'd immediately noticed the tension between she and Maxi. When I asked Maxi about it later, she said, "When I first moved here, Leon took me under his wing and did everything he could to help me feel at home, especially at school. Lucy has had a crush on Leon for years, and immediately took a disliking to me. When Leon caught her one day making a rude comment about my weight, he chewed her out about it, and she's hated me ever since."

I'd only seen and spoken to Lucy a handful of times, but I always had the feeling that she didn't liked me very much either and as I quietly sipped my water, I could feel her eyes boring into me.

"Hello, Lucy," Leon grinned flirtatiously.

"Where have you been lately?" Lucy wanted to know, her perfect red lips turning into a pout as she lightly poked at his forearm. "You promised you'd come to the dance at my house last Friday night, and you never showed."

Dances were often held at the houses of young, single girls, especially during the summer when school was out. Maxi had told me just last night that I'd missed out on several wonderful dances at their own home. She didn't know I'd never learned to dance, and I didn't bother mentioning it.

"Sorry about that, Lucy," Leon apologized, his big hazel eyes beseeching her forgiveness. "I had to help Mother with some repairs around the house, and it was too late to come over once I had finished."

Before Lucy could continue, Leon turned to me and said, "Lucy, you remember Savannah, don't you? She just recently moved back to live with her aunt and uncle."

"You're living here now?" Lucy asked, barely masking the disapproval in her tone.

"Yes, I am," I said, summoning up a friendly smile.

"Would you like to join us?" Leon offered.

When she eagerly nodded her head in agreement, I quickly announced that it was past time for me to be getting home and stood to leave. Saying my goodbyes, I made a quick getaway, thankful to be away from the snobbish girl. I'd only gotten a few steps down the sidewalk when the bell above the door jingled loudly and Leon walked out behind me.

"Wait for me," he called, hurrying to catch up.

"What about your friend?" I asked, glancing over his shoulder through the window. I could see Lucy sitting in the booth, a scowl on her face.

Leon crammed his hands in his pockets and shrugged nonchalantly. "She said some of her friends are meeting her in a bit, so she'll be fine," he said with his familiar, lazy half-smile. "It's getting late, so if you don't mind, I'll walk along with you."

"Of course, I don't mind."

I slid a hand through his offered arm and we slowly began our trek back home.

Moments later, I smiled at him through the growing shadows of dusk and said, "Do you remember when we were about, oh I don't know, six or seven, and we acted out a "play" on your back porch?"

Leon thought for a moment, then threw his head back and roared with laughter. "Oh my, yes, I remember! You were pretending to be Sherlock Holmes, and you stole a pair of Connor's pants, tying them on with his belt. I was Watson, wasn't I? Anyway, I remember Connor was so angry when he discovered you'd accidentally torn a hole in his favorite pair of trousers, and you simply stood there quietly while he ranted with your arms crossed and stuck your tongue out at him when he'd finished."

I laughed, remembering how angry I'd been at Connor for, once again, ruining our fun. "He said I was far too spirited for a girl," I said, for once smiling at a memory in which Connor was a part of.

"And he was right," Leon winked.

I offered no reply in my defense, for I wondered if perhaps he had been right after all.

Once we were back home, I thanked Leon for the escort and, after a quick hug, he left me on the front porch, saying he'd see me at church the next morning. I turned and walked inside to find Uncle Ray sitting in his favorite chair by the fireplace.

"Where's Auntie and Maxine?" I asked, leaning over to kiss his cheek.

Taking the pipe from the corner of his mouth, Uncle Ray pointed to the kitchen. "You missed supper," he said, "but be sure and get a piece of the pecan pie your aunt made. I sure am a lucky man to have married such a fine cook."

Smiling, I pulled off my hat and gloves and hurried into the kitchen to find Lizzie at the sink washing dishes while Aunt Deb and Maxi sat at the table, drinking tall glasses of sweet tea.

"Hello, my dears," I smiled, in an exceptionally good mood, and kissed them both on the cheek. "How are you feeling?" I asked Maxi.

"Better," my cousin smiled weakly.

"She barely ate a thing at supper." Aunt Deb patted Maxi's hand with concern.

I placed a palm on my cousin's forehead, noting that it was still a bit warm. "Are you drinking plenty of fluids, though?" I asked.

"I'm trying," Maxi nodded, taking another sip of tea as if to prove her point.

"Good," I said, taking the pie from the ice box.

I sat down at the table and took a large bite of the delicious dessert, pushing the thought that I'd just eaten half of a malted shake out of my mind. Pecan pie was notorious in the south, with its charming blend of crunchy pecans on top and sweet, gooey filling in the middle. It was one of my favorite desserts.

Maxi announced she was going back to bed, and Aunt Deb said she'd help her. The two of them stood and left the room, leaving Lizzie and I alone.

"Would you like something to drink?" Lizzie asked me.

"No, thank you," I shook my head. Lizzie, I'd discovered the day after my arrival, was a young, African American girl who had been working for my aunt and uncle the last few months. She came by every day to cook and clean and do the laundry, but I hadn't gotten much of a chance to talk to her yet. She looked to be about twenty years old, stood a little taller than me, and was very pretty with her smooth, ebony colored skin and sparkling black eyes. Her smile, however, was what one would notice the most about her. Her teeth were straight and gleaming white, and when she smiled, it brightened her entire face and made her eyes glitter like diamonds.

"How long have you worked for my aunt and uncle, Lizzie?"

"About seven months," Lizzie replied as she took my plate and began to wash it. "I like workin' for your family, they treat me really good."

I'd noticed Aunt Deb was a bit cross with her at times, but I supposed that's just the way things were. The rule of separation between the whites and blacks was a staunch one, but I knew a bit about the hurt that prejudice sometimes inflicted as my father was half Cherokee, and I felt the need to be extra nice to Lizzie. "Were you raised here in Savannah?" I asked.

"Oh, yes'm," replied Lizzie as she turned to lean against the counter. "My whole family lives here," she continued, "and I have a lot of family! Three brothers and a sister, a whole bunch of aunts and uncles, a couple of great grandparents, and the list just goes on and on."

I laughed at Lizzie's enthusiasm. "That's wonderful! Family is very important…"

"Lizzie," Aunt Deb scolded from the kitchen door, "you've still got work to do, young lady, and I suggest you get to it before it gets dark. You know your mother will be worried if you're out too late."

"It was my fault, Aunt Deb," I hurriedly explained. "I kept distracting her with my questions."

"Well, keep your questions for another day and let Lizzie get her work done." With that, Aunt Deb sashayed into the living room to knit.

"Thank you, Miz Savannah," Lizzie smiled gratefully, pulling out the feather duster that was peeking from her apron pocket. "Miz Debra can be a little grouchy sometimes, and I don't want to lose this job. It's very important to me."

I stood and patted the girl on the back, giving her a reassuring smile. "Don't worry, Lizzie, you won't lose your job. For the most part, my aunt is all bark and no bite. Besides, I think she's just concerned about your getting home too late."

"Maybe you're right," Lizzie grinned.

Later that night, I sat on my bed and stared at the unopened letter in my hand. Aunt Deb gave it to me after Lizzie had gone, and by the purse of her lips I didn't have to ask who it was from. I was unsure if I should open it or burn it. Curiosity finally got the best of me, and I slowly tore it open, the crisp white paper unfolding to reveal a familiar scrawl.

Dearest Savannah,

I miss you. I hope you're doing well. I know you don't care to hear from me, but you didn't give me a chance to explain and I feel that I must. As you know, Pamela and I had to work late that night. We were knee deep in paperwork when she suddenly asked if she could talk to me about something. I agreed, and she proceeded to tell me that she and my cousin Harold had been seeing each other for about six months when suddenly he told her it was over. He wouldn't tell her why, so she asked me if he was seeing someone else. When I told her he was, she started crying, and I placed my arm around her shoulders to comfort her. That kiss was never supposed to happen. I know you've accused me of flirting with her in the past, but please believe me when I say she does not mean a thing to me. You are the one I love, and if you'll only forgive me and give me another chance, I promise I'll never speak to her again. I miss you, Savannah. Please come home.
Love,
Jake

I folded the letter and placed it back into the envelope, curled up in my bed, and cried myself to sleep.

Chapter Five

-1965-

I sat in the waiting room, my stomach in knots. I hadn't been allowed to eat anything past eight o'clock the night before, but I don't think I could have forced a single bite of food past my lips if I'd tried.

"Don't be nervous, honey," my husband patted my leg. "Everything is going to be okay."

He was trying to be calm and reassuring for my sake, but I could tell he was just as anxious as I was. His left leg constantly bounced up and down, he cracked his knuckles incessantly, and his eyes were lined with puffy, black rings. The past week had been nothing but torture for the both of us. I didn't think this day would ever get here, and now that it was, I just wished it was all over.

I glanced over at Aunt Deb, my eyes following the movement of her fingers as she quietly knitted. She looked up at me and winked encouragingly, but I knew how worried she was, and I hated for her to worry about me. She was in her upper sixties now, with her own health concerns. I knew the bursitis in her hip and shoulder pained her more than she cared to admit, and she'd been struggling slightly with high blood pressure for years. I needed to be seeing about her, but it seemed that for now everything was in reverse.

Doctor Roberts stepped out from the back and surveyed the room until his eyes landed on me. I shrunk down in my seat, as if trying to hide. He smiled encouragingly, motioning for me to come, and I pushed myself up on trembling legs.

"I'll be praying for you, honey," Aunt Deb said, rising to kiss me on the cheek.

My husband took my elbow and walked with me until Doctor Roberts held up his hand and said, "I'm terribly sorry, but I'm afraid you aren't allowed back. Patients only." He glanced between us, noted our expression, and added, "I'll give you two a moment. Come on back when you're ready, Savannah. I'll be waiting."

My husband wrapped his arms around me, and I closed my eyes, breathing in his scent. I wished he could come with me and hold my hand. I'd feel better just knowing he was there.

"This will all be over soon, sweetheart," he said, gently rubbing my back. Pulling away, he grasped my shoulders and said, "You know I love you, right?"

"Yes," I whispered, nodding my head. "I love you, too. So, so much."

He stared at me for a moment, and I knew there was something else he wanted to say, and so I waited. "You know…" he paused, his voice cracking a bit, "I don't think I've ever told you this but…thank you."

"For what, honey?"

He smiled at me then, and I believe it was the most beautiful smile I'd ever seen. "For giving me a chance."

Leaning down, he kissed me sweetly on the lips, and then with a gentle push towards the door, said, "Get on back there, the doctor's waiting. I'll stay right out here, I promise."

Forcing back my tears, I turned with a smile and said, "You'd better," blew him a kiss, and walked bravely through the door.

Chapter Six

-December 1940-

Mr. Olsen, a stooped over train mechanic in his mid-fifties, glanced at his watch as he headed home from work. He'd had to stay late, and it was nearly 6 o'clock; Mrs. Olsen would be fit to be tied, but he wasn't in the mood for her jabbering. No, he was hungry and tired and ready for his pair of house slippers and soft easy chair.

He was only a few blocks away from home when he stopped in his tracks, his ears perking up at a strange, muffled sound. He glanced to his left at the old, wooden building with a sign in one of its dirty windows reading "Rooms for Rent". It was a big house, in desperate need of a new paint job, with rusty windowpanes and cobwebs hanging from the porch rafters. He took a step closer, straining as he listened. Was that moaning he heard? Old Mrs. Gibson, who was in her upper seventies and slightly crippled, and her daughter, Cathy, ran the boarding house. Could they, or one of the tenants, have had an accident, or was his imagination playing tricks on him?

Deciding to investigate, Mr. Olsen hesitantly climbed the three, rickety wooden steps onto the dusty front porch, and noticed the front door stood slightly ajar. With a feeling of foreboding, he tried to slowly push the door further open, but it only moved a few inches before it bumped into something. He squeezed his head through the small opening and, peering around the door, gasped at the sight before him.

"Oh, good God!" He cried, rearing back and striking his head sharply against the doorframe. One of the new tenants, what was her name?, was lying at the door in a pool of blood, strangled groans emerging from her swollen lips. His heart pounding, Mr. Olsen slid through the open door and knelt beside the woman for a closer look, discovering with a jolt of his stomach that her skull had been crushed.

Frantic, he jumped to his feet, his eyes flying wildly about as he half expected a murderer to emerge from the growing shadows in the dark corners of the room. He stood in a small foyer that lead to the living room, which spread out directly before him, its slightly faded sofa and chairs appearing to him more like dark, sinister figures crouched and ready to pounce rather than pieces of lifeless furniture.

The lady moaned again, bringing him back to the emergency at hand. He had to get help, but what of Mrs. Gibson and her daughter? Were they somewhere in the house, as well? Slowly, he stepped past the poor woman and ventured into the living room, reaching out with a shaking hand to flip on a lamp, casting further shadows about the room. The house was so still, so quiet, he nearly jumped out of his shoes when the grandfather clock chimed loudly to his left. *You have to hurry*, he told himself. *That woman is dying in there.*

With a deep breath, he prodded his feet to move faster as he headed for the downstairs bedrooms, but he didn't get far. There, lying in a lifeless heap in the hallway, was Mrs. Gibson's daughter, Cathy. Her brown hair was a tangled matt of blood and her throat oozed from a cut wound, while her blue, glazed eyes stared up at him blankly. She was dead.

Mr. Olsen could stand it no longer. With a strangled cry, he turned and fled, his stomach heaving as he tripped and ran as fast as his weak legs could carry him to the nearby drugstore where he planned to phone the police. He fell through the little drugstore's doorway, the bell dinging loudly as it flailed back and forth.

"Oh, Mr. Olsen!" Hank Tanner, the owner of the drugstore, cried. He hurried to poor man's side, jumping back as Mr. Olsen lost the contents of his stomach. The few people who were there doing their shopping cried out in alarm, rushing to see what the commotion was all about.

"They're dead...murdered," Mr. Olsen gasped, his stomach churning and his chest aching. "Call...police...hurry!"

"A Revolting Crime! Two Women Killed and Another Will Die," the headlines read the following morning.

"Last night, victims of a revolting crime, Mrs. Gibson and her daughter, Mrs. Cathy Carlisle, were found dead in their home. Mrs. Willingham, a boarder living in the house, was also found dying at the front door with a crushed skull. Police believe the murderer, using an axe taken from the woodshed behind the house, beat Mrs. Gibson to death, struck down Mrs. Willingham, and after assaulting Mrs.

Carlisle, finished his terrible work by beating in her skull with the weapon."

"Mrs. Gibson evidently was attacked from behind as she sat in an easy chair reading. On the floor beside the body were found the newspaper she was reading and her spectacles. One or possibly two blows were dealt her. Her grey hair, blood matted, showed the imprint of the blunt axe."

"It is probable that Mrs. Willingham was the first to be struck down; that she met the murderer at the door as he entered and was struck before she could escape."

"Then the murderer, stealthily approaching aged Mrs. Gibson, killed her. It is believed that Mrs. Carlisle was attacked as she left her room to enter the hallway, was assaulted and killed. As of yet, no suspects have been brought in, and no one seems to have seen or heard anything. If anyone has any information related to this case, please come forward. The mayor has offered a reward of $1,000 for the capture with evidence to convict the slayer of these women."

I slowly lowered the newspaper, my face drained of all color. "Dear God," I breathed, shocked that something so gruesome had happened in our very own city.

"I know that may not be the most reputable part of town," Aunt Deb said as she sipped her coffee, "but I can't believe anyone could do such a terrible thing. Those poor women," she shook her head. Giving Maxi and I a stern look, she added, "Until the police have apprehended the killer, I don't want you two girls out alone."

"After reading that, I have no desire to be alone," Maxi shuddered.

Two days later the newspaper read "**How two women could have been killed with an axe and a third left in a dying condition, without a scream or the sound of a struggle being heard outside seems inconceivable**". Bloodhounds from a local county farm were taken to the murder scene, but no scent was found. The townspeople seemed to go out of their minds like a mob of witch hunters, tearing madly about the city and storming into people's homes as they searched for the murderer. Over one hundred negro men were arrested, as rumors that a black man had committed the crime came to light, although no one could prove it. Everyone hoped and prayed Mrs. Willingham would wake from her coma and tell the police what really happened.

All of Savannah seemed to be on pins and needles, whispers and rumors spreading like wildfire. Some said Cathy had been ravished before she was killed, and poor Mrs. Gibson had been completely oblivious when the killer snuck up behind her and sunk the ax into her skull. It was a grim time in the city of Savannah, and until the crime was solved, everyone feared what might happen next.

Chapter Seven

-December 1940-

Much to mine and Maxi's relief, Christmas break was finally upon us. It seemed all that everyone talked about was the murders, and the gruesome details were so much in the forefront of my mind that I'd even started having nightmares about them. I needed a break, some time to relax and enjoy the season with my family without whispered rumors emanating throughout the classroom.

I'd received two more letters from Jake, and he even tried to call once, but I never answered. I thought it best to break all communication with him. It still, however, didn't stop me from thinking about him. I no longer cried myself to sleep at night, but there were times I'd smell something or hear a particular song that would make me think of him. It hadn't been easy, but I felt that I was finally starting to get over him.

After suffering for so long during the Depression, things were finally beginning to feel normal again, and so the city of Savannah went all out for Christmas. Light poles and tree trunks were wrapped with garland and gold ribbons, and huge, beautiful poinsettias lined the sidewalks, their deep reds adding vibrant splashes of color throughout the town.

Mrs. Emma had gotten a letter from Connor, informing her he wouldn't be able to make it home this year. Leon, hoping to take her mind off the sad news, suggested they host a Christmas party at their home the Friday before Christmas. Aunt Deb, Maxi, and I pitched in to help, and by the time Friday arrived, the house was gleaming with Christmas cheer, excitement emanating throughout each room. A massive red, green, and gold wreath hung from the front door, causing a loud racket each time it was opened or closed, and a beautiful tree sat proudly in the corner of the living room, reaching nearly nine feet tall with ribbons draped on its green branches and a gleaming, silver star perched on top. The wooden floor had been polished until it sparkled, and a heavenly aroma drifted from the kitchen as we carried trays of finger foods to sit on the dining room table.

"Leon, what on earth are you doing?" I heard Mrs. Emma exclaim, and I peeked around the corner to see what the commotion was about. Leon was perched on top of a ladder, hanging mistletoe from the ceiling near the front door.

"This is what I call planning ahead," he grinned, wiggling his eyebrows. "Plus, it's tradition," he added when his mother scoffed at him.

"Wishful thinking, if you ask me," I teased.

"Better watch out, smarty, or someone just might catch you under the mistletoe," he returned with a wink.

"I'll make sure to stay on the opposite side of the room," I replied dryly.

"Killjoy," he called as I walked back to the kitchen, and I couldn't help but smile.

At seven o'clock sharp, people began arriving in droves, and soon the house was filled with happy, chattering friends of all ages. Mrs. Emma and I were standing at the door when a couple in their mid-fifties entered, and my eyes immediately fell upon the woman's beautiful, and obviously very expensive, fur coat.

"Alvin, Marie," Mrs. Emma cried, pulling them both into a hug, "it's so wonderful to see you!" Pulling back, Mrs. Emma proceeded to introduce us. "Alvin and Marie Cox, I'd like you to meet Savannah Adair. She's Debra and Ray's niece and has come to live with them. She's about to graduate with her nursing degree in a few months. Savannah," she turned to me, her eyes bright with happiness, "Alvin just happens to be one of Candler's best doctors."

"It's very nice to meet you both," I said, shaking both of their hands.

"And you, as well," Doctor Cox smiled. "I'm always glad to hear that the hospital will be receiving new nurses. Especially when they're as pretty as you."

Blushing, I thanked him with a smile and then asked how he and his wife knew Mrs. Emma. "Her husband and I grew up together," he explained. "We were very good friends."

I nodded, remembering that Mrs. Emma's husband had been several years older than her.

"We were heartbroken when he passed away," Mrs. Cox stated, her voice soft as she reached for Mrs. Emma's hand. She was a very small woman, with alabaster skin and wide, doe brown eyes, and I could tell by the diamond earrings that hung delicately from her ears that she and her husband were quite wealthy.

"Where is Matthew?" Mrs. Emma asked, glancing over their shoulders at the door as if expecting him to suddenly appear.

"He had other plans," Doctor Cox stated, waving his hand. "You know how he can be."

I thought I caught a look of annoyance in Mrs. Emma's eyes, but before I could ponder it further, Leon appeared, giving the doctor a hug and his wife a kiss on the cheek. They had only been talking for a few moments when Doctor Cox glanced at his pocket watch and said, "Well, I hate to leave so quickly, but my sister is actually having a party tonight, as well, so we'll have to be going." Retrieving a small box from his pocket, Alvin handed the gift to Mrs. Emma and said, "We just wanted to stop by and give you a little something. It's not much, but I know this time of year is hard for you and we want you to know we love you and your family."

Her eyes filling with tears, Mrs. Emma opened the box and gasped, pulling out a sparkling, diamond bracelet. Dangling from the beautiful piece was a small sapphire, and Mrs. Emma breathed, "Frank's birthstone was a sapphire. Oh, it's beautiful!"

After they had gone, I asked Leon about Matthew.

"He's their thirty something year old son who acts like he's still twelve," he explained, rolling his eyes. "How two such nice people could raise someone like him, I'll never know. Mama always said they spoiled him too much."

As Leon walked away to greet more newcomers, I found myself wondering about Matthew Cox and the meaning behind Leon's comment of "someone like him". I also tried to remember if I recalled seeing the Cox family at Mr. Danes' funeral, but finally shrugged off the lack of memory to the fact that I'd been too young to pay much attention to those in attendance.

Later, after the food had been eaten and cleared away, all of the "old, married folks" went out onto the back screened in porch where they could socialize and drink hot chocolate around a small fire, while the young people pulled the rugs back inside the large living room and began to dance.

"Oh, isn't this fun?" Vivian Parker, a friendly girl from church, exclaimed, her green eyes sparkling with excitement. Her family owned one of the best restaurants in town, known for their unique, secret recipes and delectable desserts. I'd soon learned upon meeting Vivian that she was an extremely hard worker and very ambitious, with big ideas on how to expand the business once it was hers someday.

"I'm so glad you could make it tonight, Vivian," I smiled warmly, giving her arm a squeeze. She was such a genuinely nice person, with an ever-ready smile and never-ending supply of energy, that one couldn't help but like her.

Soon, nearly everyone was out on the dance floor swinging to the popular dances such as "The Lindy Hop", "The Jive", and "The Balboa". I stood back and watched, claiming I'd eaten too much and was feeling too nauseas to dance. *Someday*, I thought, *I really should learn how.*

The front door opened suddenly, pulling my gaze away from the dancers, and a stranger stepped inside, taking in the scene before him with dark, raised eyebrows. I watched with curiosity as he walked, unnoticed by everyone else, to the other side of the room and helped himself to one of the few remaining sandwiches left on the table that had been pushed against the wall. He propped a hip against the shiny, solid mahogany, making himself at home as he chewed slowly and watched, with a slight smirk, the wild group of dancers before him. He seemed slightly familiar, but I couldn't quite place him. My gaze took in his simple light blue, button down shirt and navy pants, not failing to notice the broad shoulders that strained at the seams. He was tall, very tall, and his black hair was cut short, framing a tanned, chiseled, clean shaven face. He wasn't necessarily a man one would call "devastatingly handsome", but there was something very attractive about him, in a manly, rugged sort of way.

He looked in my direction then, catching my eye, and I immediately looked away, feeling self-conscious for being caught staring. When I looked back, he was gone. I glanced around the room in search of him, only to come up empty.

"Are you sure you don't feel like dancing?" Leon spoke into my ear, giving me a start.

"Goodness, you scared me," I laughed, placing a hand on my chest. "Leon, who was that man that just came in?"

With a furrowed brow, Leon looked around and shrugged. "I don't know, I didn't see anyone." Glancing above my head, a slow grin spread across his face and he said, "How do you feel about tradition?"

"Oh, dear," I muttered, looking up to find I was standing under the mistletoe.

Laughing, Leon grabbed my hand and leaned forward, but before I could protest, his mother called to him from the porch. With a sigh, he leaned over and kissed me quickly on the forehead.

"You owe me," he winked, turning to walk across the room and out the back door.

Feeling slightly relieved, I watched Leon go. Jake was the only man I'd ever kissed, and I wasn't ready to kiss anyone else just yet.

As if reading my mind, the song changed to one of mine and Jake's favorites, and feeling a bit melancholy, I watched as the couples began to slow dance. I wrapped my arms around my waist and swayed gently back and forth to the music, pushing thoughts of Jake aside as I closed my eyes and soaked in the beautiful melody.

I was so engrossed in the song that I didn't sense his presence, but as soon as he touched my cheek my eyes popped open in surprise and I found myself looking into the most unusually beautiful silver-blue eyes I'd ever seen. Before I realized his intentions, he leaned over and pressed his lips against mine, his thumb gently caressing my chin. Startled, I simply stood there, my heart pounding as I realized this was the stranger who had entered the room moments ago.

Pulling back, he smiled down at me and said, "It's good to see you again, Savannah Rose. You've changed since I last saw you."

Taking a step back, I frowned and asked, "Who are you?"

"I didn't think you recognized me," he grinned. "If so, you'd have never let me kiss you."

"I didn't know you were going to," I snapped, my face flushing.

"That's normally what happens when you're standing under the mistletoe."

"Trust me, it wasn't intentional," I said, tapping my foot in annoyance. "Are you going to tell me who you are or not?"

Before he could answer, Leon's loud voice boomed from across the room, "Connor!"

Chapter Eight

-December 1940-

I couldn't believe it. Connor Danes was home, and I hadn't even recognized him. Granted, it had been six years since I'd last seen him, and he'd looked much different as a boy of eighteen compared to the mature man that he was now, but I still felt like a fool. How could I have allowed Connor, of all people, to kiss me? And to make matters worse, Aunt Deb informed me that we were going to spend Christmas Eve Sunday with the Danes family. I never wanted to face Connor again, and here I was being forced to spend the afternoon with him.

The morning dawned cold and bright, with a heavy frost in the air. I'd received a beautiful red dress from Daddy as a Christmas gift, and I slid it over my head as I got ready for Sunday morning service. It was a deep, red velvet with tiny sequins around the high neck, and a black, snug belt that accentuated my small waist. The full, flowy skirt dropped just below my knees, and since it was sleeveless, I wore a little black sweater with it and black, high heeled pumps. My hair was twisted up on the sides and pinned back with two of my mother's pearl combs, while the rest hung in loose, shiny waves just below my shoulders.

All during the service, I noticed from the corner of my eye that Connor kept looking my way. I dreaded going to his home after church and wondered if I could fake an illness.

After the service, Maxi, Vivian, and I stood talking in the foyer when Vivian said, "I noticed Connor Danes is home, isn't he dreamy?"

"More like a nightmare," I muttered.

"Stay away from him, Viv," Maxi warned, absently twirling a loose curl around her finger. "Leon says he's a real heartbreaker. He's apparently the "love them and leave them" type."

"Leon's got a lot of room to talk," Vivian scoffed. "He's just as bad."

Uncle Ray called to us then, announcing that it was time to leave. We went home first to grab the chocolate layered cake Aunt Deb made that morning before we headed next door. At our knock, Leon opened the door with a welcoming, excited smile on his handsome face. "Merry

Christmas!" He cried, as if we hadn't just seen him at church.

Mrs. Emma came running around the corner from the kitchen, a stained, pink apron tied around her waist. "I'm so glad you're here, Debra," she said, grabbing my aunt by the hand. "I need help with the dressing, I don't think it tastes right…" Her voice trailed off as the two hurried into the kitchen with their heads together.

I fleetingly wondered where Connor was as I took my coat off but was soon distracted by Leon's loud whistle. "I didn't get a chance to say this at church, but that's a knock-out dress," he exclaimed, his eyes sweeping over me appreciatively.

I laughed and twirled around, showing off the new dress from Daddy.

Leon took my hands in his, squeezing them lightly as he smiled down at me and said warmly, "You look like a million bucks."

"She most certainly does," Connor's voice rumbled from the kitchen door, and I felt my face flush as I glanced over Leon's shoulder to meet Connor's gaze. He'd obviously been in the kitchen helping his mother, for his burgundy shirt and black pants were spotted with flour, and I couldn't help but laugh.

"I can't say the same for the cook," I smirked.

Connor looked down at his clothes and chuckled. "You're right, I'd better go upstairs and change."

The food was finally ready, and with rumbling stomachs, everyone hurried to be seated and say grace. Mrs. Emma used her finest china, which was a soft, pearl white with tiny pink roses dotting the exterior, and we all filled our plates with moist turkey, dressing, cranberry sauce, creamed corn, green beans, macaroni and cheese, and fluffy biscuits.

"So, did y'all hear the news?" Mrs. Emma asked over the tinkling of china. "Connor just received word that he's going to be stationed at the new Hunter Army Airfield when it opens next month. Isn't that wonderful?"

Everyone exclaimed that it was, except for me. I simply nodded and gave a tight smile.

"Yes, I'm very excited about it," Connor said, glancing across the table at me. "Aren't you happy that I'll be around more, Savannah Rose?" He asked in an innocent voice.

Ignoring the smirk on his face, I forced a tight, fake smile and said sweetly, "I'm just thrilled."

He coughed back a chuckle at the underlying sarcasm in my words, while everyone else continued talking.

We finished off every bit of Aunt Deb's cake, and after everything was cleaned and the dishes were washed, Mrs. Emma suggested we play a game. "Don't you have that new board game, Debra?" She asked. "I think it's called Scrabble."

"Oh, yes, it's in our living room," Aunt Deb said, clapping her hands with excitement. "Run over and get it, Savannah, it's on top of the bookcase. Oh, it will be too high for you to reach. Connor, you're tall, go and help her."

"I'm sure I can get it myself, Auntie," I said, hurrying out the door.

"No, you can't, it's too high and you'll break your neck!" I heard her yell just before I closed the door.

With a sigh, I waited for Connor to join me. He walked slowly out onto the porch and smiled pleasantly. "After you, m'lady," he bowed.

As I walked next door, he followed at a leisurely pace, hands in his pockets, and whistling an annoying tune.

I stood on the porch and waited, tapping my foot impatiently. "Would you hurry?" I rubbed my arms and shivered. "It's too cold to be such a slow poke."

"Do you need someone to warm you up?" He grinned, walking slowly up the steps until he stood, towering, in front of me. Aunt Deb was right, he really was very tall, at least 6'4".

"No, thank you," I replied curtly, spinning on my heel to hurry inside.

I could hear Connor chuckling as he followed me into the house, and I fought to control my irritation. Something about this man never failed to rub me the wrong way. After hurriedly flipping on the lights, I marched over to the bookcase, my heels clicking against the wooden floor.

"Don't get your feathers ruffled, Savannah Rose, I was only teasing," he said as he walked up from behind, amusement lacing his words.

Ignoring him, I pointed to the top of the bookcase and said, "It's up there."

"You know," he said, making no move to reach for the game as he crossed his arms and leaned against the bookcase, "I get the feeling that you don't like me very much, Savannah Rose."

"It's not just a feeling," I said, immediately regretting my words. I normally wasn't so rude, what was wrong with me?

A look of surprise flashed across Connor's face, and he threw his head back and laughed loudly. "You always were honest to a fault, weren't you?"

"I shouldn't have said that," I smiled sheepishly, my cheeks flushing. "Now, are you going to get the game, or not?"

"Just give me a minute, will you?" He chuckled, raising a hand. "I want to know why you don't like me."

I hesitated, crossing my arms over my chest. "To be honest," I said, eyeing him with straightforwardness, "I've never liked the way you treat me. You tease me, you're condescending, and quite arrogant."

"I always did give you a hard time, didn't I?"

"Yes, you did…and still do," I pursed my lips.

His face immediately turning sober, he straightened to his full height and said, "Well, I am truly sorry, and I promise to do better, if you'll give me a chance. What do you say, Savannah Rose? Can we start over and be friends?"

I studied him warily for a moment, surprised at the olive branch he was offering. He looked sincere enough, but I didn't completely trust him.

"No more teasing?" I asked hesitantly.

He paused for a moment, his mouth twitching, before he held up his hand and said, "Scout's honor."

"You were never a scout," I pointed out dryly, cocking an eyebrow.

Connor laughed. "Alright then, cross my heart," he tried again.

"Well..." I hesitated, a smile beginning to tug at the corners of my lips. "Okay."

As we walked back to his house, the game curled under Connor's arm like a football, I asked, "Why do you call me by my full name?"

"It's what your mother named you, is it not?"

I stopped and looked up at him. "You remember her?"

"Of course, I do," he nodded. "I remember Mother took us to see you in the hospital when you were born. Leon was only a couple of months old, but Mother was determined to go. She said nothing could keep her from her best friend during such an important time."

"Goodness, I'd forgotten Leon and I had such close birthdays," I said, a small smile forming on my lips. "Our mothers were very close, weren't they?"

We had arrived back at Mrs. Emma's house, and Connor stopped at the front door before going in, turning back to look at me. "Yes, they were. Mother was heartbroken when she died. She was a wonderful person, your mother," he said, his eyes so thoughtful and gentle it took me by surprise.

"I remember she placed you in my arms and said "Isn't she beautiful, Connor? Just like a tiny, perfect little pink rose". She thought the world of you."

My throat became choked with emotion at his kind words, and I fought to control the tears welling in my eyes. I suddenly wondered at this complex man standing before me. How he could be so irritating one moment and sweet the next was beyond me.

"Thank you for telling me that," I said, smiling sincerely up at him.

"You're welcome." His eyes took on a mischievous spark as he added, "And by the way, when I come back next month, young lady, you'd better know how to dance."

I gasped. "How did you know?"

"I'm very good at reading people," he grinned. "In my experience, when a beautiful, young woman isn't dancing at a party it's because she doesn't know how."

My cheeks flaming, I tossed my hair over my shoulder and said saucily, "Well, don't worry about me, Mr. Danes. Instead, just concentrate on preparing your pride for its soon upcoming defeat, as I never lose at Scrabble."

Connor's eyes twinkled at the challenge. "We'll just see about that, Miss Adair."

I beat him by ten points.

Chapter Nine

-1965-

My eyes slowly fluttered open, and I stared up into a blurry, unfamiliar face.

"I'm glad to see you're awake," the young woman said as she adjusted a bit of tubing that seemed to be attached to my arm.

My mind felt fuzzy as I lifted my head to look around the room. I appeared to be in the hospital, and slowly it all started coming back to me.

"How…" I cleared my dry throat and tried again, "how did the surgery go?"

"Splendidly," the nurse smiled. "You'll be able to go home in a few days."

"When can I see my family?" I wanted to know.

"You can see them in a few hours when we move you to another room."

She finished what she was doing, gathered her supplies, and left the room. I lay there, drifting in and out of a light, fitful sleep, when someone to my right softly cleared their throat. Startled, I turned my head to find I wasn't alone. The woman I'd seen last week occupied the bed next to me, the curtain that separated us drawn back.

"Hello," she nodded at me. She was sitting up and sipping on a glass of water, the hospital gown loose and hanging from her thin frame. "How are you feeling? I've been waiting for you to wake up."

"I feel very tired," I answered, blinking my dry eyes. "And a little strange."

"So do I," she nodded, her short blonde hair falling across her face. She reached up to shove it behind one ear, and I noticed the bruises that lined her arm. "I've been here since yesterday."

"Did you have a mastectomy, as well?" I asked.

"No," she shook her head. "I had ovarian cancer, so the doctor had to remove my ovaries."

"Was the surgery successful?" I asked hopefully.

She glanced down at the glass of water in her lap, the ice tinkling against the sides as she swirled it around, and I had the feeling she was fighting tears. "He said he's afraid we didn't catch it in time and that the cancer may have spread, but we'll see," she shrugged with a sigh. "I've got to come back every week for treatments."

My stomach clenched at her words. "I hope everything turns out well for you," I said. "I've got to come back for treatments, too."

"Well, since we may be seeing more of each other, we might as well introduce ourselves," she smiled, the gesture brightening her drawn face. "I'm Abby."

"I'm Savannah." Trying to sit up a bit, I squirmed about in the uncomfortable hospital bed, the I.V. tugging painfully at my arm. "Was that your little girl I saw in the waiting room last week?"

"Yes," she nodded, her face once again growing sober. "Her name is Hannah, she's six."

"She's a very pretty child," I said.

"Yes, she's my little angel. I don't know…" her voice trailed off, and I noticed her eyes grew distant, as if her mind were somewhere else. Not wishing to bother her, I settled back down in the bed, my mind racing. What if my cancer had spread, as well? I'd been so terrified of the surgery and everything it entailed that I hadn't even thought of any other possibilities. I could only hope the treatments would take care of anything that may be left.

Chapter Ten

-January 1941-

When I came home from school on the afternoon of January 5th, I was surprised to find Lizzie sitting on my bed, crying.

"Lizzie, what's wrong?" I asked, sitting down next to her.

"Oh, Savannah," she sniffled, reaching out to grasp my hand, "they think…" she glanced at the open door, and leaned closer as she whispered, "they think Joseph killed those women."

My eyes widened. Joseph was Lizzie's fiancé. "Why on earth would they suspect him?"

Lizzie stood up and began to pace in front of me. "Because he does carpentry work for Miz Gibson sometimes, and he was there that morning fixin' her stove. People saw him, and he even admitted it when the police asked him."

"But that doesn't mean he killed them, for goodness sake!" I exclaimed.

Lizzie hurriedly sat back down, her voice filled with desperation as she said, "I know he didn't do it; he was with me when it happened, but the police won't believe me. They say I'm trying to protect him. What should I do? I've got to help him!"

"I don't think there's anything you can do, Lizzie, at least not right now," I reached out and took her hand, giving it a squeeze. "But if he goes to trial, I feel certain my aunt and uncle will help you find a good lawyer. Joseph will be just fine, I'm sure of it."

The next morning, Lizzie and I went down to the station to visit Joseph. We were forced to wait for over an hour for no apparent reason, and when we were finally allowed to see him, we both gasped at his bruised face and swollen, bloody lip.

"Joseph, what happened to you?" Lizzie cried, reaching through the bars to gently touch his face.

"They found my fingerprints on that ax," Joseph said, hanging his head. "I tried to tell them I'd used it many times to chop wood for Miz Gibson, but they don't believe me."

"That is no reason to abuse you!" Lizzie said, her voice growing louder.

"They believe I killed those women, Lizzie," Joseph said, his deep, gravelly voice strained. "In their minds I deserve to be beaten. I heard one cop say to the other that they shouldn't have to wait for a trial, that I should be killed right now, and last night some men tried to storm the place, screaming like maniacs that I needed to be taken to the nearest tree and hanged."

I felt the blood drain from my face at Joseph's words. "We're going to see that you get a good lawyer, Joseph, don't worry," I told him in an encouraging tone. "You'll be out of here soon "

"I just hope I make it 'til then," he shook his head. He looked exhausted, and I wondered if they'd even given him anything to eat or drink since his arrest.

I felt terrible that Joseph was being treated so badly. I knew why they were abusing him this way, but I kept my silence, as I didn't want Joseph to think I was taking their side. Those murders had been beyond gruesome, and whoever committed them deserved the maximum amount of punishment possible. That wasn't, however, any excuse to treat another human being so badly. Unfortunately, Joseph was the most likely suspect, and the police were convinced they had the right man, but I felt that they were wrong. I believed Lizzie when she said he was with her when the murders took place.

"Is there anything you need, honey?" Lizzie asked him, tears in her eyes.

"Prayer," he reached out and took her hand. "A lot of prayer."

I told him we would do everything we could for him and went outside to give he and Lizzie some privacy. I couldn't imagine how frightened Lizzie must be, and when she joined me moments later, I tried my best to encourage her as we walked home.

The next morning, Joseph was shot and killed in an escape attempt. The chief of police said he choked out the guard, took his keys, and tried to escape through a back door. I didn't know whether to believe them or not. I felt that he'd been set up, but I also knew that desperation and fear often made one do things they shouldn't in order to survive. I attended the funeral alone, and as I tried to find a seat in the First African Baptist Church among the hundreds of people in attendance, I felt many eyes upon me.

"Is this seat taken?" I asked an elderly lady who wore a large, black hat with black lace and tiny pearls.

"No, honey, sit down," she smiled kindly at me.

Once in my seat, I looked around until I found Lizzie. She was sitting on the front row next to Joseph's mother, her face blank and eyes glassy. My heart ached for her.

The service was both beautiful and heart wrenching. The closed, wooden casket stood beneath the pulpit like a lonely island in the midst of a sea of people. I went to the graveside service, as well, and tears slid down my cheeks when Joseph's mother broke down, falling to her knees and sobbing as she reached through empty air for the open grave. The elderly lady I sat by in the church moved to stand beside me, and chills ran up my spine as she slowly began to sing "In the Sweet By and By" in a deep, soulful voice. The others soon joined in, and I closed my eyes as I tried to control my emotions. Never had I heard anything so moving, so powerful. Once it was over, everyone stood in silence for a moment, as if in reverence.

Someone lightly touched my arm, and I turned to see Lizzie, her eyes red and swollen, a wrinkled, white handkerchief clutched in her hand. Without saying a word, I gently pulled her into a hug, rubbing her back as she cried on my shoulder.

"Thank you for coming, Miz Savannah," she said, pulling back to blow her nose.

"Of course, I came," I said. "Please let me know if there is anything you need, Lizzie."

"I will," she smiled, her lips wobbling.

Two days later, Mrs. Willingham awoke from her coma, and in her delirium told Doctor Cox that her ex-husband was the real killer. She died the next morning.

Chapter Eleven

-February 1941-

It was almost February 14th and our local Red Cross was holding their annual Valentine's Day dance fundraiser at the Tybee Island pier. For two weeks leading up to the event, flyers were hung all over town. The dance was to start at six o'clock, the tickets were $.50 a piece for soldiers, and $1.00 for everyone else. Finger sandwiches, hot chocolate, and cookies would be served along with a fun night filled with dancing to a live band. Maxi, Vivian, and I signed up to help, and on Saturday at noon we, along with the other volunteers, rode out to the island to start setting up.

I helped with the placement of the tables while Maxi and the other girls decorated the pavilion with red and pink hearts, Valentine's Day sweetheart cards, streamers, and flowers.

"Let's put the table for the hot chocolate and cookies over there," I told Lionel, one of the Red Cross volunteers. He was in his mid-twenties, with mousey brown hair and an awkward, somewhat unfriendly disposition. "Yes, ma'am," he muttered under his breath.

I paused and glanced over at him, noting his jerky movements. "I'm sorry, Lionel, I wasn't trying to be bossy," I told him.

Glancing up at me in surprise, Lionel's face turned a bit red as he cleared his throat and walked away without another word.

As I spread a red cloth on top of the long, wooden table, I heard some of the girls begin to talk about the Willingham trial.

"I find it strange that Mrs. Willingham married a man thirty years her senior," one girl said.

"I think she needed money," said another.

"He hasn't admitted to anything, you know," Vivian stated, handing Maxi another decoration.

"Surely he's guilty, though, since his wife said so," Maxi muttered over a mouthful of tacks as she attempted to balance atop a step ladder.

"No one but the doctor actually heard her say that, though," I joined in.

"Are you insinuating that he's a liar?"

We all turned in surprise to find a tall man in his mid-thirties standing behind us, a notepad and pencil in hand.

"Who are you?" I wanted to know, raising an eyebrow at Vivian when she coughed loudly.

"Matthew Cox," he stated coolly, his blue eyes piercing mine. "I work for the newspaper and stopped by to cover the dance. My father is the man you were just gossiping about."

My cheeks flushing, I said, "We weren't gossiping..."

"What were you doing then?" He interrupted, his tone condescending. "Perhaps you believe your black friend is the real murderer instead of Mr. Willingham?"

My temper flaring, I placed a hand on my hip and said, "I never once believed that Joseph committed those murders, but I don't intend to discuss it further with someone who was so rudely eavesdropping."

His jaw clenched, Matthew spun around and stalked off without another word.

"That certainly went well," Vivian said dryly, cocking a brow at me.

I sighed, my temper deflating like an overwrought balloon. "I'll never get a job at the hospital after that," I groaned.

"He had it coming, Vannie," Maxi stated, attempting to make me feel better. "He was quite rude."

"He's always a bit rude, though, isn't he?" Vivian shook her head. "It's no wonder he never got married. How old is he now? Thirty-four? Thirty-five?"

I shrugged, wondering if I should apologize when I saw Ben, a young man stationed at Fort Screven, arrive with his band, "The Soldier Boys", and I hurried over to show them where to set up.

"This is our drummer, Mark, our saxophonist, George, and our bass player, Kevin," Ben politely introduced the band members.

I smiled at the three men and introduced myself as they each shook my hand.

"What instrument do you play, Ben?" I asked. He looked very handsome in a khaki, army uniform and beret, his blue eyes twinkling with excitement over the upcoming event.

"I'm the star," he winked. "I play the guitar and sing." He then turned to another soldier who was setting up the sound system and patted him on the shoulder. "This is Robert, our sound guy."

Robert stood and nodded at me with a smile. He stood about 5'9", with thick, dark hair and a dazzling, white smile. Before he could speak, however, Maxi suddenly burst onto the scene, her face pale and eyes wide as she grasped my arm.

"Vannie!" She gasped, her tone panicked. "Where are the cups for the hot chocolate? We can't find them!"

"Calm down, Maxi," I laughed, patting her hand. "Ms. Darlene is supposed to bring them just before six; she should be here any minute."

Maxi sighed with relief and slowly let go of my arm. "Oh, good," she laughed.

"I don't believe we've met," Robert interrupted, his voice smooth as he took a step closer to us. His eyes were on Maxi, and they gleamed flirtatiously as he gazed down at her.

She turned to look at him, immediately blushing at his bold, approving gaze. "Oh, um, I'm...I'm Maxine," she stammered, nervously smoothing a hand down her red and white polka dot dress. "I...I'm terribly sorry I shoved past you so rudely just now."

He stepped closer and, with relish, took her hand and bowed over it, kissing it lightly. "It's very nice to meet you, Maxine," he winked at her. "And you can shove me around anytime you like."

Raising my eyebrows, I slowly turned and walked away, leaving the two to get better acquainted. I walked to the entrance and stood back to survey the beautifully decorated, old pavilion. It was built in 1891 by the Central of Georgia Railroad, and was a well-known destination for visitors, as well as the many dances and events held there each year. It was a huge, wooden platform covered with a rounded roof that went up to a point, and was supported by several, thick wooden posts. Just opposite of the entrance, where I stood, was the long pier that stretched straight out into the ocean. Surrounded by palmetto bushes, palm trees, sand, and water, this was as close to paradise as it got.

Ms. Darlene finally arrived with the cups, and soon the party was underway as people began arriving in droves. Maxi and Vivian sold tickets at the entrance, Ms. Darlene and I served the hot chocolate, and two other volunteers served sandwiches and cookies.

I couldn't remember the last time I received so many compliments. It seemed that nearly every soldier at Fort Screven was there, and they all passed through my line with a hopeful smile or flirtatious wink. While I was flattered by the attention, soldiers were notorious flirts, and I took the compliments with a grain of salt.

"It would seem that you have a string of admirers here tonight," Leon wiggled his eyebrows as he stepped up to my station. He looked quite handsome in a crisp white shirt, navy plaid sports coat, and matching vest. Lucy stood beside him with her fingers wrapped possessively around his arm.

Smiling at his comment, I nodded to his date and said politely, "Hello, Lucy, you look very pretty. I love your dress."

Lifting her chin, she curled her lips slightly and said, "Thank you, so do you. I've liked that dress every time you've worn it."

My cheeks flushing at the underhanded insult, I self-consciously ran my hands down the dress Daddy gave me for Christmas.

"I've actually only worn it once, but thank you," I forced a smile.

"And you look even more beautiful in it than I remembered," Leon said, his eyes warm as he stared fondly at me.

Her jaw clenched, Lucy tugged at his arm and said, "Let's dance, Leon, I've decided I don't want any hot chocolate after all."

As I watched them walk off, I hoped he wasn't serious about her. He never seemed to get too attached to any girl, and I found myself wondering why. I didn't, however, have a chance to dwell any further on my thoughts, as the next person in line was Matthew Cox.

"I'd like some hot chocolate," he said, his tone cool.

As I handed him a steaming cup, my conscience got the best of me and I said, "I'd like to apologize about what happened earlier, Mr. Cox. I was rude, and I'm sorry."

With a sniff, he raised one haughty eyebrow and said, "You should be," before walking away.

Sighing, I finished serving my line and told the other girls to go enjoy themselves, that there was no point in all of us missing the fun when the line was dying down. They readily agreed, and an hour later, I stood alone behind the serving table, watching as everyone had a good time. I tried to cover a yawn, wondering if anyone would notice if I pulled up a chair and took a nap.

"You look bored, Savannah Rose."

I gasped, in mid yawn, and spun around, colliding with a broad chest. Quickly taking a step back, I raised my head and met the amused gaze of Connor Danes.

"I could be wrong, though," he grinned down at me.

What had he said? Oh, yes, that I look bored. "What are you doing here?" I asked, ignoring his first statement.

"It's good to see you, too," he huffed, a mock look of hurt coming over his face.

"I'm sorry," I sighed, "it's good to see you. Now, what are you doing here?"

With a chuckle he said, "I arrived this morning at Hunter. It's finally open, you know, so I am now going to be living there."

I scrunched my forehead as memory struck me. "Oh, yes, I'd forgotten." I then graced him with a smile and added, "Well, it's nice to have you home."

"Why aren't you dancing, Savannah Rose?" Connor reached around me and snitched a chocolate chip cookie, cramming the whole thing in his mouth. "Or haven't you learned how yet?"

"Maybe I just don't want to dance. Have you considered that?" I pursed my lips.

"I'm fairly certain that's not the case," he laughed, reaching out to grab my hand. "Come on," he said, pulling me with him.

"Where are we going?" I tried to pull my hand away. Connor was headed directly towards the dance floor.

"Calm down, it's just a slow dance," he grinned at me over his shoulder.

"What?" My mouth fell open.

"Anyone can slow dance," he said, his smoky eyes twinkling down at me. "Trust me."

I stared at his outstretched hand, glancing uneasily at the other couples, Ben's soft, soothing tone calming my nerves a bit. With a sigh, I took Connor's hand and allowed him to pull me close, my eyes watching our feet as Connor told me what to do. I stepped on his toes numerous times, but halfway through the song, I realized I had loosened up and was enjoying myself.

"I told you I was terrible," I chuckled when I stepped on his toe once again.

"You weren't lying," he teased. His left hand held mine gently, while his right rested warmly at my waist. He was so close, I could smell the musky scent that always seemed to cling to his clothes, and his warmth radiated about me like a soft embrace.

"Hey, I'll bet you couldn't set a broken leg or sew up a cut wound. So there," I playfully returned.

"Can you really do all that?" Connor asked, pulling back to stare down at me with a look of surprise, and a little awe, on his face.

"I most certainly can," I nodded proudly. "I only have a few months left of school before I become a registered nurse."

Connor looked impressed. "I didn't realize you were already about to graduate." He then added with a wink, "Now it's time to get married."

"Very funny," I wrinkled my nose at him.

"You were engaged, weren't you?"

I nodded, immediately sobering. "Yes."

He tilted his head to the side, studying me. "What happened?"

I didn't want to answer, I hated discussing it. I'd received another letter from Jake last week, one I hadn't opened yet and wasn't sure I even would. I wanted to let go of the past, of him, but couldn't quite do so if I continued reading his letters and dwelling on what might have been.

"He was unfaithful," I stated, my words short and to the point. I couldn't meet Connor's gaze, as I didn't want to see the sympathy in his eyes. I half expected him to make a joke or say something obnoxious, but instead he pulled me closer and gently kissed me on the forehead.

"His loss," he whispered, and I blinked rapidly, fighting off the tears that suddenly flooded the backs of my eyes.

We stayed that way until the end of the song, his chin resting on top of my head as we swayed gently to the music, and it wasn't until he stepped away that I realized the song was over.

He smiled warmly down at me and opened his mouth to say something when Leon appeared.

"Savannah Adair, I can't believe my eyes," Leon exclaimed, pushing his brother out of the way. "You're actually on the dance floor, and I'm not waiting another minute to take my turn. Step aside, big brother, you've had her long enough."

Connor grinned and stepped back with a graceful bow, handing me over to his little brother. I stared at him frantically, silently begging him not to abandon me. I didn't want Leon to know I couldn't dance, but all Connor gave me in return was a wink before he walked away.

"Leon, where is your date?" I asked, a sigh of relief passing my lips when the band began to play another slow song.

Leon took my hand and pulled me close. "You were supposed to be my date, remember?"

"Yes," I nodded, wincing when I stepped on his foot, "but as I'm sure you recall, I'd already signed up to help out tonight when you asked."

"I think you turned me down because Maxi didn't have a date and you felt bad."

He was partly right, but I wasn't going to tell him that. "Well, you could have asked Maxi," I stated.

"I was going to, but Lucy asked me before I could," he shrugged.

I couldn't help but point out, "That's a bit forward, don't you think?"

"Not really," he shook his head. "You know she and I have been friends since we were kids."

"Yes, I know," I murmured.

"Well," he smiled down at me, "I'm glad I got to at least dance once with you tonight." The dim lighting above shown down on him as we moved slowly across the dance floor, illuminating his handsome face and heavily lashed eyes. His hair was parted on the side, slicked down and shiny with Brylcreem pomade, and he smelled slightly of Old Spice.

"You and Con seem to be getting along better these days," he suddenly commented.

"Miracles still happen," I grinned.

"Apparently so," he chuckled. Pulling back a bit to look down at me, his eyes serious for once, he said, "Just be careful, Savannah. Okay?"

"What do you mean?" I asked, my brow wrinkling.

Leon hesitated for a moment. "Much as I love him, Con is known to be a bit of a heart breaker, and I would hate it if he ever did anything to hurt you."

I stared incredulously up at Leon, too shocked to reply. I'd never in my life heard him speak ill of his brother; he adored Connor.

"Don't be ridiculous, Leon," I finally said with a laugh. I didn't bother to mention that he, too, had a reputation as a heart breaker. "There isn't anything at all romantic between Connor and I, nor will there ever be, so there is nothing to worry about."

"Well, just make sure of that," he muttered, pulling me close against his chest as he wrapped an arm around my waist.

Chapter Twelve

Maxi sat in one of the wooden chairs that lined the pavilion floor and sipped her hot chocolate, watching as Savannah danced with Leon. Although Savannah would never admit it, Maxi knew her cousin didn't know how to dance, and she was surprised to see how well she was doing.

She sighed as she watched Leon pull Savannah closer, her heart squeezing tightly in her chest. Why couldn't he have asked her to dance instead? She loved her cousin dearly and had never been jealous of her, but she couldn't deny feeling just a little envious of how nice they looked together. Maxi couldn't blame Leon, however, for being attracted to Savannah. She was so beautiful and independent and always seemed to know what to say, when Maxi herself was the complete opposite.

"Why don't you just tell him how you feel?"

Maxi started in surprise. She'd forgotten Vivian was sitting beside her. She turned to her friend and smiled wanly. "You know I can't do that," she said, her voice small.

Vivian sighed. "If you'd only try, it just might open his eyes to the fact that you're the one he should be with."

Maxi gave a half-hearted laugh. "Don't be silly. He asked two other girls to be his date tonight, and he's danced with nearly every female here except for me. I think it's pretty obvious how he feels."

"Well, you have danced quite a bit with Robert," Vivian pointed out. "Maybe he just didn't want to intrude."

"I didn't dance every dance with Robert," she stated.

As Maxi continued to watch them dance, a bittersweet feeling swept over her. She remembered the first time she'd come to live here; she'd been so nervous and unsure of life, and Leon had immediately taken her under his wing. He'd been her friend, her champion, her confidante, and somewhere along the way, she'd fallen very much in love with him. She could never let him see it, though. She couldn't bear to lose his friendship.

Her eyes traveled past the couple until they finally landed on Robert. He was watching her, and when their gazes met, he grinned, his dark eyes sparkling. She had to admit, he was very handsome, and he'd paid her an exceptional amount of attention tonight. He was a bit older at twenty-six, but she didn't mind. Perhaps he would be just the man to ease the pain in her heart and help her to move on. Perhaps he would overlook her faults and love her anyway. She needed that; she needed someone to love her, to make her feel special and secure.

Maxi was so lost in her thoughts that she didn't notice the dancing had stopped until Cynthia, one of the Red Cross workers, stepped up to the microphone. The twenty-two-year-old auburn-haired volunteer cleared her throat loudly and, after getting everyone's attention, smiled brightly and said, "Alright girls, the time we've been waiting for has arrived. The next dance is lady's choice. So, ladies, pick your partners!"

There were loud squeals of excitement as the girls, some shyly and some more boldly, began to make their way to the gentleman of their choice. Taking a deep breath, Maxi stood to her feet and, with a determined set of her shoulders, walked to the other side of the room until she stood before Robert.

"Well?" She smiled up at him, her heart pounding and her hands shaking. "Shall we give it another go?"

He stood along the sidelines, silently watching as happy, dancing couples swirled around the room. He wondered what they would all think if they knew a murderer was in their midst.

Everyone was talking about RJ's trial, yet only he knew that the man was, in fact, innocent. The thought made him want to laugh, to tell them all what fools they were, but none of the elation he felt at getting away with the perfect crime erased the fact that Margie was gone. She'd left him, forcing him to do what he hadn't wanted to, and now he missed her. He saw her face every time he closed his eyes, and could even hear her soft, gentle voice whispering into his ear when he tried to sleep at night. Just yesterday, he thought he'd seen her out on the street and ran after her, only to lose her in the crowd. He was beginning to think she'd come back to haunt him, to make him pay for what he'd done.

It was slowly and surely driving him mad.

Chapter Thirteen

I gladly stepped aside as Lucy reclaimed her dance partner and made my way back to my serving station. A few men without dates were standing nearby waiting for a cup of hot chocolate, and I gladly poured it for them.

"Hello, Miss Savannah," a voice said from behind, and I turned to find a man in his mid-thirties with thinning curly, red hair.

"Hi," I smiled, wracking my brain as to how I knew this man.

"How are you?" He asked, pushing his hands into the pockets of his pants.

"I'm fine, and you?" There was something familiar about his face, but I couldn't quite place him.

"You don't recognize me, do you?" He smiled tightly, a bit of something akin to irritation flashing in his eyes.

"I'm sorry, but no, I don't," I shrugged in embarrassment, biting my lower lip.

"I'm Peter, the new milkman in your neighborhood."

"Oh, yes, I should have known that!" I laughed sheepishly. I'd only seen him a couple of times, and I wondered how he remembered my name.

"It's okay, I get that a lot," he shrugged good-naturedly. "I didn't know you volunteered at the Red Cross?"

"This is my first time actually," I said, "but I plan on volunteering more in the future."

"That's nice," he nodded, glancing down at his feet.

We both grew silent then, and I was beginning to feel a bit awkward when suddenly, a string of yelled expletives erupted from the dance floor. I turned to see the crowd of dancers jumping out of the way as two men in the center began throwing punches at one another. The music stopped, girls were screaming, and I craned my neck to see who the culprits were, my eyes widening when I recognized Lionel as one of them.

Pushing past Peter to get a closer view, I rushed around the table to stand next to Maxi and Robert. The lights were turned up to reveal Lionel's red face and dark eyes bulging out with fury as he lunged at the other man, bringing them both to the floor with a loud thud. They were swinging wildly at each other, cursing at the top of their lungs, when Connor, Ben, and the bass player, Kevin, jumped onto the scene. Connor grabbed Lionel, while Ben and Kevin grasped onto the other man's arms, yanking the two men apart.

"Calm down," Connor growled, wrapping a thick arm around Lionel's shoulders. Lionel was breathing heavily and sweat dripped from his forehead as he glared at the other man, who was struggling against Ben and Kevin.

"What on earth is going on here?" Cynthia cried, stomping into the cleared circle the crowd had made. She placed her hands on her hips and glared at Lionel. "Just wait until Ms. Mason hears about this, Lionel."

"It's his fault," Lionel spat, jerking his head towards the other man.

"My fault?" The man cried incredulously. "He wouldn't let me cut in on his dance! Everyone knows it's a perfectly acceptable thing to do, and when I tried, he lost his mind."

"I-I didn't lose my mind!" Lionel cried, and Connor once again tightened his hold on the man. "I told him 'no', and he tried to shove me out of the way." The look of anger on his face sent chills down my spine.

"I think you both should leave," Connor announced, his jaw set and tone firm. "Now."

He, Kevin, and Ben lead the men outside, where they waited until both men were gone. Murmurs and whispers began filling the quiet room, and Maxi turned to me, her face pale.

"Pretty wild, isn't it?" She whispered.

I nodded, watching as Lionel's shadow faded into the darkness. The three men returned to the pavilion, and the music started back up, but no one could stop talking about the fight.

"Something has always got to happen to make things extra exciting," Connor said later in a droll tone as he joined me once again behind the serving table.

"Men and their need for power," I cocked a brow at him. "It's ridiculous."

Connor laughed. "Some men are born with it, while others have to try and prove themselves."

"I guess you're one of the few who were born with it?" I smirked.

Connor stood up straighter and took a deep breath, poking his chest out. "Well, I didn't want to brag," he sighed, "but I'm glad you noticed."

I laughed and shook my head. The dancing started back up, and squeals of laughter filled the air as the band played a lively jazz tune.

"Are you doing anything next Saturday?" Connor asked, breaking the silence between us.

I paused to think, and then shook my head. "I don't think so. Why?"

Connor pushed his hands into his pockets and shrugged. "I want to show you something."

"What do you want to show me?" I asked suspiciously.

"It's a surprise," he grinned. "Just say you'll come with me."

"I...don't know if I should," I said hesitantly, Leon's warning immediately popping into my mind.

"Come on, Savannah Rose," he sighed, "we agreed to be friends, didn't we? It'll be fun. Just trust me."

I stared at him warily for a moment, pursing my lips as I considered his request. There wouldn't be any harm in going with him, would there?

"Alright," I finally agreed, curiosity getting the best of me. I glanced to my right and noticed Peter walking out the door, and I suddenly realized I'd forgotten all about him.

"Connor," a loud voice suddenly called, and I realized the music had stopped. "Connor Danes."

We all looked at Ben, who stood in front of the microphone beckoning to Connor with a guitar pick in his hand. "Come show everyone how this thing is really played," he said, holding up his guitar.

Grinning, Connor walked to the front and took the instrument from Ben, flipping it around so he could pick and strum with his left hand. I had forgotten that Connor was left-handed and could play nearly every stringed instrument he came across. The boys started off with a fast paced, bluegrass style song, and everyone hooped and clapped and stomped their feet as Connor played along with ease, showing off with some special cords and runs. I smiled, clapping along, and when he looked back at me and winked, I wondered once again what he had up his sleeve for next Saturday night.

Chapter Fourteen

-1965-

I'd been home for three weeks with orders to rest and take it easy. I was tired, very tired, but slowly starting to regain my strength. I was to start my treatments today, and as I began to take off my night gown, I stopped to stare at myself in the mirror. An angry, red gash was all that was left. I had seen it many times before but wasn't prepared for the disfigurement on my own body. Tears flooded my eyes, and I hurriedly slid my shirt on, covering and hiding the ugly scars beneath.

My husband drove me to my appointment but had an emergency at work he had to run and see about.

"I'll be back in an hour," he promised, kissing my forehead.

When I walked into the doctor's office, I was surprised to see Hannah sitting in the waiting area alone.

"Hello," I sat down next to her and smiled. "You're Hannah, aren't you?"

She looked up at me suspiciously, a lock of dark brown hair falling over one eye. "Yes ma'am."

"I'm a friend of your mother's." I stuck my hand out and added, "You may call me Savannah."

She hesitantly took my hand, and I nearly laughed at her overly cautious nature. Apparently, her mother had done well in teaching her not to talk to strangers.

"What's that?" I pointed to the picture she was coloring.

"It's a unicorn," she said, holding it up for me to see. "My teacher says unicorns aren't real. What do you think?"

"Well…" I paused, as if giving it a great deal of thought, "if you take a horse and put a horn on its head, what does that make?"

Her dark eyes widening, Hannah smiled brightly and said, "A unicorn!"

"Precisely," I grinned.

The door to the back room opened, and Abby slowly walked out. This would be her second treatment, and she already looked exhausted. Hannah leapt to her feet and ran to her mother's side, gently taking Abby's hand as she helped her walk.

"Hello, Abby," I greeted her warmly, walking to stand beside her. "How are you doing?"

"I've had better days," she smiled wanly, her eyes sunken and black. Squeezing her daughter's hand, she added, "But with all the help this girl has given me, I'll soon be on the road to recovery."

Hannah smiled up at her mother, but I didn't miss the look of concern in her eyes. She was so young, yet already bearing the burdens of an adult.

"I'm sure you're right," I said, reaching out to squeeze her arm.

"I think I'm too tired to drive right now," she said, motioning to the chairs Hannah and I had just vacated. "Would you sit with me until they call you back?"

"Of course," I nodded, and we sat down. "I'm glad for your company, my husband won't be back for another thirty minutes or so."

"You're lucky to have a husband who takes care of you," Abby said, watching as Hannah sat on the floor to do a puzzle.

"Yes, I am," I agreed, wondering about Hannah's father but not bold enough to ask.

"I had a husband, but he ran off and left us when Hannah was only a year old," Abby said, as if reading my thoughts. "As hard as it's been raising Hannah on my own, we're better off without him. He used to beat me, and I knew it was only a matter of time before he started with Hannah." She turned to look at me, her eyes sober. "It's not easy, you know, being on your own. Especially now that…that I'm sick. But I have faith that we'll make it through this."

I reached out and took her hand, my heart aching for her. "Isn't there anyone that can help you?"

"Not really," she shook her head. "I was raised in the foster system, and my husband's family lives in Cuba. The only person I have is an elderly neighbor who can keep Hannah, but only during emergency situations."

So, Hannah was half Cuban, which explained her nearly black hair and eyes. She was a beautiful child; I wondered how her father could just run off and leave her.

"I'm so sorry, Abby," I said, giving her hand a squeeze. "If there is anything I can do..."

She turned to look at me, her eyes filling with tears as she began to shake her head. "Oh, no, you've done more than enough by just talking with me." She laughed suddenly, reaching up to swipe at her eyes. "I've never opened up to a complete stranger like that before, I hope I didn't overstep myself."

"I'm not a stranger, Abby," I smiled reassuringly. "Sometimes I think when you meet someone who is going through the same thing you are, you feel an instant connection with them, like you've known them your whole life."

"That's very true," she nodded thoughtfully. "Do you have a sister?"

"No," I shook my head.

"Then we can be the sisters we never had," she beamed. "I always wanted a sister."

"What was it like, being raised in the foster system?"

"Dreadful," she sighed. "Like I didn't truly belong anywhere, like no one really cared about me or wanted me. I remember when I had Hannah, I made a promise I would never let that happen to her."

My husband walked in then, and I introduced him to Abby and Hannah, watching with a smile as Hannah shyly took his hand and lead him over to look at her puzzle. *He would have made such a wonderful father*, I thought. The nurse stepped out and called my name just then, and I gave Abby a quick hug.

"I'll see you next week," she called, waving goodbye as I walked nervously to the back, clutching my husband's hand. As frightened as I was, I couldn't imagine not having him there with me, to support and encourage me. I realized right then and there that I needed to start counting my blessings instead of feeling sorry for myself.

Chapter Fifteen

-February 1941-

The week flew by, and before I knew it, Saturday afternoon had arrived. I slid into a dark green, button down day dress, pulled my hair back on the sides, and grabbed a khaki sweater. I still hadn't any idea what Connor had in mind, and I was growing anxious to find out.

Maxi entered the room then and asked if I needed her help with anything.

"The only thing I need is that you don't mention this little outing to Leon," I said. He was still at work and wouldn't see me leave with Connor. "I don't care to hear more of his disapproving comments."

"He's only trying to protect you," Maxi laughed, "but I won't tell him."

At the sound of a car door, I went over to the window and peered out, catching sight of Connor's teal blue, two door Sedan.

"I'll see you later." I kissed Maxi's cheek and hurried out the door, yelling to my aunt that I was leaving.

"Ready?" Connor asked when I stepped out onto the front porch. He wore a brown leather flight jacket over his uniform shirt, along with khaki pants and brown boots. His shirt was neatly tucked in, but the top two buttons at the collar were undone, giving him a relaxed, almost carefree appearance.

"I am," I nodded, and he opened the car door for me. I slid onto the tan, leather seats and waited for him to walk around and get in. "Are you going to tell me where we're going?" I immediately asked.

"Nope," he shot me a grin. "Be patient, Miss Adair."

With a sigh, I reached out and flipped on the radio, leaning back into my seat as the smooth voice of Frank Sinatra floated over the air waves, the soft way in which he crooned the words to "All or Nothing at All" instantly putting me at ease.

As we drove, I gazed out the window at the beautiful farmland that stretched out before us. Acres upon acres of green grass passed by, with cows grazing peacefully and bales of hay perched sporadically in the midst. At times, the scenery changed into blue rivers and golden marshland, and I couldn't help but breathe a sigh of contentment.

After driving for nearly thirty minutes, we reached a heavily wooded area with a dirt road and closed gate, which Connor pulled up to and stopped. I spotted a sign that read "Hunter Airfield", but before I could comment, a man wearing a uniform stepped out and peered into the car, smiling when he recognized Connor.

"Go on in, Danes," he waved us through after opening the gate.

"You brought me to see the new base?" I questioned. "That's the surprise?"

Connor looked hurt. "Well, you don't have to sound so excited about it."

"I'm sorry," I laughed. "This just isn't what I was expecting."

"I rarely do what one expects," he winked as we pulled into a huge clearing which could only be the airstrip. "Just wait. There are more surprises to come."

Connor stopped the car and I hurriedly climbed out to watch as a large plane, which had at first been a tiny dot on the horizon, lowered itself down to the ground like a mighty bird of prey with a loud, ear piercing screech.

"That was amazing," I breathed as the pilot expertly shuttled the plane down the runway.

Connor grabbed my hand and pulled me towards an enormous building with an arch shaped roof. He slid the massive door open and we walked inside what I immediately realized must be the hangar.

"It can certainly get loud out there," Connor commented, slamming the door closed with a thundering echo. "The pilots are flying maneuvers today, so that's why there are so many planes out."

"Why aren't you flying with them?" I asked as I assessed the few planes that remained inside the hangar. Some were larger than others, but my gaze was immediately drawn to the massive, silver bird resting a few feet from the rest. Its wingspan was at least 100ft, and I guessed it to be around 20ft tall. I walked over to the shiny beast and tentatively reached out a hand to touch the smooth, cold surface.

"I did mine earlier," Connor answered, moving to stand beside me. "This is our B-17 Flying Fortress," he said, his voice filled with pride as he, too, reached out to run his fingers across the plane's exterior.

"It's huge," I breathed, wondering how on earth anyone could fly such a thing. "What does a B-17 do?"

72

"This baby is a four engine, heavy bomber aircraft," he explained. "It's also able to defend itself, which a lot of bombers can't do. It's new, so it's a very sought-after machine. We're really lucky to have one."

"Hmm," I murmured, walking slowly around the plane as I thoughtfully assessed it. "Better aircraft is being manufactured, new military bases are popping up all over the country, and there is a war going on in Europe. Are we preparing for war, as well?" I asked, coming around to stand back at Connor's side.

Surprise crossed Connor's face, but instead of denying my question, he sighed and leaned against the large, solid plane, crossing his feet at the ankles. "I'm afraid so," he said, his voice low and heavy. "I don't know how much longer things can hold on with the direction Hitler is going, not to mention the tension between America and Japan over the situation with China. It's a war that we do not want to become involved in, but many have come to feel that it's inescapable."

I'd suspected as much. Most women thought it improper to discuss politics and world events, but I wanted to know what was going on around me. I read the newspapers and listened to Uncle Ray's radio and felt within my heart that it wouldn't be much longer before America joined this awful war. It frightened me to think of what it would be like; our men leaving to kill and be killed. War was a dark, ugly thing, but sometimes necessary.

Pushing away from the plane, Connor said, "Enough of that kind of talk. It's time we get to that surprise I promised you."

"I thought this was the surprise?" I pointed to our surroundings, but Connor grabbed my hand and lead me to the far side of the hangar.

He had apparently set up a small table with a record player against the back wall and, pointing a finger at the phonograph, he announced, "You, my dear, are going to learn how to dance."

"What?" I laughed incredulously, pulling my hand away. "Are you serious?"

"Very," he nodded. "I'm tired of watching you miss out on all the fun at parties. Shall we?" He held out his hand, waiting with a cocked brow.

I stared at him for a moment with pursed lips and took a deep breath, a slow smile beginning to tug at the corners of my mouth. With a shrug, I took his hand and said, "Oh, why not?"

Grinning triumphantly, Connor proceeded to show me a few steps. "You already know the basics of how to slow dance, so let's try something a little faster." At my look of apprehension, he added with a chuckle, "Don't worry, I won't throw you across my shoulder or jump over your head just yet. We'll start with something simple, alright?"

It took several tries, but I caught on relatively quickly to the new dance steps.

"This is fun," I smiled up at Connor after a bit of practice. His beautiful blue-gray eyes sparkled down at me, and his hand gripped mine firmly, swallowing it whole.

"Let's try the Susie Q now," he declared, taking a step back to show me the newest dance move.

After watching, I gave an awkward try, but Connor quickly shook his head and told me to stop. He moved forward and placed his hands on my hips, twisting them gently back and forth. "Remember, it's all in the hips," he winked.

I slapped his hands away and, with intense concentration, mimicked his earlier move to perfection, my skirt swinging out around my calves.

"Good job," Connor clapped.

We practiced for almost an hour when Connor decided it was time for some music. He walked over to the phonograph, placed a record on the turntable, and "Boogie Woogie Bugle Boy" by The Andrew Sisters blared loudly from its solid, brass horn.

The music was fast and frantic, and I tripped countless times, but with a lot of mistakes and laughter, the song was finally over, and we were both out of breath.

"You did great!" Connor beamed, wiping his brow. "I guess I'm a better teacher than I thought."

Laughing, I clutched at my stomach and tried to catch my breath. "It…it was fun," I heaved, "but I can see I have a lot of practicing to do."

"That's why I'm going to give you lessons every other weekend," he declared. "Alright?"

I hesitated for a moment, considering his statement. "Alright," I finally agreed with a smile.

Chapter Sixteen

-April 1941-

"RJ Willingham, convicted of murder and sentenced to the death penalty," Uncle Ray read aloud from the newspaper one Saturday morning.

I glanced at Lizzie's back, wondering if she would react to the news. Willingham's trial had been going on for nearly four months now, and although I didn't necessarily like the thought of the death penalty, I knew it was good for the city to finally have some closure.

"Y'all want any more pancakes?" She asked, her tone flat. She stood at the stove with her back turned, but by the set of her shoulders I could tell she was trying not to cry.

"When will he be executed?" Aunt Deb asked, her coffee cup clinking against the saucer as she sat it down.

His eyes sweeping the fine print, Uncle Ray replied, "Next month."

"Do you think he's guilty?" Maxi asked, nibbling on a piece of bacon.

"They found a bloody rag and shirt stuffed in his fireplace," Uncle Ray said. "I'd say that's plenty of evidence."

"Yes, I suppose so." Pushing away from the table, Maxi announced she was about to go over to Vivian's house. "Vannie, are you sure you don't want to come along?"

I shook my head no and waved goodbye as she left, pouring syrup over my last bite of pancake as I listened to my aunt and uncle continue the conversation of RJ Willingham.

"I still can't imagine someone doing something so horrible," my aunt shivered.

"Well, at least he's paying for it."

Lizzie turned and, without a word, left the room. As I stood to follow her, I whispered to my aunt and uncle, "Did y'all have to discuss this right now?"

"Honey, it's being discussed all over town," Aunt Deb said defensively, and I knew she was right. Still, I couldn't help feeling sorry for Lizzie.

I found her out on the front porch holding a broom, her eyes staring blankly into the distance. At the sound of the screen door slamming shut, she started sweeping fiercely, the dust creating a cloud in the air.

"I'm sorry, Lizzie," I said, laying a hand on her arm.

"It's not your fault, Miz Savannah," she stepped away, avoiding my gaze.

"As much as it hurts, at least they found the real killer so that Joseph's name can be cleared."

"I'd much rather he be alive," she snapped, her voice shaking.

I grabbed the broom handle, forcing her to stop, and waited until she looked up at me. "I'm not the enemy, Lizzie," I said gently. "I'm on your side, remember?"

Her eyes flooding with tears, she nodded her head and whispered, "I know. I'm just hurting so bad, I guess I'm taking it out on everyone around me. I'm sorry, Miz Savannah, truly I am."

"It'll get better," I said, pulling her into a hug. "I know that's not much comfort to you now, but I promise it will get better."

I let her get back to her work and walked next door, my mind still on Lizzie as I rang the doorbell. It was Leon's day off, and we'd planned to go shopping for Maxi's birthday. As soon as he opened the door, Leon noticed my sober expression and asked, "Hey, what's wrong?"

As we walked to Broughton Street, I told him about Lizzie and my concern for her.

"Give her time, Savannah," he told me, his brown Fedora slanting over one eye. "Losing someone you love isn't easy, and it takes some people longer to adjust and move on with life."

I glanced over at him, the trees along the sidewalk casting shadows on his face, and I knew he was speaking from experience.

"You still miss your father, don't you?" I asked.

"Every day," he nodded. "Just because you move on doesn't mean you stop missing them."

I laced my arm through his as we crossed the street, my mind considering his words. "Would it be silly to say I miss my mother, even though I never knew her?"

"Of course not," he shook his head emphatically. "Just because you didn't know her doesn't mean you can't still love and miss her. Growing up without a mother had to feel like a huge void in your life, like a part of you was missing."

76

Leon couldn't have described my feelings better.

"I remember there was a Mother/Daughter luncheon at my school in Atlanta when I was eleven or twelve," I told him, "and I ended up sitting by myself. One of my friends kindly asked me to sit with she and her mother, and I don't remember ever feeling so relieved. It's got to be the loneliest feeling in the world for a child to be alone when no one else is."

"Well," he reached up and patted my hand, "you're not alone anymore."

"No," I smiled, "thank goodness for that."

ONE MONTH LATER

The execution of RJ Willingham was set to be held the following day when, much to everyone's shock, the governor suddenly reduced his sentence to life in prison. Word around town was that Doctor Cox asked to see Mr. Willingham and was so moved by the man's protest of innocence that he plead clemency on his behalf, a plea that was readily accepted. I expected the townspeople to be furious, but at this point everyone was just relieved to have the killer behind bars.

With mine and Maxi's graduation closing in, I called Daddy to ask if he would come.

"I haven't been feeling well," he told me over the phone. When I asked what was wrong, he said, "I've had a cold that just won't go away, and I've been feeling very tired. I will, however, do my best to come to your graduation, I promise."

I was never more surprised than when he showed up on our front porch the following week, mere hours before the ceremony. I threw my arms around his neck and cried, so happy was I to see him. I hadn't realized until that moment how much I'd missed him. When I pulled away to wipe my eyes, I realized he wasn't alone.

"Hello, Savannah."

Feeling the blood drain from my face, I stared in shock at my ex fiancé.

Chapter Seventeen

-1941-

"Jake, what are you doing here?" I asked in a near whisper. I turned accusing eyes on my father, but he averted his gaze and pushed past me, mumbling something about wanting to see Debra and Ray.

"It wasn't my idea, I promise," Jake said, raising his hands in a defensive manner. "Your father invited me."

"Couldn't you have told him no?" I crossed my arms.

"He and I are good friends, Savannah, you know that. He hasn't been feeling well and asked if I would drive him down because he didn't want to take the train. I just couldn't say no." He sighed and raked his fingers through his hair, eyeing me with those same piercing, blue eyes that used to haunt my dreams. "You and I were once good friends, too, or have you forgotten?"

"I've forgotten nothing," I snapped, my meaning clear.

Wincing, he opened his mouth to reply, but was cut off when Aunt Deb came out onto the porch, her eyes stormy as they quickly assessed the situation.

"Savannah, are you coming inside?" She asked, intentionally ignoring Jake.

"Yes," I nodded, relieved. I moved to follow her into the house, stopping when Jake placed a hand on my arm.

"This is an important time for you, Savannah," he said gently. "You've worked hard for this; no one knows that better than I do. Let's call a truce so we don't ruin it, alright?"

I hesitated, my thoughts and emotions at war with one another. I heard a door slam and turned to see the Danes' walking over to our house.

"Fine," I said, not wanting to cause a scene in front of our neighbors. I turned to walk inside, throwing over my shoulder, "You can come in if you want. We'll be leaving in a few minutes."

Jake followed me into the living room, and I tried to ignore Aunt Deb's look of disapproval and Maxi's wide-eyed stare as I gathered my things, my earlier nerves of walking out on the platform to retrieve my diploma forgotten.

"Is everyone about ready to go?" Mrs. Emma called as they entered the house, a smile on her face. When she saw my father, her eyes brightened and she exclaimed, "Edward, it's so good to see you!" and rushed over to give him a hug.

"It's been too long since I've visited," he admitted sheepishly, patting Mrs. Emma on the back. Turning to Connor and Leon, he added, "Surely these two grown men aren't your boys?"

"Yes, sir," Leon grinned.

"It's good to see you again, Mr. Adair," Connor nodded, gripping my father's hand firmly.

When they all turned to look curiously at Jake, Daddy proceeded to make the introductions, and I watched as recognition, followed quickly by surprise, lit upon all three of their faces. Mrs. Emma played it off with a pleasant smile and "It's nice to meet you, Jake", while Leon simply nodded, his jaw clenched tightly. Connor stepped forward to politely shake Jake's hand, his expression passive, yet I got the feeling the two men were sizing each other up.

"Well, we'd better go if we don't want to be late," Aunt Deb cleared her throat, and we all hurried outside.

Jake, thankfully, climbed into his own car, announcing that he would be pleased if my father, aunt, and uncle would ride with him. Aunt Deb shook her head "no", giving my uncle a dirty look when he elbowed her and said, "Why, yes, that would be very nice."

Maxi and I rode with the Danes', and the moment we all got into the car, Leon asked, "What is he doing here?"

"I'd say it's pretty obvious why the man is here, Leon," Connor said in an even tone, his forefinger tapping the steering wheel.

"He says he only came because Daddy asked him to," I shrugged.

"Have you been answering his letters?" Maxi whispered in my ear.

"No," I shook my head. "I had no idea he was coming."

"What I'd like to do to that man," Leon muttered, balling up one fist and smacking his palm.

"But you'll do no such thing," Mrs. Emma spoke up from the front passenger's seat, her tone firm. "Savannah is perfectly capable of handling this situation on her own."

I only hoped she was right.

"And," Connor said, adding to his mother's statement, "we don't want to do anything to ruin Savannah and Maxine's special night." He winked at me in the rearview mirror, and I smiled my thanks. He was right. This was something Maxi and I had worked very hard for, and I intended to enjoy the moment.

Surprisingly enough, the night flew by in a whirlwind of nerves, speeches, and well-wishes. Robert and Maxi had been seeing quite a lot of each other since meeting at the Valentine's Day dance, and I didn't miss the thrill in her eyes when he showed up, carrying a bouquet of roses. My aunt and uncle opened their house afterwards for a graduation party, where we were showered with gifts and congratulations. Having so many people that cared meant the world to both Maxi and me.

Later that night, Jake asked to speak to me privately. I agreed, and we walked out onto the front porch, the night air surprisingly cool.

"Thank you," he said, turning to face me, "for allowing me to stay. I was afraid you might be angry enough to send me away."

"You had a lot of nerve coming here," I stated, crossing my arms

"I know," he sighed. "I suppose I could have turned your father down when he asked me to come, but if I'm totally honest, I wanted to see you."

"Why did you want to see me, Jake?" I asked. "It's been over between us for a year now."

"What's one year in the span of a lifetime?" He asked, his eyes glinting in the moonlight like two, twinkling sapphires. "We were going to be married, for Pete's sake, how am I supposed to just forget that and move on?"

"You betrayed me, Jake," I stated, my hard gaze piercing his. "How am I supposed to forget that?"

Wincing as if I'd slapped him, Jake took a step back and closed his eyes, his jaw clenching. "If I could go back," he said, his voice ragged, "that never would have happened. It was a mistake, Savannah, one that I've tortured myself over for an entire year. Why can't you forgive me? Haven't you ever made a mistake before?"

I didn't answer at first. I didn't want to discuss this. I had planned on never seeing Jake again, and yet here we were, face to face. What was I supposed to say? Of course, I'd made mistakes. Did that mean I should forgive and forget and give him another chance? I didn't trust him, didn't want to even consider going down that road again. As Aunt Deb always said, "fool me once, shame on you, fool me twice, shame on me". Did I still love him? I honestly didn't know. Was it even possible for one to completely stop loving another after investing so much time and energy into the relationship?

"What exactly do you want from me, Jake?" I finally asked, my tone flat.

"I'm not foolish enough to ask that you give me a second chance," he sighed, "but I would like to at least have your friendship back. What would it hurt to write a few letters? To simply keep each other up to date with what's going on in our lives?"

I hesitated, my eyes narrowing. I missed his friendship, as well, I couldn't deny that. Before we began courting, he was one of my closest friends. Was it harmless to renew our friendship, or opening a door that should remain closed?

Finally, I gave in and agreed.

His face relaxing in relief, he stuck out his hand and said, "Friends?"

With a nod and small smile, I accepted his handshake. "Friends."

"Well, I'd say it's time I headed to my hotel," he said, taking a step back. "See you in the morning?"

"Yes," I nodded. "At church."

As I watched him drive away, I wondered if I'd done the right thing. Perhaps it would have been for the best if I'd told him "no".

"That certainly was entertaining."

Jerking my head to the left, I squinted through the darkness to see Connor standing on his mother's front porch.

My eyes widened. "You were listening?" I gasped.

"It was pretty hard not to," he chuckled, walking down the porch steps to hop over the fence that separated our property. "That guy is relentless," he said as he joined me on our porch.

I crossed my arms indignantly. "Don't you know it's rude to eavesdrop?"

"I wasn't eavesdropping," he smiled innocently. "I just happened to be sitting on my mother's swing while you two were having your little...conversation."

"You could have gone inside," I pointed out.

"True, but I didn't want to."

With a sigh of frustration, I sat down on the swing, its old hinges creaking as I slowly pushed it back and forth with my foot.

"So, how do you feel about being forced to make a decision?" Connor asked, watching me closely for a reaction.

My eyes jerked up to meet his. "I wasn't forced into anything."

Connor raised his eyebrows in disbelief. "You haven't spoken to him for a year, and the minute he shows up and quotes a few rehearsed lines, you agree to patch things up with him." He hesitated before adding in a nonchalant tone, "I'm guessing things didn't work out with the other girl?"

It felt as if he'd punched me right in the stomach. He was right, but I didn't want to hear it, not from him anyway.

My jaw clenched, I stood to my feet and said coolly, "You've got a lot of nerve, Connor Danes. I wouldn't think that a womanizing man with your reputation would dare speak a word against someone else, but apparently, I was wrong. If you don't mind, please keep your opinions to yourself from now on."

I was so angry that my hands shook. I moved toward the front door, anxious to get away from Connor, but he quickly grabbed me by the arm.

"I may have a "reputation", but I've never been unfaithful to a woman in my life," he said, his jaw clenched. "I'm sorry I made you angry, I guess I thought we were good enough friends that I could give you some advice without your jumping to his defense."

"Advice?" I laughed humorlessly. "You weren't giving me advice; you were attacking me."

"Well, I wasn't trying to," he said, his voice raising a bit. "I was just shocked that you let him manipulate you like that."

I took a deep breath, trying to rein in my emotions. "I told him we could write a few letters," I ground out. "I never said I was going to change my mind and marry him."

"But you're opening the door again to that possibility."

"Jake was one of my closest friends before we began courting, Connor, and whether or not I choose to write letters to a friend is none of your concern." Jerking my arm away, I walked inside and slammed the door in his face.

I stood quietly for a moment in the foyer, took a deep breath, and leaned back against the door, feeling drained. I knew I shouldn't have let my temper get away from me, but I was tense and on edge, and somehow Connor always knew how to push my buttons and make me feel like a foolish, silly little girl.

My father was sitting on the sofa reading when I walked into the living room moments later, and when he saw the expression on my face, he immediately wanted to know what was wrong. With a sigh, I sat down beside him and asked, "Why did you invite Jake to come with you?"

Removing his reading glasses, he pinched the bridge of his nose and said, "Honey, you know I always liked Jake, and I just thought…"

"You thought I should forgive him and go back to the way things were like nothing ever happened?" I asked incredulously.

"He said the kiss was unintentional," he replied, jumping to Jake's defense.

"Whether or not it was unintentional, it still shouldn't have happened." I sighed, feeling very tired. "I know you always liked Jake, Daddy, but he crossed a line and I don't think I could ever completely trust him again."

He reached out to pat my knee, but I could see from his expression that he wasn't quite ready to give it up. "We all make mistakes, Savannah. Just remember that. I believe that Jake is a good man."

I didn't feel like arguing anymore, so I simply nodded my head and kissed him on the cheek. "Good night, Daddy," I said softly as I stood to my feet. "And thank you for coming to my graduation. It meant the world to me."

Chapter Eighteen

-1965-

I hurried to the restroom, one hand over my mouth as I launched myself towards the toilet, barely making it in time before emptying the entire contents of my stomach. I sat there, weak and dizzy when a damp, cool cloth was placed on my forehead.

"Thank you, honey," I said, taking the cloth and wiping my mouth.

"We've got to tell the doctor the treatments are too strong," my husband said, sitting on the floor beside me.

"No," I shook my head. "I'll be fine."

"Honey, between your upset stomach and the ulcers in your mouth, you're hardly able to eat anything," he argued. "Perhaps he could lessen your treatments to twice a week instead of three times."

I sat up straight, folding the rag so I could lay it on the back of my neck. "I want to get this over with," I told him, trying to cover a wince when my teeth scratched against the sores in my mouth as I spoke. "The sooner I do, the sooner we can both get back to living a normal life." I glanced at him through lowered lashes and muttered, "If you still want to, that is."

"What do you mean?" He wanted to know.

"That you didn't marry a woman who was disfigured, and you may not want to stay married to one who is now."

There. I said it. Finally, the subject we'd both been avoiding was now open.

"Don't you ever say that again," he said, his voice so harsh that I jumped in surprise. Raising my eyes, I saw a look of real pain on the face of the man I loved, and immediately felt ashamed. "Do you think that's why I married you? For your appearance?" He demanded, his brow furrowing. "Is that why you married me?"

"Of course not," I whispered.

"Then don't ever let such a thing cross your mind again." He reached out and took my hand, his fingers wrapping firmly around mine. "Do you know how frightened I've been this whole time, scared to death I was going to lose you?" He asked, his eyes filling with tears for the first time in years. "Don't you remember that I was the one who encouraged you to have the double mastectomy? I want to do whatever it takes for you to live, honey, I don't care about anything else. And," he added, gently pulling my chin up with his forefinger and forcing me to look at him, "neither should you."

I crawled into his lap and, my head buried in his shoulder, cried until there were no more tears left to cry. I'd been afraid to broach the subject to him, I guess I feared discovering how he really felt. Now, however, I only felt ashamed. This man loved me. I knew it now; I'd always known it. He'd stood by my side through thick and thin, and knowing I'd doubted his love and commitment had hurt him terribly.

"I'm sorry," I said, accepting the handkerchief he offered. "I should never have said anything."

"I'm glad you did," he smiled as I loudly blew my nose. "It was something we needed to discuss. I'm just sorry I didn't tell you sooner how I felt."

He helped me up and walked with me to our bed, my legs so weak I could barely walk. He helped me off with my robe and house slippers, pulling the covers back as I climbed in.

"Do you remember," he asked as he tucked me in, "when we were on our honeymoon and you got food poisoning?"

"Yes," I moaned, covering my eyes with my hand as I began to laugh. "It was so humiliating to throw up all over the hotel room while my new husband held my hair back."

"I believe that was grounds for annulment," he sighed, ducking as I threw a pillow at his head. "Just kidding," he grinned, leaning over to kiss me. "I love you," he said, and with everything I was going through, I couldn't remember feeling more content.

Chapter Nineteen

-1941-

Ida Miller climbed from the smoking car and slammed the door, sighing heavily with frustration. She was already late for work, and now would have to walk the rest of the way. She only hoped Vivian would understand.

Gathering her purse, she hurried down the two-lane road, glancing up with uneasiness at the dark, heavy clouds that still lingered from an earlier rain. An unusually thick fog was rolling in, and Ida looked as far up and down the road as she could see, hoping some passerby would come along and offer her a ride.

Soon enough, a pair of headlights pierced through the fog, shining like two round lanterns as they slowly crept towards her. She raised her hand and waved the car down, breathing a sigh of relief when the man pulled over and asked where she was headed.

"Just a couple of miles down this road to a small country club," she explained, sticking her head through the passenger's side window as she spoke. "I was supposed to be there thirty minutes ago for work, but my car broke down."

"Hop in," he motioned with his head, "I'll take you."

With a grateful smile, Ida got into the car, thanking the man profusely for his kindness. They rode in silence, and after a moment, Ida found herself tapping her fingernails impatiently against the console and glanced nervously over at the speedometer. Why was he driving so slowly?

"You have very pretty hair," the man said, startling Ida from her thoughts.

"Oh...thank you," she replied, reaching up to absently pat the dark tresses that were tucked behind her ear.

Finally, the front gate came into view, and Ida groaned at all the cars that were lined up in arrival for the party.

"Just turn here, if you don't mind," she said, pointing out a small, heavily wooded driveway just off to the right. Without a word, the man did as she asked, the beam of his headlights bouncing along the trees. "This will lead us to the back entrance," she explained as they bumped along the rutted, dirt road.

The road wound around at least a half mile before it reached the club, and they'd only gone a few yards when, suddenly, the man stopped the car, his brakes squealing a bit as they came to a halt.

"I think I have a flat," he muttered, and Ida stared at him in confusion as he put the car in park and climbed out. She hadn't any idea why he thought one of the tires was flat, but she didn't have more time to waste.

"I'll just walk from here," she said, irritation in her voice as she climbed from the car. "Thank you so much for your help."

She left him kneeling by the front driver's tire and hurried on alone. There wasn't a single person in sight, but Ida could hear music playing softly in the distance, and she breathed a sigh of relief when she spotted lights from the country club twinkling just up ahead through the trees.

Her high heel suddenly caught on a stone and, stumbling, she gasped in surprise, barely able to keep herself from falling. Between the twilight of evening, the fog, and dense tree branches that draped overhead, the path was a bit difficult to see.

Suddenly, a loud pop sounded just to her left, as if someone or something had stepped on a fallen tree limb and snapped it in half. Ida stopped and peered through the thick trees; her eyes narrowed as she fought to see what hid beneath the shadows. A deer, maybe? Or perhaps a wild dog? Unable to see a thing, she knew something was there, watching her, and felt a sudden sense of foreboding.

"Margie," a low, ragged voice whispered, and Ida felt the hair on the back of her neck rise. Every nerve in her body screamed that her life was in danger.

Without hesitation, Ida spun on her heel and broke into a dead run. She could hear the sound of leaves and twigs breaking beneath his feet as the man followed in hot pursuit but was unable to tell from which direction he came. The world seemed to spin madly about as she pushed herself to go faster, her eyes glued to the lights just up ahead.

Her breaths coming in short gasps, Ida glanced over her shoulder and cried out as a large, gloved hand reached out to her through the shadows. Her foot caught on a root, and she spiraled wildly through the air, arms flailing, before slamming hard against the moist earth. The air forced from her lungs and rendering her unable to scream, she lay in a heap of leaves, gasping helplessly as a figure slowly came to stand over her. Her eyes widened as she recognized the stranger who had just given her a ride and felt her stomach sink with dread when his lips twisted into an evil, leering sneer.

"You shouldn't have left me, Margie," he breathed, reaching down to take hold of her hands.

She tried to fight, to kick and bite and scratch, but she was no match for him, and no one was there to help. She'd taken the wrong path that night, and now would pay with her life.

I hadn't spoken to Connor since our argument almost two weeks ago, and although I'll admit I missed him, I was too prideful to apologize.

Three days after Jake's departure, I received a letter from him, and we'd been writing ever since. We reminisced about our days in college, and he spoke of both the challenges and fulfillment that came with his work. I made certain to keep my letters basic and mostly impersonal, but I'll admit it was nice talking with him again. It was almost as if we were starting all over, redeveloping and redefining a brand-new friendship.

I was sitting in the living room reading a book when I received a call from Vivian. Apparently, Lucy was celebrating her twenty-first birthday and hired Vivian to do the catering for her party that night. Vivian's father was sick, one of the servers never showed, and she said they were sorely understaffed and running behind.

"I hate to ask this," she said, her tone tight from stress, "but would you and Maxine consider coming to help?"

I didn't particularly relish the idea of working at Lucy's party, but knew Vivian would never ask unless it was an emergency.

"Maxi is out with Robert," I replied, closing my book, "but I'll be happy to come."

It was after seven o'clock when I arrived at the party, which was being held at a country club about three miles out of town. I hurried in through one of the back doors in search of Vivian, not entirely certain of what to expect.

"Thank goodness you're here," Vivian cried when she spotted me, her tone frazzled. "Please, follow me."

She led me into the large, main room, where an orchestra played and at least a hundred people lingered about, sipping champagne and snacking on Hors d'oeuvres. The party was quite formal and already underway, and I immediately spotted Lucy standing front and center, my eyebrows raising slightly when I realized the young man at her side was none other than Leon. He'd never mentioned the party to us, and I wondered why.

As Vivian stopped to speak to one of the workers, my eyes were drawn to a vaguely familiar face moving slowly through the crowd, and I silently studied the tall waiter with curiosity, wondering how I knew him. He looked my way then, and I blinked in surprise, realizing it was Lionel. I remembered meeting him at the Valentine's Day dance, when he'd come with The Red Cross to help set up tables.

"Hi, Lionel," I spoke to him as he passed by. "I didn't know you worked with Vivian."

Frowning, Lionel turned to look at me, his face blank. "Savannah, right?" he finally asked, recognition flitting through his eyes. When I nodded, he said, "I actually work for several different catering companies. I only volunteer part-time at The Red Cross. Are you going to be working with Vivian, as well?" As he spoke, I couldn't help but remember the fight he'd gotten into at the Valentine's Day dance and how angry he'd been, yet he didn't strike me as the fighting type. His voice was very monotone, and I noticed he looked everywhere but directly into my eyes.

"No," I shook my head, smiling. "I stopped by to help out, but only for tonight. Vivian and I are very good friends."

An awkward silence followed, and I cleared my throat, searching for something else to say. "So, how have you been?" I finally asked.

Lionel looked at me then, his eyes narrowing. "What do you mean?" he wanted to know.

I blinked; a bit taken aback. "Well, it's been awhile since I've seen you, so I was only trying to be friendly," I replied with a smile.

"Yes, the last time you saw me was when I was thrown out of the Valentine's Day dance for a fight that wasn't my fault," he stated defensively.

This isn't going well at all, I thought. "I'm sure it wasn't your fault, Lionel," I replied smoothly.

With a nod, Lionel turned and disappeared back into the crowd without another word, and I watched him go, my brow furrowed.

"Strange sort of fellow," I murmured, shaking my head as I followed Vivian across the room into the kitchen, where she hurriedly explained everything that needed to be done.

Nearly two hours later, I stood at the large kitchen sink, my arms elbow deep in dish water. The meal was complete, the dishes almost done, and I was glad for it; I couldn't remember the last time I'd worked so hard. At least four other workers scurried around behind me, chattering and laughing as they cleaned the kitchen, and I couldn't help overhearing parts of their conversation.

"Why do you think Ida didn't show up?" One girl asked in a low voice.

"Who knows," the other shrugged. "All I can think about is the amount of money Lucy's father must have spent on this party. He's the president of some major shipping company, you know."

"That explains a lot," I muttered under my breath.

"You've taken to talking to yourself, I see," a familiar voice suddenly spoke from behind.

Eyes widening, I slowly turned to face Connor, the wet sponge I held dripping all over his shoes.

"Whoa, you don't have to throw dirty water at me," he laughed, jumping back.

"What are you doing back here?" I asked, flinging the sponge back into the sink.

"I came to congratulate Vivian on a job well done," he replied, leaning closer to add in a low, mischievous voice, "If I'd known you were back here, however, I'd have come much sooner."

"Vivian called me in a panic and asked if I'd help her out tonight," I explained, turning back to my dishes. "So, here I am."

"You're such a good friend," he sighed, leaning back against the counter beside me.

"Speaking of friends, I didn't realize you and Lucy were so close," I sniffed. I was still annoyed with him over our argument about Jake but was making an effort to act normal. It was childish, after all, to hold a grudge.

"Neither did I," he chuckled, crossing one ankle over the other. I glanced sideways at him, not failing to notice how handsome he looked in a striped, light gray sports coat and dark gray pants. "I only came because Leon wanted me to," he explained, "but it's been the most boring night of my life. The food was the only good thing about it."

His last words were spoken a bit louder, and I glanced over my shoulder to see Vivian heading our way.

"Thank you, Connor," she smiled at him, acknowledging the kind compliment. Turning to me, she said, "If you'd like to leave now, Savannah, we can finish everything up. You've done more than your share, and I can't tell you how much I appreciate it. I really couldn't have done it without you!"

"Savannah Adair, is that you?"

Surprised at the sudden interruption into our conversation, we all turned to find Ben, George, and Kevin standing in the doorway, and I waved to the three men, pleased to see them. We'd all bumped into each other around town several times since the dance on Tybee Island, and had come to be somewhat friendly with one another.

"I didn't know you boys were here," I smiled as they moved to stand closer, not missing the look of irritation on Connor's face at the intrusion. "Have you been enjoying the party?"

"Heck, no," Ben shook his head.

"Too fancy for us," Kevin replied.

"The food, though, was delicious," George, the most flirtatious of the three, grinned at Vivian, receiving a blush in return.

"Vivian?" A sharp tone interjected.

We all turned to find Lucy standing in the doorway, a frown on her face. Vivian hurried to her side, and as I finished up with the dishes, I realized the whole kitchen had grown silent as we listened to Lucy's raised voice.

"I tried to overlook the fact that the food was late," she snapped angrily, "but one of your waiters just spilled a tray of champagne all over one of my guests, and I've had enough. Please get rid of him, and I'm sorry, but we won't be using you again."

She breezed from the room as quickly as she'd entered, leaving Vivian red faced as she struggled to hold back tears. With a quick swipe at her eyes, Vivian cleared her throat and hurried after Lucy to clean up the mess, the door swinging back and forth desolately behind her.

"Poor Vivian," I shook my head as I put away the last of the dishes.

"Yeah, she didn't deserve that," Ben sighed.

"You know," Connor said, his jaw clenched as he stared after Vivian, "we should do something to get Lucy off her high horse."

I turned to raise my eyebrows at Connor in question. "What do you have in mind?" I wanted to know.

He tapped his chin and shrugged. "How about a dance off?"

Ben, Kevin, and George jumped at the idea. "At least that would liven things up," George said, his eyes bright with excitement.

I laughed, staring at the four men incredulously. "And just who would be brave enough to start a dance off at a fancy party like this?"

A slow smile began to spread across Connor's face, and he wiggled his eyebrows at me. "Oh no," I shook my head, realizing his implication. "Find yourself someone else."

"I know my date will do it," Kevin said, "but we've got to have at least one more girl."

"What's wrong, Savannah Rose?" Connor asked, eyes twinkling. "Afraid you're not ready for that kind of dancing yet? Or are you just scared of Lucy?"

I closed my eyes and sighed. Under normal circumstances, I would have immediately said no, but after the way Lucy treated Vivian tonight, I was just in the right frame of mind to burst her snobby little bubble.

I also very rarely backed down from a challenge, something Connor knew all too well.

"Fine," I sighed, and the men whooped loudly. Sliding out of my apron, I followed them into the main room, my stomach doing little flip flops. I took a deep breath and pushed my nerves aside, slipping my hand into Connor's as we made our way to the center of the room. I'd worry about the repercussions later.

Connor and I stood silently waiting as Kevin approached the orchestra leader and whispered into his ear. I don't know what he said, but the man's face lit up and he eagerly nodded his head, smiling broadly. The slow, intimate music came to a stop, and the room grew quiet as everyone seemed to sense something was going on. I heard the drummer quickly tap the symbols eight times, and as one of the liveliest tunes I've ever heard blasted throughout the room, we began to dance.

The crowd stepped back, allowing us room as they created a large circle around us. I could hear both whistles of encouragement and murmurs of disapproval emanating throughout the room, but I soon forgot my nerves and lost myself in the fun as Connor spun me around and flipped me over his shoulder, directly into Ben's open arms. I danced back and forth between the two men as they "battled" to win my affections, grinning when the crowd began to cheer us on.

After a few, short minutes, it was time to allow another couple their turn, so Connor, Ben, and I spun off to the side, out of breath, as Kevin, his partner, and George took the floor.

"I can't believe we just did that," I laughed, placing my palms against my flushed cheeks. I turned to smile at the two men, surprised to find that only Connor remained.

"You did great, Savannah Rose," he said warmly.

"I had a good teacher," I shrugged, grinning.

"You know what this means, don't you?"

I tilted my head to the side. "What?"

"That we're friends again." Before I could blink, he leaned over and kissed me on the cheek. "I'm sorry about our little argument. Don't get so upset with me next time, okay?" He murmured, his face only inches from mine. "I've missed you."

He turned then and walked away, leaving me to stare curiously at his retreating back, when I noticed Leon heading in my direction.

"Why didn't you ever tell me you could dance like that?" He wanted to know, eyes wide.

"You don't know everything about me, Leon Danes," I laughed, shrugging my shoulders innocently.

"Obviously," he grinned. "I'm a little surprised you had the guts to do this," he added, nodding in the direction of the dance floor. "Lucy is furious."

"Good," I grinned.

"Where is Maxi?" Leon wanted to know, glancing around as if in search of her.

"She's out with Robert."

Leon hesitated before saying, "They seem to be getting a little too thick, don't you think? She doesn't really know anything about him."

"I agree," I sighed, frowning slightly. "Don't tell her I said this, but I don't really think I like him."

"Why?" Leon narrowed his eyes.

"I can't put my finger on it, but there's something about him that rubs me the wrong way," I shrugged.

"Maybe we should talk to her about it?"

"Maybe you should," I laughed. "I live with her, remember? I don't want to cause a rift between us."

"Hmm, I'll have to see what I can do," he murmured, rubbing a hand over his face.

Suddenly, the feeling that someone was watching me swept down my spine, and I turned to find Matthew Cox standing along the sidelines, his gaze cold as he stared at me. Surprised to see him there, I voiced my thoughts to Leon, who shrugged and said, "I guess Lucy invited him because of his rich, successful father."

When I turned back, Matthew was gone, and I rubbed my bare forearms, suddenly feeling chilled. I'd seen him a handful of times since the Valentine's Day dance, and on every occasion, he made me feel uncomfortable. I had a hunch he'd never forgive me for making that comment about his father.

Leon asked if I wanted to dance then, and I eagerly nodded my head, forgetting all about Matthew.

Over an hour later, Connor found me sitting along the sidelines, rubbing my feet. The party was still going strong, and I was exhausted, my feet swollen from all the dancing.

"Tired?" he asked, sitting beside me. His tie was pulled loose and the top two buttons of his shirt were undone, giving him a sense of carelessness. A thin layer of sweat beaded along the top of his forehead, and his hair was slightly mussed, a stray lock curling casually over his brow.

I nodded, covering a yawn. "I think I'm ready to head home," I said, slipping back into my shoes.

"Me, too," he stood, reaching for my hand to help me up. "I'll walk out with you."

As soon as we stepped outside, I realized we'd come out the wrong door. "I parked at the back of the building," I sighed in frustration.

"I'll walk back there with you," Connor offered. "It's too crowded to push our way through inside."

The night was dark, and a thin layer of fog still drifted lifelessly at the tops of the trees. As we circled around the building, lights from the windows casting shadows all around, I stuck close to Connor's side, relieved that he'd walked out with me. There was something about the desolate silence of the thick, black woods that made me uneasy.

"There's my car," I pointed to the shadowy silhouette just up ahead.

Suddenly, my eyes were drawn to something that lay on the ground at the edge of the woods to our right, and I stopped, my eyes narrowing as I peered through the darkness.

"Connor," I whispered, clutching his arm. "What is that?"

I looked up at him, the country club lights flickering in his eyes, and the look of alarm I saw there sent chills racing down my spine.

"Stay here," he told me in a wary tone. Slowly, he made his way to the large heap, his steps cautious. He bent over, only to stumble back a step when he realized what it was.

"Savannah Rose," he said, "go back inside and get help. This is the dead body of a young woman."

Chapter Twenty

-1941-

By mid-morning, the whole city was in an uproar. Another murder? How could this happen?

The question everyone wanted to know was, "Did the killer use an axe?"

The newspaper Monday morning read, **"Saturday afternoon, the beaten and bloodied body of twenty-two-year-old Ida Miller was found. Her skull was crushed, yet it appears that strangulation was the cause of death. All the money was still in her purse, which lay by her side. The police are investigating, but so far no suspects have been brought in for questioning.**"

Two weeks later, the body of another young woman was found. Our city had a serial killer on its hands, and the police had nothing to go on.

Maxi and I were to start our new jobs at the hospital the following week when I received an unexpected phone call from Harriet, my stepmother.

"Savannah, your father has had a stroke."

My knees giving out, I sank onto the love seat, the phone clutched tightly between my fingers. "Is…" I swallowed, "is he going to be alright?"

"The doctor feels he will make a full recovery in time, but his left side is partially paralyzed, he needs special care, and I…" she hesitated, "well, to pay the bills while your father recovers, I'll have to go back to work at the post office."

My eyes narrowed. "I thought father had enough money set aside to cover any emergency?"

"The money is gone," she snapped, and I immediately knew she was somehow to blame. I had to bite my tongue to withhold the question burning in the back of my throat: *Is that why he had a stroke? He found out his life's savings are gone?*

"I'll come," I said, rubbing the back of my neck. "I'm a trained nurse, so I'll know how to care for his needs."

"Thank you," she cleared her throat. "How soon can you get here?"

"Two days, at the most," I replied. "I'll let you know."

I immediately told Aunt Deb the news, my eyes filling with tears at the thought of my strong, hard-working father lying in bed, helpless and unable to care for himself.

"Savannah, can Maxine go with you?" Aunt Deb asked in a low voice, her lower lip pulled between her teeth.

I hesitated, surprised at the question. "Of course, if she wants to," I nodded. "But why?"

"I'm afraid for either of you to be here while a maniac killer who is targeting young, unmarried women roams the streets." She reached out and grabbed my hand, her eyes beseeching mine as she said, "Please convince her to go with you, Savannah. It would give me peace of mind."

I promised I would do what I could, and later that evening I told Maxi about father and asked if she'd go to Atlanta with me.

"You know I'd love to go with you, Vannie, but I hate to think of leaving Robert," Maxi said, her lips pulled into a frown.

"I don't think we'll be gone long," I assured her. "Three, four months tops. Besides, it might do you good to have some space from Robert for a while."

"Why do you say that?" Maxi stared at me inquisitively.

"Well…" I hesitated, "you don't really know much about him."

"I know enough," she said softly, glancing down at her fingernails.

"You only know what he's told you." The words slipped out before I could stop them, and by the defensive look in Maxi's eyes, I immediately regretted saying them. "Aunt Deb is worried about our being here right now," I added, trying to soften my tone.

"Alright," she sighed. "I'll go."

The next evening, Leon stopped by and asked if I wanted to go to Leopold's with him before we left for Atlanta. He'd started his job at the bank last month and stated that he missed our ice cream sundaes.

"I'd love to," I smiled. "I'll get Maxi."

I turned to call out for Maxi when Leon grabbed my arm and said, "Let's just you and I go. I'm sure she has a date with Robert anyway."

"Actually, I do have a date with Rob," Maxi's voice from the kitchen doorway startled me.

"Y'all can come with us," I offered with a smile. "Please? It'll be fun."

"No, thanks," she stated abruptly, glancing coolly in Leon's direction.

"You two have fun."

As we left, I scolded Leon for his words. "Now she thinks you didn't want her to come with us."

"It's her own fault," he said defensively. "I tried to talk to her about her boyfriend a few days ago, and she acted like a brat. So, just let her go out with him tonight."

"Leon," I stopped in my tracks, eyes wide, "are you jealous?"

He looked at me in surprise. "What?" He asked, brow furrowed, and I could tell the thought had never crossed his mind. Still, I wondered if he just hadn't admitted it to himself yet.

Maxi watched as Savannah and Leon drove away, irritated with herself for wanting to cry. Would she ever get over him? Oh, she was courting Robert and had grown to care a great deal for him, but her feelings for Rob could never match what she felt for Leon. How could he have been so cruel as to intentionally exclude her tonight? The least he could have done was ask if she and Rob would like to go, just as sweet Vannie tried to do. But no, he didn't like Rob. He'd said as much a few days ago, when he cornered her about the relationship.

"You'd better be careful with that guy, Maxine," he'd abruptly stated.

"Why is that?" She questioned.

"He's a little too friendly with the ladies if you ask me," he replied. "Plus, you know absolutely nothing about him. You don't even know his family."

"Leon, you're too friendly with the ladies, too, so please forgive me if I take your opinion about Robert with a grain of salt." She'd never said anything so rude to anyone in her life, least of all to Leon. Seeing the surprised look of hurt on his face should have made her apologize, but instead she asked, "Why do you care anyway?"

"Why do I care? Really, Maxine?"

"Yes," she crossed her arms, heart pounding. "Why do you care who I go out with?"

"I've been your best friend for over six years, and you ask me a question like that?" He was angry, but she didn't back down. "I've always looked out for you, Maxine, and that's all I'm trying to do now. You're like a sister to me."

A sister? His words had been like sudden shards of glass being flung in her direction, bypassing her skin to sink directly into her heart. She should have known that's what he'd say, and deep down she'd expected it, but that still didn't dull the sharp twist of agony at finally hearing the words spoken out loud.

"In case you haven't noticed, I'm not a child anymore, Leon Danes," she snapped, too hurt to back down now, "and I don't need you to 'look out for me' any longer."

He was still angry with her, she'd heard it in his tone just now, and she hated herself for allowing his actions to hurt her so badly.

The faint sound of a honking horn drifted in through the open window, and with a start, Maxi realized Robert was waiting. A feeling of guilt rushed over her as she slipped on a pair of gloves and hurried out the door. Here was a man who loved her and made her feel special, yet all she could do was pine away for someone else.

With a sigh, she realized it was time to forget about Leon. Robert wasn't perfect by any means; he was a bit possessive and demanding, and at times a little too flirtatious with other women, but for the most part he treated her well, and most importantly of all, he made her feel wanted, something she'd craved since she was a little girl.

After driving for a bit, Robert parked under a large oak tree, a spot that was well shaded in the growing darkness and pulled her into a kiss.

"I'm going to miss you," he breathed, his lips traveling to the curve of her neck.

Before Robert, she'd never been kissed, never even had a beau, and the longer they were together, the more demanding he became, always pushing her to go further intimately. She wasn't certain of how to make him stop, as she didn't want to make him angry, but tonight she finally gave in. She was hurt, once again, over Leon, and needed to feel loved, needed to feel the comfort of someone who actually wanted her. No matter the cost.

Chapter Twenty-one

-1941-

Leon and I had just entered Leopold's when I spotted Connor sitting in a corner booth. Both surprised and pleased to see him, I raised my hand to catch his eye, only to snatch it back down again when I realized he wasn't alone. Sitting across from him was a slender, unfamiliar woman with long, auburn hair. Connor glanced up, a look of surprise flitting across his face when our eyes met.

"Come on," Leon said when he saw Connor, taking my hand to pull me along behind. "I didn't know you were coming to town tonight, Con," he grinned, slapping his brother on the shoulder once we reached their table.

"Uh, yeah," Connor cleared his throat, motioning to his date. "This is Grace. Grace, this is my brother, Leon, and…Savannah. Savannah Rose."

"It's very nice to meet you, Grace," Leon smiled, an obvious look of admiration lighting his eyes.

Grace smiled pleasantly up at him, gushing over how thrilled she was to meet Connor's brother. Her voice was light and airy, and I didn't fail to notice the long, slender legs that were crossed under the table. She wore a short, fitted green dress that enhanced the color of her eyes, and when she finally took the time to acknowledge me, she openly surveyed me from head to toe. I suddenly wished I'd taken the time to pin my hair back and put on a prettier blouse.

"Did you know that Savannah is leaving us tomorrow?" Leon slipped an arm around my shoulders, giving them a gentle squeeze.

Connor's eyes widened as he looked at me and said, "No, I didn't. Where are you going?"

After I explained, he nodded and said, "I hope your father gets well soon. And," he added, smiling warmly at me, "I hope you won't be gone too long." Glancing at Grace, he turned back to us and asked, "Do you two want to join us?"

Before I could decline, Leon did it for me. "No, thanks," he shook his head. "This is Savannah's last night, so I'd like to spend some time with her before she leaves."

We sat at a booth across the room, and every so often I would catch Connor's eye. I realized I would miss him while I was gone, wishing he didn't have a date tonight and could join us.

Nearly an hour later, Connor came over to our table to tell me goodbye. I stood to give him a hug, feeling silly when my eyes welled up with tears.

"I don't know why I'm crying," I laughed, pulling back to dab at my eyes. "I won't be gone that long."

"You're upset and worried about your father, Savannah Rose," Connor said, reaching up to gently wipe away a stray tear. "It's normal to cry."

How was it that he always managed to know exactly what I was feeling?

"Connor," Grace called, tapping her foot impatiently. "Are you ready?"

"You'd better get back to your date," I sniffed, taking a step back.

"She's not..." before he could finish, Grace came over and interrupted.

"I'm not trying to be rude," she smiled sweetly at us, "but I've got to get back. Have a good trip, Savannah." With a small wave at Leon, Grace took Connor's hand and pulled him away.

"We should probably go, too," I said, turning to Leon. "My train leaves pretty early in the morning."

Darkness surrounded us as we slowly walked back home, and I slipped my arm through Leon's, suddenly wishing the night wouldn't end so quickly. A glow from a nearby streetlamp cast soft beams of light across our faces, and Leon suddenly stopped walking to look down at me.

"I'm going to miss you, Savannah banana," he said, his voice soft. A gentle breeze blew the stray tendrils around my face, and he reached out to gently push them back.

"I'll miss you, too," I replied.

Leon stared down at me for a moment, a far-away look coming into his eyes. I wondered what he was thinking, but before I could ask, he said in a light, nonchalant tone, "You know, everyone always said we'd get married someday."

He was smiling as he spoke the words, and I returned his smile, shaking my head with a chuckle. "I don't think I'm the marrying kind."

"Oh, please," he huffed. "I have a feeling you'll see a lot of your ex while you're in Atlanta."

The same thought had crossed my mind, as well, and I wasn't sure how I felt about that.

"Maybe," I shrugged. "Maybe not. We'll see."

"Promise you'll use your head and not do anything foolish?"

If those words had come from Connor's mouth, I wouldn't have let it go so easily. I couldn't, however, get angry with Leon.

"I promise," I nodded, patting his hand reassuringly.

With a smile, Leon draped his arm across my shoulders, and we began making our way back down the street, the chirping of frogs and crickets loud in the still, dark night. We stopped in front of my house, and I hugged him fiercely, thanking him for a wonderful night.

Kissing him lightly on the cheek, I said, "See you soon, old friend."

Chapter Twenty-two

-1965-

I slowly ran the comb through my hair, wincing at the soreness in my scalp, and my throat tightened painfully as a handful of my thick, dark tresses floated to the floor. I looked into the mirror, noting the black circles around my eyes and sunken hollows in my cheeks. My hair was thinning quickly, and I wondered if I should see about getting a wig.

My spirit heavy, I pushed away from the vanity and began getting dressed. This would be my second month of treatments, and they were taking their toll on my body. I was, however, doing better than Abby. I'd seen her two days ago, when the nurse was pushing her out to a taxi in a wheelchair.

"I'm too weak to walk," she told me as she rubbed her temples with trembling fingers.

"Where is Hannah?" I'd asked, gently rubbing her back.

"With my neighbor, the poor dear," she sighed. "She's having such a hard time with all of this."

I knew Abby's words were true, I'd seen it for myself. The bright-eyed, beautiful little girl was slowly shrinking into herself, her face always sober and serious, her gaze never leaving her mother. She was terrified, anyone could see that, and I wondered what kind of effect this would have on her permanently.

"Listen," I said, "it's going to be awhile before I'm through here, so why don't you let my husband drive you home? That way you won't have to worry about taxi fare."

"Oh, I don't know…" she hesitated. I could tell she wanted to say yes but hated accepting favors.

"I'd be glad to do it," my husband said, stepping forward.

She finally agreed, and I wondered if she was feeling any stronger today. When we arrived at the doctor's office, my question was soon answered. Hannah was in the waiting room, clinging to her mother and sobbing uncontrollably while a nurse attempted to pull her away.

"What's wrong?" I asked, hurrying across the room.

"My numbers aren't good, and the doctor wants me to stay the night," Abby explained. She was crying, as well, and looked to be on the verge of collapse. She looked down at Hannah and, rubbing her small, shuddering back, added, "They won't let Hannah stay with me."

"We'll find someplace for her to stay, Mrs. Lopez, don't worry," the nurse said.

"No," Abby stated firmly. "I won't leave her with just anyone. I'm going home."

"She can stay with us," I spoke up. I glanced at my husband in hopes that he would support me, relieved when he immediately nodded his head.

"No," Abby shook her head, her whole body swaying with the motion. "You're too sick."

I reached out and took Abby's hand, my eyes beseeching hers. "I'm not too sick," I assured her. "We would love to keep her, Abby, please let us."

Her eyes once again filling with tears, Abby whispered, "But I can't pay you."

"We wouldn't let you if you tried," my husband spoke up, his tone firm. "She'll stay with us, and that's that."

Pulling me into a hug, Abby said, "Thank you so much. You two are Heaven sent." Leaning back, she took Hannah by the shoulders and gently pushed her away, wiping the child's wet cheeks with her thumbs. "You'd like to go stay with Mrs. Savannah, wouldn't you?" At Hannah's hesitation, she forced a bright smile and added, "I'll be fine, sweetie, and I promise I'll see you tomorrow, okay?"

Her lower lip trembling, Hannah nodded and obediently took my hand, waving to her mother until Abby and the nurse disappeared around the corner. I was called back within minutes, and after my treatment I walked weakly back to the waiting room to find Hannah and my husband both sitting Indian style on the floor working on a puzzle.

"Ready to go, you two?" I asked, forcing the exhaustion from my voice.

We stopped at the store on the way home to pick up some things for Hannah, and when we finally got home, I was so nauseated I could barely make it to the bathroom in time. I hadn't realized until I was finished that Hannah had followed me and stood in the corner watching me.

"Would you like a rag, or something to drink?" She asked in a quiet voice.

"Oh, honey, I didn't know you were in here," I said, pushing myself off the floor. "I'm sorry you had to see that."

"Mama gets sick and has to throw up a lot, too," she said.

"Hannah?" Aunt Deb called. We'd just introduced her to the little girl, and I could tell they both took an immediate liking to one another. Since Uncle Ray's death four years ago, Aunt Deb moved in with another widow friend. She didn't like to drive very much, as her eyesight wasn't the best, but she came over to help take care of me as often as she could. We'd tried talking her into moving in with us, but she'd refused, stating matter-of-factly, "And give up my independence? Never!"

"She's in here," I called, walking on trembling legs over to the sink to wash up.

"We need to fix her some chicken noodle soup," Hannah told my aunt when she joined us in the bathroom. "Mama always says that makes you better when you're sick."

Smiling, I cupped her cheek in my hand and said, "She's right, too. Are you hungry, sweetie?"

When she nodded, I took her hand and we walked to the kitchen to find something to eat in the ice box.

Later that night, after Hannah had taken a bath and Aunt Deb left, we fixed up the guest bedroom for her, and when she asked my husband to tell her a bedtime story, I climbed in the bed beside her, wrapping my arm around her little shoulders while my husband began to tell her a story. She leaned against my shoulder; her eyes wide as she listened intently to the story of a beautiful, young woman who lived with seven dwarfs. Pretty soon, her head began to droop, and just before the end of the story, she fell asleep.

"The poor dear," I said as I tucked her in, leaving the lamp on beside her bed. "She's exhausted."

"You look a bit tuckered out yourself," my husband said, placing his hands on my shoulders as he followed me out of the room and down the hall.

"I am," I yawned, "but somehow seeing about someone else takes your mind off your own needs. I didn't even realize until now just how tired I am."

As we settled into bed, I curled up next to him and slowly began to relax as the beating of his heart thumped rhythmically against my ear. I'd just drifted off to sleep when Hannah cried out and I jerked awake, my heart pounding.

"I'll go to her," my husband said as he jumped out of bed and hurried from the room. After a moment, I heard him singing a lullaby, the deep, comforting tone of his voice floating gently into the room. When he came back to bed, I asked him if Hannah was okay.

"Yes," he said, kissing my forehead. "She was crying for her mother. She's gone back to sleep now."

I lay awake most of the night, worrying about both Hannah and Abby. What would become of the child if...no, I wouldn't think like that. Abby would be okay, she just had to be.

Chapter Twenty-three

-1941-

The next morning, I woke early and decided to get up and make myself a cup of tea. Lizzie wouldn't be here for another hour, and I couldn't go back to sleep; I had too much on my mind. Pulling on my robe, I slipped quietly downstairs and into the kitchen, careful not to wake anyone. I'd just put the water on to boil when I heard a thump on the front porch, and realized Peter had arrived with the milk

Wishing for a bit of milk in my tea, I went to the front door and opened it, nearly jumping out of my skin when I found Peter still standing there.

"Oh, you startled me," I laughed self-consciously. "I thought you'd be gone already."

His eyes blatantly sweeping over my robed clad body, he smiled and said, "Sorry, I guess I'm just moving a little slow this morning." He handed me our newspaper and added, "Here you go, this was lying on the driveway. Looks like they're still searching for that killer."

Feeling a bit uncomfortable, I pulled awkwardly at my robe, holding it together at the throat as I reached for the paper with my other hand and thanked him.

"You're up awfully early," Peter commented as he continued to stand there and watch me.

"Yes, well, I'm leaving in a couple of hours and I never can seem to sleep before a trip." I edged my way back through the door, hoping he would take the hint.

"Oh, where are you going?" He wanted to know.

"Back to Atlanta."

His eyebrows shot up, and he asked, "Alone?"

I blinked, the question unexpected. "Uh, no. Maxi is going with me."

"You're both going to live in Atlanta?"

Tiring of his nosey questions, I stepped back into the house, one hand on the door as I slowly began to close it in his face. "No, we'll be back in a couple of months or so," I told him. "Well, I'd better run, I've got some last-minute packing to do. Goodbye, Peter."

He was still standing there when I shut the door, and with a sigh, I hurried back into the kitchen, the teapot whistling from the stove.

As I sipped my tea and read the newspaper, I discovered that Peter was right; they'd yet to find any leads on who murdered those two women. It was stated that both were out alone in the twilight of evening, unmarried, and brunette. Chills shot down my spine as I imagined what those girls must have gone through before they died, fighting desperately for their lives, their lungs screaming for air, the killer's face looming over them in the darkness.

"Good morning."

I jumped, my heart thumping in my chest at the unexpected sound of my uncle's voice. With a nervous chuckle, I turned to wish him a good morning, hurriedly finishing my tea as I really did have some last-minute packing to do.

Nearly two hours later, we headed to the train station, and I couldn't help but think of the last time I was there. I'd been just arriving, still grieving over my broken engagement, and I wondered what it would be like to see Jake again on a regular basis. We would attend the same church on Sundays, and as Daddy's doctor, he would be making house calls regularly.

Maxi and I hugged Aunt Deb and Uncle Ray goodbye before we climbed on board, giving them one last wave from the window once we found our seats. As I looked out at the crowd, I noticed a man standing just behind my uncle, his hat pulled down over his face. He was wearing a trench coat, which was unusual as it wasn't raining, and there was something oddly familiar about him, but I couldn't quite place who he was. Something about the way he stood so still amongst the moving crowd made me feel uneasy, and I had the sudden urge to wave a warning to Uncle Ray. I'd just raised my hand when he turned and walked away, and I sat back in my seat, feeling a little silly.

As we pulled away from the station, I flipped through a magazine and tried to relax, forgetting all about the strange man.

He stood among the crowd; his collar pulled high around his chin while the dark gray Fedora shadowed his features. The train whistle blew, reverberating throughout the station like a chorus of trumpets, and he watched as the rumbling locomotive began to pull away. His jaw clenched in anger, he turned and stalked away, pushing his way rudely through the crowd without a care.

She was leaving him again. He'd been following her for a week now, tracking her every step before he made his move. Everyone was on edge, and he'd been trying to lay low and wait for the perfect moment. Now, it was too late. She was gone.

She'll be back, he told himself. *She'll be back, and I'll be waiting.*

Chapter Twenty-four

-Atlanta 1941-

The next few weeks were exhausting, both physically and mentally. I hadn't been prepared for how hard it would be to see my once healthy, boisterous father lying in bed so feeble and powerless. It was all I could do not to run from the room crying when I first arrived.

It didn't take long to settle into a routine. As Daddy was unable to feed himself, I would spoon feed him a bowl of grits or oatmeal every morning, and then we would start with the exercises Jake prescribed. After he settled down for his mid-morning nap, Maxi and I would do the laundry, clean the house, and cook lunch. In the evenings, when Harriet got home from work and after Daddy had eaten supper, we would do his exercises again. I would talk and tell him about my time in Savannah the past year, and he would watch me intently, his eyes never leaving my face. He'd try to respond, but the only sound he could push past his lips was a distorted word or grunt.

Jake came by the house three days after my arrival to check on Daddy. It was strange being back home and receiving visits from Jake again, even if the circumstances were different. I had to admit that I didn't mind seeing him, and even enjoyed discussing Daddy's progress. He was a good doctor, and I couldn't help but admire how kind and gentle he was with Daddy during the examinations. He came by twice a week, and his visits were always professional. We would talk of Daddy's condition, go over medication and any additional exercises that needed to be added to the routine, and then he would leave. He kept his distance, and I was thankful for it.

Dealing with Harriet, I found, was the worst part of all. She always found something to complain about, and never once did she say, "thank you" or "I appreciate everything you girls are doing". Instead, she would complain and point out things we hadn't done right, or comment about how hard she had to work every day. She also resented any additional time I spent with Daddy and would interrupt my nightly talks with him to announce it was time for me to go to bed. It was all I could do to bite my tongue, but I did it for Daddy's sake. I didn't want to do anything to upset him.

A month passed, and Daddy was doing much better. He was able to speak more clearly and move his left arm and leg slowly without my help. I was thrilled with the progress he was making.

It was a Thursday night, and we'd just finished his exercises when Daddy suddenly looked at me and said, "You remind me so much of your mother."

Blinking, I stopped what I was doing to stare at him in surprise. "Really?" I asked, pleased.

Growing up, Daddy wouldn't talk much about Mama. I'd always wanted to know any and everything I could about her, but anytime I asked he would hardly answer, and after he married Harriet it was like Mama had never existed.

"Yes," he nodded, a soft, faraway look coming into his eyes. "You look like me for the most part, but you have her beautiful smile and spirit."

As he spoke, I sank slowly into the chair beside his bed, drinking in his every word. "Her spirit?" I questioned. "How so?"

"She was so compassionate, so caring. She would do anything in the world to help another human being. You certainly didn't get that from me," he chuckled, and I couldn't help but join in. "She used to visit the widows in our church every Saturday. She'd take them little cakes and pies, and sometimes help them clean their houses. She was the same with animals, too. I remember once she found a bird in our yard with a broken wing. She brought it inside and, with tears in her eyes, said she wanted to help it fly again."

"Did she?" I asked.

"She did," he nodded, and I thought I saw a tear glistening in the corner of his eye. He reached out and took my hand, giving it a squeeze as he said, "She wanted children so badly. We had three miscarriages before we had you."

"You did?" My eyes widened. "I had no idea."

He didn't say anything for a moment, and I watched as a deep look of sadness came over his face, making him appear much older than his fifty-two years. "I told her we should stop trying, that we were getting too old, but she didn't want to give up. When she found out she was expecting you, that was the happiest I'd ever seen her. She told me "I'm going to have a healthy baby this time, Edward, you just wait and see", and when she held you in her arms for the first time, she beamed like the sun."

I didn't realize until he stopped talking that I was crying. "I miss her," I whispered. "I wish I could have known her."

"So do I, honey." He reached up to gently wipe away my tears. "I'm sorry I never told you any of this. I meant to, but I kept putting it off and time just got away from me."

"It's okay," I smiled, squeezing his hand. "Thank you for telling me now."

"I love my girl," he said, his voice raspy. "I never said it enough, but I hope you know I do. And I appreciate your coming to take care of me."

Sometimes, people say, when sickness comes along and forces you to slow down, you re-evaluate your life and realize you were focusing on the wrong things. This, I believe, is what happened to Daddy, and I couldn't be more grateful.

I lay my head over on his shoulder, my tears soaking his bed shirt, and said, "I love you, too, Daddy."

Chapter Twenty-five

-Atlanta 1941-

Two weeks later, on a Friday afternoon, Jake came by for Daddy's check-up. He seemed distracted, if not a little upset, and when the examination was finished, I asked him what was wrong.

Placing his doctor's bag on the table, he ran a hand down the side of his face and sighed. "Do you remember my Aunt Mary?"

"The one who lives in London?"

"Yes," he nodded. "We received a letter from her this morning. She said the conditions over there are unbelievably bad. The constant bombing is destroying the city, they're running low on food and medicine, and they're in desperate need for doctors."

"How awful," I said, my heart clenching.

"I want to help, but short of going over there I don't think there's anything I can do."

My eyes widened. "You're not thinking of going, are you?" I asked.

He didn't answer for a moment. Instead, he stood silently, his blue eyes clouded with thoughts and concern, his brow heavy and brooding. Finally, he sighed and shrugged his shoulders. "I don't know," he said. "Maybe."

Clearing his throat, he asked in a lighter tone, "Would you like to go out tonight? We could get something to eat and see a movie. I'm sure it would do you good to get out of the house for a while."

I hesitated, caught off guard. "I don't know," I hedged. "I really shouldn't leave Daddy."

"I can see about him." Maxi, apparently eavesdropping, stepped into the room and smiled at us. "Jake is right, you need a break."

"So do you," I pointed out, giving her a look.

"I'll be fine," she said, her eyes twinkling. "Please go."

Frowning, I wondered why she was pressing the issue when I knew she didn't approve of Jake, and I opened my mouth to protest further when Jake said, "Alright, it's all settled. I've got one more patient to see, and I'll be back to pick you up in an hour."

After Jake was gone, I turned to face Maxi. "What gives?" I wanted to know, hands on my hips.

"I think it'll do you good to get out for a while," she replied innocently.

"With Jake, the mortal enemy?"

"You agreed to write and be friends," she pointed out. "Why not go see a movie and have some fun?"

I crossed my arms. "Because I don't know if I'm comfortable with that," I stated.

"Vannie," Maxi sighed, "you were hurt last year and broke things off so quickly that I don't know if you ever really got the closure you needed. Maybe now you'll have the chance to see things more clearly."

"What makes you think I didn't get closure?" I asked, my brow furrowed.

"Because you agreed to write him."

"Can't I simply be friends with him?" I pressed, feeling a bit defensive when her words brought back to mind the argument with Connor.

"Of course, you can, but if you're truly "just friends" now, then you shouldn't feel uncomfortable going out with him tonight," was her simple answer.

I watched her turn and walk quietly from the room without another word, and I knew she was right. With a moan of frustration, I stalked up the stairs to get ready, wondering the entire time if I should call Jake and cancel. Connor had said I was opening the door again, and Maxi said I needed closure. They were both right, but what I couldn't figure out was how to get that closure while keeping the door firmly closed.

I sat down in front of the vanity, staring at my reflection. "Will you look back years from now and wonder if you did the right thing?" I murmured, wishing the girl in the mirror could answer. What would it be like if one could see into the future? How many mistakes would be avoided, how many decisions changed?

With a sigh, I began to pin up my hair. When Maxi walked into the room minutes later, she looked at me with hesitant eyes and asked, "You're not upset with me for interfering, are you?"

Smiling, I shook my head and moved to stand before her. "No, dear Maxi, I could never be upset with you. Besides, you were right."

Her face sagging with relief, Maxi pulled me into a hug and said, "I'm so glad. I couldn't stand it if you were angry with me."

She helped me finish getting ready and I'd just slid my shoes on when we heard a knock downstairs. "You'll have to deal with Harriet's complaints all by yourself, you know," I pointed out to Maxi as we hurried downstairs.

"I'll just ignore her," Maxi giggled, waving goodbye to Jake and me as we walked to his car.

The ride to the restaurant was a bit tense and awkward, but once we were seated and our drinks arrived, things started to loosen up.

"So, how does it feel to have your first assignment as a real nurse?" He asked.

"Exhausting, rewarding, trying, fulfilling." I sighed. "I certainly never imagined that my first patient would be my father."

"You're doing a wonderful job, though."

"I'm trying, and he does seem to be getting better. I couldn't do it without Maxi, though," I said, my gaze moving about the room of one of the most unusual restaurants I'd ever been in. Dozens of private booths lined the walls, each with a small window one could peer through to the outside. A buzzer rested just beneath the windowpane, and whenever we needed something, Jake would alert our waiter by pressing the button. The best part, however, was in the center of the darkened room, where a painted, glowing ceiling that resembled a beautiful, starry night hung. The restaurant was famous for their slogan of, "Come dance under the stars", and a small band played softly in the corner while couples did just that.

"It's good that Maxi came," Jake smiled warmly at me, and I had to pull my gaze away from the peaceful scene. "It's good that you came, too."

The conversation flowed relatively easy after that, and once we'd finished the delicious meal, Jake asked, "Do you remember Susie Cowart?"

"Of course," I nodded. "She's an old childhood friend of mine."

"She's dating one of my colleagues, and I ran into them this evening at the drugstore on my way back to your house. They said the Masons are holding their annual dance at their lodge tonight, and I wondered if you'd like to go?"

I readily agreed, Jake paid the bill, and fifteen minutes later we arrived at the Masonic lodge. Cars were lined up in front of the old, brick building, and as we walked inside, I was glad I'd worn a full skirt and comfortable shoes. The room was rectangular and very large, and couples danced gaily in the center to a live band. Metal chairs lined the walls, and a table of finger foods and punch was surrounded by smiling, laughing people.

"Shall we?" Jake asked, motioning to the dance floor.

Having never danced with Jake before, I immediately noticed he wasn't as skilled of a dancer as Connor or Leon, and when he tried to pull me closer only to kick me in the shin, I couldn't help but laugh.

"Now you know my secret," he said, his face flushing. "I'm not very good at dancing."

"I couldn't dance at all until someone gave me lessons this past year," I confessed, feeling a twinge of homesickness at the thought of Connor and the fun times we'd shared. I nearly shook my head in amazement at the sensation, as I never would have placed "Connor" and "homesickness" in the same sentence before.

"You'll have to teach me now," Jake grinned, and I had to remind myself what we were talking about.

"I might be persuaded to show you a thing or two," I smiled.

We'd danced through three songs when I said I wanted something to drink. We were walking through the crowd when Jake spotted a colleague and said he'd meet me at the punch table in a moment. I walked the rest of the way alone and had just taken my first sip of the cool, tangy drink when someone called my name.

"Savannah Adair, is that you?"

I turned to find Susie Cowart walking my way, and I squealed with delight at seeing my old friend again.

"Susie, how wonderful to see you!" I cried, pulling her into a hug.

"I thought it was you dancing with Jake just now, but I couldn't be sure," she said, pulling back to smile at me. "Are you home for good?"

"No," I shook my head with a sigh. "I'm just here to help with Daddy until he gets better."

"I heard about his stroke," she said, sympathetically reaching out to touch my arm. "Is he doing any better?"

"Yes, thank goodness," I nodded, taking a sip of my punch.

"I'm so glad to hear that," she smiled genuinely, her hazel eyes crinkling around the edges. "You know…" she hesitated, glancing around. Taking a step closer, she lowered her voice and said, "I'll admit I'm a little surprised that you came with Jake."

"We've agreed to be friends," I shrugged, "so why not?"

"Oh, well good," she sighed, her shoulders lowering in relief. "He and Pamela broke up not too long ago, you know."

I'd just taken another sip of punch when she spoke, and I almost choked on the cool, red liquid. "They…they were dating?" I asked, my eyes widening.

"Yes," Susie nodded, studying me closely. "They began officially dating about two months after you left last year, and they just broke up at the beginning of May. You didn't know?"

"No," I shook my head, the words in his first letter after I left running through my brain: *Please believe me when I say she does not mean a thing to me.*

"What happened?" I asked.

"I'm not entirely sure," she replied, her brow furrowing, "but I think he grew tired of her flirtatious ways."

"Interesting," I murmured.

"Susie," a man called out, and we both turned to find a young, handsome man beckoning to her. "They're playing our song," he said, "come on!"

"I'll see you later," Susie winked at me before hurrying to join her date on the dance floor.

As I watched them dance, my thoughts were running a million miles a minute. I almost couldn't believe that Jake courted Pamela after vowing to me he didn't care about her, but deep in my heart I wasn't really surprised. He never would have allowed that kiss to happen if there hadn't been something between them, and I knew that now.

Shifting my gaze, I searched the room for Jake, wishing to go home. I didn't see him, and so I walked over to one of the windows, thinking perhaps he'd stepped outside for a breath of fresh air when my eyes finally found what they were seeking. Only, he wasn't alone. Standing at his side, her hand on his arm, was Pamela. They were in deep conversation, and I could see that Jake was angry. I'd always been very good at reading lips, and it looked to me that they both mentioned my name a few times before Jake jerked his arm away and very clearly said, "I gave you a chance, Pamela, and you blew it. It's over for good this time."

He turned and stalked away, and I could see that she was crying. Strangely enough, I felt sorry for her.

I walked back to the food table and waited for him to find me. When he did, his eyes were clear and he was smiling, as if nothing had happened.

"Sorry about that," he said, coming to stand beside me. "I got caught talking with a colleague and couldn't get away."

"Anyone I know?" I asked innocently.

"Uh…" he hesitated, avoiding my gaze, "no, I don't think so."

He was lying, and I wondered just how many lies he'd told me while we were together. "I know it's still early," I suddenly said, "but I'm actually very tired. Would you mind terribly if we left?"

With a look of surprise flashing across his face, Jake agreed, and we made our way through the crowd. As we walked to the car, I saw Pamela still standing under the oak tree, her features shadowed beneath its branches, and I had the feeling that her shadow would have always haunted me had I chosen to stay with Jake.

On the way home, Jake asked if he could take me out again soon. My stomach in knots, I took a deep breath and did what I had to.

"No," I shook my head. "I don't think that's such a good idea."

"What?" He asked in surprise. "Why not?"

I hesitated, searching for the right words. "I know about you and Pamela, and…"

"There's nothing…" he interrupted, but I held up my hand to stop him.

"Please," I said, "let me finish."

His face tense, he nodded tightly, his knuckles white against the steering wheel.

"I know about you and Pamela," I continued, "but instead of feeling anger, I honestly only feel relief. Maxi told me that I left in such a hurry last year that I didn't get the closure I needed, and she was right. Tonight, I got that closure, and I mean it when I say that it is over between us. Everything. You were once my very best friend, and I'll admit sometimes I miss that, but I see now that it's impossible to get that part of our lives back, and it's unwise to even try. I appreciate what you're doing for my father, and I hope we can still maintain a professional relationship, but anything else is out of the question."

I took a deep breath, the pounding of my heart the only sound in the silent car. I knew what I'd just done was the right thing, but it hadn't been easy.

"Whatever you wish," were the words he finally spoke, his voice cool. "But I hope you know you're making a mistake," he added, turning to look at me with eyes so hard I barely even recognized him.

"No, Jake," I said gently, "I'm not making a mistake."

Neither of us spoke another word after that, and when we arrived back at the house, I thanked him for the meal and climbed from the car without his help. I closed the door and he drove away, and as I stood on the sidewalk and watched him go, I felt a giant weight begin to lift from my shoulders. I hadn't even realized until that moment that I'd been carrying it for over a year now. I may have been blunt, and perhaps even a bit harsh, but I'd made the right decision and surprisingly enough, it didn't even hurt.

As I turned to walk inside, I heard sirens in the distance, and it seemed as if they were continuously drawing closer. Before I'd made it halfway up the driveway, the front door flew open, and Maxi stumbled out, her face as white as a ghost.

"Vannie," she cried, crumpling to the wooden slats beneath her feet.

"Maxi!" I gasped, racing to her side. "What's wrong?" When she didn't answer, I grasped hold of her shoulders and shook her. "What's happened, Maxi? Tell me!"

"Your father," she sobbed. "I think…I think he's dead."

Chapter Twenty-six

-Atlanta 1941-

I stood by the graveside, my face solemn and stiff from crying. I couldn't pull my gaze away from the casket that rested so peacefully before me, waiting to be lowered down into that deep, desolate black hole.

My father was dead. I was an orphan. Never having a mother, I'd always been terrified of losing my father, and now here I was, parentless. My father and I had finally begun to connect, to find common ground and grow closer to one another, and now he was gone, and it even felt as if the connection to my mother was fading away, too.

"Mr. Adair and his wife got into an argument over money," Maxi explained to the police officer that night, her shaky, tear-muddled words echoing through my mind. "She told him she wasn't making enough at the post office to pay the bills, and he said if she hadn't so foolishly used all of their savings, they would have all the money they needed. The argument grew more and more heated, they started yelling at each other, and the next thing I knew Mrs. Adair was frantically screaming at me to call an ambulance."

More tears began to drip from my chin, splashing against the front of my black mourning dress. I wanted to hate Harriet, to scream that this was all her fault, but knew Daddy wouldn't want that. He wouldn't want a scene.

Aunt Deb wrapped an arm around my waist, squeezing gently. I was never more grateful for her presence than at that moment. She, Uncle Ray, Mrs. Emma, and Leon had all come for the funeral, their support being the only glue that had held me together the last few days. Connor wasn't granted permission to leave, so he sent a beautiful wreath made of sunflowers, my favorite, and a warm note with his regards. All I wanted was for the next couple of days to be over so I could go home.

Once the funeral was over, we went back to Daddy's house to receive visitors, and I prayed I'd be able to make it through the day without breaking apart.

"Savannah," a voice called softly, and I turned to find Jake standing behind me, his eyes full of sorrow. Daddy had been both his friend and patient, and I knew he felt quite a bit of pain, and even some guilt, over his death.

Without saying a word, I pulled him into a hug. Although I'd decided that anything romantic between us was over, that didn't change the fact that I still cared for Jake.

"I'm so sorry, Savannah," he said, his voice heavy as he pulled back. "I should have gone inside to check on him that night…"

"No, Jake," I insisted, shaking my head. "Don't blame yourself. You can't be on call twenty-four hours a day, and there probably wasn't anything you could have done anyway."

"If there is anything you need," he said, squeezing my hands gently, "please don't hesitate to call me."

"Thank you," I nodded with gratitude.

The next day we all went to the attorney's office for the reading of the will. Daddy left everything to Harriet, with the exception of his pocket watch and a trunk filled with some of Mama's things he'd packed away for me after she died. They were supposed to have gone with me when I got married.

The following day, while Uncle Ray and Leon loaded the trunk into the taxi that would take us to the train, I walked through the house for what I knew would be the last time. I thought of all the homework I'd done on the living room floor while listening to the radio, and as I walked past the back door, I glanced out the window at the old oak tree I used to climb. I touched the ruffled curtains in my old bedroom, my mind seeing visions of giggling girls whispering in the night during weekend sleep overs. As I walked past Daddy's bedroom, I stopped and pressed my eyes closed, thinking of our last conversation and wishing I could see him just one more time.

"Vannie? Are you ready?"

I opened my eyes, meeting Maxi's concerned gaze, her small suitcase clutched in one hand.

"Yes," I nodded, taking a deep breath as I followed her to the front door. When we passed the dining room, my eyes fell upon the china cabinet, and I wished all over again that Harriet would let me take Mama's beautiful, hand painted dishes she and Daddy had received as a wedding present. When I'd asked Harriet about it last night, she'd snapped, "Those dishes may have been given to your mother, but they're mine now."

126

We walked outside, I told Harriet goodbye, and we left. As we drove away, I looked out the back window of the taxi, silently telling my childhood goodbye.

Chapter Twenty-seven

-1941-

It was mid-August, and both Maxi and I had been working at Candler Hospital for three weeks. The practice I'd gotten caring for Daddy was coming in handy as I worked tirelessly day in and day out changing bedpans, giving medication, taking blood pressure, and stitching up small wounds. The heat was almost unbearable, and I couldn't stop hoping that cooler weather was just around the corner.

I was sitting with a small and very ill little girl when Maxi popped her head into the room to let me know her shift was over. "Are you ready to go home?" She asked.

I glanced at my wristwatch, surprised to find that it was nearly six o'clock. "I think I'll wait until Sally's mother gets here," I said in a low voice, nodding my head in the little girl's direction. "She's afraid to be here by herself, and her mother should be back within the hour."

"I'll wait with you then," Maxi said, stepping further into the room.

"No, you haven't been feeling well," I said, waving her away. "Take the car, go on home, and get some rest. I'll be there shortly."

"Okay," she nodded, trying to cover a yawn. "Try to be home before dark, you know how Aunt Deb worries."

As I watched her walk slowly from the room, I couldn't help feeling concerned. She hadn't been acting right the last few weeks. She was always tired and low on energy, and the circles under her eyes were growing darker and darker. I'd tried to talk her into seeing a doctor, but she insisted she was okay.

"Well, well, how is our little patient tonight?"

The deep, booming voice startled me, and I turned to find Doctor Cox standing in the doorway, a clipboard in one hand as he smiled at Sally and me.

"She still has a fever," I said, and proceeded to relay all her symptoms and the medication we'd given her that afternoon. Doctor Cox usually worked the morning shift, but he'd just gotten back from a business trip and had apparently wanted to check in with his patients. I'd been apprehensive about working with him after the argument with his son at the Valentine's Day dance, but soon learned I had nothing to worry about. Doctor Cox never mentioned the incident, and I found that I rather enjoyed working with him.

Sally's mother ran later than I'd expected, and it was after seven when I finally left the hospital. The thick humidity in the air made it hard to breathe as I walked, and I glanced up at the sky, noting it was already growing dark. Traffic bustled loudly around the hospital, the sounds of car engines, sirens, and honking horns filling the silence, but the further I went the more quiet it became, and soon the only sound I could hear was the clicking of my heels against the pavement.

It was soon a dark, still evening as I neared home, frogs and crickets contentedly chirping their lullabies. It felt as if everyone had gone to bed early and I was the only person up and about, and I shivered a bit as a feeling of wariness crept up my spine.

There hadn't been anymore murders in over a month, but a killer was still on the loose and I suddenly realized it wasn't a very good idea to be out walking alone so late. It was almost as if everyone had relaxed over the course of the past month, refusing to acknowledge the possibility of danger still lurking on our streets, but when a sudden breeze swept past me and rustled the bushes just ahead, I paused, squinting nervously through the shadows. Was someone there? I didn't see anything, and so I pushed myself to move forward, trying to ignore the strong sense of foreboding that nipped at my heels.

Minutes later, as I rounded the corner to our neighborhood, I breathed a sigh of relief. *Just a little further, to the end of this street, and I'll home*, I thought, quickening my footsteps. As I neared the middle of the street, I slowed a bit and blinked, my heart skipping a beat. I'd seen something, or someone, just up ahead. A shadow, slipping quietly through the darkness. *It was probably just a cat*, I thought warily, *or the wind casting shadows from overhead tree branches*. Shaking off my fears, I hurried on.

I was nearing Mrs. Emma's house when I noticed Connor's car parked on the curb. He must be spending the weekend with them, I mused. I hadn't seen much of him since my return home and couldn't help but wonder if he was still seeing Grace.

Glancing ahead, I noticed our front porch light beaming like a beacon in the night, and I gasped in surprise when a cat suddenly screamed from a nearby alley. I looked in the direction of the noise and rubbed my forearms, the haunting cry sending chills racing down my spine.

Just then, another, more faint sound caught my attention. Rustling leaves, branches snapping, footsteps. I quickly swung my head around and searched through the darkness, my eyes widening when they landed on the large figure of a man emerging from a mass of nearby bushes. Dressed all in black, he appeared to have some type of hood pulled over his face, and I felt panic shoot through my body, my knees beginning to shake like reeds in the wind. Before I could gather my wits enough to scream, he grabbed my arm and pulled me against his chest.

"Margie," he whispered, hot breath skimming across my forehead. "Finally, I have you in my arms again. I've waited so long."

"Let me go," I heaved breathlessly, struggling to pull my arms away. I opened my mouth to scream, but he was too quick. A large, rough hand slapped over my lips as he twisted me about, gripped me tightly around the waist, and lifted my feet off the ground.

"You're coming with me," he growled, moving in the direction of a nearby car parked on the curb.

I knew once he got me into that car there was no turning back, and I felt my adrenaline kick into overdrive. I began to swing my feet wildly back and forth, managing to connect with his shin and therefore causing him to momentarily loosen his grip on my waist. Using the moment to my advantage, I twisted my elbow around and struck him as hard as I could in the temple. With a grunt, he let me go, and I leapt away from him, stumbling slightly as I forced my trembling legs into a sprint. I'd gotten only a few feet away when he sprang forward and grabbed the back of my dress, causing me to stumble and fall face first. I threw my hands wildly out before me and crashed onto the ground, barely noticing the sharp stab of pain as the asphalt took the skin off my palms. The man grabbed my elbows and jerked me back, but before he could stop me, I opened my mouth and let out a blood curdling scream, continuing to fight him, yet knowing my strength could never match his.

Suddenly, the Danes' front porch light came on, and I saw a tall figure step out onto the porch. Cursing, the man let me go and ran to his car, gunning the engine as he raced madly away.

"What's going on out here?" I heard Connor yell as he hurried down the sidewalk in my direction, Mrs. Emma and Leon close behind. Several other neighbors did the same, and the mingling of voices and footsteps soon overtook the still night.

A sob caught in the back of my throat, and I felt my body begin to hyperventilate, the adrenaline fading away to leave behind a jittery, shaking heap sitting in the middle of the road.

"Savannah Rose?" Connor gasped when he knelt by my side. He pushed my hair away from my face, his concerned eyes not missing a single detail. The tears, my torn dress, and bleeding palms. He immediately scooped me into his arms, murmuring words of comfort as he pushed his way through the inquisitive neighbors.

Through blurry vision, I could see my aunt, uncle, and Maxi standing on our porch, peering through the darkness. All three of their eyes widened in horror when they realized who Connor was carrying.

"What on earth!" Aunt Deb cried, while Maxi gasped and covered her mouth.

Uncle Ray hurried to open the front door, and Connor carried me inside while everyone, including Mrs. Emma and Leon, followed closely behind.

Placing me gently on the sofa, Connor reached for a nearby Afghan and draped it around my shoulders, his gaze never leaving my face.

"Here," he said, pulling a hanky from his back pocket. "It's going to be okay. Just take a few deep breaths and, when you're able, tell us what happened."

I did as he said, trying desperately to calm myself. Maxi sat at my feet, her eyes filled with fear as she watched me hesitantly. Aunt Deb fluttered about the room like a wild bird, unable to get a clear thought as she asked Connor over and over what he'd seen.

"I think we should call the police," Uncle Ray said quietly.

"I agree," Leon nodded firmly, heading for the phone.

"One of the neighbors already did," Mrs. Emma stated as she walked into the room and handed me a cup of warm tea. "Can you tell us what happened, dear?" she asked me gently.

I nodded, finally calm enough to breathe normally. In a slow, trembling voice, I told them what happened, tears slipping down my cheeks as I relived it all over again.

"I knew I should have waited for you," Maxi cried, her eyes filled with guilt.

"Did you get a look at the man's face?" Connor wanted to know.

"No," I shook my head. "He was wearing some sort of mask."

There was a knock at the door just then, and Uncle Ray went to see who it was. He returned seconds later with an Officer Pane and Lieutenant

Masters.

"Did he say anything?" Officer Pane asked after I'd finished, once again, with the story.

"Yes," I nodded slowly, my brow furrowing. "He called me 'Margie' and said it was good to have me back in his arms again."

The two officers glanced at one another in surprise, and Connor asked what was going on.

"Mrs. Willingham, one of the women that was murdered earlier this year?" Lieutenant Masters waited until we all nodded before continuing. "Her first name was Marge."

We all stared in confusion, Leon finally breaking the silence. "I thought RJ Willingham was in prison for committing those murders? What does that have to do with what happened here tonight?"

"We're not at full liberty to say," Officer Pane sighed, "but none of us are entirely sure that Mr. Willingham is responsible."

"I can say this," Lieutenant Masters added, "all of the women we've found had crushed skulls, just like the women Mr. Willingham was supposed to have murdered."

"Could it be a copycat?" Uncle Ray asked.

"It could," Pane nodded. "There's really no way of being certain, but one thing we do know is there's a serial killer roaming our streets, and he's after your niece."

Chapter Twenty-eight

-1965-

I lay in the hospital bed, fading in and out of consciousness, my whole body in pain. I'd taken a turn for the worse. Abby, it seemed, was doing a little better, and I couldn't have been happier. I thought perhaps we were both going to make it through this when, suddenly, my body turned on me. I started vomiting uncontrollably, my temperature shot up to over 102 degrees, and my blood pressure went through the roof. My husband rushed me to the hospital, where I'd been poked and prodded innumerous times with no real results. The doctor said my blood counts weren't looking good, and although I wasn't certain of what that meant, I knew I was dying. The cancer had won.

Three days passed, and I was only growing worse. I'd been allowed to see my husband once, and had begged him not to leave, but the nurse said he wasn't allowed to stay. I fought to stay awake, to fight the darkness that pulled unmercifully at me, to resist the same horrible nightmare that repeated itself every time I closed my eyes. I was always running, trying desperately to get away from the black, hooded figure that chased me. I hadn't slept peacefully since I arrived, and my nerves were shot. Each day I could feel myself growing weaker and weaker, sinking further and further away.

Through the haze of medication, fever, and weakness, I heard my hospital door open, and a tall man wearing a white shirt, tie, and dark gray suit entered my room. He was holding a Bible in his hand, and the look of kindness in his warm, dark eyes instantly made me feel at ease.

"Hello there," he smiled down at me, his voice strong and a bit raspy. "I'm Reverend J.E. Burton."

My eyes widened slightly as I recognized the name. "You have that radio program, don't you?" I asked. I'd listened to many of his sermons while cooking or doing the housework. He was a very powerful preacher, and quite well-known in the area.

"Yes, ma'am, I do," he nodded. "I've come to pray with you, if you don't mind?"

"I'd greatly appreciate it," I said, my throat as dry as sandpaper. "I could use all the help I can get."

He reached out and lay a large, warm hand on my forehead, closing his eyes as he began to pray with such conviction that tears began seeping past my eyelids and dripped down my cheeks. Once he'd finished, he pulled back and asked, "Are you a Christian, young lady?"

I couldn't help but smile, as he couldn't be much older than I was, and nodded. "Yes sir, I am."

"Good, good," he nodded. "Just keep the faith and believe on Him. He's the Great Physician, and He promised to never leave us or forsake us."

He then proceeded to open his Bible and read a few passages about Jesus and His healing of the sick, and once he was finished, I asked him to keep me, and my friend Abby, in his prayers.

"I will," he stated. "And if you're still here next week, I'll come pray with you again. But," he added with a warm smile, "I'm sure you'll be better and back in the comforts of your own home by then."

Once he was gone, I noticed that my pain had lessened, and with a sigh of relief, I slowly closed my eyes, drifting off into the deepest, most peaceful sleep I'd had in weeks.

Chapter Twenty-nine

-1941-

I awoke the next morning, my mind still whirling over the events from the night before. The suspicions of both officers kept running through my brain, sending chills down my spine and putting my nerves on edge. I couldn't help but think of the mysterious man I'd seen at the train station the day I left for Atlanta. Had this man, this killer, been stalking me, planning the whole thing out slowly and meticulously all this time? The thought made me sick to my stomach.

I was frightened, to say the least, and uncertain of what I needed to do. The police officers advised me to never go outside alone, and that we should always keep our doors and windows locked. I couldn't help but wonder, however, if I would still be completely safe.

I pushed myself out of bed, tiptoeing over to the next room to check on Maxi. She'd been overcome with dizziness and nearly fainted last night after the police left, and we all immediately insisted she go to bed. Aunt Deb assumed she was simply overwrought over the events of the evening, but I thought differently, as she hadn't been herself in weeks.

The bedroom door creaked as I slowly pushed it open, and I found Maxi propped up on three pillows, her skin pale and pasty.

"Good morning," I smiled, walking in to sit beside her. I reached up to feel her forehead, relieved that she didn't seem to have a fever. "How are you feeling?"

"Weak, nauseous," she sighed. "I vomited in the bathroom just now. Do you think I have the flu or something?"

"I don't think so," I shook my head. "You haven't been feeling well for a couple of weeks now."

"Honestly, I haven't been feeling right for a couple of months," Maxi admitted, her eyes worried. "I'm so tired all the time, like every bit of my energy is just gone. I've been nauseous on and off, but no diarrhea. It's very strange."

I stared at her for a moment, a thought niggling in the back of my mind.

Surely…no, certainly not. But all the symptoms pointed in that direction, and the more I thought about it the more suspicious I became.

"Maxi," I said hesitantly, a knot growing in the pit of my stomach, "you're not…I mean, you haven't…"

Maxi stared curiously at me, her brow furrowing. "What's wrong, Vannie?" She asked, laying her hand over mine. "I haven't what?"

Taking a deep breath, I slowly raised my eyes to meet hers and asked pointedly, "When was your last menstrual cycle?"

Maxi blinked, as if trying to understand the meaning behind my question. When it finally sunk in, her eyes widened with realization and the blood drained so quickly from her pale cheeks that I feared she might actually faint this time. She jerked her hand away and lowered her eyes, but not before I saw the guilt in their blue depths.

"I…I don't…" Maxi stuttered, raising two, trembling fingers to press against her left temple. After a moment, tears flooded her eyes and she whispered, "Oh, Vannie, what am I going to do?"

I hesitated, uncertain of what to say. During those days, it was shameful to become pregnant out of wedlock, and I hated to think of how our aunt and uncle would react. "You need to talk to Robert," I finally said. "Perhaps you can get married before anyone starts to suspect."

"But what if he doesn't want to marry me?" She sniffed, wiping her face with the back of her hand.

"He has a responsibility to you and the baby, Maxi," I stated firmly. "Robert seems to care for you. I'm sure he'll want to do the right thing."

With a shuddering sigh, Maxi nodded and pushed herself out of bed. "I'll go see him now. If he can't see me, I'll wait until he can." She began to change clothes, pausing to look back at me. "Please don't tell Aunt Deb about this."

"You know I won't," I said, standing. "But I'd better go with you or she'll have a fit if you go out alone after everything that happened last night."

"What excuse do we give for leaving?" Maxi asked. "She said I needed to rest today."

"We'll tell her you're feeling better and the two of us are going to spend the day at the beach getting some fresh air," I shrugged, hurrying to get ready.

Thankfully, Aunt Deb didn't protest much when we left. She simply asked us to stay together and get home before dark. The train ride to the island was quiet and tense. I didn't know what to say, and I could tell Maxi didn't feel like talking. Once we arrived, I told Maxi I would wait for her on the pier while she went to see Robert. As I watched her walk away, I could only hope things went well.

Maxi paced back and forth in the waiting area at Fort Screven, her stomach in knots as she wondered just what she was going to say. How on earth had she not known she was pregnant? Was she really so naïve? She hoped against hope he would agree to marry her today. They could go to the Justice of the Peace, and then everything would be alright. Her aunt and uncle would be angry at first but hopefully soon get over it, and she had no doubt that if she and Rob couldn't marry today, they would at least get engaged.

Taking a deep, calming breath, Maxi sat down and leaned her head back, closing her eyes. Everything would be fine. It was all going to work out, she just knew it.

A few moments later, she heard someone enter the room and opened her eyes to see Robert walk in.

"Maxine," he said, his voice filled with surprise at seeing her. "What are you doing here?"

"Rob," she cleared her throat nervously, "we need to talk. Is there someplace private we can go?"

He eyed her for a moment, question in his gaze, and slowly nodded his head, leading her outside to sit at a lone picnic table under a large oak tree.

"What's going on?" He asked as he took the seat across from her.

Maxi swallowed, her throat suddenly very dry as she glanced down at her clenched hands. This wasn't how she'd imagined her life; this wasn't how she'd planned to announce she was expecting a baby. She was supposed to be happily married, not unwed and uncertain. But she had confidence in Robert, and so with a deep breath, she said, "Well…I, um…" her voice was so small, he had to lean closer to hear her, and she stopped for a moment, too nervous to go on.

"Maxine, look at me and tell me what's wrong," he demanded, his voice stern.

She squeezed her eyes shut for a moment, then looked up at him and blurted, "I think…I think I'm pregnant."

His eyes grew wide as he stared at her, his mouth dropping open, completely speechless.

"Say something," she whispered after an agonizingly long moment passed.

He moved his elbows off the table and sat back. "Are..." he swallowed, "are you sure?"

"I'm not positive, but I'm fairly certain," she nodded. "I have all of the symptoms."

With a groan, Robert abruptly stood and began to pace back and forth before her. She didn't know what was going through his mind and wasn't sure she wanted to by the look on his face. She'd known this was going to be a shock and felt dreadful about it. She felt she needed to give him time to get used to the idea, but they didn't have much time to waste.

"I know our getting married so quickly will cause people to talk," she said, not doubting for a minute that they would, indeed, get married, "but it doesn't matter. Do you think we should do it today? Or wait until after we tell my aunt and uncle? I was hoping..." her words trailed off as she realized he'd stopped pacing and was staring at her like she was crazy. "What's wrong?" She asked.

"I can't marry you," he said, his words so short and to the point that Maxi's brain wouldn't process them at first.

She shook her head, as if to clear her ears. "I'm sorry...what did you say?"

"I said..." with a heavy, defeated sigh, he sank back down onto the bench across from her. "I said, I can't marry you."

It was now Maxi's turn to stare at him in utter shock. In all the scenarios she'd imagined, she never thought their conversation would go like this. Surely, she'd misunderstood. Perhaps he meant he couldn't marry her right now.

"Why not?" She wanted to know, expecting him to simply say that they would need a home or to save some money first. When he stared down at his hands, neither answering nor meeting her gaze, her heart began to sink with dread.

"Why not, Robert?" She asked again in a firmer tone.

He ran his fingers through his hair, still refusing to meet her gaze. "Because..." he swallowed, shaking his head, "because I'm already married."

If someone had tried, they could have knocked Maxi off that bench with a feather. "You're…what?" She choked out, thinking she'd heard him wrong.

He stood up once again and backed away a bit, as if afraid of what she'd do. "I'm already married, Maxine," he said, pushing his hands into the pockets of his uniform khakis.

She tried to swallow, but her throat had gone too dry. He was married? She felt dazed and couldn't seem to make sense of her jumbled thoughts. "What…why…why didn't you tell me?"

He continued to simply stare at her, not saying a word, and she suddenly realized with each passing second his eyes were growing cool and his face impassive.

With a nonchalant shrug, he cleared his throat and replied, "If I'd told you, then you wouldn't have dated me. Right?"

Anger coursed through her veins at his insolence. "Of course, I wouldn't have dated you!" She yelled, suddenly finding the strength to raise her voice, yet Robert didn't even flinch. He just stared back at her, a slight, knowing smirk forming on his lips.

"Exactly."

A sick feeling formed in the pit of her stomach as Maxi stared up at him, and the realization that she didn't know this man at all washed over her like a cold chill. "How many times have you done this?" She wanted to know.

"Only a couple," he replied, shrugging again as if it were nothing. "I'm a man, honey, and I have needs. It doesn't hurt to fill those needs a bit while I'm out sacrificing for my country."

She couldn't believe what she was hearing. "While your wife sits at home and waits for you to come back?" Maxi spit out, utterly disgusted. She fought back tears when he didn't answer and struggled to control herself. "Did you even care for me at all?" She whispered, her lower lip trembling pathetically.

He looked at her, his eyes filled with pity, and in that moment, she realized she hated him. "I did care for you, Maxine," he smiled, as if that would take all the hurt away. "I never meant for you to become pregnant, but…well…I'm sorry. There's nothing I can do about it."

Maxi shook her head, unable to completely understand what was happening. All she knew was that she needed to leave immediately, before she made a worse fool of herself.

On trembling legs, she stood, lifted her chin, and said, "Goodbye,

Robert. I hope…I hope I never see you again."

She turned and walked away, hoping to make it around the corner without fainting. She hadn't realized she was crying until she felt the tears drip from her chin, and she angrily wiped them away. How could she have been so stupid? *I've turned out just like Mama,* she thought, shame and guilt filling her heart and threatening to suffocate her. All the fears and insecurities she'd wrestled with since childhood came flooding back with full force. What would happen now? What on earth was she going to do? And what would her aunt and uncle do when they found out? She'd be an outcast, the laughingstock of town. They'd surely kick her out, and she wouldn't blame them. She'd be all alone, with nowhere to go, and no one to turn to.

Maxi had been half walking, half stumbling, not paying attention to where she was going, but when she tripped and fell onto a mound of soft, warm sand, she realized she'd somehow gotten turned around and was on the beach instead of at the pier where Savannah was waiting. Turning her head swiftly to the side, she vomited violently, emptying every bit of substance from her stomach. Her head spun, her body shook all over, and she wondered if she'd die right then and there; a broken hearted, worthless tramp. Wiping her mouth, Maxi pulled her knees up to her chin and sobbed, wondering, with dread, what was going to happen to her.

Chapter Thirty

-1941-

After an hour or so of waiting, I finally found Maxi huddled on the beach, her eyes red and swollen. I could only guess what had happened with Robert, but I didn't ask. Instead, I helped her to her feet, and we walked back to the train in silence. Once on board, she leaned against my shoulder and in a small, shuddering voice told me what happened.

"What am I going to do?" She sobbed. "I can't bear to see the look of disgust and...and shame on Aunt Deb and Uncle Ray's faces, not after all they've done for me." She sat up straight and, clutching my arm painfully, plead with me not to tell them. "Give me some time to think first. Please?"

"It's not my news to share, Maxi," I assured her gently. "I won't say a word, I promise."

Once we arrived back home, Maxi was calmer and more composed. When Aunt Deb asked how she was feeling, she said she was very tired and wanted to go to bed. For the rest of the evening, I paced back and forth in my bedroom, anger at Robert eating away at me. How could he do such a thing, not only to Maxi, but to his wife? And what was this going to do to our family? Would our aunt and uncle stand up for Maxi, or send her away? Uncle Ray's job could possibly be put on the line, along with their reputation and position in the community. It could ruin them.

The next couple of days went by excruciatingly slow. Everyone heard what had happened to me and kept asking questions, but I couldn't seem to get my mind off of Maxi. She didn't go into work with me on Friday, and when I got home that evening our house was buzzing.

"Savannah, is that you?" Aunt Deb called from the living room, rushing through the house to meet me at the front door. "You're supposed to call us when you leave work so we can be on the lookout for you," she snapped, closing and locking the door behind me.

"I forgot, I'm sorry," I sighed, following her into the living room. "What's going on?" I asked hesitantly as I took off my hat and gloves.

Everyone, including Mrs. Emma and Leon, were there, all apparently waiting for me with concern in their eyes.

"This came for you today," said Aunt Deb, pointing to a vase full of wildflowers. "And this," she added, handing me a folded-up note, "was with them."

I opened the note, my stomach sinking as I read the rough, handwritten sentence before me: *You escaped me once, Margie. It won't happen again.*

"Did anyone see who delivered these?" I wanted to know, my heart thumping.

"No," Uncle Ray said. "None of us were home, and none of the neighbors saw anything."

"This man is stalking you, Savannah," Leon stated, hands on his hips.

"Did anyone call the police?" I asked, sinking down on the sofa next to Maxi. She reached out and took my hand, giving it a squeeze.

"Yes, but they said there's nothing they can do," Uncle Ray sighed. "They're the ones that questioned all of the neighbors, but since no one saw anything and the flowers are apparently hand-picked instead of store bought, their hands are tied."

"I think you should take some time off from work for a while," Aunt Deb said, her hands clenched in front of her stomach.

"What?" I cried.

"It's not safe for you to be out and about by yourself," she replied, her voice raising a bit.

"But Maxi is normally with me," I pointed out.

"What is Maxi going to do if a man really wanted to hurt or kidnap you? I think you need to stay home where it's safe until this man is caught."

I opened my mouth to argue, only to be interrupted by Mrs. Emma. "Perhaps there's another way," she said, and we all turned to look at her. "What if Savannah went away for a while."

"Go away?" I raised my brows. "Where?"

"Do you have family anywhere?"

"I have some distant relatives that live in Pembroke," Uncle Ray suggested.

"No, that's only an hour away," Mrs. Emma shook her head. "If this man really wants Savannah, a few miles won't stop him."

I shuddered at the thought, my eyes roaming back down to the note, and I wrapped my arms tightly around my waist.

"I may have an idea," Mrs. Emma said, "but give me a day or so to think it through and I'll let you know. In the meantime," she added, giving me a stern look, "you stay in for the weekend, okay?"

"I will," I nodded, wondering just what she had in mind.

That night, Maxi crept quietly into my room and sat on the edge of my bed, keeping her voice low as she said, "Vannie, if they find a place for you to go, will you take me with you?"

I sat up, peering at her through the darkness. "Why, Maxi?"

"Don't you see? It would be the perfect opportunity for me to get away from here without ever having to tell anyone about the baby."

"But, honey, they're trying to find family members for me to stay with," I said gently. "Don't you think they'd write to Aunt Deb and Uncle Ray and tell them once they found out you're pregnant?"

"Maybe I could convince them not to," she said, her voice pleading.

"And what about after you have the baby?"

"I...I don't know, maybe I could find someone to adopt it. All I know is I've got to get away from here." She started to cry then, and I couldn't help but console her.

"Alright," I sighed, pulling her into a hug. "I'll see what I can do."

Chapter Thirty-one

-1941-

Sunday after church the Danes' came over for lunch, and Mrs. Emma stated that she'd done some checking and wanted to tell us what she'd found out.

"I couldn't tell you Friday because Connor wasn't certain of his orders yet," she said, glancing at her eldest son who sat at the table across from me, "but it was just confirmed that he is being transferred to the base at Pearl Harbor for the next few months."

"In Hawaii?" We all gasped.

"Yes," Connor nodded, not looking particularly pleased about the news. "I was just informed that I'll be sent around the U.S. to teach new pilots everything they need to know about the B-17 planes, and Hawaii is my first post."

I glanced down at my hands, feeling a bit depressed at the news. There was no way of knowing how long Connor would be gone, and I would miss him.

"One of our old school friends, Barbara Swanson, is living in Honolulu," Mrs. Emma continued, turning to look at my aunt. "She and her husband run a boarding house out there. Do you remember her, Debra?"

"Of course," Aunt Deb nodded. "I'm a few years older than she is, but I do remember her. Her husband is from Hawaii, isn't he?"

"Yes," Mrs. Emma nodded. "They met when he was here one summer on furlough. Anyway, I sent her a wire yesterday morning asking if she would be interested in having Savannah come stay with her for a few months. There's a hospital there that I'm certain Savannah could work at to pay her way, and she replied last night that she would be delighted to have her."

We all sat in stunned silence, staring at Mrs. Emma as if she'd lost her mind.

"That is the most ridiculous thing I've ever heard," Aunt Deb finally cried.

"Where else is she going to go, Debra?" Mrs. Emma wanted to know, her voice calm.

"Surely there's somewhere closer…"

"I don't think it's such a bad idea," Uncle Ray interrupted, his usually quiet tone carrying a bit of strength.

"What?" Aunt Deb's mouth fell open. "You mean to tell me you want our niece to travel all the way to Hawaii by herself?"

"She wouldn't be alone, Mrs. Coleman," Connor spoke up. "I'm leaving next week and would be glad to escort her "

"By yourself?" Aunt Deb asked, cocking a brow at him.

"I could go along," Maxi piped in.

"It wouldn't be just us," Connor assured my aunt. "My commanding officer and his wife are going, as well, and said they wouldn't mind chaperoning."

"There really isn't any other alternative, Debra," Uncle Ray said gently. "If she stays here, she could get killed. She almost did, for Pete's sake."

"We could watch her…"

"There's no way we can keep an eye on her twenty-four hours a day, and if something happened to her I'd never forgive myself."

Her eyes filling with tears, Aunt Deb didn't reply, and Mrs. Emma turned to me and asked softly, "What do you want to do, Savannah?"

I hesitated, my eyes searching those around me. I didn't want to leave, and I certainly didn't want to go nearly 5,000 miles away from home. I also thought the whole idea a bit extreme, but before I voiced those thoughts, my gaze landed on Maxi, and the desperate look of pleading I saw in her eyes made me hesitate.

"I…I think I should go," I said, adding quickly, "but only if Maxi will go with me."

"Honey, we can't afford to send both of you," Uncle Ray stated gently.

"We both got some money when we graduated, didn't we, Vannie?" Maxi spoke up, her eyes hopeful. "I'm sure we could afford at least one ticket."

"Yes," I nodded, "I'm sure we could."

"That's not such a bad idea," Leon spoke up. "After all, who's to say the creep won't come after Maxine, as well?"

After much deliberation, it was finally decided; Maxi and I were going.

Saying our goodbyes were dreadfully hard. Aunt Deb cried the entire week up until we left, and even Uncle Ray had gotten a little misty eyed at the station. Mrs. Emma and Leon were both solemn faced, as well, at having to tell us all goodbye.

"Be safe, son," Mrs. Emma said, pulling Connor into a tight hug. "Come home soon."

"Look after my girls now, you hear?" Leon instructed, shaking Connor's hand. He then turned and kissed me on the cheek, whispering that he'd miss me. "I hope you can come home soon," he said warmly.

The train ride across the country was exciting, to say the least. Maxi and I kept our eyes glued to the windows, thrilled to watch the passing scenery as we roared through the diverse countryside. From flatlands and marsh to mountains and lakes, we drank it all in, each documenting what we saw in our diaries. Connor slept in a berth out in the corridor while Maxi and I shared an adjoining room with his commanding officer, Captain Marshall, and his wife, Victoria. The apartment was tiny and horribly cramped, but we didn't mind. Captain Marshall and "Vicki" were the sweetest couple, both in their mid-forties. They'd never had children of their own and were thrilled to accompany us to Hawaii.

"Maxi, do you want to go to the dining car with me?" I asked one evening. "I'm hungry for an early dinner."

"No, thanks," she shook her head, looking a bit tired.

I headed to the dining car alone and had just been seated when Connor helped himself to the chair across from me. He'd kept his distance the last few weeks, and I was a bit surprised, and pleased, to see him.

"Mind if I join you?" He asked, reaching for a menu.

"Do I have a choice?" I raised a brow playfully at him.

"Not really," he winked, glancing up to tell the waiter what he wanted to drink. "So," he said, turning back to me, "are you homesick yet?"

"Very much so," I nodded, "I didn't really want to leave in the first place."

"It's not every day you get to travel to one of the most exotic places in the world, you know."

"Correct me if I'm wrong, but you didn't seem overly excited about going either," I pointed out.

"You're right," he chuckled. "I hated to leave Mother again."

"And Grace, too, of course."

He glanced at me in surprise, but before he could reply the waiter arrived with our drinks. After placing our orders, he took our menus and left, and I leaned back in my chair, glancing out of the window at the constant, changing flow of scenery. We were passing through Oklahoma, and I couldn't help but admire the rugged landscape that stretched out before me.

"I'm sure you were sad to leave my brother's side again so soon."

My brow furrowing, I quickly turned back to stare at Connor in confusion. "What do you mean?"

"It's been talked for years that you and Leon would get together one of these days," Connor replied with a shrug.

"Leon and I have always been friends, you know that," I stated.

Connor's eyes narrowed as he studied me. "You seemed very cozy that night at Leopold's, and again at the train station yesterday morning. If I were a bystander, I'd say you were a couple."

"Well, we're not," I sniffed, my ears burning. *Do Leon and I act too "cozy"?* I wondered to myself.

"You don't have to get upset about it," Connor chuckled. "Why don't you like the idea of courting my brother?"

"Because I'd have you for a brother in-law," I stated matter-of-factly.

"Oh, come on," he laughed, "tell the truth. Or is it simply because he's never asked you?"

"That's not the reason," I shook my head.

"What, then?"

I hesitated, giving it serious consideration. "I don't know," I shrugged. "I just never really thought of Leon in a romantic kind of way. He's one of my oldest and dearest friends. Besides," I added, "after everything that happened with Jake, I don't care to think about another relationship anytime soon…if ever."

Our food arrived then, and we were both momentarily distracted as we began to eat the delicious, hot meal. After a few bites, Connor reached for his glass of water and asked, "Did something else happen between you and Jake while you were in Atlanta?"

"Sort of," I nodded. We continued eating in silence, and once we finished, Connor asked if I'd like to go to the lounge. I agreed, and once we were seated on a comfortable settee, he leaned back against the cushions and asked if I'd tell him what happened, giving me his full attention.

Taking a deep breath, I poured out the whole story. I hadn't told anyone, not even Maxi, and surprisingly enough I found myself spilling out even the tiniest of details. I went through not only the incident with Jake and how it made me feel, but also everything that happened with Daddy. Connor studied me, totally silent, his silver gaze never missing a thing. Once I'd finished, I sank back and sighed, feeling both relieved to have finally talked about it and exhausted at the same time.

"Do you regret your decision about Jake?" He asked.

I immediately shook my head. "No."

"Then why are you so hesitant to get involved in another relationship?"

"I think…" I paused, considering my words. "I think it would be very hard for me to trust anyone again. It would definitely take a lot of time and patience."

"Any man can see you're worth all the time and patience in the world," Connor replied, catching me off guard. "As long as he stays on your good side, though, because that temper of yours can get a little testy," he quickly added with a wink, dodging my hand as I reached out to playfully swat at his arm.

"If only you brought out the best in me, you wouldn't know so much about my temper," I shot back, and we both laughed.

"On a more serious note," he said, his eyes growing somber, "I'm truly sorry about your father. I am glad, though, that you were able to spend some quality time with him before he died. It sounds like you really connected, and I know without a doubt that he loved you. I understand how much it hurts, though."

My eyes filled with tears, and I nodded, thanking him for his kind words. The clock on the wall chimed, alerting us to the late hour, and we agreed it was time to head to bed. Connor walked me to my cabin, and just before I opened my door, he said, "By the way, Grace is not my girlfriend. She's one of my officer's daughters, and I was asked to show her a good time. The night you saw us together was the first and last time I've seen her."

With those words, he said good night and walked away, leaving me to stare after him in surprise.

Chapter Thirty-two

-1941-

When we finally arrived in San Francisco, we boarded a ship and set sail for O'ahu. I experienced a bit of seasickness the first two days, but thoroughly enjoyed the remaining three with ping pong, shuffleboard, going to the movies, and nightly dances with the soldiers traveling with us. On the fifth day, when the captain announced we would soon arrive on the island, everyone anxiously gathered on deck to gaze out at the breathtaking scenery surrounding us. Crystal clear, aqua blue water stretched out around the Hawaiian island, with giant, graceful mountains dotting the background. As we drew closer and began sailing around the point, I noticed an odd, circular like mountain, and an attendant explained that it was called "Diamond Head" but was actually a volcanic tuff cone known as "Le'ahi" to the local Hawaiians.

We arrived at the port to crowds of happy, smiling people who anxiously waited to greet the ship's passengers. A band played in celebration of the new arrivals, their pleasant tunes drifting peacefully upon the breeze, and ladies wearing grass skirts threw brightly colored leis for everyone to drape around their necks. It was a sight to behold.

A car sent by Mrs. Emma's friend picked us up at the port, and after saying our goodbyes to Connor and the Marshall's, we climbed into the back of the car and pulled away, both Maxi and I keeping our noses pressed to the car windows as we drove. The car took us several miles out of the sleepy town of Honolulu and turned down a long, narrow dirt road. Large houses passed by sporadically on my right, their pale hues of greens and blues reminding me a bit of the beach cottages on Tybee Island. A pang of homesickness washed over me then, and I sighed. I missed my home and family so much and wondered if Aunt Deb was coping well or worrying herself sick over us.

We finally arrived at the boarding house, and as I climbed from the car, my eyes took in the beauty around me. A white, picket fence surrounded the property with wild, exotically colored flowers growing all around. The house itself was a huge, two story home with a Victorian style wrap-around porch and several white-washed rocking chairs that bumped back and forth in the breeze, as if occupied by ghosts.

The front door swung open, and a woman in her early forties rushed out onto the porch, a smile as large as the state of Texas on her freckled face. She was wearing a long, flowery dress with a half apron knotted at her thick waist, and her curly, slightly frizzy blonde hair was piled high atop her head with stray ringlets flying in every direction. She skipped down the porch steps and greeted us with such kindness and enthusiasm that I couldn't help but immediately like her.

"I'm Barbara," she said, pulling us both into a hug. "I can't begin to express how delighted I am to have you girls staying with us."

She grabbed our hands and pulled us inside, chattering the whole way as we followed the driver, who was struggling with our trunks, through the house and up the stairs.

"Put them in the second room on the right, Henry," she told him as he grunted along, the stairs groaning with each step. Turning back to us, she asked, "Would you like something to eat? I made some sandwiches and lemonade for your arrival in case you were hungry."

We gratefully accepted, both of us famished after the long morning, and after we'd eaten Barbara showed us to the room we would be sharing.

"I'm sure you'll want to unpack and rest, so please take all the time you'll need," Barbara smiled from the doorway. "Supper is at seven. Let me know if there is anything you need, alright?"

We nodded and thanked her for everything, and after she was gone, I glanced slowly around the room, taking in the two beds, a vanity, one closet, and a chest of drawers. The room was small, but thankfully we had a window to allow in a bit of fresh air. Pink and yellow flowered curtains fluttered in the breeze, and the realization that nearly every decoration I'd seen so far in the house consisted of some type of flower made me smile. I especially loved the Hibiscus, with its huge blooms of the most bright and vivid colors.

I began to unpack, losing myself in my thoughts as the time passed by. About an hour later, the door opened, and I blinked in surprise when Maxi entered, not having realized she'd left.

"The bathroom is down the hall to the left," she explained in a weary monotone as she closed the door behind her. Still struggling with morning sickness, she wore the mantle of exhaustion like a heavy cloak.

"I now understand and can sympathize with women who are pregnant and have to go to the bathroom every ten minutes," she sniffed as she dug through her bag for a handkerchief. "I not only feel like the baby is lying right on my bladder, I think it's kicking it, too."

Sneezing loudly, she blew her nose into a blue, lace trimmed hanky, and I walked over to rub her back. "Did you want me to go downstairs and ask Barbara for an Antihistamine?"

"I already did and she doesn't have any, but she said she'll call her husband at work and ask him to pick up something at the drugstore on his way home," she replied, her voice stuffy. The poor thing was apparently very allergic to something here. Her eyes were blood shot and watery, her nose red and swollen, and she couldn't seem to stop sneezing.

"Why don't you lie down for a while and rest?" I suggested. "I'll finish your unpacking for you."

Maxi hesitated, considering my proposal with a torn expression. She was so exhausted she could barely continue to stand, yet it was obvious she hated to leave the rest of her unpacking to me. Eventually, the aching in both her back and feet won out, and she nodded wearily. Stripping down to her slip, she kicked off her shoes and slid into the nearest bed while I busied myself with the rest of the unpacking, trying to keep as quiet as possible.

"Are we crazy for doing this?"

Maxi's sudden question startled me, and I turned to look at her, a pair of stockings dangling in my hand above the drawer I was about to place them in.

"I don't think we had much choice," I finally said.

"Would you have agreed to come if not for me?"

I hesitated, my mind considering her question. I knew the answer was "no" but couldn't be certain whether or not I would have eventually changed my mind.

"I didn't want to come," I finally admitted, "but I was also afraid to stay. Everyone, except Aunt Deb, was so set on my leaving town that I probably would have given in eventually."

Maxi nibbled on her lower lip, her eyes worried. "What if they find out...about my situation?"

"You mean Barbara and the people here?"

When Maxi nodded, I said, "There's really no avoiding it, Maxi. We can try and cover it up for as long as possible, but even if we hide it to the very end, they'll find out when it's time to have the baby."

"Maybe by then we could convince Barbara not to tell our family back home?" Maxi asked hopefully.

"Maybe," I shrugged. "But what about Connor? He's here, too, you know."

"Connor doesn't have to find out, Vannie," Maxi cried, her eyes blazing as she sat up in bed. "Promise me you won't tell him."

"I won't, I won't," I assured her, taken aback by her sudden show of passion. "We'll do our best to keep him from finding out, and maybe Barbara will even help you find a family for the baby. She seems like a very kind-hearted person."

A smile of relief replaced the frown and spread slowly across Maxi's face as she sank back down against the pillows, her eyes suddenly bright with tears. "You're always so good to me, sweet Savannah," she said softly. "Whatever would I do without you?"

"You'd be miserable," I winked, and we both laughed. Stepping around my large trunk, I walked to where my cousin lay, bent over, and placed a soft kiss of her forehead. "Get some rest now, alright? You need it."

Pulling the covers up to her chin, Maxi nodded and closed her eyes. "Good night," she yawned, and I watched as her face gradually relaxed into blissful sleep, her golden curls fanning out around her face like a halo.

As I continued to unpack, Maxi's words kept running over and over in my mind. I understood her concerns, and although I'd tried to remain positive, I was also worried that Maxi's secret would be found out too soon and by too many people. Carrying a baby wasn't something one could hide very well, especially in the later stages. If we got a job at the hospital in Honolulu, they wouldn't allow Maxi to continue working if they found out, and although I really felt that Barbara was very warm and kind hearted, I wasn't certain if she and her husband would let us continue to stay, either. We'd quite possibly be forced to go home, and as dead set as Maxi was against anyone back home finding out, I could only hope that didn't happen.

Chapter Thirty-three

Savannah, GA - October 1941

Cheryl Banks walked slowly up the stairs to her bedroom, trying not to spill the cup of hot tea she carried. The steps creaked noisily, echoing loudly throughout the massive old Victorian home. It was nearly midnight, and she couldn't sleep. Her husband, one of Savannah's wealthiest lawyers, was away on business and she found herself wishing she'd gone to stay with her sister tonight. After the death of that Miller girl, she'd been on pins and needles ever since.

She'd just reached the second floor when a shadow suddenly moved down the hall, and she stopped, her hand clutching the banister as her heart began to pound. Two small, beady eyes peered at her through the darkness, a low growl coming from the back of its throat as the shadow crept stealthily towards her.

With a sigh of relief, Cheryl shook her head and laughed. "Oh, stop it, Cocoa," she scolded the cat, reaching down to run her fingers down its silky back. "You scared me half to death!"

Without a thought, Cheryl tipped the cup a bit too far, screeching in pain when the hot tea splashed on her hand and went all over the floor. Its ears twitching and tail swishing, the cat skittered off down the hallway with a howl.

"Oh, dear," Cheryl murmured as she surveyed the mess she'd made. Turning, she hurried back down the stairs in search of a mop.

The house was dark, with only a few small table lamps lit here and there. Cheryl's shadow bounced all along the walls as she made her way to the laundry room, her house slippers making a soft swooshing sound as she walked.

She'd just turned the corner, the laundry room door in sight, when something made her pause. A strange, low sound met her ears, and she tilted her head, listening intently. It was a deep, melodic rumble, like that of a man humming a tune under his breath. And then, she heard footsteps.

Clip clop, clip clop. They echoed softly against the hardwood floors.

"William?" Cheryl called, wondering perhaps her husband decided to come home and surprise her. When she received no reply, her hand began to tremble. Backing up against the wall, her eyes flitted nervously over every part of the room and back again, coming up empty. The footsteps stopped, and she stood silently, waiting. Was someone in the house, or were her nerves simply getting the best of her?

After what seemed like hours, Cheryl finally breathed a sigh of relief and moved away from the wall. It must have been the cat again. Shaking her head, she hurried into the laundry room, grabbed a mop, and stepped back out again. Her foot landed on something soft, and with a scream, the cat jerked its tail and swatted angrily at her leg. Gasping, Cheryl jumped back, the mop bouncing against the floor as it slipped from her hand and she fought to maintain her balance. Her foot slipped across the slick surface of the mop handle, and she tumbled to the ground, striking her head against a nearby table.

She lay on the floor, trying unsuccessfully to blink the stars out of her eyes. The ceiling swam murkily above, and the pain in her head was almost more than she could bear.

Suddenly, from the corner of her eye, a shadow moved. It crept closer and closer, until it loomed like a ghost over her. Her breath catching, Cheryl struggled to cry out, but all that slipped past her lips was a small moan.

The shadow squatted down at her side and, with gloved hands, reached out to touch her face. In a low voice, the man breathed, "Hello, Margie."

Chapter Thirty-four

-October 1941-

We'd been in Hawaii for two months, and things couldn't be going better. With Barbara's help, we'd managed to secure jobs at the hospital in Honolulu. The environment was relaxed and fun, and everyone we worked with was kind, friendly, and very welcoming.

After buying a car, Connor began to come over on Saturday nights to eat supper with us. He, Maxi, and I went sightseeing a couple of times, and he even took us on base once to show us around. There were tennis courts, picnics, swimming at the beach, and dancing every Saturday night. The whole island was so beautiful and relaxed.

Maxi and I made several new friends, but chose to keep mainly to ourselves, preferring not to go out very often on the weekends. The party scene could get a little too wild for our taste, and the fact that Maxi wasn't herself made it difficult to enjoy very many outings. I kept an eye on her, noticing how distant she kept herself from the men who tried to pay her any attention. She was, thankfully, over the morning sickness, and her allergies had adjusted to the surroundings, but she still cried in her sleep sometimes at night, and I knew her heart was broken over Robert.

The boarding house rested about twenty minutes from the hospital, so we bought a couple of bicycles and rode to work every day. The exercise was a bit of a strain at first; I hadn't been able to stand up straight for the first week, and although Maxi was pregnant, she had actually begun to lose weight. Once our bodies adjusted, however, we began to enjoy the scenic, invigorating ride down the two lane, country road. We worked Monday-Friday from 8:00 a.m. to 5:00 p.m., coming home in the afternoons to help Barbara with the cooking, sewing, and cleaning, and attended church with the Swanson's on Sundays. Life had fallen into an easy rhythm, and I was growing to enjoy it. I'd become quite fond of Hawaii, with its graceful mountains and white, sandy beaches, and I simply adored the Swanson's.

It was a Saturday evening, and I was in the kitchen helping Barbara slice tomatoes for supper when Maxi burst into the kitchen, waving a letter above her head like the white flag of surrender.

"Savannah, look what came in the mail!" She cried with excitement, her eyes sparkling in a way I hadn't seen in weeks.

"Good heavens, Maxi, what on earth are you carrying on so about?" I huffed, wiping my hands on my apron.

"Leon sent us both a letter, and you have another from someone else, but I didn't see who from," Maxi gushed as she shoved two of the letters into my hand before exiting the room as quickly as she'd entered.

Shaking my head, I glanced at the second letter, my eyes widening when I saw Jake's name at the top. Why would he be sending me a letter? Deciding to read it later, I shoved it into my apron pocket, opting to read Leon's letter instead:

Dearest Savannah Banana,

To say I miss you would be an understatement. I hope you are doing well and adjusting to life in Hawaii...as long as you don't get TOO adjusted (wink). I don't know whether or not your aunt and uncle have told you, but there's been another murder. A woman's body was found inside her home yesterday, with a nasty blow to the back of her head. The newspapers, though, stated that the actual cause of death was strangulation. One of the neighbors noticed a pale green sedan parked down the road the night before, so the police are taking that as a lead and are searching for it as we speak. Although you're sorely missed, I'm glad you're out of harm's way. I only hope they catch this man before someone else gets killed.

He went on to speak of his job, his mother, and just life in general, but all I could think of was that poor, helpless young woman whose life had been ended far too soon. It made me sick to my stomach.

"Leon is Connor's younger brother?" Barbara asked, eyeing me as I folded the letter and put it in my apron pocket.

"Yes, he is."

"Is he doing well?"

"He's doing just fine," I sighed, proceeding to tell her of his news.

"Oh, my," she gasped. "How tragic!"

"Yes, it is," I nodded, scraping the chopped tomatoes into a nearby bowl.

"I'm sure they'll catch this man any day now," she said, reaching out to touch my arm.

"I hope so," I sighed, wondering why it was taking so long. How many more women would have to die before this man was put behind bars? Perhaps now that the police had a more definite led, they would be able to track him down.

Later, Maxi and I hurried to set the huge dining room table, making a place for everyone. Besides us two girls and the Swanson's, there were three other guests living at the boarding house, as well, so meals were always filled with noise and lively discussion.

"Please don't place me next to Mr. Hanks," Maxi whispered. "He gives me the heebie jeebies."

I snickered as I sat out the plates. "He's a foot doctor, Maxi, he can't help it if he's...well...different."

"But his work is all he talks about, and no one wants to hear about toe fungus and heel spurs. It makes me sick to my stomach!" Maxi exclaimed, her eyes wide and so full of disgust that I couldn't help but burst into laughter.

"What's all the commotion about?" A deep voice rumbled from the foyer.

I would recognize that voice anywhere and turned to smile over my shoulder at Connor as he walked into the room and leaned causally against the doorframe, looking quite handsome in his uniform.

"Maxi is afraid that Doctor Hanks will catch sight of her cute little feet, fall madly in love, and insist on marrying her," I grinned at Connor as I reached into the sideboard for the silverware.

"Savannah Adair, hush before someone hears you!" Maxi hissed, her cheeks turning red.

Connor laughed and walked over to wrap an arm around her shoulders. "Don't worry, Maxine, I'll make sure he doesn't sit by you."

"Tell Connor about the letters we received today, Vannie," Maxi said a moment later as she brought glasses brimming with lemonade in from the kitchen.

Maxi hadn't mentioned anything about the murder to me, so I assumed Leon hadn't told her, and I didn't want to concern her. Pasting on a smile, I said, "We both got letters from Leon, but I suppose you got one, too?"

"I did," he nodded. "I also got one from Mother, and she asked me to give you two her regards."

"Who was your other letter from?" Maxi asked as she busied herself with the napkins.

Attempting to keep a neutral face, I said nonchalantly, "It was from Jake."

Both Maxi and Connor looked at me in surprise.

"What did he want?" Connor asked, his tone cool.

"I don't know, I haven't read it yet," I shrugged.

In a matter of minutes, the dining room was filled with chatter and the scraping of chairs as everyone took their seats. Thomas, Barbara's husband, sat at the head of the table, and his brother, Mike, sat on his right. Mike was a Captain in the Navy and was stationed at Pearl Harbor, and his stiff posture and stern, brown eyes always made me feel uncomfortable, as if I were back in school and he was my schoolmaster. It was no surprise that he'd never gotten married.

The conversation soon turned to the war, a usual occurrence when both Mike and Connor were in the same room together. The other women continued to talk amongst themselves, ignoring the men, but I listened on with interest.

"I don't know how much more England can take," Connor was saying in a heavy tone. "Churchill is determined not to surrender and is doing everything he can to hold on, but it seems that Hitler is relentless and gaining more ground every day."

"If Roosevelt hadn't signed the Lend Lease agreement, things would be much worse for them," Mike agreed in his deep, raspy voice. "I don't think we can remain neutral for much longer."

"And what about the Japs?" Thomas piped in over a spoonful of stew. "They're not being as peaceful as Roosevelt would like. Word is, they've had several negotiations this year, but can't come to an agreement. I have a feeling that things are only going to get worse."

Mike, in a very uncharacteristic show of bad manners, rested his elbows on the table and leaned forward, his eyes serious. "Remember when, back in August, Roosevelt warned Japan that we were prepared to take steps against them if they attack any "neighboring countries"? Everyone thought Japan would back off, but there are now rumors that they're planning an attack, maybe somewhere in the Philippines, but I personally think they'll attempt to attack America directly somehow."

"Surely they wouldn't be foolish enough to attack America!" Dr. Hanks exclaimed in a shocked voice, his eyes wide.

"Why wouldn't they?" I suddenly said, joining in the conversation without thinking. "We cut off their oil supply three months ago, we can't seem to negotiate with them, and we're supporting China, with whom they're at war. I'm of the same opinion as Captain Pinckney; war with Japan seems imminent."

The men stared at me for a moment, speechless, some with surprise on their faces, others with distaste. Connor simply looked on with a slight smile of admiration, not shocked in the least at my frankness.

Maxi, sensing the sudden change in the atmosphere, turned her attention to us and, taking note of the men's expressions, cleared her throat nervously and asked, "Why-why don't we all talk about something else? Discussing the war always puts such a damper on the mood."

Dr. Hanks pulled his gaze away from my face and looked apologetically across the table at Maxi. "I'm sorry, Ms. Coleman, we shouldn't have discussed something of such negative nature around the more delicate sex. Women shouldn't have to worry about such things." He then leaned forward a bit, his eyes suddenly sparking with interest as he regarded her with open admiration. "They should worry about other things, like getting married, raising children, and cooking for their husbands. Don't you agree, Ms. Coleman?"

Maxi's face flamed red, and I cleared my throat in irritation. "That is not all a woman is good for, Mr. Hanks," I stepped in, frowning at him.

"Oh...well...of course...you're absolutely right, Ms. Adair," he stuttered, clearing his throat.

"Yes, you are absolutely right, Savannah Rose," Connor interrupted, his eyes sparkling as he regarded me from across the table. "That is most certainly not all a woman is good for."

When Connor ended his words with a wink, my eyes widened and I kicked him, hard, underneath the table. I could feel my cheeks turning red but felt a twinge of satisfaction when my foot connected with his shin and a look of pain flashed across his face.

"I was only kidding," he laughed, reaching under the table to massage his leg.

The air around the table had grown thick, but the tension was soon broken when Barbara pushed away from the table and announced it was time for dessert.

I stood to help clear away the dirty dishes but was waylaid when Connor grabbed my hand and pulled me towards the front door. "I don't want dessert," he said. "Let's go for a drive instead."

I pulled free and crossed my arms, still annoyed with him. "No, thank you," I said coolly.

"I'll go with you, Connor."

I glanced over my shoulder at Betty, the young journalist from Maui who also lived at the boarding house. Several people had mentioned that she and I favored, with our dark hair and eyes, but that's where the resemblance ended. Betty's face was more round and flat and her eyes a bit slanted, features carried down from her Polynesian ancestors. Her hair was longer, and she was very pretty, and I suspected she had a crush on Connor.

With a smile pulling at his lips, Connor nodded and said, "Sure, Betty, come on."

As Betty rushed upstairs to grab a sweater, Connor looked at me and sighed, shaking his head with a tsk tsk. "I'm afraid you're going to end up old and lonely one of these days, Savannah Rose," he said, his eyes crinkling at the edges.

"How I end up in my old age has nothing to do with you, so please don't concern yourself," was my reply as I breezed past him and began to help Barbara clear the table.

Connor laughed, taking Betty by the arm when she arrived back with her sweater, and the two waved goodbye as they breezed from the room. Watching them go, I found myself fighting the urge to throw the dish I held at the door. Connor could irritate me faster than anyone else, and he knew it, always taking full advantage of that fact. I never could seem to get the best of him. Sometimes he made me so angry I could wring his neck, yet on other occasions he would make me laugh or say something so kind that I would wonder if I truly knew him at all.

With a sigh, I went into the kitchen and helped Barbara slice the chocolate cake she'd baked earlier that afternoon, pushing thoughts of Connor out of my head.

That night, after everyone was asleep, I opened my letter from Jake. It read:

Dear Savannah,

I'm writing to let you know that I've decided to go to England after all and offer my services as a physician. I know you probably don't care, but I wanted you to know anyway. I tried calling, but your aunt told me about your situation, so I only hope this letter reaches you. I'm sorry that you had to leave your home again, and I hope the police catch this

man so you can return soon. I may never see you again, Savannah, I may never even return home, and I won't be writing to you again, so this is the last time you'll ever hear from me. That being said, I didn't want to leave things between us as they were the night your father died. It's over for good between Pamela and me, I ended it after you left. I love you, I always will, and I'm sorry things turned out the way they did between us. I can't blame you for making the decision to end it once and for all, but I only hope one day you'll come to forgive me. Have a wonderful life, Savannah, I wish you the very best.
Sincerely, Jake

I folded the letter, put it back in its envelope, and after a moment of consideration, finally threw it in the trash. I would pray for his safety, and even think of him from time to time, but I couldn't begin another correspondence with him. I'd made up my mind not to go down that road again and was determined to stick with it.

Chapter Thirty-five

-1965-

The nurse wheeled me out of the hospital, stopping at the entrance while my husband hurried to get the car. I took a deep breath, closing my eyes as a slight breeze stirred through the air. I felt like a bird out of prison, like I wanted to leap from the chair and run through an open field in my bare feet.

I was doing so much better that I was allowed to go home. The doctor cautioned me to take it easy as I "wasn't out of the woods yet", but I couldn't help wondering if Reverend Burton's prayers had worked, and I could only hope I was on the path to recovery. I couldn't have any more tests or scans done right now, but in a couple of weeks I was to come back in to see how the treatment was doing. I prayed the cancer would be gone.

My husband pulled the car around and hurried to my side to carry me to the passenger seat, but I held up my hand and said, "No, I think I can walk. Just take my hand and help me."

He gripped both my hand and elbow, gently escorting me to the car. My legs were weak and trembling and hardly able to hold me up, but it felt wonderful to be able to walk again.

Once we were on the road, I asked about Abby. "Have you heard from her?"

"She called the hospital a couple of days ago and asked about you," he nodded. "She wants you to call her as soon as you can. She and Hannah have been very worried about you."

"I'm so glad to be going home," I smiled, rolling down the window to enjoy the cool, autumn air.

"I'm glad, too, honey," he said warmly, reaching out to take my hand.

Once we were home, my husband helped settle me in bed, and I immediately called Abby from the phone on our bedside table.

"I'm delighted to hear your voice, Savannah, we've been so worried," Abby declared over the phone.

"How are you doing?" I wanted to know.

Abby hesitated, and then said she was doing better. "I'm getting stronger, but I'm ready for these treatments to be over."

"Me, too. The doctor is hoping I can stop with mine in a couple of weeks, so we'll just have to wait and see," I sighed.

"I won't know for another month," Abby groaned. "Since I was so sick, they had to stop with my treatments and then start back, so who knows how much longer I'll have to wait."

"I'm sorry, Abby," I said, wishing we could both receive a clean bill of health and get back to living normal lives.

"How are you going to see about yourself for the next few days?" Abby asked. "Is your husband going to take off of work and stay with you?"

"No," I shook my head, although she couldn't see me. "My aunt is going to come stay with me, the sweet dear. She hasn't been feeling well the last week or so, I think it's her arthritis."

"Why don't Hannah and I come stay with you, as well, during the day so she won't have to do quite so much?" Abby suggested.

"Oh, no, I couldn't ask you to do that," I declared. "You're sick, too, you know!"

"I'm doing better than you are at the moment, and whatever your aunt and I can't do, Hannah can. She's a good little nurse, and she would love to see you."

"I don't know…"

"Please, Savannah," Abby interrupted, her tone pleading. "You and your husband have done so much for Hannah and me, please let us do something for you."

I finally agreed, and we hung up. I'll admit I missed them, too, and knew my aunt would secretly be glad for the extra help.

Chapter Thirty-six

-1941-

Two weeks later, on a Friday afternoon, I sat at the hospital's front desk doing paperwork, my eyes drifting to the clock every few minutes. It had been a slow day, with only a few nurses on staff, and I was ready to go home for the weekend.

The double front doors swung open suddenly, illuminating the foyer with a stream of light as a tall, young man sauntered through, the sun casting an ethereal glow about him.

"Well, hello there, gorgeous," he leaned against the desk, grinning down at me with twinkling black eyes. His hair was every bit as dark, and I immediately knew he was a native Hawaiian. With his tan skin and broad shoulders, he was one of the most handsome men I'd ever seen, and he knew it.

"Hello," I smiled politely, keeping my tone professional. "What can I do for you?"

"I'm sure there's a lot you could do for me," he winked. When I simply raised a brow and stared silently back at him, offering no reply to his comment, he cleared his throat and said, "I cut my hand, and the Captain said I needed to get it stitched up." He held up his hand as evidence, blood stains already seeping through the ripped rag he'd tied around it.

I reached into the filing drawer by my desk, pulled out a piece of blank paperwork, and, pen poised midair, asked, "Can you give me some information about yourself first? Starting with your name."

"Yes, ma'am," he nodded. "My name is Kanani Kealoha, I'm a freelance electrician, twenty-five years old, single, and looking for a date. You got plans tomorrow night? There's going to be a dance down at the beach, and I'd love to have a gorgeous dame like you on my arm."

I blinked, raising my eyebrows slightly. This one certainly moved fast. If any man had the right to be arrogant and self-assured, this one did, but Kanani (pronounced Kah-NAH-nee) was a bit over the top.

Clearing my throat, I stood to my feet and motioned for him to follow me. "Let's get that hand seen about first, alright?"

Leading him through a set of double doors, I spotted SuAnne, one of the nurses on staff, and asked, "Hey, Su, can you take care of this fellow's hand? He's got a bad gash." I glanced around, noting that the other two nurses on staff, one of which was Maxi, were still assisting the doctor with a kidney stone surgery.

"Sorry, honey," SuAnne said in her thick, New York accent, "but I just did my nails. See?" She wiggled her fresh, bright red nails as evidence. Eyeing Kanani with interest, she popped her gum and added, "But if he can wait a few minutes, I'll take care of him."

"Never mind," I waved a hand, pushing Kanani into the room on our left, "I'll do it."

"Sit there, please," I pointed to a chair against the wall. He complied without a sound, and I pointed to his hand. "May I take a look?"

He pushed his hand into mine and I gently removed the bloody towel, wincing at the deep cut just above his wrist. "This is going to need stitches," I said, holding his hand closer as I examined it. "How long has it been since you've had a Tetanus shot?"

"About three years," he replied.

"Good, you won't need another one then." I moved to the cabinets above the small counter in the corner and removed the supplies I needed, then quickly washed my hands in the sink. Pulling up another chair, I sat in front of him and laid his large, roughened hand in my lap. "How did you cut it so badly?" I asked while I cleaned and began to stitch up the cut.

"I've been doing some work for the Army and caught my hand on a wire," he said, watching my actions closely. "Sliced my hand wide open."

I grimaced. "Good thing it wasn't your wrist," I muttered. He leaned a bit closer, and I got the feeling he was sniffing my hair.

"I never got your name, you know," he stated matter-of-factly.

"You never asked," I smiled, glancing up at him. "It's Savannah. Savannah Adair."

"Hmm, that's pretty," he said, and I thought I heard a smile in his voice. "You don't look like a Malihini, but you have an accent. Where are you from?"

"Savannah, Georgia," I replied, recognizing the familiar Hawaiian word, which meant "Caucasian".

"Wow, you're a long way from home," he exclaimed in surprise. "You know Lieutenant Connor Danes?"

I nodded. "I certainly do." Unfortunately. I'd only seen Connor once since our "disagreement" two weeks ago, and I couldn't help but wonder where he'd been.

"Yeah, me too," he grunted, and I got the feeling he didn't care much for Lieutenant Danes.

I finished the stitches, cut and tied the thread, and proceeded to bandage up his hand. "Alright, there you go," I said once I was through, gently patting him on the knee. "If your hand begins swelling or you get a fever and start vomiting, come back in immediately. You don't want it to get infected." I stood and began to clean up. "Otherwise, come back in two weeks so we can cut those stitches out and make sure your hand is healing properly."

"Yes, ma'am," he saluted. He stood and moved to the door, then hesitated as he began twisting his hat uncertainly in his hands. "Are you sure you won't go to the dance with me tomorrow night? The Lieutenant will be there, you know, and most of the nurses, too, so it won't be a lot of strangers or anything."

SuAnne and a few of the other girls had mentioned the dance before, but I hadn't planned on going. When Kanani mentioned Connor, however, his last words immediately came to mind, "You're going to end up old and lonely one of these days, Savannah Rose" and I paused, reconsidering. Would it be childish of me to go out with this man, this stranger, just to prove a point?

Kanani watched me expectantly, and after a moment of hesitation, I finally gave in and said, "Alright, I'll go." I gave him my address, hoping I wouldn't regret the decision.

A grin slowly began to spread across Kanani's face, and I couldn't help but smile back. The man was incorrigible. "Pick you up at eight," he winked and sauntered out, whistling a tune.

Chapter Thirty-seven

Savannah, Georgia 1941

He jerked the paint sprayer from the cabinet and, after filling it with orange auto paint, plugged it in, the nerve by his eye twitching continuously. He'd made a mistake this time, and only hoped no one would be able to connect that green car to him once it was painted. He couldn't believe he'd been stupid enough to park on her street, a fact that upset him so badly he'd come home after the newspaper article was released and angrily ransacked his entire house, trying to blow off steam. Once he finished smashing glass, putting his fist through the wall, and overturning tables, he'd decided he would have to lay low for a while. Perhaps even stop killing altogether.

"*You ain't worth spit on the sidewalk*," his mother's words crept into his mind. "*Why'd you have to be born? You're worthless, completely worthless and stupid.*"

He could feel the anger building in his chest, and with one smooth motion he sat the sprayer down, picked up a nearby rake, and broke it against the side of a tree, relishing the sound of cracking, splintering wood.

"I made one small mistake," he muttered, breathing heavily as he paced back and forth. "But they won't catch me. They won't."

His mother's disgusted, sneering face flashed before his eyes, and he angrily shook his head, trying to erase the painful, childhood memories. She'd always hated him, never once trying to disguise her feelings.

"First Mother, then Margie," he groaned, closing his eyes. "Why did you leave me, Margie?"

He sank to the ground, sobbing like a small child as his mind swirled like a merry-go-round. Flashes of memory flitted in and out, pictures of better times when he and Margie were together and happy. She'd loved him, she said so. He'd loved her, too.

But then she left, and now he couldn't remember why. He'd followed her, and then…then he…

His eyes popped open, and he stood to his feet, the tears gone. He walked back to the paint sprayer, picked it up, and got back to work.

Margie wasn't dead, she was just gone for a while. But she'd be back, and that would be the last time he killed her.

1941 – Hawaii

The next evening, I met Kanani at the door, wearing a knee length, dark purple dress with a black sash.

"Wow," Kanani whistled. "I'm speechless."

"I doubt that," I laughed as I followed him down the front porch steps to his 1932 blue Coupe. I glanced back at the house and, spotting Maxi watching from the upstairs window, smiled and waved goodbye. I'd tried to talk her into coming with us, but she'd politely refused, stating that she was tired and wanted to rest.

Kanani and I arrived on Waikiki beach fifteen minutes later, music streaming loudly from the large Tiki hut as we stepped from the car. The sun had already gone down, but I could hear the waves crashing against the shore as I breathed in the familiar scent of salt and sand, the gentle breeze tousling my hair.

"Are you coming?" Kanani asked with a smile.

We walked toward the hut, which was lit up by torches on the outside, their golden flames dancing in the wind like sparkling little stars in the night sky. The beach was crowded with couples, and we had to push our way inside, where the interior was filled with palm trees, tribal masks on the walls, and dancing hula girls wearing lei's and grass skirts. A sea of uniforms and brightly colored dresses clashed against the rustic setting, and the click of heels on the rough, wooden floor sounded like the beating of drums as couples danced to the lively tunes.

I spotted SuAnne and some of the other girls with their dates sitting across the room, and grabbed Kanani's arm, leading him to their table.

"Hon, you look like a million bucks!" SuAnne smiled, pulling me into a quick hug. Her bright red lipstick perfectly matched her red, sleeveless dress and high heels.

"So do you," I replied, thinking that she looked exactly like the actress, Rita Hayworth.

Time passed quickly, with a lot of chit-chat, laughter, and dancing, yet I couldn't count the times my eyes wandered across the room in search of a certain Lieutenant, only to come up empty.

Kanani turned out to be a great date, always making everyone laugh with his outrageous tales and fun-loving personality. We'd danced countless times, and I was finally beginning to get tired when he asked for yet another dance.

"This is the last one," I laughed as he pulled me into his arms, "I'm exhausted."

"Party pooper," he teased, his black eyes twinkling.

The music was slow, and when Kanani pulled me closer, I glanced over his shoulder, my gaze colliding with Connor's. He stood across the room against the wall, watching us with a closed expression.

"So, do you have someone waiting for you back home?" Kanani asked, his voice soft against my ear.

"No," I shook my head, unable to see Connor anymore as Kanani twirled me around.

"That's good to know."

I shifted uncomfortably when Kanani began to rub circles on my back, and I tried to put some space between us. He'd apparently gotten the wrong idea, and my cheeks flushed with embarrassment.

"You know," I said, pulling back a bit, "I think I'll join Su at the table. My feet hurt, and…"

"I'd like to cut in," a sharp, deep voice interrupted.

Kanani stopped so abruptly that I stumbled in surprise, and he gripped me tightly around the waist to steady me.

"I'm sorry, Danes, but she's with me," he replied coolly, pulling me against his side possessively. "Find yourself another girl."

"I just did," Connor stated, his jaw clenching and unclenching. "Now move aside, Kealoha."

I stared wide eyed as the two men sized each other up. Kanani was a good four inches shorter than Connor, but his shoulders were every bit as wide, and he didn't seem too willing to back down.

Couples twirled all around us, oblivious to the tension between the two men. A fight was brewing, I could feel it, and that was the last thing I wanted.

Or was it? Wasn't this why I'd come tonight? To prove to Connor that I could have a beau if I wanted one? Somehow, though, I hadn't expected it to turn out quite like this. I hadn't any idea Connor would actually confront Kanani.

"Um, Connor," I cleared my throat, "I came here with Kanani tonight, so if you don't mind...?"

"Actually, I do mind, Savannah Rose," he turned his hard stare on me, and I nearly shrunk to the floor. He reached out and took me by the arm, pulling me away from Kanani. "You're my responsibility, and you're coming with me. You don't have any business being here with him."

My eyes widened, and Kanani moved to step between us. "What exactly do you mean by that, Danes?"

"Kanani, please..." I rested my hand on his arm, my voice pleading.

"And what do you mean," Kanani continued, "by saying she's your responsibility?"

"Her aunt and uncle entrusted her to my care."

My mouth dropped open. "I don't exactly remember them doing that," I spoke up, taking a step forward. I could feel my temper rising and fought to keep myself under control. Connor, however, was treating me like a child, and I had no intention of letting him get away with it. "I came here tonight with Kanani, and I'll leave with Kanani," I stated, my eyes steely as I glared up at Connor, "and I would appreciate it, Mister Danes, if you minded your own business."

His jaw clenched, Connor released my arm and made a show of bowing at the waist before he stalked away.

"The nerve of that man," I muttered under my breath, watching him go. Turning back to Kanani, I apologized profusely and said, "I think I'd like to rest for a bit, if you don't mind?"

Kanani nodded, muttering that he would join me in a bit, and I pushed my way through the crowd, embarrassment flushing my cheeks over what he must think.

I was halfway back to the table when I saw Connor talking to SuAnne. Sighing, I turned quickly to the right and stepped outside for a breath of fresh air, the cool breeze soothing my hot face.

I walked a bit further, stopping to take my shoes off so I could sink my toes into the soft sand. I wasn't paying attention and didn't realize I was getting further and further from the crowd. My thoughts were still on Connor and Kanani, and I jerked in surprise when a large hand reached through the shadows and grabbed my arm.

"Hey, honey, want some company?"

The words were slurred, and I peered through the darkness into the face of a stranger. He was quite large, with red rimmed black eyes, a protruding stomach, and stubbly, five o'clock shadow. He'd apparently been following me, and I'd been too caught up in my thoughts to notice.

"N-no, thank you," I shook my head, trepidation creeping up my spine as I tried to squirm away, but his grip was too strong.

"Oh, come on," he chuckled, a leer on his face as he grabbed my other arm and pulled me closer. "I only want to have a little fun."

"Let me go," I cried. His breath smelled so strongly of alcohol that I gagged, and by the look in his eyes, I knew he had no intentions of letting me go.

With a laugh, he licked his lips, and I jerked my gaze toward the twinkling lights of the Tiki hut, my heart pounding. I knew there wasn't any point in screaming, as no one would hear me over the music. All I could think was that Connor was right; I didn't have any business being here. Why hadn't I stayed at the boarding house with Maxi?

The man yanked me against his chest and leaned in for a kiss, his hot lips grazing my cheek as I quickly turned my face away. Panicking, I kicked him as hard as I could in the shin and he cursed loudly, his hold on my arms loosening a bit. Grasping the opportunity, I tried to slip out of his reach and jump away, only to catch my foot and trip in the soft sand. His hand slithered out through the darkness and grabbed me painfully by the arm, and we tumbled to the ground in a heap.

I felt his fingers grappling at the buttons on my dress, his other hand reaching to grasp painfully at my thigh. Suddenly, through a haze of fear and panic, I heard a voice calling my name.

"Savannah Rose?"

"Connor!" I screamed, my arms flailing as I fought against the man.

Within seconds, Connor was there. He grabbed the man and flung him across the sand like a sack of flour, and I scurried to my feet, my entire body trembling violently as I watched the man push himself up. Connor reared back and hit him across the nose with a resounding smack, and the stranger slumped to the ground, unconscious.

Connor hurried to my side, his touch gentle as he peered at me through the darkness. "Are you alright?" he asked in concern.

Fighting against tears, I couldn't answer just yet. Instead, I kept my head down and nodded.

"Come here," he said, pulling me gently into his arms. He rocked me back and forth, softly rubbing comforting circles on my back.

After a moment, I whispered, "I'd like to leave now."

"I'll get Kealoha," Connor said, his voice tight as he pulled back.

"No, wait," I said, placing a hand on his arm to stop him. "I don't want to be left alone, and I don't want to go back inside. Will you just take me? I'll call Kanani tomorrow and explain."

Connor nodded and, wrapping a supportive arm around my waist, we walked to his car. I slid into the passenger's seat and leaned my head back against the headrest, feeling absolutely exhausted.

"Are you sure you're not hurt?" Connor asked as we pulled out of the parking lot.

"I'm sure," I said, taking a deep breath. "Thank you, Connor, for once again coming to my rescue."

"You're welcome," he said softly, and I could tell there was something more on his mind.

We rode in silence for a moment, and I glanced over at Connor, watching as shadows from streetlamps played along the handsome lines of his face.

"So," he finally broke the silence, "you and Jake are talking again?"

"No," I shook my head. "He wrote to tell me he was going to England, and I threw his letter away."

He looked over at me, his expression filled with surprise. "You didn't answer him?"

"Nope."

"Well…," he cleared his throat. "I'm relieved to hear that."

"I'm not as foolish as you think, Connor."

"I don't think you're foolish, Savannah Rose," he replied, his jaw clenching.

"Apparently you do," I sniffed. "You seem to think I can't make the right decisions when it comes to men."

"Listen," he sighed, "I'm sorry about tonight. I was only trying to protect you. Kealoha isn't the type of man you should be hanging around. He goes for every new girl that steps foot on the island, and once he gets her, he dumps her. I just didn't want you to get hurt."

"I appreciate your concern," I replied coolly, "but I don't like to be treated like a child."

We stopped at a traffic light and sat in silence for, yet again, another moment. Connor's forefinger tapped the steering wheel incessantly. He opened his mouth to speak, closed it again, and finally said with a sigh, "I don't think of you as a child, Savannah Rose. I'm sorry I embarrassed you."

I was shocked that he'd so humbly admitted to being wrong and glanced over at him with raised brows. "Well...alright. You're forgiven," I said. After a moment, I added softly, "I suppose I do make childish decisions sometimes. I shouldn't have gone out onto the beach alone like that tonight."

"I get the feeling the only reason you did was because of me, though, right?"

"I was trying to cool off, yes," I smiled slightly.

We pulled into the driveway of the boarding house and stopped, and Connor turned in his seat to look at me, his eyes serious. "If anything had happened to you because of me I'd have never forgiven myself. I promise I won't ever do that to you again."

I reached out and took his hand, giving it a squeeze. "It's okay," I said sincerely. "All is forgiven."

I told him goodnight and climbed from the car. He waited until I disappeared into the house before driving away, and as I made my way up the stairs, I shook my head. What a strange, tumultuous friendship we had.

Chapter Thirty-eight

-1965-

A week had passed since my return home from the hospital, and I was now strong enough to walk on my own and see about myself. Aunt Deb, Abby, and Hannah had been a lifesaver. Every morning on the way to our house, Aunt Deb would stop by Abby's to pick she and Hannah up, and my husband took them home at night after work. He, of course, never said so to me, but I knew he was glad to be able to get back to work for a while. We both craved for a little bit of normalcy to come back into our lives.

Friday night, after he got home from work, my husband told me his boss needed him to go to Atlanta for the weekend.

"I told him I'd talk to you first," he said, leaning against the kitchen counter as he sipped on a glass of tea. "I know you're not up to a road trip, so all you have to do is say the word and I'll tell him I can't go."

I didn't like staying home by myself, especially at night, but I could tell this trip was important. I only hoped Aunt Deb felt up to staying with me. She'd seemed exhausted after spending the whole week with me.

"When will you be back?" I asked.

"Sunday afternoon. I would leave the car here for you and take the train."

"I think you should go," I said.

"Are you sure?" He asked, eyeing me with concern. "What if you have a setback?"

"I'll be fine," I smiled, moving to stand beside him. "You've told your boss "no" too much on my account already. Besides, I can ask Aunt Deb, or maybe even Abby and Hannah to come stay with me."

The next evening, it was all settled. My husband was gone, and Abby, Hannah, and I sat on the sofa in the living room eating popsicles and watching "I Love Lucy" on TV. I'd asked Aunt Deb if she'd, too, like to join us, but she begged off this time, finally admitting that she needed some rest. I felt terrible that she was so tired on my account.

The clock had just struck seven when Abby began rummaging through her purse, a look of panic on her face.

"What's wrong?" I asked.

"I forgot my medicine," she groaned. "I was so focused on getting everything Hannah would need that I forgot to pack it."

"Well," I said, climbing off the couch, "let's go get it."

"Are you sure?" She questioned, chewing her bottom lip. "It's getting late."

"It'll be fine," I waved a hand. "Your house isn't that far anyway."

Fifteen minutes later, Abby hurried from her house, medicine in hand, and was about to climb back into the car when her neighbor stepped outside and called to her.

"The police were knocking on your door a few hours ago," the elderly lady said, her house coat flapping in the breeze.

Abby stopped dead in her tracks and stared, wide-eyed, at her neighbor. "What did they want?" She asked.

"Don't know," she shrugged. "I didn't ask."

Abby climbed into the car, her face pulled into a frown. "What on earth do you think they wanted?"

I wondered the same but didn't voice my thoughts. Why would the police have wanted to speak to Abby and not the other neighbors?

As we drove, Hannah fell asleep in the back seat, and Abby grew silent as the medicine started taking effect. I reached out to flip the knob on the radio, noticing a pair of headlights in the rearview mirror. That truck had been behind me since leaving Abby' s house, and I was beginning to grow concerned. Should I keep driving? Go to the police station? I turned down our street, keeping my eyes glued to the mirror and breathed a sigh of relief when the truck didn't follow. *Silly me*, I thought, laughing at my paranoia.

Later that night, I sat up in bed reading a book, the house quiet as Hannah and Abby slept in the guest room. My husband had called to check in, and I didn't bother to mention our little outing while we talked, as he didn't like for me to go out after dark. After we hung up, I accidentally knocked the telephone over and it skittered loudly across the wood floor, breaking the phone and yanking the jack clear out of the wall in the process.

Great, I thought to myself as I picked up the pieces. *Just something else to spend money on.*

About an hour later, I was just about to turn off the light when I heard an odd, scratching sound. Setting my book aside, I threw the covers back and walked to the door, peaking out into the darkened hallway. *Perhaps what I heard was just a squirrel on the roof,* I told myself, turning to go back to bed when I didn't see anything.

I stopped dead in my tracks, my heart kicking in my chest. I'd heard it again, and it wasn't a squirrel. Someone was in the house.

I rushed to the fireplace in our room and grabbed a fire poker, my knuckles white as I clutched it tightly in my right hand. I tiptoed back to the door, stopping when I heard the guest bedroom door creak open. Relief flooded my mind as I realized it must have been Abby that I heard rummaging in the kitchen for a midnight snack.

I'd just turned to replace the fire poker when my bedroom door opened.

"Savannah?" Abby whispered from the doorway. "Was that you I just heard?"

I spun around to face her, my eyes wide. "No, I thought it was you?"

A thump, followed by a scraping sound, caught our attention, and I rushed from the bedroom and out into the hall.

"Savannah, shouldn't we call the police?" Abby hissed.

"The phone in my room is broken," I whispered. "We'll have to use the one in the living room."

Abby hurried to catch up with me, and we tiptoed down the dark hall and into the living room, my hand starting to ache from the tight grip I had on the poker. We stopped in the entranceway and peered around the dim room, our eyes landing only on shadowed furniture and table lamps. I listened intently over the pounding of my heart, but all I could hear was the ticking of the Grandfather clock in the corner.

"Come on," I whispered, and we began to move slowly across the room like two ghosts, our night gowns billowing out around our bare feet. We were inches from the telephone when, suddenly, the overhead light switched on, and a man with dark hair and black, piercing eyes stepped from behind the door.

"Stop right there," he growled in a thick, Spanish accent.

"Juan," Abby breathed, the blood leaving her face as she began to sway back and forth beside me.

It was then I realized he was holding a gun.

183

Chapter Thirty-nine

-1941-

Sunday morning, I had just taken the curlers from my hair and was attempting to gently comb through the thick, tangled tresses when Barbara came to tell me I had a visitor.

"Who on earth would visit a girl on a Sunday morning?" I muttered to myself as I slipped into a bathrobe and hurried downstairs.

I rounded the corner, stopping in surprise when I found Kanani waiting in the parlor, hat in hand.

"I'm sorry to stop by so early unannounced," he said, smiling apologetically, "but I wanted to make sure you got home okay last night."

"How thoughtful of you," I said, genuinely surprised he'd made the effort to check on me. I proceeded to tell him what happened.

"Are you alright?" Kanani asked, his eyes wide.

"Yes," I nodded, smiling. "And I'm sorry again about what happened between you and Connor. He tends to get a little overprotective at times, sort of like an older brother."

"Except I'm not her brother," a voice rumbled from behind, and we both turned in surprise to find Connor standing in the doorway, dressed in a suit.

"Con, what are you doing here?" I wanted to know.

Pulling his gaze away from Kanani, Connor looked at me and replied, "I decided to attend church with you this morning."

I raised my eyebrows in surprise. "I thought you attended services on base?"

"Can't I go with an old friend this time?"

I blinked. "Well…yes, of course."

Connor moved to stand at my side and motioned toward Kanani. "What's he doing here?"

"I can answer for myself, Danes," Kanani grunted.

This can't be happening again, I thought, desperately searching for a way to divert their attention.

"Savannah, dear, aren't you going to introduce me to your friend?" A silky voice interrupted.

We all turned to find Betty leaning against the doorframe, eyeing Kanani with interest. Her red lips were curled into an inviting smile, and she didn't seem the least bit embarrassed that her hair was still up in curlers.

I quickly made the introductions, breathing a sigh of relief when Kanani's lips curled into a flirtatious grin and he sauntered over to stand before Betty, temporarily forgetting all about Connor and me.

"Look, Connor," I whispered, turning to look up at him, "I've got to go get dressed, so will you please be nice to Kanani and not cause another scene? He came by only to make sure I got home safely last night, and that's it."

Pursing his lips, Connor nodded his head in agreement, then stepped back and appraised my robe clad body. "Why do you have to change? I sort of like this outfit," he winked.

"Very funny," I stated dryly, slipping past the engrossed couple to rush upstairs and get dressed.

Betty talked Kanani into attending church with us, and by the time I came back downstairs, the two men, much to my surprise and relief, had seemingly decided to put aside their differences and were sitting on the sofa, talking congenially.

After church, everyone came back to the boarding house to eat lunch. Kanani and Betty sat next to one another, both sneaking shy looks and flirtatious smiles every chance they got, and when Connor slid into the seat next to me he leaned over and said, "I don't know how those two egos are going to work, but I think I already hear wedding bells."

Snickering under my breath, I muttered, "I'm just glad to have his attention off of me."

After dessert, Connor asked if I'd like to go for a drive with him, and I agreed. There was something different about him today, but I couldn't quite put my finger on it. Perhaps our argument last night had him on his good behavior, but I didn't attempt to try and figure it out. That simply wasn't possible when it came to Connor Danes.

We drove down to the beach, not stopping until we found a quiet, remote spot. Connor parked and retrieved a blanket from the trunk while I took off my shoes and knee-high stockings, anxious to feel the sand between my toes.

We walked for a bit, talking and laughing as we splashed our feet in the water and searched for sand dollars. We came across a huge, beautiful shell washed up on the beach, and I tucked it carefully into my bag with plans on giving it to Aunt Deb when we got home. I missed her so much. After a bit, Connor unfolded the blanket and we laid it out on the sand, quickly hopping on top as the breeze tried to snatch it away.

"It's so beautiful here," I said, sighing softly as I stretched my legs out and wiggled my toes down into the soft sand.

"It certainly is," Connor agreed. Turning to look at me, he asked, "So, what made you decide to become a nurse?"

"That's a random question," I laughed. Tapping my chin with my forefinger, I thought for a moment and said, "When I was about ten or eleven, I found a wounded squirrel in our backyard. Harriet was going to kill it, but I begged her to let me take care of it, and for once she let me do what I wanted. I took the squirrel down the street to an old neighbor who used to be a doctor. He showed me what to do, told me how to care for it until it was well, and I did exactly that. It was hard saying goodbye once it was healed and I let it go, but I can't remember ever feeling so good, so fulfilled. I'd helped another living thing to survive, and I decided right then that caring for others was what I wanted to do. After that, I spent many an afternoon with my old neighbor, asking him questions and bugging the life out of him. He died when I was sixteen, and I find myself thinking of him often."

"You have a very big heart, Savannah Rose," Connor said with a smile. "You're one of the kindest, most compassionate people I know."

"Oh no," I shook my head with a laugh. "Those words describe Maxi, not me."

"They describe you, too," he said, and I expected a wink or sarcastic comment to follow, but he simply looked at me with an open, genuine frankness that caught me off guard.

"Thank you," I said, glancing down at my hands. Clearing my throat, I asked, "I believe it's your turn now. You told us why you joined the Air Corps, but you could have become a pilot without joining the military. What made you decide to join?"

Picking up a small stick, Connor began drawing small circles in the sand, his expression thoughtful. "When Father died, joining the military was honestly the easiest thing for me to do," he finally said, his voice low. "It was up to me to take care of Mother and Leon and going to college was out of the question. The military pays good, comes with benefits, meals, and lodging, so why not?"

"You like it, though, don't you?" I asked, tilting my head as I studied his profile.

"I like the structure it gives me," he nodded, "and I've enjoyed seeing the world. I just don't like having to leave Savannah. I miss my home and family."

I'd always been so close to Leon that, up until now, I'd never thought of how hard it must have been on Connor when their father died. He'd been forced to grow up and become a man in an instant, when he really was still just a boy. He'd shouldered a lot of responsibility, and I was slowly starting to understand, and respect, him more.

Chapter Forty

-1941-

The weeks passed by so quickly I felt that if I blinked, I'd find it all to be a distant memory. Kanani continued to court Betty, and much to everyone's surprise, she had him toeing the line like a trained puppy. He quit drinking completely, didn't pay any attention to other women, and went to church with her every Sunday. Betty, Maxi, and I had become very good friends, and quite often when she and Kanani would go on a date, Maxi, Connor, and I would go along. The two men had thankfully put aside their differences and got along very nicely.

Maxi and I both received a letter from Vivian, with news that she was courting a young man who was a newcomer to Savannah. She gushed about how handsome and sweet he was, and I very much wished I could meet him. Maxi and I missed Vivian a great deal, and we told her so in our return letter, with hopes that we'd be able to come home soon.

It was Saturday, November 29th, and Connor, Betty, Kanani, Maxi, SuAnne and her sailor boyfriend, a couple of military nurses from Tripler Hospital, and I were all heading up to visit Diamond Head for the first time. SuAnne had met the two nurses at one of the many dances she'd attended and invited them to come along. Poor Maxi, now nearly six months pregnant, lingered in the back, huffing and puffing as she tried to keep up with the group in the hike up the mountain. I fell back to walk with her, leaning in to quietly ask if she was certain she was up to making the hike. She hadn't gained much weight at all and seemed to be getting along just fine, but I still worried over her.

"Yes, I'll be…fine," Maxi insisted, out of breath. "I really…want to do this. I hear the view is…beautiful from the top."

"But I don't know if this is a good idea for you or the baby," I whispered,

"We're both…doing fine, Vannie," Maxi huffed. "Everything is normal and…going as it should. The baby is growing and has a…healthy heartbeat, and the exercise is good for us both."

"You two slow pokes coming?" SuAnne called. The group had gotten a good bit ahead of us and had stopped to wait.

I waved them on, yelling that we were both out of shape and needed to take it slower than the rest. They all laughed and went on without us, all except for Connor. He walked back to join us, taking both our hands as he pulled us along behind.

"Want to climb on my back?" He joked. "I'll give you both a ride for $.50 each."

"I might just…take you up on that," Maxi laughed, swiping at a bead of sweat on her forehead.

Connor glanced over his shoulder at her, and I didn't miss the look of concern in his eyes. He was worried about Maxi, and I wondered about his suspicions. Maxi was hardly showing at all, and she'd bought bigger, baggy clothes to cover her tiny baby bump, but I wondered if Connor somehow still noticed that something was different about her. We still hadn't decided what to do about the baby, and I was starting to get worried. Maxi didn't seem to want to discuss it, but we only had three months left to get it figured out. Time was running out.

Once we finally reached the top, all of my worries faded away as I gazed out at the beauty surrounding me. Brilliant, aquamarine waves crashed against the rocks far down below, and from the 360-degree view, one could see for miles. The ocean stretched out before me and, shading my eyes with my hand, I stepped closer to the edge, spotting a red and white lighthouse rising from the rocks below like a shiny beacon of warmth and welcome. Connor and Maxi stepped up next to me, and we gazed out over Waikiki Beach, a cool, fresh breeze ruffling my hair. To our right and over the tops of the city rose emerald green mountains, sparkling in the sun like the jewels they resembled. To say the view was breathtaking was an understatement.

"So," Connor cleared his throat, breaking the silence, "there's going to be a dance down at the Hickman Field officer's club next Saturday night. Will you go with me?"

A surprised thrill rushed over me at his request. I'd heard about the dance, as it was supposed to be a big deal, and I'd hoped Connor would ask me to go with him.

Trying to keep my face nonchalant, I shrugged as we turned to rejoin the group and said, "Sure, I'd love to."

As we sat down, SuAnne asked if we were talking about the dance, and pretty soon everyone joined in, stating that they were all planning to go.

Realizing that Maxi hadn't said a word, Connor leaned around me and asked, "You're going to come, too, aren't you, Maxine? You can ride with Savannah and me, if you want."

"Psh, Max here never goes anywhere and has any fun," SuAnne interrupted. "You really should come, though, Max."

Maxi's cheeks were turning red from all the attention as everyone turned to look at her, and I quickly cut in and said, "Of course she'll come," I winked at my cousin, then proceeded to pull the potato salad out of the basket and pass it around.

"Thanks for taking up for me back there," Maxi said later as we all headed back down the mountain.

"They meant well," I smiled, patting her hand. "And we all really would love it if you came. You don't get out enough and have any fun."

"I know," Maxi sighed, shrugging her shoulders. "It's just…I don't know…I guess I feel like I don't fit in."

My heart dropped, and I stopped walking to pull Maxi up beside me. "Oh, Maxi, I'm so sorry. It's my fault, isn't it? I've been spending too much time with Connor…"

"Stop, Vannie," Maxi laughed, shaking her head. "It's not your fault at all. I never was one for running around to parties and dances anyway. You know that. I'm more of a homebody, which just makes it worse because I'm not home and I'm homesick. And," she added with a sigh, "I'm upset and worried about what's ahead of me, with the baby and everything. But please don't blame yourself over my feeling I don't fit in. You've done so much for me, Vannie, more than I could have ever asked for, and I'm just grateful you're here with me through all of this."

Maxi's beautiful eyes were so open and sincere that it was all I could do to fight back the tears that threatened to fill my own eyes. I hated the fact that my sweet cousin was suffering from her very own choices. I was homesick, as well, and I could only imagine how frightened Maxi must feel knowing she would be having a baby so far away from the comforts of home.

"I'm glad I'm here with you, too," I said, pulling my cousin into a gentle hug.

Chapter Forty-one

-1965-

Abby's ex-husband moved slowly across the room, his cold, beady black eyes sweeping over us as he picked up the telephone and threw it across the floor.

"Is there anyone else in the house?" He asked, raising the gun to point directly at my face. "I suggest you tell the truth."

I hesitated, uncertain of whether or not I should tell him his daughter was asleep in the guest room. Telling him could put her in danger, but if I didn't tell him and he found her, the consequences could be fatal.

"Hannah…" I gulped, fighting to stay calm, "is sleeping in the guest room."

"There's no one else?"

"No," I shook my head.

"Then lead the way," he said, his gun still pointed at us.

"Juan, please…"

"Shut up, Abby," he snapped, and she took a step closer to me, her eyes filling with tears.

On trembling legs, I turned and walked toward the guest room, praying Juan wouldn't hurt Hannah. When I opened the door, Juan glanced inside and motioned for me to get the child out of bed.

"I want you all to be where I can see you," he stated.

I leaned over Hannah and touched her shoulder, shaking her gently. "Wake up, honey," I said, and her eyes fluttered open. I pulled back the covers and helped her sit up, her eyes squinting from the overhead light.

"Hurry up," Juan snapped, and Hannah glanced his way in surprise. Seeing the gun, as well as the look of fear on her mother's face, her eyes widened and she quickly stood up, clutching my hand tightly.

Turning his eyes on me, Juan asked, "Where do you keep your money?"

"Juan, no!" Abby gasped, and he backhanded her so quickly it was all I could do not to scream.

With a small cry, Hannah made a move towards her mother, but I grabbed her arm and quickly pulled her back when Juan pointed his gun at her and growled, "You stay put."

Hannah sunk her face into my side and began to cry, her deep, shuddering sobs breaking my heart. I patted her back, my thoughts running in a million different directions.

"I asked you a question," Juan said to me, his gaze cold and hard.

"My...my husband keeps some money in a safe at the back of our closet," I stammered. "I don't know how much is there, but that's all we have here in the house."

"Show me," he said, jerking Abby out of the way.

Taking Hannah's hand, I hurried to the master bedroom and crawled to the back of the closet, praying there would be enough money to satisfy him. I could hear both Abby and Hannah sniffling from the doorway, and I took a deep breath, trying to remain calm. I opened the safe, retrieved the money, and handed the roll of cash to Juan, my hands trembling.

As he counted the money, I noticed a bead of sweat dripping from his forehead. He was pale, his eyes wild, and I wondered what had brought on this sudden appearance. Did it have anything to do with that visit to Abby's house from the police earlier?

"There's close to a thousand dollars here," Juan said, the corners of his mouth turning up into a callous smile. "That's more than enough to get me out of the country."

"Juan, why are the police after you?" Abby asked suddenly, her voice shaking. She and Hannah stood wrapped in each other's arms, and my heart stopped beating for a moment when Juan threw an icy glare in their direction.

"Because I killed someone," he said, his tone flat and low. "And if you say another word, I'll add you and your little brat to the list."

Turning his attention back to me, Juan asked, "Where is the cellar?"

I told him, and he herded us all in that direction, pushing us down the steps as we entered the dark and damp room below. He asked for the key, I gave it to him, and then the door slammed shut and he was gone as quickly as he'd come. Abby, Hannah, and I stood huddled together in the darkness, our muffled sobs the only sound in that pitch-black prison.

Chapter Forty-two

-1941-

Before I knew it, the week had passed and Saturday, December 6th finally arrived. All day long the girls chattered with excitement over the dance that night at the officer's club, each discussing what they would wear and how they would fix their hair, until the chief nurse finally told them to, "Please talk about something else before I lose my mind."

She then approached me, a clipboard in hand and spectacles perched on the end of her nose and asked if I could come in the next morning.

"On a Sunday?" I asked in surprise.

"If you don't mind," she nodded. "Macy is, as you know, out sick with a stomach virus, and since you're doing so well and assigned to light duty in the surgical ward this week, Dr. Stanley said he'd like to have your assistance with an appendix surgery. Will you do it?"

Pleasantly surprised, I smiled and nodded. This really was a wonderful opportunity, and I couldn't be more pleased that Dr. Stanley had requested I be there. "Yes, ma'am, of course. What time shall I be here?"

"Eight o'clock will be fine."

I watched her walk away, excited but already feeling tired just thinking about the long night ahead followed by such an early morning. Perhaps I should forego the dance and get to bed early, but it was supposed to be a big event, and Connor was planning to escort me. Plus, he'd bought me a new dress specifically for the occasion, and I couldn't wait to wear it. He'd seen me eyeing the beautiful, light blue gown in town last week through a store window, completely ignoring my protests as he marched right inside and bought it for me, stating I should accept it as a "thank you" gift for agreeing to go to the dance with him. The draped neckline hung gracefully about my shoulders, while silky soft chiffon gathered snugly at the waist and fell to my ankles, making a soft "swooshing" sound when I walked. The sleeves were short and loose, fluttering about my arms like soft, delicate angel wings. I felt like a queen when I tried it on later that night and couldn't wait to wear it at the dance.

At seven o'clock, I was seated before the vanity while Maxi fixed my hair. We were chattering excitedly about the letter we'd just received from Aunt Deb. The police, it seemed, had captured a man along the Savannah River who was accused of killing a local girl. He hadn't confessed, but they felt sure it was the same man who had killed those other poor women.

"So, once the baby comes, we can go home," I beamed.

"Yes, once the baby comes," Maxi smiled wanly. She'd pulled my hair into an elegant up do and reached into the top drawer, pulling out Mama's sparkling comb. As she placed it in my hair and began arranging a few curls around my face, she noticed my expression had changed and asked, "What's wrong, Vannie?"

I hesitated, staring at my reflection in the mirror. "While you were securing Mama's comb in my hair, I just started thinking of Daddy and...I don't know," I sighed, shaking my head. "Maybe I shouldn't have agreed to go tonight."

"Why?" Maxi asked, leaning against the vanity to study my face.

"Because it could quite possibly give Connor the wrong idea."

"Why did you agree to go with him then?"

"I don't know," I moaned. "It's hard to explain, but I think being out here so far away from home has blinded me a bit to reality."

"Vannie, quit speaking in riddles and talk plainly," Maxi sighed, placing a hand on her hip.

"I don't want another relationship right now, Maxi," I stated, standing up to pace about the room. "Thinking of Daddy made me think of Jake and I just can't go through that again."

"Who says you'll have to?"

"Maxi, I've never trusted Connor," I stated. "You even said yourself that he's a heartbreaker."

Her brow furrowed in confusion over my sudden outburst, Maxi watched me pace around the room for a moment, her eyes suddenly widening as she stood to her full height and said, "Vannie, have you fallen for Connor?"

"What?" I stopped and stared at her, blinking. "No," I insisted, firmly shaking my head, "of course not."

"Then why are you so concerned?" Maxi raised her eyebrows.

"Because it looks like a date," I cried.

"Okay," Maxi laughed, holding up a hand to stop me, "you're blowing this way out of proportion. You're going to a dance, not the Justice of the Peace, and you've gone out with both Leon and Connor before without giving it a second thought, so tonight shouldn't be any different. Besides, Connor hasn't done or said anything to make you feel he's interested in being more than friends, right?"

"That's true," I nodded, beginning to feel a bit silly. "I guess I'm overreacting."

"Just a little," Maxi laughed. Tilting her head to the side, she glanced at the bedroom door and said, "I think I just heard the doorbell."

"Oh, that must be Connor," I sighed, fidgeting. "Are you sure you won't come with us, Maxi? I really wish you would." I couldn't understand why I was so nervous. Like Maxi said, I'd gone out with Connor plenty of times before, so why was tonight any different?

Maxi smiled and shook her head. "No, dear, but thank you for inviting me." Adding one final touch to my hair, she patted me on the back and pushed me towards the door. "Now, go have a good time. You look beautiful!"

I thanked Maxi with a kiss on the cheek and grabbed my small purse, hurrying down the stairs to meet Connor. He was waiting in the foyer, quite dashing in a black, pin striped suit, matching black tie, and crisp white shirt. He turned at the sound of approaching footsteps, a low whistle emerging from his lips when he saw me.

"Wow," he exclaimed, his gaze warm. "I didn't realize how pretty that dress was until now." Smiling softly, he stepped toward me and took my hand, squeezing gently. "You take my breath away, Miss Adair."

"Thank you, Connor," I said, quickly pulling my hand away. "You look very nice yourself."

He extended his arm, and I accepted with a smile, waving goodbye to Barbara as we walked out the door to his awaiting car. With a deep breath, I slid into the passenger's seat, both apprehensive and eager for the night ahead.

Chapter Forty-three

-1941-

Maxi watched from the kitchen window as the couple drove away, a melancholy smile slipping past her lips. Poor Savannah, she was falling for Connor and didn't even know it. Maxi only hoped she would relax and enjoy the evening.

With a sigh, she turned away from the window, wondering why things couldn't have turned out differently with Robert. She'd struggled with bouts of bitterness and depression the last few months, trying desperately not to let it show. The letters from Leon had been like a beam of light and warmth in a dark, cold night. They'd been writing since October, and Maxi couldn't deny that it brightened her day every time she saw his handwriting on an envelope addressed to her.

"Why didn't you go to the dance tonight, Maxine?"

Barbara's voice startling her out of her reverie, Maxi reached for a nearby knife and began to help Barbara chop carrots for supper.

"Oh, I just didn't feel like it, I guess," Maxi said lightly, making sure to handle the sharp blade carefully.

Barbara eyed her for a moment as she peeled an onion, and Maxi could feel her concern. "Do you have a beau waiting for you at home?" She asked, as if that might be the reason behind Maxi's boring lifestyle.

Maxi shook her head, a sad smile pulling at her lips. "No, ma'am, we broke up before I left."

She didn't offer any further explanation, and Barbara didn't press it. As the two women continued to work in silence, Maxi's thoughts began to drift, and she found herself asking the other woman why she and Thomas never started a family of their own. She didn't know where the question came from and was immediately embarrassed.

"I'm sorry, Mrs. Barbara, I didn't mean to be so nosey," Maxi apologized. "I'm sure that's personal."

"Don't be silly," Barbara laughed. She then stopped her chopping and a thoughtful, almost sad look came into her eyes. "We actually tried to have children for years. But it seems…it seems that it just wasn't meant to be."

When Barbara's eyes filled with tears, Maxi felt ashamed. She laid down her knife and went to her side, resting her hand on Barbara's arm. "I'm so sorry, Mrs. Barbara, I had no idea."

Sniffling, Barbara raised a corner of her apron to dap at her eyes. "It's alright," she smiled bravely. "We want God's will to be done, and if we're not meant to have children, then we're just not meant to."

A sudden thought crossed Maxi's mind, and she was almost afraid to voice the question on her lips, but she felt that she had to. "Did...did you and Thomas ever consider...adopting?" She asked, trying to keep her tone nonchalant.

"We talked about it, and if we ever found a child in need and felt like it was God's will, then yes, we'd definitely consider it," Barbara nodded.

They went back to chopping vegetables, and Barbara continued to rattle on, but Maxi wasn't paying attention. Instead, she was deep in thought as excitement and hope began to flood her soul. Was this the reason they'd come to Pearl Harbor in the first place? It was all so perfect! The Swanson's wanted a baby, and Maxi could give them one. She'd been so worried, wondering how on earth she would go about finding a good, God-fearing family to adopt and raise her child, and now she had the answer. She didn't doubt for one minute that the Swanson's would take her baby, and she suddenly felt as if the weight of the world had been lifted off her shoulders.

And then, the melancholy hit home again. She'd spent over six months with this child inside her body and had grown to love it more than she'd ever imagined. She'd felt it move, heard its heartbeat. How was she possibly going to give it up? It would break her heart.

Excusing herself with complaints of a headache, Maxi went upstairs and lay down, tears flooding her eyes. She was doing the right thing, wasn't she? She couldn't possibly keep the baby and raise it on her own. She was counting on returning home to live with her aunt and uncle, and she couldn't expect them to take her back with a baby in tow. No, this was for the best, and the fact that the Swanson's were such wonderful people was a comfort to her.

Turning her head, a smile tugged at her lips when her eyes landed on Leon's last letter. She still loved him, she always would, and wondered if maybe she and Leon could ever have a chance. She wasn't sure how he felt about her, but he'd faithfully written to her for months and that was something, wasn't it?

Hope once again raising her spirits, Maxi sat up and pulled out her ink pen and notepad. If Leon didn't love her now, that didn't mean there was no hope for the future. She'd go home in a few months, and everything would be different. She was determined to be happy, and knew she had to do whatever it took to make that happen.

Chapter Forty-four

-1941-

The Hickman Field officer's club was alight with music and happy, laughing couples when Connor and I arrived. Chatter and the tinkling of crystal drifted through the air while a band played softly in one corner, their instruments blending together in perfect harmony. The women were all dressed in long, flowing gowns, and many of the men wore tuxedos, while others their "Dress Blues". A magnificent ice sculpture rose gracefully from the center table, with sparkling glasses of champagne and delicious Hors d'oeuvres artfully surrounding it. A massive chandelier hung from the high paneled ceiling, diamonds dangling like icicles from its golden arms as it beamed brightly off the freshly waxed wooden floors.

We walked through the huge room, admiring all of the elaborate decorations as we searched for our friends, and I pointed with delight at the massive, hunter green Christmas tree that rested in the corner, stating that it reminded me of the one we had last year.

"You mean last Christmas when I kissed you under the mistletoe?" Connor winked.

My eyes widening, I pinched his arm and he laughed, my own lips twitching as I tried to hold back a smile. In a way, his teasing put me more at ease. I felt ridiculous over my earlier conversation with Maxi. Connor and I had been friends for almost a year now, and he'd never once crossed a line or done anything out of order. I felt silly even thinking he might assume this was a real date.

Scanning the room, my face lit with a smile when I saw Vicki Marshall and her husband standing among a small group of people. I pulled Connor in that direction, stopping to give Vicki a hug.

"You look beautiful, my dear," Vicki gushed, stepping back to admire my dress.

We'd seen quite a bit of each other since our arrival to Hawaii, as Vicki made certain to keep her promise to Aunt Deb to keep an eye on us girls. She, Maxi, and I had gone shopping a few times, and she and her husband had eaten supper at the boarding house once or twice. They were such a nice couple, and I was very pleased to see them both.

We finally spotted our friends sitting at a large, round table with an ivory colored satin tablecloth that flowed gracefully over the sides. Red and green bows were tied to the backs of all the chairs, and I hurried over to sit next to SuAnne.

"You were right, Su," I smiled at my friend as Connor pulled out my chair for me. "Your gown is lovely."

SuAnne stood to show off the full length of her sparkling green dress, twirling around with a giggle as it billowed out around her like a bell. "Isn't this thrilling?" She squealed when she sat back down. Her cheeks were flushed with excitement, and I readily nodded my head in agreement. This, indeed, was going to be a night to remember.

Time seemed to pass slowly, and I found myself enjoying every minute of it. Charlotte and Lola were there, as well, with their dates, and I listened with interest as the two women described life as military nurses. I had to admit it sounded very exciting. I didn't know them well, but they were two of the nicest girls I'd ever met, and when they invited SuAnne, Maxi, and myself to go shopping with them the following weekend, I readily accepted.

We were served a delicious five course meal that ended in a choice of delectable desserts and a variety of flavored, hot teas. Connor, of course, was the ever-charming companion, as he and Kanani raced to tell the best joke or the funniest story. He and I danced nearly every waltz together, and by the end of the night, I felt as light as a feather. I was tired and my feet hurt, but I felt warm and happy and…something else I couldn't quite put my finger on.

The night finally came to an end, and after saying our goodbyes, Connor and I made our way outside. Once outdoors, I shivered as a cool breeze ruffled my skirt, twirling it around my ankles. The temperature had dropped a good bit since we arrived, and I began rubbing my hands along my bare arms.

"It feels like we're in for a storm," Connor muttered to himself, glancing up at the dark sky. "Are you cold?" He asked, noticing my shiver. "Do you want my coat?"

I nodded yes, and when he slid his suit coat off and slipped it gently around my shoulders, his hands lingered there for a second longer than necessary, and I found myself wanting to lean back against him. *You're being silly*, I scolded myself, trying to shake off the warm, giddy feeling that seemed to have crept up on me.

"Did you have a good time?" Connor asked.

"I had a wonderful time," I nodded, smiling. "Thank you for inviting me."

"Thank you for coming," he replied warmly.

The drive home was quiet, but it didn't matter. As we bumped along the dark, rutted dirt road, we kept glancing over at each other, only to quickly look away again with a smile. There was something between us, something that hadn't been there until now, but before I had a chance to further explore what I was feeling, a sudden, deafening boom blasted through the silent night, and the car jerked roughly to the left, throwing me against Connor's side.

"What on earth?" I gasped as Connor gripped the wheel in both hands and stepped firmly on the brakes, bringing the car to a skidding stop.

"What happened?" I asked, my eyes wide.

"I'm not sure, but I think I now have a flat tire." Connor climbed out to inspect the damage, returning to say that his diagnosis was, indeed, correct. "And the worst part is it's too dark to change it."

"Great," I groaned. "Now what?"

"Now?" Connor raised his eyebrows. "We walk. We've only got about a mile left."

"You can't be serious. I can't walk that far in these shoes!"

"I'm afraid we don't have any other choice, Cinderella," he laughed, coming around to the passenger side to pull me out. "Want me to carry you?"

Smiling, I shook my head. "No, thank you, Prince Charming, I'll just walk barefoot."

As I slipped out of my shoes, Connor reached into the back seat and retrieved a small flashlight, stating that it would be better than nothing.

We headed off down the dirt road, side by side, talking softly as thunder rumbled off in the distance. The wind whistled through the trees with a high-pitched moan, the sound like that of a woman searching for her long-lost love, her whispered breaths blowing tendrils of hair around my face. It suddenly seemed that there was something magical, and almost unearthly, about this night. The darkness formed a sort of cocoon around Connor and me, wrapping us up in our own little world, far away from everyone else.

"See? This isn't so bad." I could hear the smile in Connor's voice as he spoke. "What better way to end such a wonderful night than with a romantic, moonlit walk home? I couldn't have planned it better myself."

"Except it's a flashlight we're walking by, and not the moon," I teased, laughing. "And is it really so romantic?"

Connor stopped walking then and took my hand, pulling me gently up next to him. "It could be," he whispered, his face a shadow, and yet I could feel his warm, piercing gaze.

Heat washed over my body, and I felt my breath quicken. His intentions were clear, but before I could wrap my mind around it, a drop of water splashed against my cheek, followed by a dozen more.

"It's raining!" I exclaimed, laughing at Connor's groan of frustration.

"Come on," he said, pulling me along as we turned to make a dash through the field that stretched between us and the boarding house.

The inn could be seen through the shadows, looming up in the darkness before us like a beacon in the night as we raced through the wet grass, my skirt hiked up to my knees. Connor tried to hold his jacket above my head, but we were both getting soaked and soon laughing so hard we could barely continue to run. I stopped suddenly, yelping in pain when my bare foot landed on a stick, and Connor swooped me up into his arms, carrying me as if I weighed nothing more than a feather.

By the time we made it to the front porch, water was dripping into our eyes and splashing from our clothes. Connor leapt up the stairs and gently set me back on my feet. His hands remained at my waist, and when a bolt of lightning flashed through the sky, illuminating his face, our eyes met, and I suddenly found it very hard to breathe. There was something in those silvery depths, something I hadn't noticed before, and when he slowly backed me up against the door, I felt my hands begin to tremble. There was something between us, like a current of electricity, and it was so strong that I couldn't pull away.

We were so close I could feel the beating of his heart thumping a rapid rhythm that matched my own as our breaths mingled together in the damp, night air, and through the dim shadows, I saw his head slowly lower until his lips were only inches from mine. I felt dizzy and disoriented, barely noticing the storm that thundered angrily around us. Connor was giving me the option to back away, but I didn't want to; I wanted him to kiss me.

I slowly slid my hands up his arms and buried them in his hair, pulling his head closer until I felt his lips touch mine. A low groan slipping past his throat, Connor moved his hand to the back of my neck and pressed his mouth hungrily against mine. I'd kissed Jake a few times during our courtship, but never had I felt like this. I couldn't think, couldn't breathe. All I knew was that I could stay like this forever. It was like our hearts had been searching for each other all this time, finally coming together in one single, beautiful moment.

Suddenly, through the haze that surrounded us, reality came crashing in with a thundering boom that shook the ground beneath our feet. We jerked apart in surprise, turning to watch as a magnificent tree crashed to the ground, missing the house by only a few feet.

Is it a sign? I thought, stepping away from Connor as I crossed my arms protectively about my waist. What I was feeling frightened me, and the urge to run was so strong I looked quickly at the door, mentally judging the distance between us.

Connor turned to look at me, and I could see the wariness in his eyes. "Savannah…" he began, reaching for me, but I shook my head.

"No, Connor, stop," I said, taking another step back. I couldn't make sense of the jumbled thoughts in my head, and knew I needed to get inside and away from Connor so I could think.

When he made another move toward me, I swiftly sidestepped him, opened the front door, and ran inside, locking it quickly behind me.

"Don't do this, Savannah," I could hear him say on the other side, and I slumped against the door and began to cry.

Everything had happened so fast, yet I'd known he was going to kiss me. Why hadn't I stopped him? Instead, I pulled him closer, and now wondered if he'd really wanted to kiss me, or if I had thrown myself at him? With a moan of embarrassment, I turned to press my forehead against the door, closing my eyes as the thoughts continued to swirl wildly about in my head.

I felt so confused. A part of me wanted to open the door, run back into his arms, and talk this out, while another part screamed at me to run as far away from him as possible. How could I do this to myself again, and so soon after Jake?

Needing time to think and sort through my feelings, I hurried up the stairs and into my room, trying to keep quiet so as not to wake Maxi. The last thing I wanted to do was explain what had just happened, especially after the conversation we'd had earlier. After quietly changing my clothes, I slipped into bed and buried my face in my pillow, finally allowing the tears to flow freely.

Had I fallen for Connor somewhere along the way, or did I simply get caught up in the moment? As my mind travelled back over the last year, I slowly began to realize just how much had changed between us. I thought of that kiss under the mistletoe and how annoyed I'd been. I'd disliked him a great deal and wanted nothing to do with him. But, as time moved forward, we slowly started to become friends. I smiled as I thought of how he took it upon himself to teach me how to dance, and I realized now that when I thought he and Grace were dating, I was jealous. I remembered how he came to my rescue the night I was almost kidnapped, and how he stuck by my side these last few months in Hawaii, always there if I needed him. Somehow and somewhere along the way he'd become a very important part of my life, an important person in my life, and if I were completely honest with myself, I'd come to care a great deal for him.

"He's a heart breaker, a 'love them and leave them' type," Maxi's words from so long ago crept back into my mind, and I groaned quietly. Was that possibly all Connor was doing with me? Using me to add another name to his little black book?

Needless to say, I didn't sleep all night. I tossed and turned, my mind running in a thousand different directions. One minute I thought maybe Connor truly did care for me, as well, and the next I had myself convinced he was just using me, stringing me along until he got bored. I didn't want to get hurt again. Jake had broken my heart, and I'd promised myself that would never happen again.

I finally got up around 6:45 and readied myself for work, dreading the long day ahead of me. I only hoped I would be alert enough to assist the doctor with his surgery. I glanced into the mirror, cringing at the mussed-up hair and swollen, puffy eyes staring back at me. I looked a fright. After splashing my face repeatedly with cold water, I hurried downstairs and gulped down a cup of cold coffee I'd saved from the day before, cramming a banana into my mouth as I went back upstairs to brush my teeth.

It was just after seven when I stepped through front door, and I stopped dead in my tracks, my eyes widening as I slowly closed the door behind me. Connor's car was parked in the driveway, and he was sitting on the hood, staring at me, his bleary eyes red from a sleepless night. His face was covered with a shadow of stubble, his hair uncombed and curling at the ends, and he wore the same clothes from the night before, wrinkled and still damp from getting caught in the rain.

"Have...have you been here all night?" I asked, finally finding my voice.

Connor nodded, his steady gaze piercing a hole through my heart as he studied me. "I went back and changed my tire at dawn," he rasped, and I felt a pang of guilt when I realized he must have caught a cold from spending the entire night outside in wet clothes.

Sliding from the hood, Connor moved toward me, not stopping until he stood on the porch a few feet away. "Why did you run off like that last night?" He wanted to know, stuffing his hands into his pockets.

Embarrassment flooding over me, I searched desperately for words, unsure of what to say. Why was he still here? I needed more time to think. Perhaps he intended to apologize, but I couldn't be certain by the guarded look in his eyes.

"Because it was the right thing to do," I cleared my throat, my own voice strained.

He stood silent for a moment, his eyes narrowing as he studied me, as if trying to read my mind. "Why do you say that?" He asked, his voice soft. "Tell me what you're thinking, Savannah Rose...what you're feeling."

Not on your life, I thought, stepping forward as I moved to walk past him. "I don't really have time to talk right now, Connor, I have to get to work."

When I tried to step around him, he grabbed my arm, stopping me. "Please don't do this, Savannah Rose," he ground out, his jaw clenched. "Don't push me away."

I pulled my arm free and, taking a step back, looked up at him. I could see his throat bobbing with frustration, his hands clenching and unclenching at his sides, and I felt confused by his actions. Connor was a man who was ever the epitome of calm, cool, and collected, yet here he was so upset that he'd waited outside for me all night. It couldn't be because he cared...could it? Perhaps he felt guilty over crossing a line with such a close, family friend.

"I've handled this all wrong," he muttered, his voice heavy as he shook his head with a sigh.

"What do you mean?" I asked, bracing myself inwardly.

Connor shoved his hands into his pockets and studied me for a moment, and I found myself wishing I could read his thoughts. He seemed to be at war with himself, as if he didn't know exactly what it was that he wanted to say.

Finally, he sighed and, running his fingers through his hair, asked in a low voice, "Do you really not know?" Stepping closer, he reached out and took my hand, pressing it firmly against his heart. "Is it not obvious how I feel about you?"

I could feel the steady rhythm of his heart thumping against my palm, and I raised my eyes to meet his, questions warring within my mind. His words, the earnest expression, the way he held my hand against his chest, it all took my breath away, and in that moment, I wondered if he truly did care for me.

Connor opened his mouth to speak again but was interrupted by the sudden whir of airplane engines. We both turned in surprise to stare up at the sky, and I asked, "Are the boys at Ford Island flying maneuvers today?"

"No," Connor shook his head, his brow puckered in confusion as he shaded his eyes with his hand. We continued to watch as the planes drew nearer, and the sudden catch of Connor's breath brought my gaze quickly to his profile. "Oh, my God," he whispered.

"What?" I asked, fear tightening my chest. "What's wrong?"

Connor looked down at me, his eyes wide and face as white as a ghost. "Those are Japanese planes, and they're headed straight for Pearl Harbor!"

I stood in stunned bewilderment and watched as Connor took off at a dead run and leapt into his car, not yet able to comprehend what was happening.

"Stay here," he shouted out the window, his tires spinning and throwing up gravel as he jerked his car into reverse and drove away like a madman.

I raised my eyes once again to watch the planes grow smaller and smaller as they flew away, and when the boom of a sudden explosion vibrated the earth beneath my feet, it finally sunk in.

Japan was attacking Pearl Harbor.

Chapter Forty-five

-December 7, 1941-

It's strange how life can change in the blink of an eye, isn't it? One moment everything is going just fine, maybe a little rocky at times, but nothing you can't handle. Then in an instant, a split second, everything changes, and life as you know it disappears into the air like a thin, weak vapor, and you start to wonder if life, if humankind, really ever was good and decent, or if it was all just a dream.

Everyone lives in hopes of finding true peace and happiness, but there always comes a time in each life that will test our belief in those things. Whether it be war, a fatal accident, the death of a loved one, or harm to a person's body or mind, it never fails to make us question what we truly believe, and if there really is such things in life as truth and goodness. Some overcome tragedy, while others let it overcome them.

I remember hearing later all the stories that were told, of the men who slept peacefully within the battleships that morning, unknowing of the danger that crept undetected through the sky. It had all been such a surprise, the attack at Pearl Harbor. One nurse, who stood on one of the hospital's balconies that morning, waved as the planes went by, and received a friendly wave in return. She wouldn't realize until later that they were Japanese planes instead of American.

The Oklahoma and West Virginia sank within minutes of the initial explosions, their oil and fuel gurgling to the top of the water as men tried to swim through the muck, their skin burning and whelping with blisters. I read of the many brave men on deck of the Nevada who fired back at the enemy aircraft with their heavy artillery before diving off into the water as the ship, sinking and ablaze, had to be run ashore. The Arizona, by all accounts, held on for an amazing amount of time, receiving hits over and over until finally one bomb penetrated the vicinity of her forward magazines and detonated with a massive, ear splitting blast that quickly sank the brave warrior. Screams and pleas for help from the men trapped inside could be heard for hours.

I can still see myself, giving no thought whatsoever to my own safety as I leapt onto my bicycle and pedaled towards the base. All I could think was, *They'll need help. The hospitals will need nurses.*

Once I finally arrived at the entrance to the base, my breath was coming in short spurts, and already the smoke was burning my lungs. The attack had begun nearly thirty minutes ago, and still there were planes flying overhead, bullets ricocheting off the ground and nearby buildings. Glass was shattering, buildings exploding, and people were running and screaming, throwing their arms over their heads as they tried to duck out of the way. A spray of shrapnel burst on the ground in front of me, and with a gasp, my bicycle went down. A flash of pain ripped through the side of my body as I fell onto the hard cement, and I quickly crawled for cover against a small building, the bullets barely missing me.

I sat huddled against the concrete wall for a moment, my heart pounding and eyes wide as I stared out at the chaos before me. Through the thick smoke, I could make out bleeding bodies lying on the ground, some severely injured, some already dead. I could feel the heat from the fires that seemed to be burning all around me, and the smell of singed flesh made my stomach turn. I hadn't fully realized until now how severe of an attack this was.

Forcing myself to move, I stood on trembling legs and began running down the streets, pushing my way through the people and stepping over bodies. A lady ran screaming past, her face severely burned, a bullet wound pouring blood from her shoulder. Men were carrying their injured comrades and brothers, their faces tight with shock and fear. I searched every face, looking for Connor, wondering if he was okay. Several planes passed overhead, and I glanced up, noticing that a few of them were our planes. I wondered if Connor was up there, fighting for his life, for the lives of the people below. I could barely make out one solid thought in my jumbled mind, but one that prevailed above all others was, *Please, protect him, God, please protect us all.*

At the sound of thunder, Maxi sat up in bed, her heart pounding from being so suddenly awakened. The boarding house shuddered, and she leapt out of bed to look out the window. Instead of dark, billowing clouds flashing with lightning, she saw a clear, sunny sky, with smoke rising off in the distance towards Pearl Harbor. Movement caught her eye then, and she glanced down to see Savannah riding her bike at breakneck speed towards the base, and fear began to creep up the back of her neck. What was happening?

Suddenly, her bedroom door burst open, and Maxi spun around to find Betty staring at her with wide eyes.

"I think Pearl Harbor is being attacked," she gasped. Her hair was mussed and blouse half buttoned, as if she'd gotten ready in a hurry. "I was out in the garden drinking my coffee when I saw Japanese fighter planes fly over us. I ran inside and had barely gotten my skirt on when the explosions started. I'm going down there, my boss will want a story on this. Tell the Swanson's for me, will you? Oh, my God," she suddenly gasped, her eyes widening, "Kanani is there! He went in early this morning to finish up a job before church."

Maxi could hardly make sense of Betty's ramblings, but when the frazzled young journalist turned and ran from the room towards the stairs, Maxi jumped into action. She yanked her nightgown off, hurriedly pulled a dress over her head, and grabbed her shoes on the way out. It was difficult to run down the stairs in her condition, but she managed, and by the time she made it outside, Betty was already in her car backing down the driveway.

"Wait!" Maxi shouted, waving her hands at the girl. She jumped into the passenger seat, out of breath. "I'm…coming with you," she heaved.

"No, Maxine, you don't need to go…"

"Savannah just left!" Maxi cried. "I have to go with her, I have to help. She'll need me…the hospitals will need me…hurry!"

Betty drove like a madman, her knuckles white as she clutched the wheel with both hands, her eyes wide as she stared out at the chaotic road ahead of them. Tires were screeching and horns blowing as doctors, nurses, and soldiers raced to get on base. Officers and men were scurrying to report to duty in any way they could: on foot, by car or bicycle, some even commandeering taxi cabs in their frantic attempts to get to their stations of duty. Maxi could hear the thundering of explosion after explosion, and for a moment, the car stalled from all the vibration. Clenching her jaw, Betty tried for what seemed like ages to get the old Coupe to start up again, and finally it roared back to life. Maxi leaned up and looked out the windshield, watching as smoke billowed up into the sky like black, angry clouds. Instinctively, she placed a hand over her stomach, praying for God to protect her baby.

When they finally arrived on base, Maxi gasped in horror at the sight before her. There were too many people and too much chaos to continue driving, so Betty pulled over and the two girls jumped out. Maxi spotted Savannah up ahead, huddled against the side of a building, her face white with fear.

"Savannah!" Maxi shouted, just as a bomb landed only yards away. Screaming, Maxi dove onto the ground and covered her head, but by the time she got back up, Savannah was gone.

"Come on, we need to get moving," Betty cried, grasping Maxi's hand in her own.

The two girls joined the rest of the throng of scared, frightened people as they hurried down the street, hearts pounding in their ears. They spotted Lola, one of the military nurses, frantically making her way down the street toward Tripler Hospital, and the two girls scurried to catch up.

"I'm heading down to the port," Betty shouted in Maxi's ear, and Maxi nodded, giving her a quick hug.

Lola spotted Maxi and slowed her steps, reaching out for Maxi's hand. "I'm glad you're here," she shouted, her eyes wide with fear.

"Yes, the hospital will need my..." before Maxi could complete her sentence, a spray of bullets suddenly rained down from the planes overhead, catching them both unaware.

The entire world seemed to stop moving at that moment. The hand clutching hers fell away, and Maxi watched as a red hole formed in the side of Lola's head, and blood began to run down her beautiful face. She stared at her as if in a daze or dream, not fully understanding what had just happened. Lola crumbled to the ground, her eyes open but glazed over as death quickly and silently stole her away. Maxi shook her head violently from side to side as if trying to clear her vision, to make this horrible scene go away. This had to be a nightmare. Surely, she was still asleep.

Someone bumped hard into Maxi's shoulder, jarring her from her trancelike state, and with a gasp of air, she fell to her knees and desperately felt the side of Lola's neck, confirming what she already knew to be true. There was no pulse. Choking back a sob and a wave of nausea, Maxi kissed the girl on the cheek and stood to stumble down the street, her stomach in knots. The fog surrounding her brain lifted, and everything that was happening suddenly became clear with a gut-wrenching sense of shock and fear. America was now at war.

Chapter Forty-six

-December 7, 1941-

I raced through the hospital corridors, the crowd of injured men nearly unbelievable. I could still hear the whir of planes and unrelenting explosions of bombs outside and wondered if the attack would ever end.

"Savannah, thank God you're here!" Charlotte cried, her face stark white. I stopped and stared at her, not recognizing her for a moment as my mind struck a blank. "We need all the help we can get," she said, shoving a stack of bandages and medicine into my trembling hands. "We don't have enough medical supplies for the amount of injuries on hand, but just work with what you can get." She glanced up, taking in my dazed, almost lost, expression, and gripped me firmly by the shoulders, giving me a quick shake. "Snap out of it, Savannah, we need you. Now, hurry!"

With a gulp, I spun on my heel and rushed to the nearest man, who lay on the floor in a puddle of blood. He was crying and gripping his shoulder; his clothes were torn, and his skin covered in soot. I squatted next to him and gently pried his fingers away from the injury, trying my best to control the trembling in my own fingers. The hospital was filled with such chaos and noise that I could barely concentrate, and the fear of what was happening hung in the air like a thick, poisonous gas.

For what seemed like hours, but was in reality only a matter of minutes, I ran from patient to patient, doing what I could for them. Some were badly burned, others were missing limbs, and some were so near to death that I had to force myself to leave their side and help someone else. The doctor's face was like steel as he operated on one man after another, removing bullets and shrapnel and bandaging up amputations, and we all hoped that the less than sterile environment wouldn't later lead to infection. Nurses scurried about in a hurried and nervous frenzy, each of us trying to ignore the fear that we may all die at any minute. They were running short on supplies, and the endless number of patients seemed overwhelming.

The building shuddered time after time as bombs detonated all around, setting our teeth on edge. Connor flitted in and out of my mind, my stomach twisting painfully as I wondered yet again if he was still alive.

Trying to concentrate on the task at hand, I pushed thoughts of Connor away for the time being and bit my lip as I readied the arm of a young sailor for an I.V., gasping in shock when the skin on the entire length of his forearm came off. Glancing around to call for help, I spotted Maxi down the hall, and my eyes flew open wide in surprise.

"Maxi!" I cried.

Somehow hearing me through the noise, Maxi turned and searched the room until her eyes met mine. She started towards me, and at that very moment, bullets came bursting through the window she'd just been standing by, missing her by only a few inches.

Leaving the poor sailor, I rushed to my cousin, gripping both her hands in my own. "Maxi, what on earth are you doing here?" I cried, pulling her further away from the shattered window. "You should have stayed at the boarding house!"

"I had to come help," Maxi replied, and I noticed that her dress was splattered with blood. "Savannah," she said, her eyes sad as she squeezed her cousin's hand, "Charlotte's friend, Lola, is dead. She got hit by a spray of bullets."

My breath catching in my throat, I shook my head, my eyes filling with tears. "Oh no," I whispered, glancing around the room until my eyes landed on Charlotte. My heart broke for her.

Before I could dwell on the news for long, the head nurse interrupted and pushed us in opposite directions, yelling at us to quit wasting time.

"I'll see you later," I called to Maxi as I rushed back to the sailor, and I wondered how many others would die before this day was over.

Time seemed to stand still for Maxi as she struggled to maintain a steady method of work: Stay calm, clean and bandage the wounds, sew up the cuts, don't think about all of the blood, tune out the screams of agony, turn over the worst cases to the doctor and surgeon, stay calm, fight the nausea.

She felt her baby kick, and the thought that she shouldn't be here crossed her mind once again, but she pushed it aside. To say that the hospital was in complete mayhem was an understatement, and she knew every bit of extra help the staff could get was appreciated. This is what she'd decided to do with her life, yet being a nurse for the next fifty years was starting to hold less and less appeal. Maybe she wasn't cut out for this after all. Perhaps she'd only decided to do it because that's what Savannah wanted to do. She'd always been a follower, and that little character trait hadn't always been in her best interest.

Maxi smoothed a burn salve onto the leg of a middle-aged Major in jerky and not so gentle movements, apologizing as the man cried out in pain, the puffy red skin blistering and oozing under her fingers. The sounds and smells were about to overcome her, and she tried desperately to tune it all out and think of something else. Something not so dark and morbid.

Suddenly, thoughts of her mother drifted to the center of her mind, and for once, she gladly welcomed the reprieve. There weren't many good memories related to thoughts of her mother, but she did remember a couple of good times. Like on her sister's birthday that one year when her mother had helped her make a cake, or the time they all went for a rare trip to the movies. She'd never understood her mother, yet she'd never been around her enough to get the chance to even try. Her mom had always been too busy with her boyfriends, leaving Maxi at home to care for her younger sisters.

A wave of pain passed over Maxi as she thought of her sisters. Oh, how she missed them. She hadn't heard from them since she came to live with Aunt and Uncle Coleman. She'd tried to get in touch with them, but didn't know where they were, and her mother wouldn't answer any of her letters. All she knew was that they'd been placed in the homes of distant relatives and nothing more. She hoped they were safe and happy. She hoped their adoptive families had been as wonderful as her own. She hoped they'd been lucky enough to have someone like Savannah around as a replacement sister.

At the thought of Savannah, Maxi looked up from her work to seek out her cousin once again, a smile coming to her lips when she found her working tirelessly across the room. As if sensing her thoughts, Savannah looked up and their eyes met. Savannah gave her a brave half smile, but suddenly, her expression changed to one of shock and horror. At the same time, Maxi heard a loud explosion, and the window to her left shattered into pieces, spraying her with shards of glass. A flash of pain sliced through her side like a knife, and she fell to her knees, her arms instantly covering her stomach to protect her baby.

The sounds around her seemed to fade into the background as Maxi raised her hand to gaze at the blood dripping from her palm, confusion wrinkling her brow. She couldn't understand what was happening, but when Savannah suddenly appeared before her, Maxi saw the answer to her question in her cousin's fear filled eyes.

She'd been hit.

"My baby," she gasped brokenly, reaching down to clutch her stomach as she fell into Savannah's arms. The pain was nearly unbearable, and tears began to stream down her face, for she knew in her heart that her baby was already dead, and that she was dying as well. *Oh, God, why didn't I stay at the boarding house? What have I done?*

She'd failed. She'd failed this child, this precious life she'd carried within for the last six months. She'd never have the chance to meet him or her, and it would never have a chance at life. Thoughts raced through her mind, jumbling together like an overturned jigsaw puzzle. Savannah was pressing something against her wound as she shouted frantically at her, at the doctor, at someone who could help, but no one seemed to be listening. Maxi knew it didn't matter, though, because it was too late.

A picture of Leon suddenly floated across her mind's eye, and she began to sob openly, ignoring the pain, wishing she'd had a chance with him. She loved him so much, but now she'd never be able to tell him. She'd hoped for so long that one day she would know how it felt to kiss him, to be held in his arms, to see the look in his eyes when he finally realized he loved her. Now, she'd never know. If only she hadn't held back. If only she'd just taken a chance and told him how she felt. She placed her hand over her heart, trying to ease the pain.

Something wet fell onto Maxi's face, and through blurry eyes, she looked up to find tears dripping from Savannah's cheeks. With a sad smile, she reached a weak hand up to cup her cousin's face, her voice barely a whisper as she said, "Dear Savannah, my dear, sweet Savannah, don't cry."

Savannah clutched Maxi's hand so tight that she winced in pain but didn't pull back. "Hold on, Max, I'll get help. Please, just hold on."

"I...I don't think I can," Maxi rasped, feeling the blood gurgling up in her chest. She coughed, and Savannah sat her up a bit, still trying to get help, but not wanting to leave her.

It was getting harder to breathe, and as Maxi lay in Savannah's arms, struggling to hold on, she wondered what would become of her cousin. Would she go back home and get married some day? Would she realize that she loved Connor, or would she continue running away from her feelings? The thought that she would never know the answers to these questions broke Maxi's heart. She didn't want to leave Savannah behind. She wanted them to stick by each other for the rest of their lives, to stay close and share secrets until they were old and gray.

Still clutching Savannah's hand, Maxi looked up at her and said, "I love you, sister of my heart."

Sobbing, Savannah held her close. "I love you, too, sweet Maxi," she whispered in return. "I'm sorry this happened, so sorry. Please hold on. I'll find the doctor, I'll get help."

Savannah's pleas began to grow dimmer and dimmer, and, her eyes drifting shut, Maxi thought of her aunt and uncle, and desperately wished for one of Aunt Deb's comforting hugs, or the sound of Uncle Ray's contagious laugh. She could see them now, as if they stood before her, and suddenly, a strange warmth swept over her, almost as if her wish had come true, and she began to wonder if this is what it was like to die. Would angels soon come to carry her to Heaven? Would she see Jesus?

With a feeling of peace, Maxi took a deep, shuddering breath, and slipped away. Like a broken, blonde haired angel, she lay in her cousin's arms, another casualty of that day at Pearl Harbor, another lost loved one, another soul gone into eternity.

Chapter Forty-seven

-December 7, 1941-

Tears dripped onto Maxi's face as I stared down at my cousin, unable to comprehend what was happening. Maxi's lids slid shut, her lips were pale and no longer moving, and her face had grown lifeless, but still I clung to her, asking God to please not take her. I couldn't accept that Maxi was dead. I wouldn't.

"Maxi, wake up and look at me!" I cried, shaking her by the shoulders. "You can't leave me, you can't."

I raised my eyes to search for the doctor and felt a rise of hope when I saw him rushing by with a glass jar in his hands.

"Doctor!" I reached out and gripped his coat, desperate to get his attention. He spun to face me, his eyes drifting down to the woman I held in my arms.

"Oh, dear," I read his lips as he knelt down, for I couldn't hear his murmur over the noise. He reached out to lay a hand on Maxi's neck, his face falling when he couldn't find what he had hoped to. He raised sorrow filled eyes to meet mine, confirming what I already knew to be true, and said with a shake of his head, "I'm sorry, but I'm afraid she's gone. There's nothing I can do."

I felt as if the breath had been stolen from my very lungs. I stared at the doctor, shaking my head in denial, murmuring, "No, no, no…she's not dead…God, please, no." My eyes filled with tears as I looked down at the dearest friend I'd ever had, and it felt as if someone began to punch me in the chest. Pulling my cousin close, I laid my face against Maxi's and sobbed, rocking back and forth. Nurses and doctors, patients and those seeking to help, scurried around me as if I were invisible. Voices yelled, men screamed in pain, but the only thing I could think was, *This can't be happening. No, God, please, this can't be happening.*

By the time SuAnne spotted me sitting in a corner, a half hour had passed, and the attack seemed to finally be over, but I hadn't noticed. Airplane engines and bombs and shouts of fear still rang in my ears, and Maxi died countless deaths as it all replayed over and over in my head.

SuAnne rushed to my side, her face turning white when she realized the corpse I clutched to my breast was Maxi.

"Oh, honey," she moaned, falling to her knees at my side. "I came to offer my help, and…" reaching out to touch Maxi's limp hand, she closed her eyes, as if saying her goodbyes as a tear slid down her cheek. After a moment, she looked around at the chaos surrounding us and, taking a deep breath, said gently, "Come on, Savannah, you've got to let go now. They need our help."

I looked up at SuAnne with red, glazed over eyes, as if I didn't even know where I was. I was in shock, and SuAnne knew it.

"Savannah," SuAnne said, reaching out to pat me on the cheek, "you don't need to think about this right now. Let me take Maxi, and you can get something to drink, okay? The Red Cross brought blankets, bandages, and refreshments a few minutes ago."

While she continued to talk, SuAnne was able to pry my arms away from Maxi and lift the dead girl away with a huff. She was heavy, but SuAnne was used to pulling on men who were much heavier. She laid Maxi on a nearby table, said a quick prayer as she pulled a sheet up over her face, and turned back to me. I still sat in the corner, my eyes blank and staring. Rushing to the small cart that held water and lemonade, SuAnne grabbed a cup of the latter and brought it to my lips, forcing me to drink.

"I want Aunt Deb. I want to go home."

SuAnne had to lean her head in closer to hear my hoarse whisper, and she placed a finger on my chin, forcing me to look her in the eye as she said in a calm, firm voice, "I know you want to go home, Savannah, but you can't, not yet. Right now, we need you. Your country needs you. You've got to snap out of it and help us. Please, Savannah. Do it for Maxine."

My eyes blinking, I looked around, taking in what was happening around me as if I'd forgotten where I was. I turned my eyes back to SuAnne's, and with a tired nod, stood to my feet and, without another word, turned and walked to the nearest gurney.

Hours passed, and I wondered if it would ever end. My head was hurting, eyes blurry, and body so exhausted that I moved about like a robot. After SuAnne's good, stern lecture, I knew what I had to do, although I didn't want to. I wanted to scream and cry and kick the wall, I wanted to ask God why this had happened, I wanted to crawl into bed and sob my heart out for as long as it took for the pain to subside, but I couldn't. Not yet. I was on the verge of losing it if I didn't get a grip on myself, and so I forced thoughts of Maxi away for now and told myself to hold on for a little bit longer, that these people needed me. I tried focusing on thoughts of Connor, my mind's eye seeking him out and grasping on like a lifeline. I wondered where he was, if he was okay, and wished desperately to see him, if only for a moment. I needed him, needed his strength.

The day passed into the night like a blur. My stomach rumbled and pinched with hunger, but I couldn't eat. Each time I tried, I vomited it back up. I'd had to see and face things that I never thought I could endure, and I was exhausted and stretched utterly to the limit, but still forced myself to press on.

In the case of another attack, the windows of the hospital had been covered with black cloth, and the staff was forced to work in very low lighting, but that didn't slow us down. I accidentally bumped into another nurse, causing the girl to leap back with frightened eyes and drop the bandages she'd been carrying. Everyone it seemed, civilians and military alike, were suffering from the jitters. Every sudden movement or sound caused everyone to jerk to attention, our eyes and ears straining for any sign of danger. We were all on edge, and every time the whir of airplane engines would pass overhead, we would pause and hold our breath until we realized it was, once again, our own men keeping guard up in the sky. I wondered with each time if Connor was among them, hoped and prayed he was.

Dawn had just broken when I finished bandaging a young marine and moved to the next table, my mind hardly comprehending a thing, my hands going through the motions. I didn't even flinch when my gaze rested upon a face so badly burned that it could hardly even be called a face any longer. I instead focused on doing what I could to help him. Pulling out a tiny bottle of morphine, which had only a few drops left inside, I was startled when the blistered hand reached out and grasped mine with surprising strength.

"S-Savannah?" The voice rasped, and my eyes flew down to meet those of the young man.

"Yes?" I whispered, unsure to whom I was speaking. I swiftly pulled my hand away and continued with my work, studying him closely as I tried to place from where I knew him. I wasn't positive, but I guessed him to be only a few years older than me. His left ear hung by a thread and was bleeding heavily, most of the skin on his face had peeled off and was covered with red, angry blisters, and his left eye had been badly damaged. My heart nearly stopped when the sudden realization that it could be Connor hit me, but when he once again opened his swollen eyes and looked up at me, I breathed a sigh of relief. His eyes were black.

"H-have you…heard from or," he paused to heave a dry, raspy cough, "seen B-Betty?"

My heart slammed against my ribcage and I caught my breath in a gasp. God in Heaven, it was Kanani! Tears hit the back of my eyes so fast I had to quickly turn my head and blink them away before he saw them. Clenching my teeth so hard that my jaw began to ache, I took a deep breath, steeled myself, and turned back to look at the mangled mass of flesh who had once been among the most handsome of men.

"Savannah?" He croaked, bringing his original question back to surface.

Gulping past my emotionally swollen throat, I forced a smile and shook my head. "No, hon, I haven't."

At the mention of Betty, Maxi immediately leapt to the forefront of my mind, and I squeezed my eyes shut, trying desperately to push the painful thoughts away as they ripped at my heart. I couldn't think about this, not yet, for I feared if I ever allowed myself to cry, I wouldn't be able to stop.

With a deep breath, I cleared my throat and smiled reassuringly at Kanani, slipping a bit of morphine under his tongue. "This will make you sleep and help with the pain," I said, gently patting his arm. "Don't worry, Kan, the doctor will be around to see you shortly."

I turned to move on to the next patient before he noticed the torture in my eyes, but Kanani's grip on my hand stopped me. I looked back at him, my heart twisting at the look of fear on his face, causing me to momentarily forget my own pain. His eyes reminded me of those belonging to a frightened little boy.

"Am I g-going to…die?" He wanted to know.

I didn't know the answer to that. His injuries were extreme, but miracles happened, didn't they? Forcing a positive attitude, I moved closer and gently patted the hand that clutched mine.

"No way," I shook my head. "You're tough, remember?"

My words seemed to help soothe his troubled mind, but I stayed at his side until he finally drifted off to sleep. My shoulders drooping, as if they carried the weight of the world, I turned and surveyed the room through tired, bleary eyes. Patients were lying on beds, tables, and the floor, covering nearly every inch of space, and still more were being brought in. Would there ever be an end to the injured and dying? Most of the windows had been shattered, while instruments, broken bottles of medicine, and linens lay scattered on the floor, and the smell of ammonia, vomit, blood, and death mixed together to create a sickening combination that filled my nostrils and curdled my stomach.

Glancing over my shoulder once again at Kanani, I felt utterly and completely overwhelmed. In the matter of only a few hours, my life as I knew it had crumbled down into a pile of ashes. Maxi was dead, Kanani may die at any moment, but if he didn't, he'd never be the same. And what of Connor? Was he lying among the dead, as well? Pain clutched at my heart. I couldn't lose Connor now, not when I was finally beginning to realize what he meant to me.

With a sigh, I forced myself to get back to work, my body steadily growing more weak and tired by each passing hour, but I, along with the rest of the workers, refused to rest. It must have been nearing nightfall, I hadn't looked at the clock in several hours, when I realized my skin had grown clammy and my head was pounding more than normal. I thought I should try and eat something, but when my stomach rejected the cold coffee and ham sandwich, my body couldn't handle the strain. Sparks floated before my eyes before everything suddenly went black.

Chapter Forty-eight

-1941-

My eyes slowly drifted open, and I had to blink several times to remove the film that seemed to rest heavily upon them. I felt so odd, like my body weighed only as much as a feather, and when I tried to raise a limp, pale hand to touch my face, I had only enough strength to lift it a couple of inches from the quilt on which it rested. My brow wrinkling in confusion, I slowly appraised the unfamiliar room in which I lay, trying unsuccessfully to remember where I was.

I lay in a large, queen sized bed with a lovely lace canopy on top, and a massive, mahogany Armoire stood in the corner by the door, its tall, heart shaped figure taking up nearly half of the wall. The room was large, the wallpaper was pale and feminine, but I could find nothing at all that seemed familiar. Where was I? What had happened?

I opened my mouth to call out for help when the door suddenly opened and Vicki Marshall walked in, a look of pleasure coming over her face at seeing her young friend awake.

"Savannah, my dear girl, how are you feeling?" The kind Captain's wife asked as she rushed to my side, placing a cool, small hand on my forehead.

"I...I feel strange," I whispered, surprised to find my voice so weak.

"That's understandable," Vicki nodded. "You were so ill you've had me worried these last few days but thank goodness your fever broke early this morning. It looks like you're out of the woods now, my dear."

I stared up at the woman. "I've been ill...for a few days?"

"Yes, when I came by the hospital in search of my husband, one of the young nurses...SuAnne, I believe her name was?...told me that you had fainted and were sick, so I immediately gathered you up and brought you here. That was four days ago. Your body was so weak, you acquired a terrible fever and have been delirious until this morning. You've been able to keep a bit of water down, but no food, and I was so afraid..." Vicki's voice drifted off, and then she said with a smile, "Well, you're alright now, aren't you? Praise the Lord."

The more Vicki talked, the more everything began to clear up in my mind. I now strangely remembered being sick and unsure of what was happening, almost as if I'd been consciously unconscious, if that made sense. Dreams and hallucinations had filled my mind, working together with the fever to create sudden flashes of terrifying, horrific images. It had seemed almost like a projector, changing constantly from scene to scene, and I suddenly knew now that most of it had really happened. I remembered the attack, and knew that the screaming of airplane engines and blasts of bullets and explosions wasn't just my imagination playing tricks on me. It was all a blur, yet clear as crystal.

And then I remembered Maxi, and my heart stopped beating for a moment. Maxi was gone, dead. With trembling hands, I reached up and buried my fingers in my tangled, unwashed hair, squeezing my scalp as hard as my weakened condition would allow, as if trying to erase the memories and force my swirling thoughts to come to a standstill. A sob stuck in my throat as every last, heart wrenching detail came back to the surface, and an anguished, sorrowful moan slipped past my lips.

"Oh, sweetie," I heard Vicki whisper. She sat down on the bed beside me and pulled me gently into her arms, rocking me back and forth like a child as I gave in to the gut wrenching sobs that I simply couldn't hold back any longer.

Over the next two days, I drifted in and out of sleep, gaining my strength back little by little. Vicki hovered at my side, shoveling chicken broth and dry toast into my empty stomach every chance she got, and soothing my nerves when the flashbacks occurred. No matter how hard I tried to block it all out, my mind kept reliving the attack over and over.

I asked Vicki if she'd heard anything about her husband, Captain Marshall, but Vicki shook her head silently, her eyes hopeful yet brimming with concern. Everyone was frantic with worry for the loved ones they'd yet to hear from, each holding on to the hope that they were still alive.

I'd learned just that morning that America was officially at war. After the attack, we declared war on Japan, with Germany immediately following suit against us. I wondered when and where it would all end. How many more innocent lives would be lost at the hands of such evil and greed? It sickened me, frightened me, and it angered me. Why did this have to happen? I wished I were a man so I could fight back and make them pay for what they had done to us, to Maxi.

"I sent the telegram to your aunt and uncle, dear," Vicki stated on the third morning of my recovery. She'd gotten up early to go to the market, and I had asked that she send word to my family, letting them know of Maxi's death and that I was safe. "I also made the arrangements to have Maxi's body shipped home."

At Vicki's words, I felt sick to my stomach. The thought of Maxi's body being shipped thousands of miles away, all alone in that cold, hard box made me want to cry all over again. After everything she'd gone through to keep everyone from knowing about the baby, and now they would both be buried together. I promised myself that no one would ever find out about Maxi's secret. It had been her wish, and I intended to do everything I could to make it happen.

"Thankfully I had enough food in the house," Vicki continued as she sat the nearly empty shopping basket on the kitchen table, "because when I went to the market, the shelves were almost bare."

As I listened, I sighed heavily, wanting desperately to get out of the house and see all the damage that had been done. I wanted to go back to the hospital to help, to go to the boarding house and make sure everyone was alright...and I wanted to find Connor. I was nearly going out of my mind lying helplessly in bed when there was so much I could be doing.

"I'm going to visit the hospitals now, to see what I can find out about the Captain," Vicki said, using her normal reference to her husband. She held up her hand, stopping my plea to go with her. "Don't even ask, because you can't go with me. You may be strong enough to get out of bed and move about the house a little, but that's as far as you've gotten. I'll ask about Connor, too, while I'm there, okay dear? Now, please go lie back down, you look as pale as a ghost!"

I laid about for the remainder of the day, feeling restless as I waited for Vicki to return. I tried to read for a bit, then got up and slowly walked through the large house the Marshall's were renting, only making it as far as the living room before I collapsed onto the sofa. I must have drifted off to sleep, for I awoke suddenly, my heart pounding as the front door opened and closed with a loud thud. I pulled myself up and looked at Vicki's tight, ashen face, almost afraid to ask what was wrong.

"Vicki?" I asked in a small voice, a world of question in that one word.

Vicki's eyes slowly moved around the room until they landed on me, and she stared silently for a moment before tears filled her eyes and she said in a broken whisper, "The Captain. He's...dead."

My heart sinking, I pulled myself to my feet and walked to stand at

Vicki's side, my throat tight with emotion as I gently lead the older woman to the sofa. We sat beside one another in silence, my mind trying to form a word of comfort as Vicki sat woodenly at my side, not crying, not saying a word. Her face was tight and brow wrinkled as she stared blankly into space with glazed over eyes, her hands lying limply in her lap.

"I want to go home," Vicki said suddenly, her voice heavy with grief. She turned to look at me, her eyes determined. "They've started evacuating the island, Savannah. This is our chance to get out of this horrible place. You'll come with me, won't you?" She reached out and took my hand, her voice desperate as she added, "We both need to go home."

I knew what she said was true, but rejected the idea at first, shaking my head in denial as I said, "No, I need to go back to the hospital and help. I can't just leave. I have to stay and find Connor."

"No one has seen or heard anything of Connor," Vicki interrupted, her eyes filling with pity. "There's a good chance he…"

"No," I shook my head vehemently, "I won't accept that. I have to be certain."

I leapt to my feet, immediately regretting the quick action when my head began to spin. Vicki stood and grasped my shoulders, her tiny hands surprisingly strong and firm as she steadied me.

"If he's alive, Savannah, he'll write to you. Now, please, don't fight me on this. Everyone is afraid we might get attacked again; it would be crazy to stay! You've been ill, dear, you need to go home. Your aunt and uncle entrusted you to mine and…" her voice drifted off on a strangled note, and for a moment she closed her eyes as obvious pain washed over her at the near mention of her husband. She took a deep breath, opened her eyes again, and continued in a steady, determined voice, "they placed you in my care, and I will not leave here without you."

I stood silently for a moment, fighting a war within myself. I knew Vicki was right; I needed to go home. But for some strange reason that I couldn't quite understand, leaving this place gave me the feeling of finality. As if I would be admitting that everything really had happened. That Maxi really was dead, that this chapter in my life was over. I would be forced to go home and face reality. I'd have to see the look of sadness on my aunt and uncle's faces. I'd be faced with looks and stares and endless questions. I'd be going back to my "normal" way of life, except there wouldn't be anything normal about it. Not anymore.

Glancing up, I saw the look of determination on Vicki's face, and knew I couldn't fight her. I simply wasn't strong enough, and deep down inside, I knew that leaving was for the best.

With a sigh, I nodded my head in reluctant surrender.

Chapter Forty-nine

-1941-

After a long day spent between taking naps and helping Vicki pack, what little bit of strength I had gained was gone. I crawled into bed that night, barely able to awaken the next morning.

"We've got to hurry if we're going to catch the boat that's set to leave this afternoon," Vicki insisted as she helped me get dressed. I noticed my friend's eyes were swollen and bloodshot, as if she'd lain awake all night crying. I could sense that she was desperate to get away from here, to get back home to her family, and I honestly couldn't blame her. I only wished I could have a little more time on the island. Time to say goodbye.

We called a bus to come out and take Vicki's trunks to the port, while the two of us took the car Vicki and her husband had brought to the Swanson's boarding house.

I leaned my head back against the car seat, my body weak and tired as we drove to the inn. Vicki switched on the radio for a moment, in hopes of hearing a relaxing tune, but all that came from the speakers was news of war. Tears filled my eyes as I listened, my gaze taking in the sights passing by that spoke so loudly of the devastation the island had suffered. It seemed that martial law had taken over the island, hence all the evacuation plans. Civilians and military personnel who were injured were being sent home. "War is inevitable" I'd said only a few weeks ago, not realizing then just how close we'd been to stepping over that threshold.

We pulled up in front of the building I'd called home these last few months, and seeing its familiarity brought a strange sense of comfort to me. The front door swung open, and Barbara stepped out, shielding her eyes from the sun as she looked to see who had pulled into her driveway. As I slowly climbed from the car, her eyes flew open and she leapt down the steps, nearly knocking me over with her embrace.

"Oh, my dear Savannah, I thought you were dead," she cried, her tears soaking my neck.

I held on to her tightly, mixing my own tears with those of my friend. Barbara must have sensed how weak I was, for she pulled back and began to walk slowly up to the porch, her arms around my waist for support. As we neared the porch, the door opened once again and Betty stepped out, her eyes widening when she saw me.

"Oh, Savannah," she cried, rushing to my other side. "What happened to you? Where have you been all this time?" She questioned when I collapsed on the top porch step.

With a soft voice, I relayed everything to the two women, from the moment Connor and I spotted the planes, to Maxi's death, and finally to my waking up in Vicki's home after my illness. Vicki stood silently nearby with a distant look in her eyes as she gazed out at the field before us, not uttering a single sound, and when I finished, she turned and said with a tight smile, "That's why we've come, Mrs. Swanson, to collect Savannah's things. We're leaving in a few hours."

Barbara wiped her watery eyes with her apron, nodding her head in approval at Vicki's words. "That's for the best," she said, her voice strained with emotion, "you need to go home. We...we all do." She stood to her feet and lead us upstairs, and it was all I could do to walk into the room that had been mine and Maxi's. As I stepped through the door and began to pack up our things, I refused to feel anything at all. Instead, I closed my emotions off into a small, dark corridor, and silently went through the motions of folding, placing in trunk, and repeating. When it was finally done, I turned and walked out of the room, never looking back.

While Thomas loaded the trunks into Vicki's car, I asked both Barbara and Betty if they'd heard from Connor. When they shook their heads, my heart dropped. "No, dear, I haven't," Barbara said. "If I hear anything, though, I'll write to you."

The car was loaded, and it was time to say goodbye, yet I didn't want to. I'd come to love these people like family, and the thought of possibly never seeing them again broke my heart. I hugged them both, promising to write, and as I walked to the car, Betty slid her arm through mine and walked with me.

"You...you didn't see Kanani while you were at the hospital, did you?" She asked, her voice hopeful.

"Yes, I did," I hesitated. With a sigh, I turned to face her, my eyes solemn. "When I last saw him, he was in very bad shape. I don't know if he made it or not."

Her eyes filling with tears, Betty nodded and said, "I tried to ask about him, but no one could tell me anything. Now that things have settled down a bit, I'll go back. I hope…I hope he's still alive."

I squeezed her arm and said gently, "I'm sure he is. Just be prepared, Betty," I cautioned. "His burns were severe."

Before I climbed into the car, I turned back to Betty and asked, "If you see SuAnne, will you thank her for looking out for me that day? I don't know what I'd have done without her." I wished I could track her down and tell her myself, but there simply wasn't time.

Betty said that she would, and after one last hug, I slid into the passenger's seat, watching as the beautiful, old boarding house slipped off into the distance as we drove away.

Connor drove the old pickup truck down the dirt road, turning the half broken down heap of metal onto the long driveway he'd grown so accustomed to. He coasted to a stop in front of the lovely old house, his mind filled with thoughts of the last time he'd been here over a week ago. A lot had taken place since then, so much that he could hardly wrap his mind around it.

After he and Savannah Rose had seen the Japanese planes flying overhead, Connor had raced to the base like a madman, reckless and fearless in his mission to reach his post of duty. He hadn't made it there in time to warn anyone, but once he arrived, he and several other men leapt into what planes they could find that weren't damaged or destroyed and headed up into the sky to defend their country.

The fighting was fast and pumped with adrenaline, but Connor had blocked away any fear that threatened to seize him, focusing instead on his training and the anger boiling over inside his chest. He shot down two Japanese planes before he began chasing a dive bomber, barely paying attention to how far they were getting from the heart of the action. On and on they went, dipping and swiveling as the Jap tried to escape. Connor had been relentless, his eyes trained on the glimmering tail before him when his engine suddenly started making a strange noise. That's when he'd realized he was out of gas. He made one last attempt at destroying the enemy plane, never to know whether or not he'd succeeded, before he turned his nose downward and prepared to make a crash landing.

That's all he remembered until waking up hours later, lying in a field. He had no idea how he'd survived the crash, but when he woke, he was lying face up and about twenty yards away from his wrecked plane, with a rather large gash on his head, several broken ribs, and a badly sprained ankle. It had taken all day and nearly all his strength to hobble to an old, abandoned shack, where he forced himself to remain until his ribs were well enough for him to walk.

Several days later, he began his journey back to the city. With no other means of transportation, he walked. And walked. It took almost two days, and when he finally came upon an old, abandoned pickup truck, he felt as if God himself had placed it there just for him, for he didn't think he could take another step on his still swollen ankle. He'd driven for another full day until finally reaching Honolulu, and now here he was at the Swanson's, hoping to see Savannah. He knew he needed to report back to duty, but he had to see her first and make sure she was alright. He wasn't sure what he'd say when he saw her, he figured he'd cross that bridge when he came to it.

With a squeak, Connor opened the truck's door and climbed out, his limbs sore and aching from exhaustion. As he walked up the front porch steps, he thought that the inn seemed quiet, almost too quiet. He opened the door without knocking and stepped inside, looking around but seeing no one.

"Is anyone home?" He called, receiving no reply.

He hesitated for a moment before making the decision to go upstairs, uninvited. If she was here, he was going to find out. He went to the second floor and walked down the hall until he stood before her bedroom door, his heart clenching hopefully within his chest as he raised his fist to knock.

"Savannah Rose? Are you in there?" He called out, listening intently for her voice to answer. When it didn't, he cautiously turned the knob and walked inside the bedroom, his eyes taking a moment to adjust to the dim lighting. As they did, he took in the two neatly made beds, and the thought that the room seemed almost bare slipped through his mind. Throwing caution to the wind, Connor opened the Armoire, went through the drawers, and even looked under the beds, but his thought had proven to be true: the room was bare. Where were Savannah and Maxine's things?

A sense of foreboding gripped at Connor's chest, and he spun on his heel and ran down the stairs, nearly colliding with Barbara Swanson on the landing.

The poor lady was so caught off guard, she gave a loud shriek and would have toppled over backwards if Connor hadn't been quick enough to grab her by the shoulders.

"Mrs. Swanson!" He exclaimed in surprise, setting her easily back on her feet. "I do apologize. I didn't know anyone was here."

"Good heavens, you gave me a fright," Barbara laughed nervously, placing a hand over her breast. "I was in the cellar and didn't hear anyone come in."

"I was looking for Savannah Rose. Have you seen her?" Connor asked, getting right to the point, his hands curling into a fist as he anxiously awaited her answer.

Barbara blinked, caught off guard by the sudden question. "Savannah Rose? Oh, yes, yes, of course, the poor dear, she's been staying with Vicki Marshall. Captain Marshall was killed during the attack, and so now Mrs. Marshall has decided she wants to leave, and since Savannah has been so ill, she's taking her along…" the woman was talking so fast, Connor could barely keep up. He raised a hand to stop her, and the way her mouth hung open in midsentence might have seemed funny if he hadn't been so intent on finding out more about Savannah.

"She's been ill? What's wrong with her? And where is Mrs. Marshall taking her?" Connor fired the questions off one after another, causing Barbara to pause for a moment before answering.

"Well, I don't know all of the details," she said, her green eyes blinking, "but it seems that Savannah simply exhausted herself working at the hospital and was so distraught over Maxine that she finally just collapsed. Mrs. Marshall said she had a terrible fever for several days, to the point that she was afraid Savannah was going to die. She's much better now, though, thank the good Lord."

"Why was she distraught over Maxi? What happened?"

A flash of pain filled Barbara's eyes, and for a moment she just looked at him, her face becoming a mask of sadness. "She…she was killed," she said hoarsely. "When the attack began, they both went to help at one of the hospitals on base, and Maxine was shot. She died…in Savannah's arms."

It felt like a wall of pain slammed into Connor's chest at those words. Maxine, sweet Maxine, was dead, and Savannah had witnessed the whole thing. How horrible that must have been for her. How she must be feeling, Connor couldn't imagine. If only he'd known they would dare to venture onto base during the attack, he would have done everything he could to stop them. He felt responsible. He was supposed to keep an eye on them. He'd never know for sure, but somehow, he felt that if he'd tried, he could have prevented Maxine's death.

Seeing the anguish on Connor's face, Barbara reached out and squeezed his forearm compassionately, her eyes brimming with tears. Connor stood in silence for a moment, breathing deeply as he tried to clear his head and stop the thoughts that raced wildly through his mind. Finally, he cleared his throat and asked, "You...you said she and Mrs. Marshall are leaving. When and where are they going?"

"They're going home, and they're leaving today."

Connor's startled eyes shot up and collided with Barbara's. "They're going home...today?" He hadn't any idea they would be letting ships on and off the island so soon.

"Yes," she nodded. "They actually just left here about an hour ago with Savannah's luggage. I believe they said they were hoping to leave sometime this afternoon. They may already be on the boat now."

With a quick "thanks", Connor turned and raced out the front door. He leapt into the truck, praying it would run long enough to get him to the port. Savannah may not care for him in the way he wanted, but he had to see her before she left. America was now officially at war, and it may be the last chance he ever got.

I stood next to Vicki on the ship's massive deck, the guard rail bearing the brunt of my weight as I leaned against the smooth wooden finish, my eyes taking in the last sights of the island before we left. A cool, salty breeze drifted through my hair, and I closed my eyes to inhale deeply of the island's scent.

"I'm going back to the cabin," Vicki said, interrupting my thoughts. "Do you want to come along?"

"Not just yet," I shook my head. "I want to stay out here for a while longer. If I get too tired, I'll sit on one of the deck chairs and rest."

"Alright," Vicki patted my hand gently before she left.

There were many people on deck, some pushing through the crowd to find their cabins, while others stayed on deck to wave to those standing on the dock below. I waved, too, not so much to the people as to the island itself. If only I could have seen Connor one last time before I left, to know he was alive and...

"Savannah Rose."

My eyes popped open, my heart beginning to race as I searched madly about for the familiar, deep voice I'd just heard. Hadn't I? Or had I simply imagined it? Pulling myself up on my tiptoes, I craned my neck and searched the face of each person standing on the dock below, hope giving strength to my weakened body, and when my eyes finally met his, it was as if the whole world stopped turning. I caught my breath and stared at him, afraid to move, afraid to blink unless he wasn't real and disappeared. But the warmth in his eyes as he gazed up at me couldn't be my imagination. No, it was real, he was real, and when a beautiful smile split his lips and he raised his hand in a wave, it was all I could do not to launch myself over the railing.

"Connor!" I cried, happiness bubbling forth and forming a laugh of delight in my throat. "You're alive."

He couldn't hear me, for at that moment the ship's horn sounded and they began to raise the gangplank. I wanted so badly to speak to him, to tell him how I felt. But it was too late. We were already moving away from the dock, and so all I could do was lean over the railing and mouth for him to write me, making a writing motion with my hand. Connor nodded in understanding, crossing his heart in a promise to do just that. With a smile, I waved until I could see him no longer.

Chapter Fifty

-1965-

The darkness seemed to grow thicker and heavier as time crept by, and I shivered from the cold, damp air. It had taken over an hour for Abby and me to calm Hannah down and convince her to stop crying, and she now straddled both our laps, her soft snores echoing off the walls as she slept.

"I'm so sorry about all of this," Abby whispered.

"It's not your fault," I replied, leaning my head back against the wall. "I'm just glad he didn't harm anyone."

"It's so strange how much someone can change," she sighed, and I could hear the heaviness in her tone. "I remember when we were young and first began courting. He was so charming, so kind. I could hardly believe it when he struck me that first time."

"How long had you been married?"

"A little over a year," she sniffed, and I wondered if she was crying. "I made excuses for him at first. I told myself he didn't mean it, that he wouldn't do it again. And then when I got pregnant, I thought perhaps having a child would change him, but he only grew worse. He beat me so bad once that I feared I was going to lose her."

Her voice caught in a sob, and I reached through the darkness until I found her hand. "Why didn't you leave him, Abby?" I asked gently.

"I didn't have anywhere to go," she sniffled, "and I was afraid he'd kill me if I left him. I didn't know what to do."

"I'm so sorry," I squeezed her hand, wondering if I would not have done the same if I'd been in her shoes. Nowhere to go, no one to turn to. It had to be a terrible feeling of helplessness, of entrapment, to be in such a situation.

"I'll do my best to pay you and your husband back for the money he stole," she said, her voice quivering.

"Don't be silly," I replied. "It's not your responsibility to do anything of the sort, so don't think another thing about it."

Abby was silent for a moment, and I was just about to drift off to sleep when she said quietly, "What is going to happen to my poor little girl,

Savannah? Her father a criminal, her mother quite possibly dying with cancer. What will become of her?"

"Don't say that, Abby," I scolded her. "You're going to be alright, just wait and see."

"I don't know," she sighed. "I haven't been feeling right the last few days. It's hard to explain."

"Your body has been through a lot lately," I said softly. "You'll feel better once we get out of this dungeon that we're in."

We both grew quiet, fading in and out of sleep throughout the night. I couldn't tell what time it was when we heard a noise upstairs, but I knew it wasn't Sunday afternoon yet, when my husband was to be home. My heart pounding, I scrambled through the darkness in search of a weapon. Hannah began to whimper, and I could hear Abby trying to comfort her. My hands landed on a brick I sometimes used to prop the door open with, and I raised it above my head, my mind whirling. Surely Juan hadn't come back. Should I call out in hopes that it was a neighbor nosing around?

I was still deliberating when I heard someone call my name, and my heart leapt with relief. It was my husband.

"We're down here," I yelled, my throat hoarse from thirst. "In the cellar."

The handle rattled for a moment as he tried unsuccessfully to open the door. "I'm going to kick it open," he called. "Make sure you're away from the door."

Within minutes, light streamed down into my face, and I could see my husband's silhouette as he hurried down the steps and pulled me into his arms.

"What happened?" He asked, pulling back to search my face.

"I'll tell you everything in a moment," I said. "But first let's get out of this hole and get something to drink."

On weak, trembling legs, the three of us walked up the steps and to the kitchen, my husband following closely behind. I filled us all a glass of water, and as we collapsed at the kitchen table to drink, my husband ran to the bedrooms to grab us all a blanket. We were chilled to the bone.

"Here," he said, gently wrapping the blankets around our shoulders. "I'll fix some hot tea."

While he made the tea, I told him what happened, my mind exhausted from the turmoil surrounding us these last twenty hours. "I thought you weren't supposed to come home until tomorrow?" I asked, welcoming the warm mug of tea in my hands as I took a sip.

"I wasn't," he said, patting Hannah gently on the head, "but when I called twice earlier today and couldn't reach you, I got worried and decided to come home early."

"I'm sure glad you did," Abby said with a sigh, exhaustion written all over her face.

The police were at our house within minutes of calling, and after we told what happened, a young officer named Lieutenant Baker said, "We've been on his tail for weeks, and about three hours ago we got word that he was killed in a shootout with the police." He turned to Abby and Hannah and said, "I'm very sorry it all turned out this way."

Pulling Hannah close, Abby nodded and said, "Thank you, Officer Baker."

While the officer spoke of returning our money to us within the next few days, I noticed how pale Abby looked, and how Hannah seemed to be supporting her, instead of the other way around. I reached out to touch her arm, about to suggest she go lie down, when suddenly she slid to the floor with no warning at all.

Chapter Fifty-one

-January 1942-

The journey to San Francisco was vastly different from our first trip to Hawaii. The laughter and gaiety on the ship was missing, as everyone was too nervous and on edge, half expecting to be attacked by a Japanese warship at any moment. The shuffleboard court and ping pong tables were occupied only by the children, and there was no singing and dancing at night. It didn't matter in the least to me. I was miserable, torn between relief that Connor was still alive and heartache over Maxi's death. I was grateful to have Vicki with me, but she just wasn't the same, either. She was quiet and withdrawn, hardly speaking a word to anyone, but I didn't mind.

When we finally reached San Francisco, I sent a telegram to my aunt and uncle, letting them know I was coming home. I didn't know the exact date of my arrival back in Savannah, so I simply told them I would walk home from the train station, leaving my luggage behind to be picked up later.

There wasn't to be a train leaving San Francisco until the following morning, so Vicki and I toured around the city a bit, regaining our land legs as we enjoyed the fresh air. We walked along the waterfront, and I shaded my eyes as I gazed out at the crystal blue water before me, allowing myself to enjoy the spectacular view. The newly constructed Golden Gate Bridge rose up before us like a giant red beauty, sparkling and shining bright in contrast to the pale blue sky in the background, and I had to smile at the noisy racket the car horns made as they crossed its lengthy expanse high above the rippling waves.

We walked a bit more, finally stopping at a little roadside café to eat clam chowder served in a bread bowl, and I couldn't remember anything ever tasting so good. I'd eaten very little on the ship, and my stomach rumbled in appreciation as I filled it with the warm, delicious meal. San Francisco was a truly delightful city, one that I would always think of fondly.

Many long and exhausting days later, I was finally home. Vicki and I gathered our things and stepped from the train, the familiar sights and smells bringing a bittersweet smile to my lips. I turned to Vicki, pulling the older woman into a tight hug. Vicki was staying at the station, where she would catch the next train to her hometown in Atlanta.

"Thank you, Vicki, for everything," I whispered, my throat tightening with emotion. I was truly grateful for everything the woman had done for me. I honestly didn't know what would have become of me had Vicki not been there to see about me. Through everything, we had bonded and become very close friends.

Vicki hugged me in return, pulling back slightly to swipe at a stray tear trailing down her cheek. "I'm glad we had each other," she smiled, fondness shining in her eyes. "Come visit me sometime?" She asked.

"I will," I nodded. "And you do the same."

As I made my way home, so many thoughts and emotions ran through my mind, and I looked up at the gray, overcast sky, struggling to fight back the tears. It was hard to fathom all that had changed since my arrival here almost two years ago. I'd come as a brokenhearted young woman, a girl, ignorant of life and completely unaware of what lay ahead. That girl felt like a stranger to me now. In the span of only a few months, I lost my father and dearest friend in the whole world, and I feared I'd never truly heal from the pain, that my heart would simply shrink and scab over.

My legs trembling and weak, I turned down our street and breathed a sigh of relief. The last month was piling on top of me with every step, and suddenly all I wanted to do was crawl into my old bed and sleep for days. As I slowly drew closer to the house, I could see a figure standing on the front porch, a hand resting above her forehead. It was Aunt Deb, and she seemed to be looking for me.

I raised my hand in a small wave, my footsteps quickening when she rushed from the porch steps toward me, her arms outstretched. In all honesty, I hadn't been certain how she would react upon my return home. I'd feared she would somehow blame me for Maxi's death, but when I saw the love shining from her eyes, I knew I'd been wrong. With a sob catching in the back of my throat, I ran into her open arms, our tears mingling together as we held each other and cried right there on the sidewalk in front of the house.

I was finally home again.

The next week passed by slowly and painfully. Upon my arrival, Aunt Deb drew a hot bath for me, immediately putting me to bed after I'd bathed and eaten. I was exhausted, mentally and physically, and hardly moved out of that bed for three days. Lizzie came and sat with me every afternoon, reading to me and bringing me special treats she knew I liked.

On one such afternoon, Lizzie began to speak about Joseph and how much she missed him. "I don't think I'll ever get over him, Miss Savannah," she sniffed, her lips quivering.

"You'll always love him, Lizzie, you can't help that," I said, reaching out to take her hand. After a moment, a thought struck me and I asked, "Have there been any more murders, or did the police finally catch the man?"

"The answer to both questions is 'no'," Lizzie replied, raising her dark, piercing eyes to meet mine. "Ever since he made a grab for you, I've been doing a little snooping."

My eyes widened. "Lizzie, what do you mean?" I wanted to know.

"Those policemen said they think it might be the same man that killed those first three ladies at the boarding house, and I tend to agree. People still wonder if my Joseph really was responsible, and I aim to prove them wrong."

"But how?"

"I've been asking some questions, among other things," she sniffed, glancing down at her fingernails. "I think I might be onto something, but I can't say what it is just yet."

"Lizzie, you had better be careful," I warned, although I knew she wouldn't listen.

"Don't you worry about me," she said sternly. "I have a little handgun my daddy gave me, and I know how to use it."

I shook my head, watching as she left the room to tend to some laundry she had out on the line. I wondered just what is was she'd found out and prayed she wouldn't cross paths with the killer.

Vivian stopped by nearly every day after work, bringing along delicious leftover desserts from her family's restaurant. It was wonderful to see her again, and she even stayed the night with me once. We stayed up late talking about Maxi and how much we both missed her, and I found myself feeling very grateful for Vivian's friendship and support.

Once everyone knew I was home, visitors stopped by the house every day, and I began to feel like I was trapped in a never-ending cycle of constant "thank you's", and the retelling of everything that happened in Hawaii. I finally reached the point of simply thanking the people for coming by but adding that I didn't want to talk about it anymore. I knew people were curious and wanted to hear first-hand about the attack, but I felt as if it was draining the very life out of me.

I'd been back a week when the day of Maxi's funeral arrived. As if in a trance, I dressed myself in black, rode to the church, and stood silently by the grave while the preacher read from the Bible. My aunt and uncle decided on a simple graveside service, and I clutched my aunt's hand as I watched the pallbearers lower the closed, wooden box into the ground. I dropped a handful of daisies, Maxi's favorite flower, into the hole, and said one final goodbye as the dirt was thrown on top.

"Savannah banana."

The hoarse voice to my left caught my attention, and I turned to see Leon standing just a few feet away, his eyes filled with tears. His mother told me he'd joined the Army a few days after the attack, as so many men did, and was shipped away for training, and as I ran into his open arms, I wondered vaguely how it was possible that he was here.

"I can't believe she's gone," he whispered against my hair.

"Neither can I."

I rested my cheek against his chest, my tears dampening the white cotton shirt beneath my skin. After a moment, I pulled back and Leon gently wiped my face with his hanky. "I thought you were in training?" I asked, taking the handkerchief to blow my nose.

Leon took my arm as we began walking slowly to my aunt and uncle's car. "I was," he said with a sigh, his face somber, "but I was rejected."

"What?" I looked at him in surprise. "Why?"

"Remember I had asthma as a kid?" When I nodded, he continued, "I thought I was over that, but apparently it's just been lying dormant. When I began the intensive training, it came back with full force. I guess my body just can't handle the stress," he shrugged, glancing down at his feet as he added, "It looks like Connor is the only man in the family that can fight for his country."

He looked so downtrodden that my heart squeezed for him, and I said, "You can't help it, Leon. Besides, I'm glad you're not going. Your mother needs you here. It really would have been terrible to leave her here alone. Plus," I added, my eyes once again filling with tears, "I don't think

I could bear to lose another friend."

With a sigh, Leon pulled me into another hug and said, "You won't ever lose me, Savannah. Not ever."

Chapter Fifty-two

-1942-

The days gradually turned into weeks, and the only word received from Connor was a quick telegram sent to his mother, Mrs. Emma, before I had even made it back home yet, which stated he was leaving Hawaii and would write as soon as he could. That was over a month ago, and we were all worried sick about him.

I received a letter from Betty and was overcome with relief when she said Kanani was going to be alright. He had a long road of recovery ahead, but she vowed to be there with him every step of the way. *I plan to marry the goof,* she wrote, *so he has no other choice but to get better.*

With most of my time being spent cooped up in the house, I began to grow stir crazy. I finally decided it was time to get back to work, and when I climbed out of bed on my first morning back, I was torn between excitement and nervousness. I hadn't done any nursing since the attack and wondered if I would be able to do it without being overcome with flashbacks.

I was on my way out the front door when I saw Peter's milk truck pull up in front of our house. I rustled through my purse for my car keys, smiling at Peter as he climbed from the driver's seat.

"Good morning, Peter," I said as I hurried to my car, which was parked just behind his truck.

"Morning, Miss Savannah," he nodded politely. "I heard you were back home, but I haven't seen you around. Going back to work?"

"Yes," I replied. "I figured it was time for me to get back to my normal way of life."

"I'm sorry about your cousin," he said, taking a step closer to me. "Is your family doing okay?"

I edged back, my backside bumping against the car. "Yes, thank you," I said, moving to open the car door.

"Oh, let me," he sprang forward to open it for me.

"Thanks," I smiled, my spine tensing a bit when he put his hand on my arm.

"If there's ever anything I can do for you, Miss Savannah, don't hesitate to ask," Peter said, his tone low.

"I appreciate that," I stated, pulling my arm away as I swiftly slid into the car and shut the door.

You're too much on edge, Savannah, I told myself as I drove away, watching Peter from the rearview mirror.

My first day back at work went better than I expected. Everyone was so nice and seemed to be genuinely happy over my return, and I kept so busy with patients and filing and paperwork that I barely had time to think of anything else. During my lunch break, I went out back to the garden and sat at a picnic table, the crisp, cold air cooling my flushed skin. I'd just begun to eat when, to my surprise, Doctor Cox appeared before me.

Startled, I gulped a half-eaten bite of my chicken salad sandwich and quickly wiped the mustard from my mouth.

"Hello, Savannah," he smiled brightly. "Mind if I join you?"

"Of course not, Doctor Cox," I motioned to the seat before me.

He sat down and opened the brown paper bag he was carrying, pulling out a whole chicken breast, two buttermilk biscuits, a small bowl of potato salad wrapped in saran wrap, and a slice of apple pie.

"Would you like one of these biscuits?" he asked politely. "I do believe my wife makes the best in the whole city."

"Oh, no, thank you," I shook my head and smiled. "They do look delicious, though."

He took a bite of potato salad, and I sipped my coffee, watching him curiously. We'd always had a good working relationship, but he'd never sought me out this way. I wondered what was on his mind.

"It's good to have you back, Savannah," he finally said, looking up at me. "How are you doing?"

This was the first time today that someone had asked how I was doing, and I forced myself not to cringe. I knew he meant well, but I didn't want to think about Maxi or what had happened or how I was doing. I simply wanted to focus on my first day back at work.

"I'm doing just fine," I said, smiling tightly at him. "How are you and Mrs. Cox?"

"She's been a little under the weather lately," he sighed, his brow furrowed. After a moment, he cleared his throat and said, "My son, Matthew, works for the newspaper. Did you know that?"

"Yes, I did," I nodded, my eyes narrowing slightly.

"I always wanted him to become a doctor, just like his old man, but he wouldn't have it," he chuckled, shaking his head. "He always was one to do things his own way."

"I see." I held back a smirk, forcing myself not to say what passed through my mind. Everyone knew Matthew Cox was a spoiled, stubborn individual who never knew the meaning of being told "no". I was just surprised he had enough initiative to get a job at all. I assumed he only did it to defy his father, but before I could follow through on that thought Doctor Cox began talking again.

"He actually seems to enjoy his work, though, so who am I to judge?" When I didn't respond, he continued, "He actually mentioned to me that he would like to interview you on your experiences at Pearl Harbor."

So that's it, I thought, taking another sip of my coffee. "Really?"

"Yes," he nodded. "I thought I would mention it to you in hopes that you'd agree to do it?"

"Doctor Cox," I sighed, "I don't want to seem rude, but I really don't care to talk about what happened…"

"Please, my dear," he interrupted, reaching across the table to rest his hand atop mine. "It would mean so much to me."

I hesitated, a bit taken aback by the beseeching look in his eyes. How could I tell him no when it obviously meant so much to him? He was basically my boss and had only ever been kind to me. I hated the thought of sharing my story, of reliving those horrible memories again, especially with the likes of Matthew Cox, but found myself nodding my head reluctantly in agreement.

"Alright, I'll do it."

"Wonderful!" Doctor Cox exclaimed, smiling brightly. "I'll tell Matthew to call you and set up a time."

"That will be fine," I smiled, my jaw clenched.

With a deep sigh, I placed my chin in my hand and watched the doctor gather his trash and walk away, hoping I wouldn't regret this decision.

After I'd eaten, I threw my trash away and went back to work. Immediately upon my return, the head nurse told me there was a man in the waiting area that needed stitches.

"I'll take care of it," I told her, taking the clipboard with his name and information. As I walked to the waiting area, I glanced down at the patient's name and was surprised to find it was someone I knew.

"Hi, Lionel," I said, smiling politely at him from the doorway. I hadn't seen him since Lucy's party nearly a year ago and wondered if he'd even remember me.

He sat with his head in his hands, and when he glanced up, I saw recognition flit across his face as I quickly surveyed his injuries. I couldn't tell what type of accident he'd been involved in, but he had a swollen, black eye, a nasty cut on his cheek, a busted lip, and his hair and clothes were dirty and in disarray.

"You can come on back now and I'll get you taken care of," I said, motioning for him to follow me.

He followed me to room three, not speaking a word. I told him to sit down, and as I gathered the necessary items I would need to tend to his cuts, I asked him what happened.

"I…uh…fell," was all he said.

My brow furrowing, I glanced over to find him staring at me, his direct gaze a bit unnerving. "How did you fall?" I questioned as I laid my utensils out on the table.

"From a ladder."

My eyes widened. "Oh, my goodness, you could have broken your neck!"

He shrugged, glancing down at his hands. I sat down before him and gently cleaned the cuts before I began to apply the sutures. "This will be a little painful," I said, "so I apologize beforehand."

"You won't hurt me," he mumbled.

The entire time I worked, I tried to ignore how close he was and how his breath, which smelled of stale cigarettes, blew against my face. He kept glancing up at me, his gaze making me feel oddly uncomfortable, and I had to force myself not to slide away from him.

"You'll need to come back in a couple of weeks to get those stitches removed," I told him once I was finished, adding with a smile, "and try not to pick at them, even when they start to itch."

"Yes ma'am," he nodded. Glancing down at his hands, he added, "Thank you for stitching me up. You're a good nurse."

With a look of surprise at the compliment, I said, "Why, thank you, Lionel, and you're very welcome."

He stood then and, taking a step towards me, said, "You're very nice, Savannah, even though…"

The door opened suddenly, interrupting Lionel as Dr. Cox entered the room.

"I'm sorry to intrude, Savannah," Dr. Cox said, his eyes on the clipboard he held in his hand, "but as soon as you get done here, I need your help in room…"

His eyes falling on Lionel, the doctor stopped talking. "What are you doing here?" He asked Lionel. "What happened?"

"I fell off a ladder," Lionel replied, his jaw clenched.

"You two know each other?" I asked in surprise.

"Oh, uh, yes," Doctor Cox cleared his throat. "Lionel has…waited on a few events my wife and I have held at our home."

"Oh, I see," I stated, my eyes moving between the two men as obvious tension filled the room.

"Thank you for fixing me up," Lionel said to me, his chair grating loudly against the floor as he stood. "I'll be back in two weeks."

And with that, Lionel left the room. As I continued to clean up my work area, I glanced at Doctor Cox, noting the strained expression on his face. "Is everything alright, Doctor?" I asked.

Shaking himself, Doctor Cox nodded and said, "Yes, yes, of course. Just come to room seven when you can."

He hurried from the room, leaving me to wonder if there was possibly something more to Doctor Cox and Lionel's acquaintance that I didn't know.

Chapter Fifty-three

-1965-

I sat in the hard back, metal chair, my fingernails biting into the palms of my hands. My husband sat beside me, his arm around my shoulders, and I glanced nervously at the loudly ticking clock which hung over Doctor Roberts' desk. He'd been gone nearly thirty minutes, what was taking him so long?

It had been three months since my surgery. Three exhausting, tedious months, and after a long morning of tests, we were waiting to get the results on whether or not I was cancer free.

"I wonder how Abby is doing," I murmured, my stomach in knots as my mind twirled back and forth between Abby's condition and my own. After she collapsed two nights ago in our home, we rushed her to the hospital, and she was immediately taken back. We waited several hours, but since we aren't family the only thing the nurses would tell us was that she had yet to wake up, but her condition was stable, and they were running tests.

Hannah had been staying with us, and last night I slept in her room with her. After everything that happened with her father and then seeing her mother collapse had been very traumatic for the child, and I couldn't help but worry about her. She was out in the waiting room now under the watchful eye of the receptionist, and I hoped for her sake I'd be able to hold it together if I didn't receive good news.

"I'm sure Abby is going to be alright," my husband patted my shoulder. "She was probably just dehydrated from spending so much time in that cellar."

If that's the case, wouldn't the hospital have released her by now? I thought, worrying my lower lip between my teeth.

The door opened suddenly, and Doctor Roberts walked in, chart in hand. I couldn't gauge by his expression whether he had good news or bad, and I held my breath as I watched him sit behind his desk and casually intertwine his fingers.

"Savannah," he finally said, raising his eyes to meet mine. He hesitated, and it was all I could do to remain silent, my heart pounding so heavily within my chest I feared I might faint. Suddenly, a smile broke upon the doctor's face, and he said, "You are cancer free."

I sat in shock, unable to move or speak for a long moment. My eyes filled with tears, and I could feel the hot liquid begin to drip down my cheeks. I couldn't believe it. I was cancer free!

With a joyous laugh, my husband leapt to his feet and pulled me into his arms, swinging me wildly about the room. I cried and laughed and cried some more, thanking Doctor Roberts for all he'd done with a hug and kiss on the cheek.

With a spring in our step, my husband and I hurried from the office hand in hand to find Hannah, and when she saw us coming down the hall, she jumped from her seat and ran to us.

"Are you going to be okay?" She asked, her eyes filled with concern as she reached out and took my hand.

Smiling, I nodded and pulled her into a hug, wondering how she'd known the reason I was here. "Yes, honey, the doctor said I'm going to be just fine."

We went out for lunch, celebrating my good news with an ice cream sundae for dessert. Hannah sat close to me, her little hand constantly touching my hand or arm. I told her we'd go back by the hospital after lunch and check in on her mother, and her black eyes filled with both apprehension and excitement.

"I'm glad you're here, Savannah," Nancy, the nurse at the front desk, said when we arrived. Nancy and I had worked together for years, and were good friends. "Abby is awake and asking to see you and Hannah."

Hannah and I followed Nancy down a long hall, hand in hand, both of our nerves on edge. I wondered how Abby was doing, and if she'd received any test results yet. Nancy finally stopped at a door to our left and, after knocking lightly, pushed it open and peeked inside.

"Abby?" I heard her say. "You have company."

She turned, beckoning us to follow, and we stepped into the dimly lit room. My eyes fell on Abby, and my heart sank a bit. She looked so small and frail in that big hospital bed, her skin as white as the sheets. She smiled when she saw us and pushed herself up into a sitting position, opening her arms to Hannah as the child walked hesitantly to her mother's side.

"Hey, Baby," Abby said, her voice weak. "Come sit up here by me."

"You know when the visiting hours are over, Savannah, so just stay as long as you want," Nancy said, patting my arm as she left the room.

I stood back and watched Hannah climb into the hospital bed and curl up next to her mother. Abby asked how she was doing, and Hannah said, "I'm fine, Mama, you don't have to worry about me. When are you coming home?"

"I don't know," Abby sighed. "They don't know yet what's going on with me."

"They haven't gotten any test results back?" I spoke up, coming to sit in the chair by Abby's bed.

"I guess not," she shrugged, absently running her fingers through Hannah's hair. "When I finally came around this morning, they said they had been running tests but would need to run some more now that I'm awake."

"Aunt Savannah got good news today, Mama," Hannah announced with a smile, and I forced myself not to cringe. I hadn't wanted to tell Abby until she got some good news of her own.

"Yes, I did," I said when Abby looked at me questioningly. "It looks like I'm cancer free."

"Oh, Savannah," Abby gasped, her face melting into a joyous smile. "That's wonderful!"

"Isn't it?" I laughed, swiping at a stray tear. "I only hope you'll receive the same news soon."

"I'm sure I will," Abby said optimistically, patting Hannah on the back.

We all three continued to talk until Hannah fell asleep in her mother's arms, and Abby glanced lovingly down at her daughter, smiling as she gently touched her cheek. "You know," she said softly, "it's the strangest thing, but sometimes she reminds me of my younger sister."

"Oh?" I asked, surprised.

"Yes," she nodded. "Her name was Claire. She was a couple of years younger than me, but I remember she was the sweetest little angel. We had different fathers, and she had darker hair and eyes like Hannah. I loved her so much." Her eyes filling with tears, she whispered, "I loved both of my sisters."

I stared at Abby, my brow furrowed. "I thought you were raised in the foster system?" I asked.

"I was put into the foster system when I was ten," Abby explained, her blue eyes filled with the pain of memories. "My mother just couldn't keep us all. My oldest sister was the first to go. I believe she was sent off to live with a family member, but that was never certain. After I was grown, I went back to look for them, but they were all gone."

Something about Abby's story sounded oddly familiar, and I nearly pushed the feeling aside, thinking myself silly. But then something told me to ask the question that burned in the back of my throat, and I found myself saying, "Abby, what was your other sister's name?"

"Maxine. Her name was Maxine."

Chapter Fifty-four

-1942-

I'd been back to work for three days, and yet somehow it felt more like a year. I was bone weary every evening when I got home, but just couldn't make myself slow down. I wanted to work and needed something to occupy both my time and mind but found myself counting down the days until the weekend.

After speaking with Doctor Cox, I received a phone call the next day from his son. The interview was scheduled for tonight, and the closer the clock drew to six o'clock the more I dreaded the appointment.

At fifteen minutes past six, the doorbell rang, and I hurried to let Matthew in, trying to hide my irritation that he was late. I showed him into the living room, graciously offering him something to drink.

"No, thank you," he shook his head. Leaning forward, he opened his notepad and said, "I'm ready to begin whenever you are."

My jaw clenched, I slowly sat down in the chair across from him, wondering how he made it as a reporter. He was arrogant, rude, and self-absorbed, and as I studied his features, I realized this was likely the reason he was still single. A rather handsome man, he stood several inches taller than me, with curly blonde hair and deep-set blue eyes. I could only assume he was even more attractive when he smiled but couldn't say for sure as I'd never been the recipient of such a gesture from him.

"What would you like to know?" I asked, folding my hands nervously in my lap.

"Just tell me of your experiences in Hawaii, both before, during, and after the attack."

Taking a deep breath, I began talking, my voice monotone as I relayed the information he was seeking. I closed my eyes as I spoke of the attack, fighting off the tears and nausea that threatened to overtake me. Once I was finished, I released a deep sigh of relief, my body finally relaxing against the cushioned chair.

"How was it, witnessing the death of your cousin?" Matthew asked, his question catching me off guard. I'd mentioned Maxi's death, choosing to keep it short and basic as I didn't like going into too much detail. I felt that his question was a bit callous and hesitated before answering.

"It was like witnessing my own death," I whispered, fighting to keep my composure. "She was like a sister to me, and I loved her dearly. Watching her die was the worst thing imaginable."

He stared at me in silence as I spoke, his cool, relatively blank expression never changing. I'd expected a reaction of some sort during the interview, whether it be sadness, anger, or compassion, but instead I received no reaction at all. It was as if I was speaking to a wall.

"Well, that covers everything I wanted to know," he said, slapping his notebook shut as he stood to his feet.

As I walked him to the door, I attempted small talk by asking about his mother. "I heard she wasn't feeling well," I said. "Is she doing better? Your father seemed quite worried about her."

"Did he now?" Matthew laughed disdainfully, and I blinked in surprise. "She's doing better, no thanks to him."

"Oh…well, I'm glad she's feeling better," I cleared my throat. "So, this morning I read the article you wrote about the murders. There really isn't any new information?"

"I believe I said there wasn't in the article. Apparently, this guy is a good deal smarter than our local law enforcement."

And with that, he walked out, shutting the door behind him. Irritated, I flung the door back open and called after him, "You're welcome for the interview."

The only acknowledgement I got was a hand thrown half-heartedly in the air as Matthew continued walking to his car, his head held high and stride that of an arrogant, self-assured jerk. I slammed the door, angry that I'd been coerced into doing this interview. I only hoped Matthew did the article justice.

I went upstairs, my mind on the interview, and found myself pushing open the door to Maxi's bedroom. I paused in the entryway, my eyes sweeping over the bed, the trunk we'd yet to unpack, the vanity with Maxi's hairbrush and perfume resting on top as if waiting for her to return and use them. It seemed so strange that everything she owned was still here in this room, but Maxi was never coming back. My aunt, uncle, and I hadn't been able to bring ourselves to clean out her room yet, and I walked over to the trunk and slowly lifted the lid. I ran my fingers over her sweater, picking it up to breath in the faint smell of her scent, when my eyes fell on her diary. I picked it up, wondering if I should read it. Would it be wrong to intrude on something so personal? What if our aunt or uncle read it and found out about the baby?

Perhaps I should destroy it, I thought, walking from her room into mine. No, I couldn't do that. Locking my door, I sat on my bed and slowly opened the leather-bound book to the pages of her last few entries. Most of what she wrote was of our time in Hawaii, of the Swanson's and our job at the hospital, but I paused on the very last entry, my eyes widening as I read:

Dear Diary,

I received a letter from Leon this morning, and I can't tell you how much it means to hear from him. I don't think my feelings will ever change. I've loved him for as long as I can remember and suppose I always will. Oh, how I wish things could have been different! I wish I'd never even met Robert. Maybe if I were a better person, stronger and more confident, Leon could have loved me. If he ever found out about my situation, I'd die of shame.

My due date is drawing closer, and I'll admit I'm very nervous, but I quite possibly have good news to share. I spoke to Mrs. Swanson earlier this evening, and she mentioned wanting to perhaps adopt a baby. Although I never intended to become pregnant, I've come to love this child and want him/her to have a good, loving home. My greatest hope is to give my baby to the Swanson's and go back home. I miss my family so much, and although I'd never say this out loud, I secretly hope that Leon has missed me and has had a change of heart towards me. Perhaps once I get back, things will finally be different between us. I realize I'm not worthy of someone so wonderful and fine, but if only I could know there is hope for us, I'd be willing to wait until the end of time for him.

I closed the diary slowly, my eyes staring at the little book incredulously. How had I not known Maxi was in love with Leon? Why had she never confided in me? It felt strange, and maybe even a little wrong, to read about Maxi's private, innermost thoughts, but now I was beginning to wonder if I ever really knew her at all. How had I missed something so obvious?

And obvious it was, looking back now. As if my mind were

magnifying all the little details that had been right under my nose, I could now see the soft spark in Maxi's eyes when she looked at Leon, the flush in her normally pale cheeks. I could read the gentle smile on her lips when they talked and hear the longing in her voice when she called his name. How could I have been so blind? How could Leon have been so blind?

Angry at both Leon and myself, I pushed the diary under my mattress and stood up, walking over to look out the window. Why had Leon never pursued Maxi? Had he been worried about ruining their friendship, or had he simply never cared for her in that way? The latter made me even more angry, for if he had cared and just told Maxi, she would never have become involved with Robert and would quite possibly still be alive today. How could I ever act normally around Leon after this?

With a sigh, I closed the curtain and turned around. I couldn't very well blame Leon for Maxi's death, that wasn't fair, but I couldn't help feeling a bit angry at him. He'd unknowingly been hurting Maxi for years, and she'd died without ever truly knowing how he felt about her. In a way, she died with a broken heart, and I wasn't sure if I could ever forgive him for that.

After what seemed like an eternity of waiting, I finally received a letter from Connor. It was Friday afternoon, and I had just arrived home from work when I saw Lizzie emerging from the front door, carrying an empty laundry basket.

"Heading home so late?" I asked, giving her a hug.

"Yes, your aunt is in the mood for a little early spring cleaning, so it's been a long, busy day," Lizzie chuckled, shaking her head.

"Do you want a ride home?" I asked, glancing up at the darkening sky.

"No, I...uh...have some other things to do first," she replied, glancing down at her feet as if avoiding my gaze.

Eyes narrowing, I asked, "Lizzie, you're not still playing Nancy Drew, are you?"

"Don't mind me, Miss Savannah," Lizzie winked. When I opened my mouth to protest further, she hurried past me and said, "Well, I've got to get going. You've got a letter from Connor waiting upstairs."

Distracted by Lizzie's announcement, I turned and ran into the house, the screen door bouncing shut behind me. I raced up the stairs to my room, my hands shaking as I tore anxiously into the envelope addressed in Connor's familiar, bold script.

Dear Savannah Rose,

I hope you are doing well. I'm sorry I haven't been able to write sooner. I'm currently stationed just outside of England, but that's subject to change at any given moment. I'll do my best to keep you, Mother, and Leon posted on my whereabouts.

I miss you, Savannah Rose. Very much. I keep replaying our last night together in my mind, as well as our conversation the following morning. There's so much I want to say to you, but I just can't put it down on paper. What I have to say needs to be said in person. Just know that I care very much for you, please don't ever doubt that.

My brow furrowing, I stopped reading for a moment and thought about his words, trying to decipher their meaning. They could be taken both positively and negatively. The "please don't ever doubt that I care for you" line was what really gave me pause, as if he were trying to let me down easy. Did he simply care for me as a friend, and wanted to tell me so in person? To apologize for kissing me? Shaking my head, I heaved a deep sigh. I honestly didn't know. Raising the letter up to the light once again, I continued to read.

Mrs. Swanson told me about Maxine. I am so, so sorry. I know how much you loved her. We all loved her, but you two had a special bond, and I'm so very sorry I didn't do something to prevent her death. Maybe if I hadn't run off so quickly that morning, I could have talked you both out of going to the base. If only I'd known what was going to happen, I'd have done everything I could to stop it. I hope you can forgive me for that, and for not being there to help you afterwards. During the attack, my plane went down, and I was injured in the crash. I'd just gotten back to town the day you left, and barely made it to the port in time to see you off. I wanted so badly to speak to you before you left, but I'm glad I at least was able to see you.

I wish I could write something a bit longer and more interesting, but I'm going on a mission early tomorrow morning and need to get some sleep. I hope to hear from you soon. I'll try to write as often as I can. When you think of me, do me a favor and smile. You're so beautiful when you smile.

With a sigh, I folded the letter and placed it in the top drawer of my vanity, with intentions of reading it over and over again until I received his next letter. I missed him very much, and as I began to change from my nursing uniform, I prayed fervently for his safety.

Vivian and her beau came over to eat supper with us that night, and I had to admit that everything Vivian said about him was true. His name was Howard, he was shy but very sweet, and it was obvious that he absolutely adored Vivian.

"I one hundred percent approve," I whispered into her ear when I hugged her goodbye.

As I watched them walk to his car hand in hand, I smiled softly, feeling a bit melancholy as I found myself thinking, once again, of Connor.

Chapter Fifty-five

-1942-

He walked along the sidewalk, his shoes clicking out a rhythm with each step. Crickets chirped, a gate creaked, a dog barked. It was late, nearly two o'clock in the morning, but he couldn't sleep. He wanted, needed, to be near her. Rounding the corner, he made certain his hat was pulled low over his face as he neared her house. He wouldn't risk getting seen by another nosy neighbor.

There it was. He stopped before her house, his eyes searching the darkened bedroom windows for a light that may give him a glimpse of her silhouette. He'd seen her a few times since her return home but tried to keep his distance. He didn't want to scare her off. It had, however, been excruciatingly hard to control himself. He was waiting for just the right moment, when everything would fall into place, but he had to be careful. After nearly getting caught the last time, he was afraid of once again making a wrong move. He couldn't, wouldn't, be put behind bars like a caged animal.

Soon. That was the word that kept floating through his mind over and over. He couldn't wait much longer. He'd be careful, but he'd make his move soon. That nosy maid was getting too close to the truth, and if he waited too long it would be too late. He'd have to take care of the maid sooner or later, but first he would be with Margie. He had to be with her one last time, and then it would all be over.

Turning, he slowly walked away, his figure melting into the black canvas of the night.

When March arrived, no one was expecting another cold spell to show its face but show it did. I bundled up in a thick sweater and hurried to my car, Aunt Deb's words floating through my mind as I dug through my purse for my car keys: *"There's always one more cold spell before Easter."*

"I guess she was right," I chuckled to myself, forcing back a yawn.

I found my keys and hurriedly slid into the driver's seat to crank the engine, only to blink in surprise when my car wouldn't start.

"What in the world," I muttered, trying once again with no luck. With a sigh, I turned and grabbed my purse from the passenger's seat, swiveling back around to open my door. I hadn't seen anyone approach the car, and when my eyes landed on the hooded figure stooped over and staring at me through the car window, I shrieked in surprise, accidentally bumping the horn with my elbow when I jerked away.

The figure jumped back, and through a haze of fear I realized it was Peter. My hands shaking, I slowly climbed out of the car and stared at him.

"I didn't mean to scare you, Miss Savannah," Peter hurriedly explained, "but I just now realized I dropped one of my gloves on your neighbor's front porch, so after parking my truck down the street, I ran back to get it. That's when I noticed you were having car trouble, and thought I'd ask if you needed help."

Taking a deep, calming breath, I cleared my throat and said in a shaky voice, "That's okay, Peter. I just didn't hear you come up." Glancing back at my car, I added, "My car won't start."

"Let me just pop the hood and take a look at it for you," he said, rushing around to the front of the car before I could object.

I stood on the sidewalk, shivering, and waited while Peter attempted to figure out what was wrong. I assumed I'd have to take it to a mechanic, but after a short moment Peter's head popped back up and he said, "Give her another try."

I did just that, surprised when the engine immediately came to life after just one try. *Apparently, Peter knows his way around a car*, I thought, climbing back out to thank him.

"Oh, no need to thank me," he smiled broadly, "I was glad to do it. I, uh," he hesitated, clearing his throat, "I would like to ask you something, if you have a minute?" I nodded, and he continued, "I was wondering if…well…if you'd like to go see a picture show with me sometime."

I blinked, totally unprepared for such a question. Although a little odd, Peter seemed nice enough, but I just wasn't interested and didn't quite know how to tell him.

"Savannah?" A voice to my left called. "Is everything alright?"

Relieved, I turned to see Leon walking my way, his eyes on Peter as he assessed the situation.

"Yes," I nodded, "Peter was just helping me get my car started."

Leon came to stand next to me, and I noticed the way Peter tensed up at his interfering presence.

"Well, that was nice of him," Leon stated, his smile forced. I noticed then that he held something in his hand. "Is this yours?" Leon asked Peter, raising his hand to reveal one lone glove. "I found it just now on our front porch."

"Yes, thanks," Peter nodded, taking the glove.

We stood there in an awkward silence until I finally cleared my throat and said, "Well, I'd better be going. I'm late enough as it is."

I turned to go, stopping when Peter said, "But you haven't answered my question."

With a sigh, I turned back to face Peter and opened my mouth to reply when Leon interrupted and asked, "What question was that?"

"I don't see how that's any of your business," Peter snapped, his face turning red.

"I just made it my business," Leon replied smoothly.

Peter glared at Leon with such force that I said the first thing that came to mind. "I appreciate the offer, Peter, but I'm actually seeing someone else."

Both men looked at me in surprise, and with a clenched jaw Peter pointed to Leon and asked, "Him?"

"No," I shook my head, refusing to say anything further.

"Well then, I hope you have a nice day," Peter hissed, spinning on his heel to stalk angrily away.

As we watched him round the corner and disappear, Leon commented, "I don't like that guy, you need to stay away from him."

"Well, it's not like I had much choice," I sighed, telling him everything that happened.

"It seems a little strange to me that he magically appeared just when you needed him and within five minutes fixed your car. Which, I might add, has never given you any problems," Leon said, frowning.

"I'm sure he's harmless," I replied, my tone not nearly as convincing as I'd hoped.

Glancing down at me, Leon raised his eyebrows and said, "So, I didn't know you were seeing someone."

"You didn't ask," I shrugged nonchalantly.

"Probably because you've been avoiding me lately."

My face flushing, I reached up to straighten my hair and replied, "I haven't been avoiding you." *Yes, you have*, my conscience told me, *ever since you read Maxi's diary.*

"Yes, you have, and now I know why," Leon stated, crossing his arms. "Just who is the lucky fellow?"

Laughed sheepishly, I shook my head and said, "Oh, I don't know that I should have said I was "seeing" someone, because I'm not. Not really."

"That doesn't make sense," Leon stated, his brow furrowed. "Either you are, or you aren't."

"It's just that I don't really know where we stand, so I can't say for certain," I shrugged, avoiding his gaze.

"Why don't you ask him?"

"Because he's off fighting in a war."

After a moment of silence, Leon reached out and raised my chin, forcing me to look at him. "Is it my brother?" He wanted to know. When I didn't answer, his eyes narrowed and he asked, "Did something happen between you two in Hawaii?"

Squirming away from him, I turned and opened my car door. "That's none of your business," I said with a sniff. "I need to get to work. I'm late."

Thankfully, Leon let me go without another word, and as I drove away, I glanced in the rearview mirror to find him still standing in the road watching me.

Chapter Fifty-six

-1965-

"Savannah, what's wrong? Are you alright?"

Abby reached out to touch my hand, the concern in her voice pulling me away from my shock. I felt as if I'd been punched in the stomach as I stared wordlessly at her, my mind racing. I studied her face, finally seeing the similarities that had been there all along. The soft, blue eyes and blonde hair. The sweet smile and gentle spirit. Had I known deep down in my heart, but never consciously acknowledged it?

"Abby," I whispered, my throat tight, "we're cousins."

Her brow furrowing, Abby asked, "What?"

"Maxi...Maxine lived with my aunt and uncle for years. She and I were like sisters. I was with her when she...when she died." I laid my head against our intertwined hands and began to cry, my tears soaking the sheets.

Abby didn't say anything for a moment, she simply sat in silence, not moving or making a sound. "Maxine is dead?" I finally heard her say softly, and I raised my head to look at her, realizing that, of course, she hadn't known.

"Yes," I nodded, wiping my cheeks. "I'm so sorry, Abby. That was very thoughtless and insensitive of me."

"How did she die?" Abby wanted to know.

Leaning my elbows against the bed, I told her everything. About the baby, about Pearl Harbor, about how I felt after Maxi's death. We both cried, each of us mourning a different memory. Abby remembered Maxi as the older sister that helped take care of her as a child before she was taken away, while my memories of Maxi were much different.

"I can't believe she's dead," Abby sniffed, dabbing at her eyes with the edge of the bedsheet. Reaching out to once again take my hand, she said, "And I can't believe you and I are cousins!"

"I know," I laughed, shaking my head. "I can't wait to tell Aunt Deb. It truly is wonderful!"

We talked for at least another hour, each sharing memories of Maxi. Eventually, Abby's eyes grew heavy, and within moments she and Hannah's heads were resting together as they slept peacefully. I stepped out into the hall, on a mission to find a cup of coffee, when I bumped into Nancy.

"How is Abby?" She asked, glancing down at the clipboard she held in her hand.

"She's resting," I replied, excitement in my voice as I proceeded to tell her the good news.

"Incredible!" Nancy exclaimed once I'd finished, her eyes wide. Glancing around, she took my arm and pulled me into a nearby corner, her face solemn as she said in a low voice, "I probably shouldn't tell you this, but since you're not only one of us but also Abby's cousin, I think you should know."

"Know what?" I asked, my stomach sinking.

"We got Abby's results back," she replied, glancing down once more at her clipboard. "I'm sorry, Savannah, but her cancer has spread. The doctor said she doesn't have much longer to live."

Chapter Fifty-seven

-1942-

Friday evening, as I readied myself to leave work and head home, one of the other nurses approached me.

"You got a telephone call earlier when you were assisting Doctor Cox in the operating room, so I jotted it down for you," she said, handing me the note.

Unfolding the piece of paper, my brow furrowed in concern as I quickly scanned over the words:

Miss Savannah, I've uncovered some very important information. Meet me at Mrs. G's as soon as you can. -Lizzie

I slowly lowered the paper, my mind racing. What was Lizzie up to now? And why did she want me to meet her at Mrs. Gibson's boarding house? Just the thought of going near that place made me shiver. I suddenly wondered if perhaps Lizzie was in some sort of trouble. Then, another thought struck me. Maybe this was a trap.

Hurriedly, I grabbed my things and rushed to the front desk in search of the nurse that gave me the note. When I found her, I asked, "Was the person that called me a female?"

"Yes," she nodded, eyeing me curiously. "She said she works for your aunt and uncle."

I blinked, surprised but relieved to know it wasn't a trap. Still, the thought of driving out there on my own unnerved me, so I went to the telephone and dialed the Danes' number.

Mrs. Emma answered and I asked for Leon. "He isn't home yet, honey, he had to work late," Mrs. Emma explained.

"Oh," I sighed. "I wanted him to go somewhere with me, but never mind. I'll see you later, okay?"

I hung up and hurried outside to my car. It was growing dark, and as I drove away, I felt a strange sense of uneasiness. Perhaps I should have called Uncle Ray, but I didn't want to waste any more time. Lizzie needed me; I could feel it.

The busy, lighted streets that were bustling with shoppers and businesses soon faded away as I neared the less than desirable side of town. I'd only been down here once, and as the sky darkened, my surroundings seemed to do the same. I could hear the train whistling through the night, and knew I was getting closer to the boarding house. Or, as locals had grown to call it, the "murder house".

There it was. Through the shadows I could make out the lone frame with its dark, bleak exterior. Obvious to anyone that passed by that it was abandoned, the lopsided shutters flopped back and forth in the breeze as if signaling that there was still some form of life there. My headlights flashed across the yard as I pulled into the driveway, and I sat for a moment, looking around for any sign of Lizzie. The front door was closed, and it appeared that all the windows had been boarded up.

I turned and dug around in the backseat until I found the large, sharp hatpin I was looking for. Feeling a bit safer with a weapon, I then pulled a flashlight from the glove compartment and climbed out of the car. Slowly, I made my way to the foreboding structure before me and hesitantly climbed the three rickety steps that lead to the front porch. I reached out and grasped the doorknob, a bit surprised when it turned so easily in my hand. I pushed the door open, my eyes immediately dropping to the floor beneath my feet. There they were. Mrs. Willingham's blood stains. From what I'd heard, Mr. Olsen found her lying just inside the door, moaning in pain.

Forcing my gaze up, I took a step inside and noticed a light seemed to be burning in the other room.

"Lizzie?" I called, listening intently.

"I'm in the living room," I heard her call in return, and I breathed a sigh of relief.

I hurried through the front room in the direction of the light, my footsteps the only sound in the lonely, old house. The living room door was pulled two, and as I pushed it open, I said, "You'd better have a good reason for..."

I stopped, my eyes widening. Lizzie was seated in a wooden chair in the center of the room, her black eyes glittering as she stared at me. Her arms were twisted and tied behind her back, and it was then that I noticed the figure standing behind her. He stood perfectly still, watching me from the shadows.

"Lionel," I breathed, my heart quickening in my chest. "What...what's going on?"

"Thank you for coming, Margie," he said, his voice monotone. He reached out a hand and motioned to the nearby loveseat. "Won't you sit down?"

I shook my head and began to back away, my eyes jerking between Lionel and Lizzie. I had to get out of here. I had to get help.

"Don't," he ground out, and I stopped, gasping when he raised his other hand and revealed the gun. "If you do, I'll kill her," he said, pointing the gun directly at Lizzie's head.

"I'm so sorry, Miz Savannah," Lizzie cried, tears dripping down her cheeks. "He threatened to kill my parents if I didn't cooperate."

"Shut up," Lionel snapped, his lip curled in disgust as he pressed the gun painfully against Lizzie's head.

"What do you want, Lionel?" I asked, desperate to divert his attention.

"I want you, Margie," he shouted, spinning to glare at me. "Why did you leave me?"

My mind scrambled to think of an answer. He apparently thought I was Marge Willingham. "I didn't leave you, Lionel," I said gently, forcing my tone to remain calm. "I'm here now, aren't I?"

"Yeah, now that it's too late and I've killed all those people," he laughed mirthlessly. "Why did you leave and come here in the first place? It's all your fault, Margie." With a moan, Lionel rubbed his head and began to pace around the room. I slowly curled my hand behind my back, trying to hide the hatpin in hopes that he wouldn't see it.

"I'm sorry, Lionel," I said, keeping my eyes trained on him. "Can't we start over?"

"No, no, it's too late," he shook his head and began to cry. "You lied to me. You said you loved me, but you lied. Why do you hate me so, Mother?"

I glanced at Lizzie, noting the widening of her eyes. He was talking out of his head, and we both knew it was only a matter of time before he killed us both. I tightened my grip on the hatpin, ready to do what I must when, suddenly, a deep laugh sounded from behind. Gasping, I spun around to find Matthew Cox standing in the doorway, smirking at Lionel.

"Lionel, Lionel," he said, shaking his head, "it seems that Father was right. You do need to be in a mental institute."

Lionel spun around and glared at Matthew, his eyes wild. "I am not crazy!" He shouted, raising the gun to point at Matthew.

With a short harrumph, Matthew leaned casually against the door frame and made a sweeping motion with his hand of the room. "What do you call this, then? What do you call murdering all those innocent women? Can you explain that, Lionel?"

His head jerking, Lionel stood in silence for a moment as he stared at Matthew. "How do you know about that?" He finally asked, his voice raspy.

"Oh, I know many things," Matthew stated nonchalantly, studying his fingernails. "I know that you and Marge Willingham were having an affair until she found out you're insane. She left you and her husband and came to live here, in hopes of getting away from you both. You followed her, though, didn't you, Lionel? And when she wouldn't take you back, you killed her. And then, like a spoiled child, you went on a rampage and murdered poor old Mrs. Gibson and her daughter." Lionel opened his mouth to speak, but Matthew raised a hand and said, "I'm not finished. You then proceeded to slowly go more and more out of your mind. You started seeing Marge everywhere and couldn't stand it. So, you kept killing, over and over again. If you don't call that crazy, then I don't know what is."

Matthew's condescending tone and manner brought a flush of color to Lionel's cheeks. I slowly backed into a corner, uncertain of what was about to unfold. Matthew was obviously goading Lionel, but why? Why didn't he do something to put a stop to all of this?

"You and your uppity ways," Lionel sneered, his voice dripping with hate. "You can threaten me all you want, but we both know I'll never be sent to an institute, because if I am, I'll tell everything, and what would that do to your dear mother's health?"

His smirk instantly disappearing, Matthew jerked away from the door and hissed, "Why don't you shut up?"

"What's the matter, Matt?" Lionel laughed, waving his gun at Lizzie and me. "Are you afraid I'll tell these two lovely ladies our dark family secrets?"

My eyes widened, and before I could stop myself, I whispered, "You two are brothers."

"Half-brothers," Matthew snapped. He turned to look at me then, the familiar smirk returning as he said, "My dear old dad had a mistress. I know it's hard to believe, saint that he is, but it's true. I didn't know I had a brother until I was a teenager and stumbled upon some old letters he'd written to Lionel's mother. Oh, he'd ended the relationship by then, but I burned those letters because I knew if my mother found out it would kill her."

"Does...does your father know that Lionel killed those women?" I asked, although I felt I already knew the answer.

"Why do you think he talked the authorities into not executing old RJ? He felt guilty, I suppose," Matthew shook his head and chuckled. "Marge told him on her death bed who was responsible, but Father refused to tell the truth for fear that Lionel would spill the beans about his parentage. So, Father lied and said RJ was the guilty one. Sly old fox, isn't he?"

I couldn't believe it. I looked at Lizzie, who stared at Matthew with the same incredulous expression I myself wore. It was incredible to think of all the lies that had been told, of the secrets that had been kept hidden all these years, and by people who were well-known and respected in our community. If anyone else had told me this of Doctor Cox, I wouldn't have believed it. But now, it all started to make sense. The tension between the doctor and Lionel that day at the hospital, and the obvious hate that Matthew had for his father. It was enough to make one sick to their stomach.

"How can you stand there and be so...so cynical?" Lionel hissed. "After everything our father put my mother and I through, and you just stand there and laugh."

"You and your mother were trash," Matthew spat out. "I never understood why my father ever lowered himself to that level."

"You forget, that was before he was so successful," Lionel said in disgust. "By the time my mother got pregnant, he had a career and reputation to protect. That's why he dumped her. That's why she became a bitter, hateful alcoholic with only one desire in life, which was to remind me daily that it was all my fault that everything turned out so horribly. She hated me, and I hated her." The more Lionel spoke, the angrier and more wild-eyed he became. I pushed myself as far against the wall as I could, praying that Lizzie and I would get out of this alive.

"Marge wasn't the first person you killed, was she?" Matthew asked in a low, steady voice.

I watched as Lionel's face lost every bit of its color, and he dropped both hands to his side in defeat. "No," he shook his head, his gaze growing distant. "Mother was."

The room was silent for a moment, and I began to hope that this whole mess was finally over. Perhaps Lionel was going to surrender, perhaps Matthew would convince him to give up, perhaps…

"It's time to join them now, Lionel," Matthew's voice broke the silence, and I glanced over at him. He was staring at his brother, his posture straight and braced as his hand slowly crept into his pocket. "You can't continue like this. It's time to go be with your mother and Margie."

Matthew withdrew his hand, and I saw a gun glinting from the lamplight between his fingers. I looked back at Lionel, who was slowly raising his eyes to look at Matthew, his brow furrowed in confusion.

"No," he shook his head, motioning to me. "Margie is here. I don't want to go anywhere else."

Matthew raised his gun and pointed it at Lionel, his gaze steely as he stared unwaveringly at his brother. "You have no choice," he whispered. "Your mother is calling."

"No!" Lionel shouted, the crazed look returning to his eyes. He raised his gun and pointed it at Matthew, and with a deafening roar, Lionel jerked backwards and crumpled to the ground.

I stood in stunned silence as I realized Lionel was dead. Matthew had killed him, his own brother.

"You goaded him into doing that," I whispered, turning my gaze back to Matthew. "Why? He may have surrendered if you'd just tried. He was your brother."

"Brother or not, I wanted him dead," Matthew stated in a clipped tone. He then raised his gaze, and his gun, to point directly at my head. "Now it's your turn."

"What?" I gasped.

"Do you think I'm going to let you two live to tell the whole world about everything you saw and heard here tonight?" Matthew laughed. "I've finally freed my family of that trash lying there on the floor, and I refuse to let my mother find out any other way. I'll tell everyone that when I got here, Lionel had just killed you both and I was forced to shoot him. No one will doubt my story. I'm sorry, ladies, but this is how it's got to be."

My hand clutching the hatpin, I lunged at Matthew, lashing at his arm with the sharp, pointed weapon. I made contact and, with a cry, Matthew jumped back, dropping the gun in the process. It skittered loudly across the hard wood floor, and I made a dash for it, but not before Matthew grasped my hair and jerked my head back with a painful snap. We struggled, Matthew's arm dripping with blood as I fought like a madwoman. I kicked and scratched and bit, doing my best to get away from him. Just when I thought I had the upper hand, he balled up his fist and punched me hard against the temple. My ears ringing, I fell to the floor, momentarily blinded as I struggled not to black out.

I heard him pick up the gun, and thought, *This is it. I'm going to die.* I tried to crawl away, but my limbs just wouldn't move fast enough. I heard the gun fire, and someone screamed, but I felt no pain. Raising my head from the floor, I looked wildly about until my eyes landed on the dead body of Matthew Cox lying lifeless on the floor. I swiveled around, my heart pounding, to find Leon standing by the loveseat, Matthew's gun in his hand.

"Leon," I breathed, dropping my forehead to rest against the back of my hand. "Thank God."

I heard the gun drop, and footsteps rushed my way. Leon knelt beside me and grasped my arm, gently pulling me up.

"Savannah, are you alright?" He asked, his eyes filled with concern.

"Yes," I nodded, my head still swimming. "Lizzie? Go help her, Leon."

As soon as Lizzie's ropes were loosed, she ran to my side and pulled me into her arms. "I'm so sorry, Miz Savannah," she cried, her tears soaking my dress. "I almost got us both killed."

"What were you doing here, Lizzie?" I asked as she and Leon helped me to my feet. I swayed back and forth for a moment, my head pounding.

"A few days ago, I discovered that Lionel and Marge Willingham were having an affair, so I've been following him," Lizzie explained, her normally strong voice a bit breathless. "When he came here tonight, I just knew that he was the killer returning to the scene of the crime, so I snuck quietly inside to see what he was doing. He caught me, tied me up, and said if I didn't call you, he'd kill my parents. I hoped you would sense something was wrong and call for help."

"I called Leon," I said, glancing his way, "but he wasn't home. How'd you know where to find me?" I asked him.

"Mother told me about the call when I got home," Leon replied, running his fingers through his hair, "so I drove out to the hospital and one of the nurses told me about Lizzie's note. I wasn't certain where "Mrs. G's" was, so I just made a wild guess. I'd say it paid off."

"You got here just in time," I said, wrapping an arm around his waist as he and Lizzie helped me walk. "You saved our lives."

We drove to the same drugstore that Mr. Olsen stumbled frantically into so many months ago and called the police, explaining what happened. They, along with Doctor Cox, my aunt and uncle, and Mrs. Emma, met us back at the boarding house within the hour.

When we returned, everyone was already inside, and the place was lit up with dozens of lamps and candles. It felt odd returning after everything that had happened, and upon entering, I immediately hurried into the comfort and protection of my uncle's arms.

"There, there," he murmured, patting me on the back.

"Savannah, you could have been killed," Aunt Deb scolded, her eyes filled with tears. She reached up and gently touched my swollen forehead, concern pulling her lips into a frown.

After assuring them both that I was alright, we proceeded to discuss everything that happened with the police.

"I don't believe it," Doctor Cox breathed as he stared in disbelief at Matthew's body. After a moment, he raised his eyes and glared at us, declaring, "It's a lie! I don't believe for one second that my son would try to harm these two girls."

"Which son, Doctor Cox?" I asked in a soft voice.

Jerking slightly, the doctor took a deep breath, raised his chin, and said in a clipped tone, "I'll admit Lionel was my son. I can't change the past, but that affair happened, and ended, a long time ago. We all make mistakes. No one is perfect, you know."

"Matthew said Lionel was responsible for all of those murders," I replied, watching him closely for a reaction. "He said Mrs. Willingham told you that before she died."

There was an audible gasp in the room as everyone turned to stare at the doctor with wide eyes. Mrs. Emma's face drained of all its color, and Leon quickly reached out to steady her when she began to sway uneasily on her feet.

"Doctor Cox?" One of the police officer's asked, notepad in hand. "Is that true?"

"No, of course it's not true," Doctor Cox said, his gaze narrowing as he glared at me. "She's lying."

"I heard Matthew say it, too," Lizzie spoke up, her lower lip jutting forward.

"Neither of you can prove it, though, can you?" He asked, cocking a brow. Turning to look at Lizzie, he sneered, "And why would anyone believe you? Your fiancé was, after all, accused of the same and killed during an escape attempt, was he not?"

Teeth clenched, Lizzie ground out, "We are not lying."

Officer Pane quickly took over, stating that we would all have to go down to the station to make an official statement. As we drove away, I glanced back and watched as the dark, gloomy house drifted further and further away, eventually melting into the blackness of the night, and wondered if I'd ever forget the terror I'd felt within its rooms. I'd almost been killed in that house, by two men I'd never suspected of being capable of such terrible things. It gave me chills to think I'd been so close to a murderer on more than one occasion and wondered if I could truly trust anyone. Who knew what dark, ugly secrets one kept buried deep within their souls?

Turning back in my seat to face forward, I grasped ahold of Aunt Deb's hand, giving it a squeeze. I was never more grateful for my aunt and uncle than in that moment, for I knew that if I could trust anyone in this world, it was them. Closing my eyes, I quietly thanked God for His protection, and for my family.

ONE

YEAR

LATER

Chapter Fifty-eight

-1943-

In the blink of an eye, an entire year had passed. Shortly after the deaths of Matthew and Lionel that horrible night, Doctor Cox "retired" from the hospital. I kept my mouth shut, giving only the barest of details when asked, but a hushed whisper flew around town about what really happened at Mrs. Gibson's boarding house. Doctor Cox refused to acknowledge that he'd lied regarding Mrs. Willingham's deathbed confession, and so RJ Willingham continued to stay in prison, with mine and Lizzie's story said to be only "speculation", since we didn't have any real proof. The story, however, was leaked to the newspaper, and within a week everyone knew about Doctor Cox's hidden little secret. After reading the article I'll admit that I did feel a moment of satisfaction, a feeling that was short lived and immediately followed by pity for his poor wife.

It wasn't long that the hospital hired a new doctor to take Cox's place, and upon meeting him I was struck by how young he looked. I soon learned that Doctor Zachary Holt was in his early thirties, with an impressive medical degree from Armstrong University. He was introduced to the staff throughout the day of his arrival, and I did my part to help him settle in as much as I could. He was very pleasant, with a nice smile and reddish-brown hair. I wondered at first why he wasn't serving his country, only soon after to notice the slight limp as he favored his left leg.

"I fell off the porch when I was young," he'd explained one day while massaging his calf. "My leg was broken so badly that the doctor feared I'd lose it. As you can see, I didn't, but it left me with a limp, and the military said I was 'unfit' to join."

"Their loss, our gain," I replied with a smile. He and I quickly became very good friends, and I was grateful our hospital had such a wonderful new physician among its staff.

As time went by, the seasons changing with what seemed rapid succession, Connor and I wrote to each other every week without fail, and I often found myself wondering if, when I saw him again, how changed we would both seem to the other. It had been two and a half years since I'd seen him last, and our time in Hawaii sometimes seemed like a distant memory. We'd shared so much in our letters, details of not just our everyday tasks, but of our innermost thoughts. We'd never ventured to discuss our feelings toward each other, however, and that was fine with me. There were just some things you couldn't write down in a letter.

I am in England at the moment, but that's subject to change at any given time, he wrote in one of his last letters. *You can't imagine how bad things are over here. Civilians, women and children, walk around town wearing gas masks, and there is so much destruction here it makes me sick. I've flown so many missions I've lost count. We're doing our best to kick their tails, but unfortunately, I'm afraid it's going to take a while. These Nazi's are some tough characters.*

London is mighty torn up, but there's still a lot of beauty left. I even saw the young princess, Elizabeth, a few weeks ago, and I rode by Buckingham Palace once. I'll send you some post cards with pretty pictures soon, I promise.

It sure is cold here! But I can't complain too much, because however cold it is on the ground, it's ten times worse in the sky. To give you an idea of just how cold, last week my men and I were flying a mission, and one of my gunners caught some flak. It didn't kill him, just got him good in the shoulder, and when my other gunner rushed over to help him, he took off his jacket to press against the wound. To make a long story short, we hit some turbulence and when he fell against the side of the plane, his bare arm stuck to the wall (like when your tongue gets stuck to ice). In his haste to continue helping his friend, he jerked away from the wall, ripping the skin completely off in the process. It was so cold up there, though, that his arm didn't start bleeding until we got back on the ground three hours later. His arm is pretty messed up for now until it heals, and the doc said it's going to leave a nasty scar, but I'm thankful that both men are going to be okay. So, whenever you feel like complaining about the cold, just look up and know there are worse places *wink*

I hope you are doing well. Sometimes, when I'm up in the air and not yet in combat, I try to imagine that I'm above all the destruction and pain. I think of you, and all the good times we shared, and I can't help but smile. I take a long, hard look at the picture you sent me every night before I go to sleep. Have I told you I miss you?

I'd never experienced so many different emotions while reading one, single letter. I laughed, frowned, cried, and smiled all within the span of five minutes. Yes, I missed him. Very much. And I told him so. I also begged him to stay safe and come home soon.

As the war progressed, life as we knew it started to change. Rationing soon began to take place, including gasoline, rubber, sugar and other certain foods, and even some types of clothing. To do my own little part to help with the war effort, I chose not to drive my car to and from work on days that it wasn't raining. I also assisted when I could with local scrap drives, as well as helping the Red Cross to sort through donations. I was proud of the citizens of my city, each of us doing what we could to support and maintain supply levels for our troops abroad.

The summer months were brutal, as usual. We got a lot of thunderstorms, due mainly to the high level of heat each day. One evening after work, it was storming and my car wouldn't start. Zachary offered to drive me home, which I gratefully accepted, and when we pulled up in front of our house, I asked if he'd like to stay for supper. It was the polite thing to do, and I was pleasantly surprised when he accepted.

"My mother passed away a few years ago," he said, "so it's been awhile since I've had a home cooked meal."

As we walked inside, I hoped Aunt Deb wouldn't have my head for not letting her know we would have company for supper. Much to my surprise, Mrs. Emma and Leon were inside, and I breathed a sigh of relief when I realized we would have plenty to eat.

After introducing Zachary to everyone, we all sat down to eat. I noticed that Leon was unusually quiet throughout the meal, and after Zachary left, he continued to sit in his chair with his arms crossed.

"Are you about ready to go, dear?" Mrs. Emma asked him, her brow furrowed.

He nodded silently, and as I walked them out, Aunt Deb called from the kitchen, "That young doctor friend of yours sure is nice, Savannah. So kind and mannerly! You be sure and invite him over again sometime."

"Yes ma'am," I smiled, glancing over at Leon to note the tense way he held his jaw.

As I watched Leon and his mother walk to their house, I wondered what was bothering Leon.

Connor stared down at the letter in his hands, his heart twisting painfully in his chest as he read.

She invited him over for dinner, Leon wrote, *and you should have seen how chummy they were! Sitting shoulder to shoulder, laughing at inside jokes. It was nauseating. Apparently, she has a thing for doctors.*

It couldn't be true. Could it? The proof was in the words of his own brother, and he knew Leon wouldn't lie.

Crumbling the piece of paper into a ball, Connor slammed it angrily into the metal trashcan by the door, his jaw clenched as he placed around the room. He'd never felt like this before. He wanted to yell, to punch something, to cry and rant until he felt nothing at all. But that wouldn't do any good. He loved her, and no amount of emotional outburst would take that away. How could she do this to him?

Suddenly, he stopped. He'd never actually told her how he felt. He'd assumed she knew and planned to tell her everything once he saw her again, which wouldn't be much longer. He'd just gotten word that he and his unit were to be rotated home after this mission. He'd been torn by the news; excited to go home, while at the same time feeling guilty for leaving when he was needed so badly. Now, all he could think about was having to face Savannah Rose when he knew she didn't love him.

"Danes, are you ready?" A sharp voice spoke from the doorway.

Jaw clenched, Connor silently nodded his head and slid into his leather jacket. They were to fly an important mission today, and as he walked outside to his awaiting men, he wished he'd waited to read the letter. He'd have to fight to keep a focused, level head.

Thirty minutes later, he maneuvered the plane expertly through the sky, glancing down at the beautiful, green countryside below. There were eight planes following closely behind, all fully loaded with bombs. On an important mission such as this, Connor usually felt an odd sense of calm and determination, but something about today was different. This time, he felt taunt and on edge, as if every muscle and nerve in his body was being prodded with a hot iron.

"Ten minutes," the navigator, 2nd Lieutenant Simmons, said over the radio, and Connor's spine tensed. Ten minutes until they were over their destination and dropped the bombs. If, that is, they encountered no interference.

Nine minutes. Eight. Five. Connor took a deep breath, trying to keep his head clear.

"Two minutes."

"Ready the package, boys," Connor spoke into his earpiece, referring to the bombs.

The two minutes passed, and the bombs were released without a hitch. Just as the smoke began to rise from the ground below, however, Connor caught movement from the corner of his eye.

"We've got company," he announced, straightening in his seat as he prepared for the upcoming battle.

Nazi aircraft filled the sky, coming at Connor and his men from all directions. What felt like hours was in reality only a few minutes as bullets shot through the air, striking the plane with full force. Connor dodged as many as he could, his eyes narrowing as he spotted a Spitfire diving right towards him. He informed his gunners over the radio, breathing a sigh of relief when the plane suddenly stalled and sputtered, its nose pointed downward as it spiraled to the ground.

"I think we've got 'em, boys," Connor said moments later when it seemed the Nazi's were in retreat.

"Not quite," he heard one of his gunners say, and he quickly turned to look around. He saw the plane just before its bullets rained all along the side of his B-17, one catching his co-pilot in the neck while the other tore into Connor's thigh.

Catching his breath, he immediately turned the plane in an attempt to get away, trying to ignore the pain in his leg. Bullets continued to tear into the plane, and Connor called into his earpiece, "Ramsey, Tanner, can't either of you get rid of him?"

When only silence met his request, he realized he was the only one on board left alive. He could see that the other remaining planes in his squadron were too far away to help, and he knew with a sinking feeling that he was all alone.

His plane shuddered violently once again, and he steered in the direction of an open field with hopes of surviving a crash landing. An image of Savannah Rose flashed through his mind, and he closed his eyes, his heart squeezing in his chest. Would he ever see her again? Ever get the chance to tell her how he felt? Would she even want to hear it?

Before he could completely ready himself for what was to come, another ray of bullets shattered through the wall, piercing his shoulder, and he groaned in pain, clutching at the control wheel.

God, help me, were his last clear thoughts as the engine exploded into a fiery blaze and his plane began spiraling through the air, out of control.

It was a Saturday, mid-morning, and the sun shone brightly, as if unaware of what was to come. I sat on the front porch swing, drinking a glass of tea, when I heard the sputtering sound of an engine coming down the street. A man in uniform rode his motorcycle past our house and stopped in front of the Danes'. I sat my glass of tea down and stood up, my eyes glued to the man's solemn, stoic face. I watched as he slowly walked through the gate and up the pathway, the click of his heels reverberating throughout the quiet neighborhood. He reached the front door, knocked, and waited, and I realized I was holding my breath. There was only one thing he could want, but I refused to believe it.

Leon was the first one to the door, and when he saw the man his face turned white. He called for his mother, his voice trembling, and when she arrived by his side, she immediately clutched onto his arm for support. The man handed her an envelope, saluted, and turned on his heel to walk back the way he'd come. I took a step closer, watching as Mrs. Emma slowly opened the telegram, her hands trembling. She read it, and it felt like a million years before her legs gave out and Leon had to catch her.

"No," she whispered, tears filling her eyes. How one word could be filled with such pain was something only a mother could describe. Mrs. Emma buried her face in Leon's shoulder and began to sob, her whole body shaking. He picked her up and carried her inside, and I hurried down our steps, my own legs trembling beneath me.

I'd just reached the Danes' porch when Leon re-emerged, holding the telegram in his hand. "What…what does it say?" I whispered, clutching the handrail tightly.

"Con's plane went down in enemy territory," was his hoarse reply. "They can't find his body. He's listed as missing in action."

I stared at him, unable to process the meaning of his words. *He can't be dead*, I told myself, my mind rejecting the very thought. His face floated before my mind's eye, his beautiful silver eyes sparkling with mischief, his lips turned into a smile, and I closed my eyes, fighting against the tears that threatened to bring me to my knees. I'd lost Father and Maxi. I couldn't lose him, too.

I heard Leon's footsteps drawing closer, but I couldn't look at him, couldn't bring myself to open my eyes and face the possibility that Connor was dead. Leon pulled me gently into his arms, and as I rested my face against his chest, it was only then that I realized I was crying.

Chapter Fifty-nine

-1943-

August, with all its heat and humidity, was upon us. I wiped the sweat that was already accumulating on my brow as I walked to work, wishing for a cool breeze to give a bit of reprieve. As I walked, my ears caught the sound of a song floating through the early morning air. Someone, it seemed, was listening to a record while they dressed for work, and the song that played stopped me in my tracks. It was "Boogie, Woogie, Bugle Boy", the same song Connor used to teach me to dance.

My heart ached for news of Connor. It had been a month since receiving the telegram, and Mrs. Emma refused to speak of it. To anyone that asked, she simply said that Connor was still alive and until they could produce his body, she wouldn't believe anything else. I, like Mrs. Emma, couldn't believe he was dead. The thought that I may never see him again was almost more than I could bear. I prayed for him every morning and evening, hoping against hope that somehow, he'd escaped that plane and was alive somewhere, safe and sound.

I finally arrived at the hospital and prepared myself for a busy day. Surprisingly enough, the morning passed by quickly, and before I knew it, I was sitting on a park bench eating the sandwich I'd prepared for myself that morning. I didn't hear anyone approach, and so when Zachary spoke to my left I jumped in surprise.

"Just a sandwich for lunch?" He tsked, shaking his head. "A hardworking nurse should eat more than that for her mid-afternoon meal."

"I agree," I smiled, "but it's a bit difficult to pack a full course meal into a paper bag."

"I know what you mean," he laughed, sitting down beside me. He opened his own bag and proceeded to pull out two sandwiches. "I'll half my second one with you, if you want," he offered kindly.

"No, thank you," I shook my head, my heart warming at his thoughtfulness. "I brought an apple for dessert, so I have plenty. Besides, a hardworking doctor needs his nourishment."

"I'd much prefer a great, big, juicy steak, though, to a ham and cheese sandwich," he snickered, taking a huge bite of his meal.

We sat quietly for a moment, both lost in our own thoughts as we ate. When Zachary finally broke the silence, I'd almost forgotten about my lunch companion.

"How come you're not married, Savannah?" He asked.

A bit startled by the question, I turned to look at him in surprise. Laughing at my expression, he shrugged and said, "Hopefully that's not too nosy of a question. If so, I apologize."

"No, no," I shook my head, "it's not too nosy at all. I just wasn't expecting it." I took a sip from my Coke bottle, trying to gather my thoughts as I prepared an answer. "I was actually supposed to get married about three years ago, but it just didn't work out. I guess I've just been too busy with work to do much courting since." My thoughts went to Connor, and I tried to push his memory away as I focused on what Zachary was saying.

"That's a real shame," he said, frowning. "A pretty girl like you should be courted."

"Well, thank you," I laughed, blushing. "Enough about me, though. What about you? Why aren't you married?"

"The same as you, I guess," he shrugged. "Too busy with school and work."

As I searched my mind for a reply, I caught movement out of the corner of my eye and glanced to my right, surprise lighting my face.

"Leon," I cried, "what on earth are you doing here?"

He walked slowly toward us, hands in his pockets, and I noticed the firm set of his jaw as he stared at Zachary. "Work was slow today, so my boss let us off early," he replied. "I came to sit with you while you ate your lunch, but I see someone else beat me to it."

"Would you like to join us?" Zachary spoke up, scooting away from me to make room for Leon.

After a moment of hesitation, Leon sat down between us and rested his back against the wooden bench.

"I was just telling Savannah what a shame it is that she isn't courting anyone," Zachary stated matter-of-factly.

"Apparently she's secretly courting my brother," Leon replied, and I felt my eyes widened. "Or she was, but he's…well…he's missing in action."

"Is that so?" Zachary turned to look at me in surprise.

"I never said we were courting," I said, my cheeks flushing.

"But something happened between you that you refuse to talk about," Leon sniffed.

I closed my eyes, trying to keep from snapping at Leon. "Why don't we talk about something else?" I asked, clearing my throat. "Zachary, why don't you tell Leon about the letter you received from your journalist cousin who is traveling through Europe covering the war?"

Zachary readily acquiesced, and soon all the two men were talking of was the war. I tried to listen, but I was too annoyed with Leon to pay much attention. If Connor ever came home, and I prayed he did, to discover I'd been telling people we were courting, I'd be humiliated! It wasn't Leon's place to share information about my personal life, and I fully intended to tell him so at the first opportunity.

I sat back against the bench with a sigh. The last year had seen a change in Leon. He'd gone from a boisterously happy and teasing friend to a distant, sullen acquaintance. I wondered if his unhappiness was due to his rejection by the army, and I'd often thought of talking to him about it, but things just weren't the same between us. I'll admit that I did push him away to a certain extent after reading Maxi's diary, but even after I decided to try and let it go and move on, I quickly found that our easy, close-knit friendship was gone. I, too, had changed, but something had shifted between us and I wasn't quite sure what it was.

The bells at St. John's Cathedral suddenly tolled in the distance, alerting us to the time. Zachary and I gathered our trash and stood, announcing it was time to get back to work.

"What time does your shift end today?" Leon asked me.

"Three o'clock," I replied. Some days I worked a twelve-hour shift, while others only eight. It all depended upon the workload and number of employees that showed up.

"I'll come back by and walk you home," he said.

"You don't have to do that," I replied as I dumped my trash in a nearby can.

"I know," he shrugged, walking in the direction of Broughton Street. "See you at three," he called over his shoulder.

At five minutes after three, I met Leon on the sidewalk in front of the hospital and we began our trek home. We hadn't spent much one-on-one time together lately, and we walked in silence for a few moments, both seemingly uncertain of what to say. I couldn't remember a single time in the history of our friendship where making conversation was ever a problem.

"There's something I've been meaning to ask you, Leon," I spoke up, finally breaking the silence.

"What's that?"

"You haven't seemed yourself lately," I spoke slowly, choosing my words carefully. "Are you alright?"

Leon was silent for so long that I feared he was going to ignore the question altogether. Finally, he sighed and said, "If you consider the fact that I'm a complete failure 'alright' then yes, I am."

"Leon," I stopped and touched his arm, "why would you say such a thing? You're not a failure."

"I'm the only man in my graduating class unable to serve his country, Savannah," Leon spat. "I work at a bank and live in my mother's house while every other man in town, including my own brother, risk their lives for me."

His eyes were so angry, and he spoke with such bitterness that I was taken aback. "Leon, you can't help…"

"That I'm pathetic?" He interrupted with a mirthless laugh. "That's what I keep telling myself, but it doesn't seem to change anything."

Leon was throwing himself a pity party, and I tried to think of a way to make him feel better. "You're not the only man in town unable to serve, Leon," I said. "Zachary was rejected, as well, because of his bad leg."

"Zachary?" Leon tilted his head, eyeing me curiously. "Ah yes, the good doctor who wants to court you."

I blinked, taken aback. "What on earth makes you say that?" I wanted to know, my brow furrowing.

"That's what he was hinting at," he shrugged.

"I don't think so," I shook my head. "He and I are good friends, that's all."

Silence once more filled the tense void between us, and I cleared my throat and said, "I didn't bring him up to talk about that, though, I was just trying to…"

"Make me feel better, I get it. Can we talk about something else now?"

Exasperated with his attitude, I dove in with what had been bugging me all afternoon. "Fine. I wish you hadn't told Zachary that Connor and I were courting."

"You told me yourself that you were "seeing" each other."

"That was for your ears only," I sighed. "And I believe I also told you I didn't know where we stood with each other."

"Why don't you want the good doctor to know about Con?" Leon demanded, turning to glare at me. "Because you're interested in "seeing" him, as well?"

"I already told you 'no'," I snapped, seething. What a fine example this was of just how much he had changed. The old Leon would have immediately apologized, despairing at the thought of anyone being angry with him. "I just don't think it's your place to be spreading gossip about my personal life, especially when it may or may not be true."

"Well, what does it matter?" Leon sniffed. "Con is dead now anyway, so you're off the hook."

I stopped in my tracks, my mouth dropping open as I stared incredulously at Leon. "How can you say that?" I hissed, my fists clenched.

"We all need to face it, Savannah," he said, glancing down at his shoes. "Con isn't coming back."

"We don't know that," I declared, my voice trembling.

He looked up at me then, his cool gaze meeting mine in a direct, almost searching way. "You're in love with him, aren't you?" He finally asked, his tone clipped.

Blinking, I took a small step back, startled at the question. My cheeks flushing, I said, "That's none of your business," and began walking again.

It wasn't long before Leon caught up with me and demanded, "Why won't you tell me what happened in Hawaii? I thought I was your friend."

"I thought you were, too, Leon." I spun to glare at him, nearly causing him to collide into me. "Don't you understand there are some things that are personal?" He was acting like a child!

"There didn't used to be," he snapped, eyes flashing. "We used to tell each other everything."

"Okay, fine," I said, my temper getting the best of me. Something in the back of my mind told me to stop, to just walk away, but I pushed it aside. "Here's a nice, juicy piece of information for you: Did you know that when Maxi was alive, she was in love with you?"

Leon blinked, his eyes narrowing. "Did she tell you that?"

I started to answer, and then stopped when I realized he didn't seem surprised. "You knew, didn't you?" I asked incredulously.

"Well," he hedged, shuffling his feet, "not really. I suspected, but we never talked about it."

"Why didn't you court her if you suspected she was interested?" I demanded, placing my hands on my hips.

Sighing, Leon ran his fingers through his hair. "She was my friend, Savannah. I didn't like her that way. Plus, I was afraid if we tried to date, we'd ruin a lifelong friendship between two families."

"You could have tried. You could have saved her, Leon," I whispered, tears of anger filling my eyes. "If you had given it a chance, she wouldn't have gone with me to Hawaii, and she'd still be alive today."

"You can't lay the blame for her death at my feet," he said, his face losing all its color. "That isn't fair."

"It also wasn't fair for you to keep stringing her along," I said. "If you suspected how she felt, you should have given her some space, left her alone until she got over you. But no, you kept flirting with her, giving her hope when there wasn't any."

"If I'd stayed away from Maxi, that means I would have also had to stay away from you," Leon said, his tone hoarse. He stepped forward until we were nearly nose to nose, wrapping his fingers around my forearms. "Maxi never would have agreed to court me, Savannah. Not when she knew I was in love with you."

Before I could comprehend what was happening, Leon bent forward, pressing his lips against mine. He pulled me closer, wrapping his arms around my waist, and I felt my head begin to spin. I squirmed against him, moving my hands up to his chest to push him away, but he wouldn't let me go. I bit down on his lip, hard, and with a cry of pain, he released me and jumped back, his eyes wide.

"Don't you ever do that again, Leon Danes," I hissed, trembling from head to toe. Spinning on my heel, I ran down the street towards home, not looking back.

I spent the next two days in complete misery. I had no idea Leon felt anything other than friendship for me, and now that I knew the truth, I was angry that Leon loved me instead of Maxi. I went from anger to tears and back again, hardly able to eat or sleep. Aunt Deb fretted over me until I finally broke down and told her everything. About Connor, about Leon, and about Maxi's feelings for Leon. She was shocked, to say the least.

"I can't believe Leon has done this," I wiped away a tear, my face pulled into a frown.

"Honey, one can't help who they love," Aunt Deb said gently.

I looked at her in surprise and opened my mouth to refute her, only to close it again when I realized she was right.

"How do you feel about Leon?" She asked after a moment.

"I've only ever loved Leon as a friend, Auntie," I moaned, guilt finally finding its way through the anger. "I judged him so harshly for not loving Maxi, and now I'm doing the exact same thing to him, aren't I? I feel horrible about the whole thing."

"And Connor?" Aunt Deb asked gently, pity in her eyes. She thought he was dead, too, just like Leon.

"He's more than a friend, so much more," I whispered, tears once again flooding my eyes. I felt like an overly emotional schoolgirl. "And with each passing day, I grow more and more afraid that I'll never see him again."

Aunt Deb pulled me into a hug, her gentle pats along my back like a soothing balm. "Don't lose hope, honey," she whispered.

That night, I readied myself to go over and talk things out with Leon. I was on my way down the stairs when a knock sounded on the front door. It was Leon.

"I was hoping we could talk," he said, looking every bit as miserable as I felt.

I stepped out onto the porch and closed the door. We walked to the swing and sat down, both of us silent as we gathered our thoughts.

"Savannah," he began, swallowing hard, "I just wanted to say how sorry I am for the way I acted. I'm embarrassed...humiliated. I never intended to force myself on you that way, and I only hope that you'll be able to forgive me."

He did seem sincere, and my heart warmed at his courage in coming over to apologize and admit he'd been wrong.

"I forgive you, Leon," I whispered, feeling emotional once again. "I was actually on my way over to your house when you arrived."

"You were?" He looked at me in surprise.

"Yes," I nodded. "I wanted to ask you to forgive me. I was wrong to lay the blame of Maxi's death on your shoulders. I've felt the need to blame someone or something, but the truth of the matter is that no one is to blame. Maxi made her own choices, one of which was to go to Hawaii with me. I'll never get over losing her, but I want you to know I don't blame you. It wasn't your fault."

"Thank you," he nodded, leaning over to rest his elbows on his knees. "What about...what about what I told you?" He asked after several moments of heavy silence. "Do I ever...stand a chance?"

I stood and walked to the nearest column, leaning my shoulder against it. My heart felt heavy; I didn't want to answer him but knew I must.

"I'm afraid not, Leon," I said gently, watching his bowed head in the moonlight. "My feelings for you are that of warmth and friendship, but nothing more. I'm sorry."

He stayed absolutely still for what seemed like an eternity, until finally he stood abruptly to his feet and, with a firm set of his jaw, forced a smile and said, "I understand."

He moved to walk past me, and I laid my hand on his arm, stopping him. "I know things may not ever be the same between us," I said, my heart squeezing painfully in my chest, "but I hope we can still be friends. I love you and...and your family dearly, and I don't ever want to lose y'all."

Leon reached up and gently patted the back of my hand, his eyes brimming with unshed tears. "You won't ever lose us, Savannah."

He walked away then, and I watched him go, feeling like a heartless, ruthless human being. I'd hurt him, badly, I'd seen it in his eyes. I only hoped he would heal quickly.

I cried myself to sleep that night, mourning the loss of a close and very dear childhood friend.

Chapter Sixty

-1965-

I pressed the gas pedal down further, my heart pounding as I searched the road signs. I had to hurry, had to get there as quickly as possible. Abby's life depended on it.

There it was. The house sat just beyond the hood of my car, and I pulled hurriedly into the driveway and parked. I climbed from the car, tugging nervously at my gloves, and walked to the front door, my legs trembling. Taking a deep breath, I raised my hand and rang the doorbell, waiting anxiously.

The door opened after a moment to reveal a woman in her mid-forties. She was very small with kind, hazel eyes shaded by a pair of glasses, and her hair was twisted up neatly in the back.

"Yes?" She spoke in a soft voice. "Can I help you?"

"Is this the Burton residence?"

"Yes," she nodded. "I'm Mrs. Burton."

"Is Reverend Burton in?" I asked hopefully.

"He's in Panama on a mission's trip," she replied. "He won't be back for another couple of weeks or so."

"Oh no," I whispered, swaying slightly on my feet. "That might be too late."

"Is there something I can do for you?" She asked, reaching out to steady me, her eyes filled with concern.

"I don't..." I began to cry then, feeling completely hopeless. Abby was dying, but I felt in my heart that if I could find Reverend Burton and ask him to pray for her, just as he prayed for me, she would get better. I'd spent the last two days searching frantically for a way to find him, and now that I was finally here at his house only to discover he was gone was almost more than I could handle.

"Why don't you come inside and sit down?" Mrs. Burton asked gently, motioning for me to step through the doorway. "You look very pale."

I followed her to the living room, where she helped me sit on the sofa.

As she went to get something for me to drink, I glanced around the cozy room, noting the many pictures along the walls. The one closest to me was a family photo, when the Reverend and Mrs. Burton were several years younger. *What a handsome couple they make*, I thought. Mrs. Burton's hair was braided very prettily along the crown of her head, and she held a baby girl in her lap. Three older boys stood smiling around their parents, and I suddenly felt a tear slip down my cheek. What a beautiful family the Reverend and his wife had. That was something I missed most in life.

"Here you go," Mrs. Burton announced upon her return moments later, a glass of iced tea in her hand. "Would you like something to eat?" She asked kindly as I took a long sip of the cool drink. "I can make a sandwich for you or…"

"No," I shook my head, smiling tremulously. "Thank you, though, you're very kind."

She sat down and watched me quietly, worry in her eyes. I felt that she could see straight into my heart. She had such a warmth about her, a quiet strength that I immediately radiated to, and before I knew it, I was spilling my story out to her. I told her of my battle with cancer and of Abby and Hannah, and I spoke of how Reverend Burton appeared and prayed for me just when I needed it most.

"The doctor said Abby's cancer has spread," I said, wiping my cheeks with the handkerchief Mrs. Burton had given me, "and I was so hoping your husband could come and pray for her, just as he did for me. If only he could, I just know she would get better."

Mrs. Burton eyes were filled with tears, as well, and all throughout my story she sat, quietly listening, and patting my hand. "I'm so sorry," she said, her voice filled with sympathy. "But you know, honey," she added gently, "even if he were here to pray for your cousin, that doesn't guarantee she would get better."

I knew she was right but didn't want to accept it. Accepting it meant accepting defeat, and I had to keep trying. "If…if he calls," I said, "would you ask him to say a prayer for her?"

"Of course," she nodded with a kind smile.

As I backed out of the driveway moments later, I hoped against hope that the Reverend would call.

Chapter Sixty-one

-1943-

It was Tuesday, the first week of September, and I glanced with dread up at the dark, densely clouded sky. It was hurricane season, and a massive, category 5 hurricane had been leaving a path of destruction throughout the Caribbean. Everyone had been keeping a close eye on the storm, listening at night to the five o'clock news for any information we could get. After leaving the Bahamas, the storm weakened to a category 3, but was still a huge threat to our Eastern shores. The latest news was that the storm was to strike Florida this morning around ten o'clock, and so all weekend Floridians had been flocking to our fair city. The hospital was a madhouse, but I couldn't complain. At least it wasn't my home and city that was being threatened, and I was thankful for that. We were, however, supposed to get some wind and quite a bit of rain, so I grabbed my raincoat and car keys as I headed out to work.

Just before noon, I glanced out the window, relieved that it wasn't raining very hard yet.

"You just got a call from your friend Vivian," the girl in charge of the switchboard told me. "She started having labor pains this morning, so she's on her way to Telfair Hospital."

"Thank you," I smiled, excitement making me feel giddy. Vivian had been married almost a year, and now she and her husband were about to have their first child. She and I had grown quite close since my return home, and I'd promised to help with the delivery. As soon as my shift was over, I'd head to the women's hospital and do what I could.

Since it was raining, I ate my lunch alone in one of the many break rooms. I'd just finished and was heading back to work when I suddenly noticed a tense, frenzied atmosphere had come over the place. When I arrived at my floor, the phone was ringing incessantly, nurses scurried in all directions with wide eyes, and patients were lined up at the desk demanding to be released.

I spotted Zachary in the midst of all the chaos and hurried to his side.

"What on earth is going on around here?" I asked.

"You haven't heard?" He blinked in surprise. When I shook my head, he replied, "The storm has doubled in speed and has changed directions. It is now supposed to lightly skim Florida's coast and then turn directly into us."

"Oh no," I whispered, my face draining of all its color. "When?"

"That's the worst of it," he said, his expression grim. "At three o'clock tonight."

He rushed off in the opposite direction, while I just stood in shock, my eyes wide. A storm of that magnitude would be devastating, to say the least, and the city hardly had any time to prepare.

I rushed to the telephone to call Aunt Deb, my hands trembling. I wondered if it was too late to evacuate.

"Aunt Deb, have you heard the news?" I asked as soon as she answered.

"Good heavens, yes," she said, and I could hear the underlying panic in her voice. "Businesses are closing, so your uncle is home trying to board up the windows. Everyone in the neighborhood is helping each other, so it shouldn't take too long. I'm trying to get together a basket of food and water and such..."

She continued to ramble until I finally interrupted. "Are we going to evacuate?" I asked.

"Your uncle just listened to the news, and the traffic is almost at a complete standstill. It would be crazy to try and leave now; we could get stuck on the highway in the middle of the storm. It's too late, we'll just have to weather it out here." As Aunt Deb spoke, I couldn't help but notice the tremble in her voice. She was terrified, as was I.

"The hospital is pretty crazy right now, and Vivian is over at Telfair having her baby," I said, my words rushed. "I'm going there in an hour or so to see what I can do. I'll be home as soon as I can."

"Okay, honey," she said, and then gasped. "Oh, there's something I almost forgot to tell you..."

The phone began to crack and then finally cut off. I figured whatever Aunt Deb needed to tell me could wait, so after taking a deep breath, I hurried back to my station.

Nearly two hours later, I told everyone to be safe and headed to Telfair. The traffic was insane. Horns were blowing, a rare sound in the south, and tires squealing. People were hurrying down the streets carrying bags full of supplies to weather the storm, and I could already picture in my head the shelves at the market quickly going bare. I turned my car into the only available parking spot I could find and hurried up the tree lined walkway that lead to the hospital's main entrance.

As soon as I entered the hospital, I realized how badly I was needed. I'd volunteered here before and knew I'd be welcome, so I hurried to the main nurse's station to ask what I could do.

"I'll do anything I can," I told one of the nurses, "but I'd like to see Vivian McCombs first. Do you know what room she's in?"

"Room 302. She's had a time of it all morning," the nurse said. "She's been dilated to about five or so, but can't seem to get any further."

As soon as I entered Vivian's room, I noticed how tired she looked. Her face was pale and covered in sweat, her breathing labored, and eyes bloodshot.

"Savannah, I'm so glad you're here," she cried with relief, her face suddenly turning into a grimace as a contraction began to hit. Immediately switching into professional mode, I hurried to her side, dipping a rag into the nearby basin of water. I gently wiped her damp forehead, offering words of comfort in soothing tones as I checked the pulse in her wrist.

"You're doing just fine," I said with a smile of encouragement, patting the back of Vivian's hand when the contraction was nearly over. "Would you like some ice chips?"

She shook her head "no", leaning back against the pillows with a long sigh. "It's so hot in here," she moaned, wiping the sweat off her neck. "Someone said the hurricane is headed our way?"

As we discussed the storm, I stood and walked to the closet, taking out the sphygmomanometer and a stethoscope. I wrapped the cuff around Vivian's arm and pumped until it was tight enough, then used the stethoscope to determine her blood pressure. *Hmm, it's a bit high*, I thought to herself, unwrapping the cuff and placing everything, except for the stethoscope, back into the closet. I then walked back to the bed and, gently resting the stethoscope's disc against Vivian's belly, listened for the baby's heartbeat. *There it is*, I thought with relief, taking note of Vivian's questioning gaze.

"Everything is fine," I assured her, placing the stethoscope back into the closet.

Suddenly, a bumping sound came from the window, causing both of us to jump in surprise. It took a moment to realize it was the shutters being blown about in the wind, and I hurried across the room, pushing the window up with a humph. I poked my head out, surprised at how strong the wind gusts were becoming. The storm was drawing closer, bringing with it a sense of urgency that rested heavily in the air. I pulled the shutters closed and latched them tightly, shut the window, and told Vivian I was going to see if there was anything I could do to help the nurses and other workers.

"I'll be back to check on you in a few minutes. Is there anything you need before I go?"

Vivian shook her head "no", and so I stepped back out into the busy hallway, barely catching the head nurse as she breezed by. "Mrs. McCombs is alright for the time being. Is there anything I can do?"

The nurse, with a grateful smile, gave me a list of things that needed to be done. Mrs. Holloway, who had delivered her baby last week, needed to be wheeled downstairs and checked out so she could go home, and her baby also had to be retrieved from the nursery. Next, every bed in the hospital had to be moved away from the windows and pushed as far across each room as possible. Once that was finished, I realized I'd been away from Vivian's room longer than intended and went back to check on her, welcoming a few moments where I could sit with my friend and rest my aching muscles.

When I stepped back into the warm room, however, and saw the red stains on the sheets as Vivian writhed in pain, my heart caught in my throat.

"Vivian!" I cried, rushing to her side. "How long have you been like this?"

"Feels like forever," she groaned, her hands clenched tightly around her stomach. "But I think…about fifteen minutes or so."

I instructed her to lay on her back with her knees up, and when I pulled the covers away to take a look, I gasped at the amount of blood on the bed. Was the baby breech? A lot of bleeding was often involved in breech births. It was also very dangerous for the mothers, as well as the babies. This wasn't good; this wasn't good at all.

"I'm going to get a doctor," I said. I saw the look of panic on Vivian's face, and stopped long enough to pat her hand reassuringly. "Everything is going to be alright, don't worry."

It took nearly ten minutes to get a doctor into Vivian's room, and once he examined her and realized the emergency of the situation, he immediately called for assistance.

"This is a breech birth. We need to prepare for surgery," he told the two nurses when they arrived. As soon as the words left his mouth, Vivian let out an ear-piercing scream. Everyone ran to her side and saw that, mixed with more blood, her water had broken, and she was dilating rapidly as contractions hit her one after another.

"There's no time to prepare for surgery," the doctor said, rushing to the basin to wash his hands. "This baby is coming now. Savannah, please stay by her side and keep her as calm as you can."

I rushed to take Vivian's hand, trying not to flinch as the girl's fingers tightened around my own in a choke hold. "It's going to be okay," I said gently as I wiped her forehead with a damp cloth. "You'll be holding that sweet baby before you know it."

"Hurts...so...bad," Vivian panted, her cheeks as red as fire. "I want...see...H-Howard."

No one was allowed to come back during a birth, not even the husband, but I didn't tell Vivian that. All I said was, "You know how men are, they never handle pressure very well. He's sitting patiently down in the men's waiting room, but as soon as the baby comes, I'll go get him, okay?"

I wasn't sure if Vivian even heard me, for the poor girl let out another heart wrenching wail, her body tight and writhing from the excruciating pain. Tears mixed with the sweat on her face and dripped like rain down onto her wet hospital gown. The doctor and nurses worked continually, their movements practiced and professional, but I didn't miss the concerned look in their eyes. They knew how dangerous breech births could be. As I kept whispering encouraging words, my hand now numb, I suddenly thought of Maxi, and wondered if this is how it might have been with her. She'd planned on having the baby in Hawaii, but what if she'd had complications, just like Vivian? It would have been terrifying, to say the least.

"Savannah, check her blood pressure," the doctor ordered, and I immediately set to work.

"Here it comes!" One of the nurses cried moments later. "I see its feet."

"I...don't think...I can...d-do this," Vivian cried through clenched teeth.

"Just keep pushing, Mrs. McCombs," the doctor said. "It won't be much longer now."

"I don't think I can," Vivian shook her head, and I could tell she was on the verge of panic.

"Savannah," the doctor said in a warning tone, eyeing me over Vivian's raised knees.

"Don't say that, Viv," I said, grabbing her hand. "The baby is almost here. You've got to keep pushing."

Sobbing, her eyes widening with hysteria, Vivian arched her back and tossed her head from side to side, her sweat dampened hair sticking to her cheeks. "N-no...can't...stand it...any l-longer."

I leaned over my distraught friend and gripped her arms tightly, forcing her to be still. "You have to do this, Vivian," I said in a firm tone, "or your baby might die. Now, push!"

Trembling from head to toe, Vivian took a deep breath and once again began pushing. Propped up on her elbows, her feet digging into the bed, Vivian pushed with all her might, receiving new strength when the nurse yelled, "It's a boy! Keep pushing, dear, he's almost here."

Suddenly, the nurse's eyes widened, and I knew something was wrong. With dread, I read the doctor's lips as he whispered, "His arm is up by his head. He can't come out like that."

Her eyes wide, the nurse whispered, "If you don't hurry, doctor, neither of them will make it."

Chapter Sixty-two

-1943-

My nerves on edge, I watched as the doctor, his jaw set with determination, reached his fingers inside and began to twist the baby's body in an attempt to get access to its arm so he could push it away from the head. I held my breath, watching and waiting for his eyes to light up with success. Vivian lay panting beside me, clutching my hand with waning strength, and I began to pray she wouldn't faint.

"There!" The doctor cried, and within seconds, the cries of a newborn baby filled the room, along with heavy sighs of relief.

Moments later, after he'd been cleaned and taken care of, little Howard Jr. lay peacefully in his mother's arms, his tiny hand curled around her finger. The doctor checked Vivian to make sure everything was normal and under control, gave her a few instructions, and left the room to see about his other patients. I could hear the wind howling outside, and glanced at my watch, my eyes widening when I realized it was nearly six o'clock. It was time to head home, but the urge to sit a few minutes longer with Vivian held me back.

"He's a beautiful baby," I said, coming to sit by the bed.

Vivian raised tired, red rimmed eyes to smile at me. "He is, isn't he?"

Nodding, I smiled back, tears pricking at the back of my eyelids as I watched mother and baby, my mind once again filled with thoughts of Maxi.

"Thank you, Savannah, for being here and helping me," Vivian said, her lower lip trembling. "I don't know if I could have done it without you."

"It was my pleasure," I smiled. Leaning over to kiss her on the cheek, I told her I needed to head home. "May God keep you and your family safe through this storm," I said, fear of the impending monster that was heading our way once again filling my thoughts as I left the room.

I'd just told Howard the good news and was on my way out the door when one of the nurses asked me to help her with a patient. One thing led to another, and before I knew it, it was nearly eight o'clock.

When I finally made my way outside, I was taken aback by the angry, billowing clouds in the darkening sky. The wind was already much stronger, and I had to hold on tightly to my hat as I hurried to the car. I'd just pulled out of the parking lot when the rain started again, and I nervously clutched the steering wheel as I fought to see the road.

Ten minutes later, the rain was worse. I inched along at twenty miles per hour, my nerves taunt. I only had a couple of miles to go when, suddenly, a small animal raced across the road directly in front of me. With a gasp, I jerked the wheel and stepped on the breaks, my eyes widening as the tires began to spin wildly on the wet pavement. Panic threatening to overtake me, I fought to regain control of the vehicle, but it was too late. My car jerked madly to the right and, with a loud crash, finally came to a shuddering stop.

I sat completely still, my breath coming in short spurts as I tried to calm my racing heart. I could barely see out of the windows, so after a moment, I pushed the door open and climbed out. Thankfully, my headlights were still on so I could see, and I groaned with frustration at what came into view. The front right side of my car was wrapped around a tree, and both front tires appeared to be busted. I'd never be able to drive it now. My only option was to walk.

Pulling the hood of my raincoat tightly around my head, I grabbed a flashlight from the glove compartment and began the trek home. It was difficult to walk against the sudden gusts of wind, but I remained on my feet and pressed on, my face dripping from the rain. Trees flailed back and forth above my head, their limbs groaning and cracking in the wind. This was just the beginning; I couldn't imagine how they could stand up against what was to come.

Another sudden gust of wind ripped down the street, pushing me forward just as a small limb cracked above my head and fell, striking my shoulder as wet leaves slapped me in the face. I stumbled in surprise, and my foot twisted on a pebble beneath me. Unable to catch myself, I fell to my knees, the flashlight crashing against the pavement and rolling away. Moaning, I reached down to clutch my throbbing ankle, tears springing to my eyes.

This is just great, I thought miserably. I was still quite a distance from home and stuck in the middle of an incoming hurricane with a broken flashlight and a twisted ankle. I wasn't certain I could walk on my own, but I had to try.

Suddenly, like a beacon in the dark night, headlights flashed through the air as a car turned down the street and slowly headed in my direction. I waved my hands and yelled as loudly as I could, hoping they would see me and stop to help.

The car inched closer and stopped, its breaks squealing slightly, and as I tried to push myself up off the ground, I heard a deep, familiar voice being carried over the roar of the storm. A voice I would recognize anywhere.

"Savannah Rose?"

I stopped, every muscle in my body frozen in place. My breath caught, and my heart jerked in my chest. I slowly raised my eyes, almost afraid to look. It wasn't possible, was it? But there he was, his silhouette rising up through the darkness as he walked toward me. *I'm hallucinating*, I told myself, unable to tear my eyes away. Had I hit my head when I fell?

He reached my side and stopped; his beautiful eyes troubled as he studied me. All I could do was stare up at him, my mind running in a thousand different directions. I wanted to leap to my feet and throw my arms around him, while at the same time feeling an overwhelming need to burst into sobs. I had so many questions to ask, so many things I wanted to say, but before I could form one coherent thought he leaned down and swooped me into his arms, carrying me to the car to gently place me inside. I watched, as if in a daze, as he walked around to the driver's side.

"Connor," I finally whispered in disbelief, hesitantly reaching out to touch his arm when he slid into the seat beside me. "It's…it's really you?"

With a slight smile, he looked over at me and nodded, his eyes dark and unreadable. Without a word, he put the car in gear, backed around, and we headed towards home.

I simply couldn't believe it. Connor was alive and had come home! But when did he arrive, and why hadn't someone told us he'd been found? My head beginning to pound, I closed my eyes and reached down to absently rub my throbbing ankle.

"Is it broken?" He asked, and my eyes popped open.

"No," I said quietly, "just lightly sprained."

We'd just turned the corner to our neighborhood when Connor stopped the car, a slight frown on his face as he leaned forward to peer through the windshield at something lying in the road.

"That's Mr. Hill!" I gasped, my hand going to the door handle.

"Stay here," Connor ordered as he jumped from the car and rushed to our elderly neighbor's side.

Mr. Hill was a widower in his early eighties and quite feeble, with no children or family to help him. As I watched Connor assist the gentleman to his feet, movement in the corner of my eye caught my attention and I glanced out the window. Mr. Hill's little dog, Missy, sat huddled in the bushes beside the car.

"Missy, come here!" I opened my door and called.

The frightened little creature immediately ran to me, and I scooped her up into my lap, hurriedly closing the door behind me before we both drowned. I wrapped her tightly in my arms, her little body quivering against mine.

"Thank goodness you got her," Mr. Hill moaned as Connor helped him into the backseat. "I let her out to do her business before the wind got too bad, but a tree limb fell against the gate and knocked it open. It scared Missy so bad that she ran off before I could stop her."

His forehead appeared to be bleeding, and I had to force myself to wait until we got indoors to inspect his injuries.

Connor pulled into Mr. Hill's driveway and I asked in a low voice, "Should we just take him to my aunt and uncle's house?"

"When I was helping Mr. Hill to his feet, I noticed a tree limb lying across the street. It appeared to have taken a power line down with it," Connor sighed. "It will be safest if we all just stay here, especially since neither of you can walk very well."

"But what about our families?" I asked, concern furrowing my brow. "They'll be worried sick."

Without an answer, Connor climbed from the car and helped Mr. Hill inside. He returned seconds later to carry me in. I clung to Missy, wincing when my ankle bumped painfully against the door as Connor carried me into the small house.

"I'll see if I can find us all something dry to change into," Connor stated, heading off in the direction of the bedroom. It wasn't the first time he'd been here. I vaguely remembered that he used to visit with Mr. and Mrs. Hill quite often when he was a teenager, before he joined the military.

"Look in my closet," Mr. Hill called weakly. "All of my wife's clothes are still in there."

Connor returned moments later carrying an armful of clothing. Picking me up once more, he took me into the bathroom. "I'll go help Mr. Hill. Call for me when you're ready," he said, sitting me on the counter with a towel, one of Mrs. Hill's old dresses, and a pair of men's socks.

I kept my arms wrapped around his neck and pulled him into a hug, a smile on my face as I said warmly, "It's so good to have you home."

I'm not sure what I expected of him, but when he grabbed my arms and pulled them from around his neck and stepped away, I was surprised.

"Thanks," he said, his tone cool as he turned and walked away.

I stared after him, wondering why my hug and words were apparently so unwelcome. Why would he push me away like that? It hurt, to say the least, and I fought tears as I began to get undressed.

It felt strange putting on another woman's clothes, especially when she was no longer living. I dried myself off as best as I could and slid the dress over my head. It was at least fifteen years old and two sizes too big, but it was dry and comfortable, and I was grateful for it all the same.

Pulling my feet up to the counter, I looked at my ankle. It was swollen, red, and painful, but thankfully not broken. I hoped Mr. Hill had some ice in his freezer. After pulling the thick, cozy pair of socks over my cold feet, I stood and tried to make my way back to the living room on my own. If Connor wanted to keep his distance, then I planned to oblige him. I'd barely made it into the hallway, however, when Connor saw me, his face pulling into a frown as he hurried to my side.

"You shouldn't be putting any weight on that ankle," he scolded as he carried me back into the living room.

"I need to see about Mr. Hill," I stated, ignoring his statement. "He has a pretty nasty cut on his head."

Connor sat me on the sofa next to the gentleman, hurrying into the kitchen to rummage around for medical supplies.

"How are you feeling, Mr. Hill?" I asked, reaching up to gently inspect his head.

"My knee hurts," he said, rolling up his pants leg to reveal a skinned and badly bruised knee. "And I have a headache."

"Do you feel dizzy or light-headed?"

"No," he shook his head.

Connor returned with a handful of bandages, rubbing alcohol, and iodine. I gently cleaned Mr. Hill's wounds, trying to maintain a focused, level head with Connor standing so close behind me. Once I finished, Mr. Hill said he'd like to lie down.

"I'll need to wake you in about an hour," I told him. "I want to make certain you don't have a concussion."

"Where's Missy?" he asked, yawning as he stretched out on the sofa.

I turned to find that Connor was sitting on the floor, the little dog between his knees as he attempted to dry her with a towel. She wiggled around, jumping continuously at his face, her little pink tongue leaving a wet streak along his cheek. I snickered at the sight, and Connor glanced up, his brow cocking as he said, "If you think this is so funny, why don't you take over?"

"Why would I do that when you're doing such a wonderful job?" I asked with a smirk.

His lips pursed, Connor stood and carried Missy to her owner. She immediately settled down, curling into a ball in the crook of Mr. Hill's arm. Within seconds, the two were snoring peacefully.

"While you were changing, I managed to get a phone call through to our families. They're all staying together, and your aunt and uncle said to tell you not to worry about them," Connor explained as he helped me to the love seat.

"I'm so glad you were able to get in touch with them," I sighed, settling back against the cushions.

Connor left the room again, returning moments later with an ice pack. "Prop your foot up on these pillows," he said, stacking a couple of cushions against the arm rest, "and keep this ice pack on your ankle as long as you can stand it."

"Thank you, Doctor," I said, hoping to coax a smile out of him. When all I received was a stiff nod, I sat back with a sigh, wincing when he placed the ice pack against my ankle.

Rather than sit beside me, Connor chose the rocking chair across from the love seat and sat down.

"I'm shocked that the electricity hasn't gone out yet," I commented, trying to make conversation. When Connor didn't answer, I began to fidget nervously. Something about him was different. He seemed so quiet, so distant.

We sat in silence, each listening as the storm steadily grew worse. The wind gusts were growing stronger and more forceful, and I jumped in surprise when the bathroom door suddenly slammed shut. Shivering, I pulled a homemade afghan from the back of the loveseat and pulled it around my shoulders.

I glanced at Connor, noting the faraway look in his eyes, and wondered what he was thinking. "What happened to you, Connor?" I finally asked, unable to restrain my curiosity any longer. "We were told your plane went down and no one could find you."

He didn't answer for a moment, and I began to wonder if he would. Finally, he sighed heavily and said, "My plane did go down, but I was able to parachute out before it crashed. I landed in a field and made my way to a farmhouse, the bullets in my leg and shoulder causing me to lose so much blood I was afraid I would die before I found anyone to help me. Thankfully, the farmer and his wife, although German, were sympathetic and let me hide in their basement. That first night was the worst," he shook his head, reaching up to rub his eyes. "The farmer's wife was able to remove the bullets, with nothing to dull the pain, and by the end of it all I'd lost so much blood she was afraid I wouldn't make it. I faded in and out of consciousness for several days, until I finally turned a corner and started to get better. I stayed with them for about three weeks, and once I was strong enough to travel, they helped me get back to safety. I owe them my life."

Connor stood, tucking his hands into the baggy pockets of Mr. Hill's pants, and began to walk around the room, glancing at the many pictures hanging on the walls. He stopped before a black and white photo of a very young Mr. and Mrs. Hill, a melancholy smile tugging at his lips.

"It's amazing how two people, in a world full of people, can find each other and fall so much in love." He spoke so quietly I had to lean forward just to hear his words. He glanced at the sleeping old man and added, "I remember Mrs. Hill. She was a lovely person, but the thing I remember most about them as a couple was their obvious love and devotion for each other. He's been lost without her."

I studied Connor, wondering about this complex man before me. One minute he was quiet and pensive, and the next contemplative and thoughtful. I'd never been able to figure him out, that much was still the same, but something was different. I felt shut out in some way, as if I almost didn't even know him. It had been so long since we'd last seen each other, but we'd written faithfully all those long months apart, further developing and deepening our friendship. Or so I'd thought.

"Are you home for good, Connor?" I asked hopefully.

"For now," he nodded. "I've been rotated home with my regiment, but if they let me, I may volunteer to go back."

My heart tightened. "Why? You've served your time."

"Because I'm needed," was his short reply. "And I have no reason to stay here."

"Your mother is here," I stated.

"She has Leon," he shrugged, continuing to walk around the room.

I fought against the tears that burned the backs of my eyes. He was being so flippant, so unfeeling. I was on the verge of telling him so when, suddenly, something crashed loudly against the house and the room was incased in complete darkness.

Chapter Sixty-three

-1965-

I paced back and forth in Abby's room, my stomach in knots. A week had passed, with no word from Reverend Burton, and Abby was steadily growing worse. I'd stayed by her side as much as I could while Aunt Deb saw about Hannah, but I felt like I wasn't doing enough. I felt like a failure. And lastly, I felt guilty for being healed of my cancer while Abby lay there dying from hers.

"If you don't sit down, you're going to wear a hole in the floor."

The weak voice, laced with humor, caught me by surprise, and I turned to find Abby struggling to push herself into an upright position.

"I didn't realize you were awake," I said, hurrying to her side to help.

"I haven't been awake long," she smiled. "What were you pondering so heavily just now? You looked as if all the problems in the world were left up to you to solve."

"Oh, I was just thinking about how nice it's going to be once you get well and can go home," I said, forcing positivity into my voice. "Won't it be wonderful, now that we've found each other? I can help babysit Hannah when needed, we can spend holidays together, and even go on vacation…"

Abby reached for my hand, the look of sadness, and almost pity, in her eyes stopping me midsentence. "Oh, Savannah," she said gently, "don't do this. You and I both know I'm never going home. I've admitted it to myself, and now it's your turn."

I stared at her, tears welling up in my eyes. "I can't," I whispered.

"Yes, you can," she said. "You have to let me go."

"No." I stood to my feet and walked to the window, my back to her as I silently watched the birds flying freely amongst the clouds, and I wondered how it felt to be so light and burden free.

After a moment, I heard Abby speak again. "Savannah," she said softly, "I need you to promise me something, but you can't do it if you refuse to admit that I'm dying."

I turned to look back at her, my heart sinking as I took in the pale, yellowish tint to her skin and black circles around her eyes. "What is it?" I asked, my voice trembling slightly.

"I know this is a very large request, but I don't have anyone else to turn to," she said, and just before she glanced down at her hands, I thought I saw tears in her eyes.

I returned to the seat beside her bed and, taking her hand in mine, asked, "What is it, Abby?"

Taking a deep breath, she said, "I...I'd like to ask if you and your husband would take Hannah and raise her as your own after...after I'm gone."

I shook my head. "Abby, you're not going to..."

"Savannah, please," Abby stopped me, her voice stern. "I need to know that my little girl will be taken care of. You can't know how hard it is for me to leave her behind, but knowing she'll be with two such wonderful people that I love and trust will give me peace. I know it's asking a lot, but..." her eyes filled with tears, and she could no longer speak.

My heart clenched painfully in my chest. I hated that this was happening, but the truth of the matter was that Abby was dying and I needed to accept it. I didn't want to, I'd been fighting against it all this time, but it was staring me in the face, and I knew I couldn't continue to run. If only it didn't have to be this way. I saw so much of Maxi in Abby, and having to face Abby's death was like losing Maxi all over again. I loved them both with a love one only has for a sister, and I wasn't sure how much more my heart could take. Abby and I had known one another less than a year, but we'd been through so much together it felt more like a lifetime.

I didn't have to ask my husband about Abby's request to take Hannah in; it was obvious how he felt about the little girl, and knowing how much Abby loved her daughter, the fact that she wanted us to raise her was like being handed a precious gift. I wouldn't let her down.

Squeezing Abby's hand, I said, "You don't have to worry about Hannah. We would be honored to raise her as our own." Swallowing past the tears, I added, "She won't ever forget you, though. I won't let her."

The sweetest smile spread across Abby's face, and the look of relief brought a sparkle to her tired, dull eyes. With the peace of my promise came renewed energy, and we sat, talking and giggling like schoolgirls for the rest of the day.

Chapter Sixty-four

-1943-

After going to investigate, Connor discovered that a partially rotted oak tree which stood between Mr. Hill's and his neighbor's house had split under the pressure of the storm, falling partly on both houses and taking down a power line with it. We were able to find some candles and a couple of flashlights, which were now resting all around the living room.

Mr. Hill, having been awakened by the crash, sat upright with a trembling Missy by his side while I checked his head and eyes, making certain he didn't have a concussion.

"You don't have any nausea, do you?" I asked.

"No, I feel fine," he said, settling down once more into the soft cushions and closing his eyes. "Just sore."

I made my way back to the loveseat, thankful that the swelling in my ankle had gone down considerably and I was able to walk, with a limp, on my own. I sat down and listened, my nerves on edge as the storm steadily grew worse and worse. The wind and rain beat loudly against the house as if a giant, angry monster was fighting its way inside. I could hear tree branches cracking and falling to the ground and feared that one of the tall pines in Mr. Hill's yard would crash down on top of us any second.

"You look worried," Connor spoke from his seat on the brick fireplace. The candles that flickered on the mantle above cast a soft glow on his face, and as I looked at him, I suddenly noticed how drawn his face appeared in the shadows. His eyes were dark and hollow, his shoulders tense and never relaxed. The war had obviously taken its toll on him, and I wondered how many scars there were beneath the surface. He'd seen so many men die, some of which were his friends, and had come so close to dying himself. It broke my heart to think of what he must have gone through.

"Aren't you?" I asked.

"Me? No way." His eyes twinkled with just enough mischief that I caught a glimpse of the old Connor and smiled, thinking of one particular stormy night in Hawaii. The night Connor kissed me.

"You've weathered tougher storms than this the last few years, haven't you?" I asked softly.

He nodded, glancing down at his intertwined fingers. "There are many different types of storms, though, and I'd say we've all been through our fair share," he replied, his gaze thoughtful as he looked at me. After a moment he said gently, "I know I said this in my letters, but I wish I could have been there for you when Maxine died."

My heart softened at his words, and I had to swallow past the sudden lump in my throat. "In all my life I've never felt so alone as I did that day," I replied softly. "I was so afraid you would be killed, too."

"If I'd known you followed me to the base, I would have done everything I could to stop you," he sighed, his eyes filled with sorrow. "I wouldn't have been able to concentrate knowing you were there in the midst of all that chaos."

His words made my heart skip a beat. "Why Lieutenant Danes," I smiled teasingly, "I didn't know you cared so much."

At my words, a hard look passed over Connor's face and he said stiffly, "That was a long time ago."

The sting of his harsh words caught me by surprise, and I shrank back. How could he be so warm one minute, and cold as ice the next?

Turning my face away to hide the hurt in my eyes, I said, "Yes, I suppose so. Although sometimes it feels like only yesterday. It's strange how a place we spent less than half a year of our lives in can hold so many memories, both happy and sad."

"Yes, it is," Connor agreed, his voice low.

Suddenly, a thought struck me, and I looked back at him and asked, "Why were you out driving around in the storm tonight? Were you looking for me?"

"That was a delayed question," he snickered. "Your aunt and uncle were worried, so I offered to go look for you."

"I guess it was a bit delayed, wasn't it?" I shrugged, smiling. "But I was so caught off guard when I saw you that I didn't think to ask. I nearly thought you were a ghost."

"Sometimes I feel like I am," he replied with a half-smile, leaning his elbows over on his knees.

"The ghost of Christmas past, present, or future?" I teased.

He kept his gaze downward for a moment, not answering, and I wondered once again if I had said something wrong. When he finally raised his gaze and looked at me, I saw a hint of pain in his eyes as he softly replied, "Christmas past," and I knew he was referring to something different, something far deeper and more personal. I just didn't know what.

"Why is that?" I asked, tilting my head.

"Sometimes I feel like a part of me died that morning in Pearl Harbor," he stated, pointing his gaze downward once more. "I wish everything could go back to the way it was, but it just can't."

"A part of us all died that morning, Connor," I said gently. "I wish every day that I could just wake up one morning and the world would be at peace and Maxi would still be with us, but my wishing it doesn't change the reality. Time has passed, life has changed, but there are still some things that have stayed the same."

"Such as?" he looked up at me.

"Home, family, friends. Your mother never gave up hope that you would come home. None of us did."

"Apparently you did," he stated with a sniff, "since you thought I was a ghost."

"I didn't want you to be a ghost, though," I replied. "I wanted you to be real."

"Ah, yes, because you were caught in a storm and needed to be rescued," he stated matter-of-factly. He then promptly stood and walked from the room, abruptly ending the conversation.

I watched him go in utter confusion, my temper slowly starting to creep up on me. He had no right to accuse me of such a thing! After a moment of battling with myself, I finally flung the afghan aside and, ignoring the pain in my ankle, stomped after him.

"I would like to know one thing, Mister Danes," I stated once I reached the kitchen and found him leaning against the counter, peeling a banana.

Connor looked up at me in surprise. "What's that?" he asked, his eyebrows raising in question.

"Have I done something to offend you?" I crossed my arms, my right foot beginning to tap with irritation.

"What makes you think that?" he asked nonchalantly as he took a rather large bite of the banana.

"Because what you just said was completely ridiculous and uncalled for," I snapped. "The reason I was glad to see you had absolutely nothing to do with the fact that I needed help."

As I spoke, I moved to stand by the sink, leaning heavily against the counter. My ankle was throbbing, and I wasn't paying attention to the fact that I was too close to a window. Before I could finish my rant, I heard a loud crack. My heart jumping, I turned my head to the side, following the sound. What I couldn't see was a giant tree limb breaking away from its trunk and being flung about like a ragdoll, its thick branches hurdling through the air directly toward the boarded-up window I was standing in front of. Connor heard it, too, and before my mind could process what was happening, he launched himself across the room and pushed me to the ground just before a deafening crash sounded above our heads.

Chapter Sixty-five

-1943-

I felt the breath leave my lungs as I lay beneath Connor's body, gasping for air. Glass shattered all around us, and I heard Connor grunt in pain as the limb crashed through the opening of the window and landed partly on his back. We both lay there, frozen in shock, and I wondered for a split, terrifying second if Connor was dead.

"Oh, good heavens," I heard Mr. Hill exclaim through all the noise. I turned my head to watch as the old man stepped carefully through the glass and debris, the flashlight in his hand trembling slightly as he made his way to our side. Connor moaned, his body twitching a bit, and I breathed a sigh of relief when he slowly raised his head and looked at me.

"Are...are you alright?" he asked, a trail of blood dripping down his cheek.

"Yes," I nodded as Mr. Hill reached down to try and push the tree limb from Connor's back.

It took quite a bit of effort, but with Connor's help, the two men were able to push the limb back out the window. Buckets of rain poured in through the opening, leaves and debris blowing all over the kitchen. It took every ounce of strength I had to help Mr. Hill hold up a thick, heavy piece of plywood as Connor nailed it over the window, and once he was done, I collapsed against the wall, out of breath.

"Do you think it will hold?" I asked hopefully, my arms burning.

"I hope so," Connor replied, wiping sweat from his brow.

"I need to see about that cut," I said, reaching out to touch his cheek.

"Later," he waved me away. "Let's get this mess cleaned up first."

It took nearly an hour to get the kitchen clean, and once we were finished, we realized there was water coming in under the back door, which was at the lowest part of the house. We stacked as many towels as we could on the floor around the door, hoping for the best. If the floodwaters continued to rise, we would be forced to climb up into the attic. My stomach clenched with worry for my aunt and uncle. I prayed they were alright.

"Here are some blankets we can use once those towels soak through," Mr. Hill said, his arms loaded down with blankets of various size and color. He stumbled a bit under the weight, and Connor hurried to his side to relieve him of his burden.

"Mr. Hill, you look exhausted," I said, worried as I watched the elderly man lean back against the ice box. "Why don't you go lie back down and I'll bring you a sandwich?"

"Alright," he nodded gratefully. As he walked from the kitchen he added, "I sure am grateful that you two are here."

I smiled, watching as he shuffled slowly away, his knees bent and shoulders stooped. I, too, was glad we were there to help him.

"I'll get us both another change of clothes," Connor stated, and I suddenly noticed we were both soaked and covered in dirt.

"Alright," I nodded. Connor turned to go, and I suddenly noticed that the dark stain on the back of his shirt wasn't a dirt stain. It was blood.

"Connor, your back," I gasped, hurrying to his side. I reached out to raise up his shirt and take a look, but he grabbed my hand, stopping me.

"It's fine," he said, pushing my hand away.

"You've bled through your shirt, Connor, you're not alright," I stated, an eyebrow arching indignantly.

"Alright, fine, Nurse Adair," he raised his hands in surrender. "I can see by the look in your eyes that I'm licked. Go on and tend to Mr. Hill and then you can see about me."

He left me standing there in surprise, as I'd been expecting a fight. With a small smile of victory, I hurriedly fixed Mr. Hill a sandwich and poured him a tall glass of milk. I delivered the tray of food to the living room where Mr. Hill and Missy sat cuddled up on the sofa, smiling as I patted Missy gently on the head.

"Shall I fix her something to eat, as well?" I asked, motioning to the little dog.

"No, she ate earlier," Mr. Hill shook his head. Glancing over his shoulder, he leaned toward me, lowering his voice as he said, "Don't continue to let time come between you two, honey. Y'all have that same, special something that my sweet wife and I had, and it's too precious to let go." He reached out and squeezed my hand, his eyes piercing through the darkness as he continued, "If you don't fight for it, you'll regret it for the rest of your life."

Shocked at Mr. Hill's sudden, passionate speech, I stared at him in silence, wondering what it was he saw between Connor and me.

"I don't think he really cares about me, Mr. Hill," I finally said, forcing the words past my suddenly scratchy throat. "I thought he did once, a long time ago, but now I'm not so sure."

"Well, why don't you ask him?"

My eyes widening, I shook my head and said, "Oh no, I couldn't do that." I couldn't risk the pain of Connor's rejection.

With a sigh, Mr. Hill released my hand and said, "I don't believe you'll regret it, dear. Just think about it, alright? Life is too short to let fear hold you back."

Swallowing, I nodded and slowly turned to make my way back into the kitchen. I'd just finished cleaning up the counter and retrieving the first aid kit when Connor returned.

"If we're not careful, we're going to run out of clothes," he smirked, handing me another dress. He'd changed his pants and held in his hand a fresh shirt. "I'll wait until you change before I let you start torturing me."

"Scaredy cat," I winked, reaching to pluck the dress from his hand.

I blinked in surprise when Connor caught my hand and held on tightly, his eyes serious as he said, "You nearly scared the daylights out of me earlier. How about staying away from windows for the remainder of this storm."

"I think I can manage that," I spoke slowly, smiling.

With a nod, Connor tried to release my hand, but I held on. He looked at me questioningly, and I said, "If you hadn't reacted so quickly, I might have been killed. Thank you, Connor."

"You're welcome," he nodded, his eyes warm.

We stood there for a moment, our hands still intertwined, and I wondered what Connor was thinking as he stood so silent, watching me with that searching gaze of his. When he let go of my hand and stepped back, I squeezed my fingers together, missing the warmth of his touch.

"I'll be right back," I muttered, hurrying past him to the bathroom.

Connor's words kept repeating themselves over and over in my mind as I changed my dress. Why was he such a mystery to me? Why was it that one minute he seemed to truly care, and the next he was pulling away with his sword and shield drawn? *Life is too short to let fear hold you back*, Mr. Hill's words echoed through my mind, and as I walked back into the kitchen, I wondered what I should do.

"Alright, Lieutenant Danes, take your shirt off and sit down," I ordered, my lips twitching. "Your torture awaits."

Heaving a dramatic sigh, Connor slid out of the shirt and sat in one of the barstools, tapping his fingers nervously on the counter.

"Don't worry," I chuckled, flashlight in hand as I walked around behind him, "I won't hurt you too badly." It felt so nice to tease with Connor again.

I shined the light on his back, wincing at the long, angry red cut that ran from between his shoulder blades to his waist. It was fairly deep, but thankfully didn't require stitches. I said as much as I gathered the medicine with which to clean it, warning him that the alcohol would sting.

"I'll try to be gentle," I said as I gingerly pressed the soaked cotton ball against his torn flesh.

Connor winced slightly, the muscles in his back contracting. I could see the scar on his shoulder, left behind from his bullet wound, the flesh still a bit red and not fully healed just yet.

"Does your shoulder cause you much pain?" I asked, trying to distract him.

"Not as much now as it did," he replied, his voice tight.

"What about your leg?"

"It bothers me a little, especially at night," he replied, his body relaxing a bit once I finished cleaning the cut. I proceeded to lightly tape some gauze all around, hoping it would stay in place, and then helped him into the new, clean shirt.

"That wasn't so bad, now, was it?" I asked, walking around to face him.

"I suppose not," he admitted. "I guess you must know what you're doing."

"Well, I have had quite a bit of practice," I smiled. I placed the flashlight on the counter with the beam pointed directly at the side of Connor's face and stepped closer, biting my lip as I eyed the cut on his cheek. "Hmm, it looks like it may need stitches, but I'll just have to make do with cleaning and bandaging it for now."

I wet another cotton ball and began to work, cleaning the cut as gently as possible. I could feel Connor's gaze boring into me, his breath warm against my cheek. We were only inches apart, and I fought to keep a steady hand.

Don't let fear hold you back.

Taking a deep breath, I dove in. "Why did you accuse me of only being happy to see you tonight because I needed help?" I asked quietly.

He didn't answer right away, and I found myself anxiously holding my breath as I waited.

"I shouldn't have said that," he finally replied.

"Why did you?" I pressed. "Have I done something to offend you?"

"No," he sighed heavily. "You're just living your life, and there's nothing wrong with that."

He was talking in riddles, and I leaned back to look at him, my brow knitted in confusion. "What do you mean by 'I'm living my life'?"

"Things are just different now, Savannah Rose, that's all," he shrugged, his voice once again growing a bit indifferent as he glanced away. "I was rude earlier, and I'm sorry. Let's just leave it at that."

As I stood there in silence staring at him, he continued to avoid my gaze, and I felt so frustrated. How were things different? Had we been writing to each other all these months for nothing? Had he simply been playing games with me? The more I pondered it, the angrier I became.

"So, you kissed me in Hawaii, and wrote all those letters to me for what reason?" I asked, my voice shaky but cold. Something in the back of my mind warned me to stop, but it was too late for that. I was angry and hurt and felt like a fool for thinking he actually cared for me. "Because you were lonely? Because you needed someone to fill the void and boost your ego? You could have found a little German girl for that."

His gaze flew back to my face and he stared at me, eyes flashing and jaw clenched. "That's not..." he began but stopped. Taking a deep breath, he said stiffly, "Are you finished with my cheek?"

"Oh, I'm finished alright," I snapped, snatching up the gauze and pressing it firmly against his cheek.

"Ouch!" Connor cried, reaching up to grab my hands. I jerked away and proceeded to roughly place a couple pieces of tape around the edges of the gauze, my fingers trembling so badly I almost dropped the tape.

I spun around to stomp from the room, needing as much space from Connor as possible, but I'd barely made a half turn when he gripped my forearms and stopped me.

"You didn't have to claw my cheek off," he stated through clenched teeth, spinning me back around to face him.

"Let me go," I hissed, trying to jerk away, "or I'll claw the other cheek, too."

"What do you want from me, Savannah Rose?" Connor asked, his voice rising.

"Obviously something you can't give," I shot back, eyes flashing. I couldn't seem to stop lashing out at him. "If only I'd heeded the warning I received long ago of what a playboy you are. Apparently, that description was quite accurate."

"Okay," he growled, shoving the barstool back loudly as he stood up. His fingers dug into my arms, but when I saw the way he looked at me I stopped struggling. His face was red with anger and frustration, but all I could see in his eyes was hurt.

"You want me to tell you how I feel?" he asked, his breath hot against my face. "Fine. I love you, Savannah Rose. I've loved you for years. You're the woman I've always dreamed of, the one I want to spend the rest of my life with, but I can't have you. There. Is that what you wanted to hear?" He stopped then, taking a deep breath as the passionate, fiery speech slowly turned into a solemn, quiet plea. "Can you please just cut me some slack and try to understand how it feels to love someone so much that you ache with the force of it, all the while knowing you can never be with that person? Just don't accuse me of not caring or playing games. I never played games with you, Savannah Rose. Never."

Before I could process what Connor's words meant, he leaned forward and pressed his lips against mine. His grip on my forearms loosened, and he slowly trailed his hands down along my elbows and wrists, stopping to lace his fingers through mine. My breath quickening, I felt his arms then move to my waist, pulling me tightly against his chest, and I slid my hands up to rest at his neck, welcoming the deep, overwhelming passion I felt in his kiss.

There are few moments in one's life that truly leave you breathless. Perhaps the first time a snowcapped mountain comes into view, or when a mother gives birth to a child. Maybe even on a simple Christmas morning, when the tree is twinkling with lights and the laughter of family fills the air and you suddenly realize you have so much to be thankful for. For me, it was this moment. When Connor kissed me that stormy night in Hawaii so long ago, a part of me was changed forever. I'd known ever since that I cared a great deal for him, but I hadn't been ready to acknowledge anything deeper.

Until now. In all my life, I'd never felt the way I did at that very moment, and I suddenly knew that this was where I was supposed to be, as if every road and path I'd ever taken was meant to lead right here, into the arms of the man holding me.

Connor moved away from me then, breaking the spell, and I felt a sudden chill sweep over me. He stepped around me to leave the room, his eyes filled with sadness. It seemed that his words and the kiss had taken something from him, and as I turned to watch him go, his shoulders stooped, I fought to find the right words to say.

"Connor, wait," I called, my voice a near whisper. He stopped but didn't turn back around. The dark void between us felt like a million miles. "I love you, too."

Slowly, Connor turned to look back at me, his face filled with doubt. For a split second, I was afraid he would simply turn and leave the room, but he finally said, "And what about your doctor? Do you love him, too?"

My brow knit in confusion, I asked, "What on earth are you talking about?"

Connor swallowed, the lump in his throat bobbing up and down in the shadows. "Leon told me you were seeing the young, new doctor at your hospital."

My brows shot up and eyes widened in disbelief. Leon told Connor that on purpose, knowing something was between us and hoping such information would tear us apart. It almost had, and I couldn't believe Leon would do such a hateful thing. But then I realized that perhaps in his jealousy Leon had believed it, too.

"That's not true," I shook my head, taking a step closer to Connor. "Zachary and I are good friends, but that's it. I promise. You can even ask him yourself."

Connor stood completely still, his face a mask of confusion, disbelief, and hope as he stared at me in silence. I could see the war in his eyes, and I slowly moved closer until I stood only a few inches away. Reaching out, I took his hand in mine and said softly, "Why do you think I wrote to you all of those months, Connor? Why did I share so much of myself and constantly say how much I missed you? Why do you think I was so angry with you just now? I wanted you to love me, to tell me I wasn't imagining there was something between us, but you kept pushing me away."

I touched his face, tears coming to my eyes as I silently plead for him to believe me. "I love you, Connor Danes," I whispered. "You're the only man for me."

The most beautiful smile began to spread across Connor's face then, and when he pulled me into his arms and kissed me once again, I knew my life was finally complete.

Epilogue

-1966-

I stood over the grave, a fresh bouquet of flowers in my hand. Today was the one-year anniversary of Abby's death, and I still thought of her every day. I missed her so much, often wondering what life would be like now had she lived. She fought long and hard, and I would never forget her bravery, nor her friendship.

"Savannah Rose?"

I turned to see my husband walking towards me, his beautiful silver eyes filled with sympathy and understanding. He knew how much I missed both Abby and Maxi, and I sometimes wondered how I could have made it this far in life without him. I hadn't thought it possible to love him more now than the day we married, but our love grew stronger every day.

As he stepped up to my side and took my hand, I was reminded of when he told me he loved me. That dark, stormy night seemed so long ago, but I could still feel the intensity of his words and the passion in his kiss as if it were yesterday. I could also remember with absolute clarity the fear I felt as we weathered that storm, afraid that at any minute old Mr. Hill's house would crash down on top of us.

It was one of the worst storms to hit our city, with wind gusts up to 120 mph. The streets had remained flooded for two days, and the electricity didn't come back on for nearly two weeks. Thankfully, Uncle Ray had a generator and was able to keep the freezer from thawing, and as soon as the water in the streets subsided, he took the generator to several of the neighbors so they wouldn't lose all their food either.

Savannah Morning News put out a special edition two days after the storm with a banner headline that read: **"HURRICANE RIPS THROUGH SAVANNAH"**, and a drop headline adding vivid, violent details: **"Man dies of heart attack during the storm, and woman killed by flying glass - Buildings unroofed, some blown down - Uprooted trees clog streets and highways - Windows smashed out all over the city and chimneys topple. The heart attack victim, a Union Bag** policeman, passed away after fleeing to his son's house during the height of the storm. The woman suffered cuts from which she died a few hours later."

"Every street and every section of the city bears evidence of the destructive force of the wind," the story continued. "Plate glass windows throughout the business district were ripped out, and merchandise from the windows was sent flying through the air. Virtually every street and every road in the section is blocked by fallen trees."

The stories didn't end there. An old tower collapsed, leaving the City Hall clock lying at a 45-degree angle. Several of the city's famous squares were damaged, with one large tree uprooting and "blowing right out of Wright Square". The city's main shopping district, Broughton Street, also sustained significant damage, with stories of wax models and mannequins being blown about, which "looked sort of silly stuck up at crazy angles". The police had to rush details down to protect the stores against looting.

It was a trying time for our city, one that we would never forget, but the main thing I remember is the feeling of thankfulness that my family was safe, and the warmth of knowing that Connor and I finally found each other.

"Are you ready, honey?" Connor asked, lightly kissing my temple.

I nodded, leaning down to place the flowers on Abby's grave.

Small fingers intertwined with mine, and a little voice asked, "Do you think she can smell our flowers from Heaven?"

Connor and I looked down at Hannah and smiled, love shining from our eyes. After Abby's death, we adopted Hannah and officially became a family. I'd always wanted a daughter, to know what it felt like to be a mother, but I'd never expected such a precious gift.

"Yes, sweetie," I nodded, squeezing her hand. "I think she can."

"Can I ask Reverend Burton to sing her favorite song?" Hannah wanted to know. We'd been attending Reverend Burton's church for nearly a year now and received so much love and acceptance there.

"Of course, you can," I smiled. "I think "In the Sweet By and By" will be a beautiful addition to this morning's service."

We turned and walked back to the car, where Aunt Deb waited patiently, the three of us walking hand in hand. When we reached the car, I stopped for a moment to take in my surroundings, thinking of that day so long ago when I sat on the train, heartbroken, on my way to a new life. I had no idea of what lay ahead of me, of the trials and hardships I would have to face, but here I was, no longer that same lost, searching young woman. I'd found myself, I'd found love from so many people, and I'd found a home.

"Coming, Mama?"

My heart fluttering, I reached up and lightly touched my chest, thinking of the scars that lay beneath my blouse. If cancer had taught me anything, it was to enjoy each and every moment God gave me. To soak in the laughter and sunshine, and even the dark, rainy days, because as Abby and Maxi and even Daddy had proven, life isn't always guaranteed.

"Yes, sweetie," I smiled at my daughter. "I'm coming."

As I slid into the car with my family, I realized once again that although life isn't always easy, it certainly has its beautiful, breathtaking moments that make it all worth it.

A note from the author:

Thank you so much for reading my book. It really means the world to me, and I sincerely hope you enjoyed it! As previously stated, this book was inspired by many true stories, real people, and true events. Although I can't possibly list every part of the book that was true, I would like to point out a few:

1. Although Savannah Rose is her own fictional character, a lot of her story is based on my maternal grandmother's life. Nana (as I called her) also lost her mother as an infant and was partly raised by her aunt and uncle. Another young female relative lived with them, as well, and she and Nana were very close (she did not, however, become pregnant and die at Pearl Harbor).

2. Reverend and Mrs. Burton were based on my maternal grandparents. Granddaddy was, indeed, a pastor, and Nana was just as I described Mrs. Burton – gentle, kind, quiet, and loving.

3. Lizzie was also based on a real person. She worked for Nana's aunt and uncle, and Nana loved her dearly. She talked of her often before she died. However, everything I wrote about Lizzie (her fiancé getting killed, etc.) was fiction.

4. The newspaper articles of the murders of "Mrs. Gibson, her daughter Cathy, and Mrs. Willingham" were real. The article of the hurricane in the very last chapter was also real but in actuality was about a hurricane that hit Savannah in 1940, instead of 1943.

5. If you assumed my descriptions of the hurricane scenes simply came from my imagination, they did not. I based those pages from my own real-life experience, as my family and I stayed to brave Hurricane Matthew in 2016. It was quite terrifying, to say the least!

6. The part where the man wearing a mask jumps from the shadows at Savannah Rose was based on a story Nana once told me. As the story goes, she and her cousin were walking home late one night when a masked man jumped out at them from behind the bushes. Nana screamed so loudly that the neighbors immediately came running, therefore sending the mysterious man quickly on his way! They never discovered who he was, or what his intentions were.

7. The story Connor shared with Savannah Rose in his letter about the airman who took his jacket off during a mission and got his arm stuck against the side of the plane and therefore ripping the skin completely off, was true. I was told of that story at a wonderful little World War II museum I visited a few years ago.

8. Just as "Uncle Ray" did, my paternal grandfather took his gas generator around to his neighbors during a power outage after a hurricane in the 1970's so their food wouldn't spoil. Being a good neighbor was very important to him, and he was always willing to help during times of trouble.

9. As previously stated, although I changed the names and some of the facts, the murders of Mrs. Gibson, her daughter Cathy, and Mrs. Willingham were based on a real crime. However, the events that happened afterward in relation to those murders (Doctor Cox, Matthew, Lionel, the other women that were killed, etc.) were all fiction.

If you have a couple of minutes, please leave a review of "The Healing Rose of Savannah". Once again, thank you so much for reading. God bless!

Made in United States
North Haven, CT
11 December 2021

12491569R00200